# THE
# GIRLS
# UPSTAIRS

An absolutely gripping crime thriller with a massive twist

# CHARLIE GALLAGHER

*Detective Maddie Ives Series Book 9*

Joffe Books, London
www.joffebooks.com

First published in Great Britain in 2024

Cover art by Nick Castle

ISBN: 978-1-83526-485-0

# CHAPTER 1

'Control, show me state six . . .'

PC Philip Jones spoke into the radio strapped to his chest and was in no doubt that *control* would be able to hear the wide grin in his voice. Just that morning he had been reminded that this was not the way to announce his arrival at a 999 call — not anymore. He should be touching the screen on his smartphone. It was the way of the world now. His sergeant, who had issued the stern reminder, had said that she would be listening out and that she didn't want to be hearing his voice. *There's no need to be taking up the airwaves, that's what we're trying to avoid!* she had said.

Human contact was what they were trying to avoid.

First the team briefings had gone, that precious fifteen minutes of bad-mouthing the previous shift and what they had left to mop up, five more minutes bad-mouthing the shift that would be taking over from you and how you would be sure to leave them some shit to deal with and then five more minutes taking the piss out of each other while you finished up the cup of tea made by the last officer to join the team. Now it was a *self-briefing*: a series of dull power-point-style slides to scroll through on the screen of your hurriedly assigned patrol car. On your own.

They'd even taken the breaks away — at least, the breaks back at the nick with the rest of your team — the last chance of some interaction, of human contact.

Phil was happy to be on the home straight of his career. The Job he loved was all but gone. All that was left for the likes of him was the pension.

'Frant Village Hall . . .' Phil had flipped open his pocket-book to read it out, lifting his eyes to take in the signage that confirmed he was in the right place. He was also supposed to be using a digital pocketbook by now — of course he was — some app on the smartphone that was in his kitbag somewhere, its battery long since exhausted.

Phil would be pen and ink until the day he died.

Nothing about the bright frontage of Frant Village Hall with its empty parking spaces and manicured bowling lawn, or the warm sunshine smothering his back like a weighted blanket gave him any clue that this, of all days, would be that very day.

## CHAPTER 2

The car was visible long before it pulled up. It was the only thing moving in the pleasant afternoon sunshine but, even if it were choked in traffic, you couldn't miss the Battenburg markings ignited by the bright sunshine.

My view out was over gently sloping grassland, the middle of which was well mowed into neat lines that got ragged around the edges, left wild so flowers could grow in the longer grass. The village green was punctured by just a few trees, with leaves almost reaching down to the ground. It was almost as if they were designed with hiding in mind.

The car stopped. The bright white "POLICE" reflected as a white shimmer across the ground when the door opened and a black boot found the tarmac.

I licked my lips. Excitement and apprehension had me seeking eye contact with the other who was hiding with me, a connection that only heightened the moment, a moment of realisation. A switch had been thrown. We were no longer two people standing in the shade of a tree; we were two people hiding with intentions, two people entering the next phase.

It had started.

I gripped the thick trunk a little tighter, stepping in closer as I did, so tightly that a branch dug at my hip. He stepped in too, his left hand over mine, a light squeeze that told me he was thinking the same.

Once out of his car, the police officer stood still long enough to cast a look around, but there was an air of laziness to him, to his stretch that ended with his hands on hips and a check of his watch. Certainly, there was no sign of any urgency in searching for the group of nuisance youths that had been the subject of the call.

The indicators flashed, the mirrors turned in and it was confirmed: he was on his own.

The officer stretched again, this time adjusting the belt that held his handcuffs and baton. I watched him angle the radio strapped to his chest so that it met with his mouth. There was a breeze. It was moving over him and right towards us, gathering up enough of his voice for it to arrive like a gentle hum but with no words discernible.

The officer made for the side door to the village hall, closest to where he had parked. The door opened easily to catch him out. He'd jerked too hard, expecting it to be locked, and so stumbled a pace back. He steadied himself, the door still in one hand. He tipped his radio back up with the other.

The breeze hummed again.

His next move was to step into the hall. The door started to close slowly behind him.

We were moving across the green long before it found its place.

# CHAPTER 3

The door was unlocked. Phil hadn't been expecting that. The call had been for nuisance youths throwing stones at the village hall. He knew this community well enough; the truth was likely to be quite different — more like a local had seen someone under the age of thirty too close to their precious bowling green. Phil had been sure to drive through the village first under the guise of an *area search*, which was actually a way of giving any nuisance kids the opportunity to run away giggling. He was always comfortable with kids running away giggling since it removed the need to actually talk to the little bastards.

Now inside, the feeling overall was one of emptiness.

'Police!' He called out and the word bounced off the polished surfaces to course down hallways and penetrate into side rooms. He stood still for a moment, listening for any reaction. He got none.

The hall was ringed by stacks of chairs that hunched like spectres observing him from the shadows. A wooden lectern was out front and centre with a closed book on top. The whole room was set up pretty much as Phil might have expected. The middle of the hall, where an audience might sit, was currently inhabited by dust falling gently through a window-shaped tunnel of strong sunlight. A closed door was to the left, marked clearly as KITCHEN.

Phil's footsteps were surprisingly loud, the acoustics were church-like, with the sounds confused by an exposed roof that pitched twice.

'Police!' he said again on his way to the kitchen door, stopping on the threshold to listen for any reply. There was a sound, a rattle, something solid flexing, like a heavy door in a storm.

Only it was behind him, from the door he had just entered?

# CHAPTER 4

The distance to close up was forty metres and we both took long strides to cover it, resisting breaking out into a run. Running attracts attention, though attention shouldn't have been a concern. There was no one in sight. The location had been chosen for that very reason. There were houses around but they were all surrounded by tall hedges or fencing. Affluent Middle England was a place where no one wanted to be overlooked.

I slipped off my glove to run my finger down the side of the police car as I passed — I couldn't help myself. I had a sudden urge for the connection. It was warm and smooth, still drenched in light. I passed the hall's entrance door next, careful of where I put my feet, avoiding the loose stones and grit that might have warned of my arrival, my strides changing to not-quite-tiptoes. There was a wheelie bin, out of sight in a three-sided shed. The two steel crowbars were still where I had left them, tucked in beside the bin. The heavy-duty bungee was still there too, hooks on each end, one of which was already wrapped back on itself to grip tightly on the handle of the wheelie bin. I scooped up one of the crowbars, it felt lighter than before with arms that were superpowered by adrenaline.

There was more eye contact, this time to check that he was ready. It was just like we had practised, only this time in daylight. Even his excited laughter and wide eyes were the same as they egged me on.

I used the hooked end of the crowbar to heave the bungee cord towards the door handle, though it fell short and I needed help. There was no hesitation, he was strongly built, but he still grunted and his face twisted with the exertion as we inched the bungee cord closer until it snapped over the handle, effectively holding the door tightly shut.

I still tested it, dropping the handle and giving it a push, then shouldering it as hard as I could. There were a few millimetres of give maybe, enough for it to rattle in its housing, but always against a powerful force intent on slamming it shut.

I no longer tiptoed when I went back for the second crowbar. He snatched it up to wield across his chest like a warrior pumped up for battle.

'You ready?' Those first un-whispered words made me realise that my throat had dried.

'What did you say? Backup's half-hour away?' He was just as croaky.

'At best.'

'I only wish we could be here to see the dopey fuck's face, when he gets let out by his mates!'

I didn't respond, my breath was so shallow I didn't think I could. The moment was getting to me, the thrill of what we were doing, the fact it had started, was going to plan, the weight and feel of the crowbar in my gloved hands. I wasted no more time, turning away to walk to the parked car and I didn't hesitate. My first strike started out a long way back, the hooked end of the crowbar swung as a haymaker for a direct hit into the centre of the windscreen. The damage shot out from the point of impact like a jagged sound wave. I hit it again and it made a deadened *pop!* where the glass was pierced. The screen still had integrity but it was opaque. TV static.

My companion was stock-still on the other side of the car. I could only see his head and shoulders, which also meant his facial expression: his bitten lip and his eyes searching all over the car with an excitement that now seemed to have him frozen to the spot. We locked eyes for a moment and it broke the spell.

His crowbar lifted up into view, his swing similar to mine as he drew a big arc in the sky that ended abruptly against the passenger side window. His entrance into the action was dramatic. Glass exploded inwards like dropped ice, covering the passenger seat, filling a police hat that had been left upside down. He stepped back and I took a moment to watch. He looked around to see if he'd attracted any attention, his shoulders rising and falling, his mouth hanging open, his tongue out to wipe dry lips.

His next swing had a whoop of excitement and he split another window into a thousand shards that spread themselves over the interior. The quarter-light followed moments later.

I smiled, and a little laughter leaked out too. Then I swung again, this time downwards into the bonnet, the epicentre was the "O" in "POLICE". The panel dented but it didn't justify the energy that ran back down the steel to spread into every part of both my hands. I almost dropped it, the pain catching me out. I took a moment to recover as more glass popped then shed over the hard standing where the other side of the car was still taking hits.

I moved round to the front, the headlights went first, the pay-off greater, the satisfaction too, fuelled by the sight and sound of falling glass.

The wing mirror bent outwards with a thud, my partner-in-crime grinning above it. His next blow unseated it entirely, leaving it swinging against the door on a black wire. He was breathing heavier still, I was too, more noticeable now that I had stopped. The crowbar felt heavy again, cumbersome. I was losing that first wave of excitement and the strength that had come with it.

'Job done!' my companion announced, beaming. A rivulet of sweat rolled down the side of his face.

But I could feel another flush coming, another wave of excitement even stronger than the first. 'I think we should hurt him,' I said and I watched closely for the reaction. His expression changed, slowly at first and he stared back at me like he was trying to read me, trying to see if I was serious.

I had never been more serious in my life.

'Say that again.'

I did, only stronger, buoyed by a malice that mixed in with the excitement, like a fire given a sudden rush of oxygen. Words can be like that, take on greater meaning when said out loud.

'We talked about the car,' he said. 'We've done more than we said. You were just gonna put a window in. look at it!' He gestured with the crowbar at the metal carcass still leaking glass from every angle. The panels had taken a beating too, even the long blue light on the roof was split open to expose white bulbs inside. 'What if someone comes! We're pushing our luck!'

'No one's coming.' And I felt so sure. It was like we had the whole village to ourselves, like we could beat up cars all day and no one would ever come. Even if they did, we had our hoods up, and we had an escape route planned and practised, one that took us away from the back of the building and into a warren of alleyways and woodland paths to where our getaway was parked. There was nothing distinctive about us either; we were two people dressed in dark clothing — even our gloves were black — and no one would get close enough to say anything different.

My decision was already made, my movements instinctive. The first of which was to reach for the zombie knife tucked in my belt, a genre of knife so-called because it would stop the undead. Its blade was clean-edged on one side, serrated on the other, both sides curved into each other to form a vicious point eight inches from where the steel handle started.

'What the fuck is that?' There was fear in his reaction, excitement too.

Shards of glass squealed and popped under my heel as I spun, my focus moving away from the stricken car and towards the door that was bungeed shut. It was when I got closer that I realised that it was making noises, hammering noises from the other side and a voice too — raised — someone trying to be heard. I took a moment to marvel at just how little I could hear. The village hall was linked to the church, built from its budget and by its people, which meant church-like features were inevitable. One such feature was the solid wooden entrance door that was effective in reducing a man's enraged shouting to nothing more than a hum on the breeze.

The knife was solid and heavy, but I was back to being powered by adrenaline and once again it lost its heft. It was light and nimble in my right hand — my strongest — as I reached out for the bungee with the other.

# CHAPTER 5

The main door flexed. The sensation was of a slight give and then a snap back in place when Phil tried to pull it back open. It wasn't locked; the feeling was more like someone was hanging onto it on the other side, or a whole group of people, based on the force that was seemingly being applied. The sounds from it had stopped, the rattling he had heard and he used a moment of stillness to listen out for giggles.

There was nothing, no sound at all.

When he cussed, he did it quietly so as not to be heard. He tried the door again, putting a little more into it this time, leaning back to use his body weight. The door was budging, but it was nothing more than a few millimetres, snapping back shut the moment his weight was removed.

Philip cussed a little louder as he turned his attention back inside the room. The hall's only windows were two thirds of the way up the walls and were long and thin. He could make it if he used the stacked chairs, but it could only be a clumsy exit ending with a graceless fall the other side. Just what a group of kids would want to see: the local bobby tumbling out of a window. He could almost feel the mobile phones already pointed at every exit from the building, waiting to fill their Instagram feeds with his idiocy.

Sod that for a game of soldiers.

He moved to the kitchen to assess any options in there. The window was more standard, the lower half frosted, made up of three panes, the one on the right was the longest. Locked. There were toilets too, a short walk from the kitchen, hidden down a short corridor. There, he found the smallest of all the windows above the urinal. The window was open, maddeningly so, balanced on an old-style metal arm with a catch that fell into a hole, the gap enough for a breeze that smelled like cut grass. But even pushed open as far as it would go, he didn't reckon he would get a thigh out of there, let alone the rest of him.

Smashing glass.

It's a distinctive sound — unmistakable — and it drifted in, bundled up in that scent. It was impossible to tell where it was coming from. He stood up on his tiptoes and pushed the window as wide as it would go so that he could peer out. He was on the bowling green side and there was nothing to see but pristine green and a memorial bench on the far side. There were more of the same sounds: something solid meeting something glass.

*The car!* The realisation powered him on his march back through the hall. The sounds of destruction kept coming, muted, where they were being filtered through the thick walls. He had already considered calling his situation in; it had been his first thought, but it had quickly been eclipsed by his awareness of the piss-taking that would follow his admission live on air that he had been locked in the village hall by a bunch of village kids. The pride that stopped him from calling for assistance was also what fuelled the rage in his fists as he swept to the door to start hammering on it.

'Let me OUT of here! You're gonna be SORRY!'

# CHAPTER 6

The knife sliced through the bungee cord as if it was nothing, the tension enough to twang the ends in opposite directions with a fizz to the air. There was a moment's silence. The banging stopped, the shouting too. It was like the police officer on the opposite side of that door had somehow got a glimpse through to us: two hooded figures with weaponry and we were now all sharing a sobering moment.

If it was a stand-off, it was utterly intoxicating.

I pushed the knife back into my waistband, my heightened senses prickled with pleasure at the feel of it against my skin. The crowbar too had a pleasing ergonomic to it. It felt indestructible. So did I.

The handle twitched and I sucked in a sharp breath, the heavy door rattled in its frame at first, like he was trying to yank it open without twisting the handle all the way. It did have a stiff mechanism, I knew that. He would work it out, though. He would yank that door open and then the next part was formed so clearly in my mind it was like I had already seen it play out. In that vision I rushed him the moment the door opened, forcing him back into the hall with a couple of quick hits, so hard and so fast that he didn't have a hope in hell of even knowing what I was, let

14

alone who and any sound would be contained within those thick walls.

The door pulled in.

I flew forwards, powered by something different, my movement like nothing before. I had the crowbar raised and I swung it like it was a twig, my aim no more specific than into the doorway. The officer on the other side was also moving forward, into the doorway, into the blow. The noise when I hit him was nothing like the strikes on his car. It was a dull thud, instantly sickening, like when you beat a mattress for dust. Only it wasn't a mattress and it wasn't dust that came from the falling shape in a splatter that painted the floor. My momentum took me into the hall just as I had pictured, but the officer fell away from me, the speed of his fall was different — wrong, too fast to be real. There was another sickening sound when the back of his head met with the solid wood of the floor and his skull popped like a blown egg. It all happened in a blur, I'd heard a gasp, felt the connection, a rush of breeze from moving forward so fast it had actually made my eyes water.

And then it was over.

I was still. My companion bundled into my side. A moment of silence passed and then there was a noise like a man inhaling deeply, it ended in a whistle.

'What did you do?' My companion spoke first, his voice deeper than I'd ever heard from him. I didn't reply. I was still looking down at the floor and the mess that was on it, that was still expanding like performance art. The police officer's back was arched, his head pushed back, one of his eyes was completely shut with the other half open. The open eye was seemingly fixed on the door to the kitchen but there was no focus and it wasn't moving, no part of him was. His limbs, rather than thrashing around or lifting in defence, seemed curled up, like they were on strings pulled tight from his midriff.

It was nothing like my vision, it was like nothing I had seen before.

Even when he finally twitched it didn't seem real, more like a movie prop where someone was playing with the controls. The fists twitched first, the hands balling themselves up tight, then a twitch from the neck that spread out to move his lips. I moved closer, squatting over him, watching as his jaw made a movement a bit like breathing, but not quite. I couldn't look away. I should have been shocked, appalled at myself at what I had done, but I was flooded with excitement instead.

I knew I was watching a man move his last.

# CHAPTER 7

Acting Detective Inspector Maddie Ives leant on the car door she had just shut and she hesitated. The moment she took her hand away she was going to have to walk towards the warm frontage of PC Philip Jones's family home and start the process of stripping away every last bit of that warmth, every last bit of everything, until there was nothing left but the shell that would remain when her news was delivered.

It was a pleasant home. Boxy in design, but softened by white weatherboarding covering the top half. It was attached to an identical neighbouring property by just a garage on the right side, the tarmac of the drive was lightened by the sun in the shape of two cars, though it was only hosting one.

The front garden was long, flat and recently mowed. It was intersected by a garden path that was bordered by a juvenile blossom tree sagging under the weight of a stunning pink jacket that was new for spring. The path ended at a porch made of newer looking bricks. The ground floor window was long, with net curtains neatly pulled into hourglass shapes at each end.

'I'll do it.' Detective Inspector Harry Blaker appeared above the roofline, his usual gruffness mixed with resignation.

'I said I would,' said Maddie.

17

'You want to?'

'Of course, I don't. Let's just get it done.'

A woman answered the door before they had even made it to the blossom tree.

'Mrs Jones . . .'

And then a moment occurred that may be unique to this very set of circumstances. A moment where two strangers look at each other and everything that needed to be said, everything one party needs the other to understand, is instantly communicated. Maddie and Harry could have turned away at that point with their job done, it might even have been better.

People always just know.

'Yes?' The shake in her voice was unmistakable.

'May we step in?'

'My husband's at work,' Mrs Jones said and she stepped back, as though she was floating. It wasn't by way of an invitation, more like she was being repelled. Maddie moved in and stepped to the right, it took her into the doorway of the living room with the perfect net curtains. The carpet had a pattern like it was just hoovered, the air smelled of polish and a disturbed chair hadn't quite been put back to cover the visible dents in the carpet. Maddie lingered on them, needing to take a moment. A pang of sharp pain coursed through her gut, forcing her to pause, to hold her breath for just a moment.

'I'm Detective Inspector Harry Blaker and this is DI Maddie Ives,' Harry spoke up. He always sounded like he was growling but he could manage warmth when he needed to. 'And we're sorry to interrupt your evening. Perhaps you would like to take a seat?'

'Phil . . .' Mrs Jones said in a way that was as if she was standing over his body.

'We work with your husband, Mrs Jones,' Harry continued. 'He attended a call this afternoon where he was badly assaulted. Phil sustained injuries that were too serious for the ambulance crew to save him. I'm so sorry, Mrs Jones, your husband died before a transfer to hospital was possible.'

And there it was. Word perfect. All the detail she needed at that point about what had happened, a nod to the fact that he was one of us and we were hurting too and then the absolute assurance that her husband was dead. Now it was a waiting game. Mrs Jones held her breath as if she had sucked in those words to keep them there until she could make some sense of them. Her eyes lost any focus, they flickered a little, side to side and her hand rose to cover her mouth.

Maddie stepped in a little closer. 'Shall we take that seat?' she said. She led Mrs Jones to a pristine sofa. There was a crackle of leather from under her slight frame as she sat back, reaching out for the reading glasses that were tucked into a unit that also contained the TV remotes. Then she put them back down.

'I'll need to . . .' she said, moving her hand towards where her mobile phone was laid out on the same table. 'I'll need to make some calls . . . He has two sons. They . . .'

Maddie took a seat next to her. Harry backed away until he was far enough to spin on his heels and leave the room entirely. A moment later came the sound of a kettle.

'Phil,' Mrs Jones said, meekly. 'He's on a late shift. I always leave his dinner in the oven.' A smile began but spluttered out. 'I never know how someone can eat that late but he's never liked eating at work. Always gets disturbed, he says. Always gets *turned out*. Skips his own dinner to go and help people. To keep them safe.'

Maddie waited long enough to know that she was finished. 'Mrs Jones, I would like to get someone here to be with you, just for now. We're not going anywhere, you understand, but maybe you've got family or friends nearby that would come and sit with you for tonight. This will be very—'

'Phil,' she said. 'The only person I ever want to sit with me, do you understand?' The flash of anger was sudden but not unexpected. Maddie had done this enough to know that it was a cyclical process. There would be shock, there would be anger and disbelief and there would be a lot of sadness and all of these things would rotate like a tombola. Maddie's job was nothing more than to roll with it.

'Of course. And there's nothing I would want more than to make that happen. But I can't, Mrs Jones, so we need to do what we can to make sure you're going to be okay.' Maddie grimaced the moment she had said it. There was a whole list of things *not* to say and any suggestion of being *okay* would be near the top of the list. Mrs Jones seized on it.

'Okay? How am I supposed to be okay *ever again?* My husband . . . my Phil is . . .' She couldn't say it. She might never be able to say it. 'Those two boys!'

Harry had been a peripheral blur at the doorway, but now he stepped back in with a steaming mug in his blunt fingers. Maddie sat back for the drink to be delivered and it prompted something, a convulsion from her throat where the stomach cramp surged back like this time it was making a break for freedom. She fought it off. This was not the time. Mrs Jones took the tea in a wordless exchange, placing it on the table. The next sound was a pop from Harry's joint as he squatted down to Mrs Jones' level. He reached out for where she had balled her hands up tight. Just one of his hands swamped them. Her focus had been lost, her eyes pointed down at the floor but they reacted now, to his warmth perhaps.

'I know how you are feeling.' His voice was deep and strong, the sort you can feel as well as hear. This was another subject on the list that should be avoided, had Maddie said it the escalation might have been untenable, but Harry had a sincerity to him that you couldn't fake. 'My wife . . .' He moved his other hand to complete the wrapping. 'My wife, who I loved with all my heart . . . I remember when I got the same message you are . . . the moment when I knew it was true, that she was gone . . . So, we are going to stay with you and we are going to give you anything you need, anything that is physically possible, we will do. But we cannot give you what you *want.*' Mrs Jones rushed a nod that shook a thick tear loose. 'And when you have everything you need then you *will* be okay, I promise you that. Okay is not a high bar, you can be okay and still be hurting, we know that. That's what my colleague meant.' She rushed another nod.

'Mrs Jones . . . could I use your loo? Sorry, I—' There was nothing more Maddie could say; an explanation could only make the timing even more odd.

'Of course,' Mrs Jones said. 'Back out into the hall and there's a door under the stairs.'

'Thank you.' Maddie got up, deliberately avoiding eye contact with Harry. She was clumsy, she clutched her bag tightly under her right arm and it caught a picture to lay it out flat on its back. She pushed on, her whole body starting to convulse. She bundled out into the hall, her hand slipping off the handle to the downstairs loo in her haste. It was tiny, a cupboard really, but it would do.

She got the door closed and dropped to her knees just as the hot rush of vomit surged through her. She fumbled for the chain, it was a circular button on the middle of the cistern and she held it down as another surge rocked her frame. The flushing toilet was oddly pleasant, it made a cool mist as it churned in front of her, mist with a hint of lavender. Another surge contorted her body, her jaw pinned open and the flush wouldn't work again to mask the sounds so she scrabbled blindly for the tap.

Two and done, not including a similar episode earlier in the day. Then came the familiar feeling of exhaustion that swept in where the cramp had been relieved — for now at least — combined with a runny nose that burned as she blew it. She kept the cold tap running and swilled her mouth as best she could, catching her reflection in the small mirror above and wishing she hadn't. She took a moment, sitting on the closed toilet and her eyes fell to her bag. It had slipped to the floor and was now slumped against her leg. She parted the top, reaching down for the white stick that had formed the pivotal part of her day: *Clearblue*.

'Pregnant.' The word tumbled from her lips to surprise her, like someone else had read the confirmation over her shoulder. It was the first time she had said it, the first time she had really accepted it. Even watching those lines appear a few hours earlier hadn't been enough.

'Pregnant,' she said again.

# CHAPTER 8

Maddie's walk back down a path smattered in pink petals was just under an hour later and came with the accompaniment of a vibration from the phone in her pocket. They were handing over to a Family Liaison Officer who had arrived with his expression already fixed on *sympathetic ear*. She couldn't stand the aftermath, the constant reassurance, the going round and round in circles while the atmosphere of sadness thickened with every rotation. Harry, on the other hand, seemed much more engaged, to the point that Maddie had left him with his hands still intertwined with those of Mrs Jones.

Maddie checked her phone while she waited. The vibration was a message from her boyfriend and just seeing the name *Vince* had her tightening her grip on her handbag, its contents and all that it meant.

*Hey, I heard what's gone on. Just checking in, seeing you're okay. I know Jonesy, one of the good ones. Thought he'd retired tbh. Bet the mood is on the floor. Keep your chin up, Mads, and go get the bastards.*

She slid the message left, then selected the option to clear it from her screen. She should reply, she knew that. The last three nights she had been going back to her flat rather than the home they shared, then ignoring his calls, his pleas to talk. But this was different; this wasn't about them, this was a message that deserved some reassurance. She would do it later.

When she looked away from her phone, Harry had separated himself from the grieving widow and was standing beside the FLO. They were in deep conversation, Harry with his hand on the man's shoulder like he was giving him advice he really needed to heed. They shook hands to end the interaction and Harry walked towards her.

'Are you okay?' he said, unlocking the car. Maddie used it as a natural delay, taking her time to get into her seat.

'Yup.'

'Tough times ahead.' She said, while Harry peered back up the path to prompt a flush of realisation and then guilt in Maddie. She'd dropped the ball in there, it hadn't gone well but it would have been a lot worse if Harry hadn't picked it up with his empathy and explanation of the loss of his own wife. She was certain he hadn't gone in there with the intent of bringing that subject to the surface. Maddie's mistake had forced his hand.

'Are you okay?' she said.

Harry shrugged in time with starting the car. 'Always.'

'I forget the impact these jobs can have on . . .' She ran out of words.

Harry shrugged again. 'I know what it's like. Makes me the right person to deal with it.'

'Or the wrong person, if we're talking about looking after you.'

Harry met her with tired eyes that held a spark of humour buried deep, 'Ain't no one talking about looking after me.' He reached down to turn up a radio channel that was playing Elton John and Maddie knew that the conversation was over. This was further confirmed by an incoming call that cut Elton off in his prime, the Rocket Man known for his vast array of spectacular eyewear was suddenly replaced by Eileen Holmans and her similarly emphatic collection of carpet slippers.

Harry did the talking while Maddie peered out of the window, occasionally closing her eyes to the swirl of scenery where she was starting to feel nauseous. She had her bag on her lap, her hand under it to lie flat on her belly, her concentration all over the place. She absorbed what she needed from the call.

Eileen Holmans was the Major Crime Data Analyst, but that didn't go anywhere near explaining her role. "In Charge" was possibly the most accurate description, despite being a civilian employee and technically standing on the bottom rung. As part of *being in charge* she had acquired a space in Cranbrook Police Station that she was now setting up as an incident room. Eileen was good at a lot of things, but *acquiring* might just be her greatest strength.

'You were in the toilet for a long time,' Harry said when the call had been over for a good few minutes. Maddie was caught out, facing away, her eyes tightly shut, seeing off another wave of nausea fuelled by cramps.

'Wordle,' Maddie said. 'It's a tough one today.'

'That's a phone game, right?'

Maddie stayed facing away.

'In the middle of a death message?'

'If there's one thing you should never ask a woman, Harry, it's about how long they were in the toilet.' She turned back into the cabin.

Harry stayed peering forward. 'But you're okay?'

'I am. I've not been feeling great, but it's nothing. I know I coulda handled it a little better back there, but there's no such thing as a good death message, right?'

'It's why we do these things in pairs.'

'In case one fucks up?' Maddie almost delighted in his grimace. Harry Blaker was well known for his dislike of profanities, so they were useful to halt conversations that might become uncomfortable.

'How's young Vince?' Harry seemed determined that this one would continue.

'Suspended,' said Maddie.

'I'm aware of that.'

'You're aware of it in the sense of him being a police officer suspended from duty. I mean it more literally . . . he's like a man suspended from a piece of string, waiting to be told what to do next, what to say and what to think.'

'He must be driving you mad,' Harry said. There was more in that question, like he already knew that Maddie had used the loss of the tenant in her flat as a way of giving him some space. Giving them both some space. She was careful with her answer.

'He's driving himself mad.'

'I asked him out for a pint.' Harry let the sentence linger.

'And he didn't go?'

'He said he couldn't. Perfectly legit excuse. Had something with the kid.'

There was another silence, another one that she was supposed to fill. Maybe she was supposed to confirm what he was thinking already, to lay out her boyfriend's state of mind, to talk about how he wasn't coping so well, that neither of them were. Maybe chuck into the mix how she was pregnant, confirmed it just that day and how she had no idea how she could deal with that right now.

'You could try again,' she said instead.

'Would I get the same response?'

'You might.'

'I imagine if Vince had lost his sister at any other time in his life, he would have thrown himself into his work. That's not the best reaction, but knowing Vince, I think it would have helped him.'

'I think you're right.'

'But he can't do that.'

'He can't,' Maddie agreed.

'Tell him to get in touch,' Harry said, then added something rather telling: 'Next time you see him.'

* * *

Cranbrook Police Station was a rural station in every sense, which meant that it was about as modern as a wooden truncheon, born of a time when buildings were built specifically

26

for the police, by the police and entirely without the input of anyone concerned with aesthetics. It presented through Maddie's passenger window as a rectangular box with square windows. The doors were right where you would expect them and painted in a "Police Blue" that had faded over time, like the memories of the cells in its belly that were now used for storage. The whole building had the feeling of a former time and place.

'Take you back?' Maddie said while the speed-gate made a noise like a grumble as it rolled open for them. Harry had history with this place. He'd mentioned it before: his first posting to Major Crime as a Detective Constable had been inside these walls.

'Had some good times here,' he said. 'We did some good work.' He nosed the car in among a row of identical looking models. 'Let's go do some again.'

There was an instant murmur on entry. It travelled down the stairs as a preamble to the chaos that filled the first floor, the space that Eileen had commandeered. The woman herself stood stationary at its centre like the queen bee, while everyone else moved and buzzed. Despite the day she had suffered, Maddie couldn't help but smile at their Intelligence Analyst directing an entire department of battle-hardened detectives in a plaid skirt and reading glasses. And those being directed included a rather bemused looking superintendent.

'Ah, you two . . .' Superintendent Banks looked relieved to have an excuse to peel away. 'I need to be somewhere else,' she said. 'There's a press release briefing. I'll be taking it in my car on the way to headquarters. I'll catch up with you after. Sorry to have to shoot off. Everything okay?' Her eyes lingered on Maddie.

'We're okay, ma'am.'

'How did the news go?' She then waved her hand. 'Actually, don't answer that. Stupid question. I'm out there myself, tomorrow. Probably the Chief Constable wants to come too, it's only right.'

'Understood.' Maddie nodded. 'Did you need anything from us, for the press?'

'Oh God, no! You know what the first response will be like. Very vanilla. So light on detail we'll all blend into the painted wall behind. We'll confirm a serious incident, a serving officer as a victim, give the ongoing investigation line and then a warning to the vultures out there that they need to be respecting the family. Then it's a straight-out appeal for witnesses. I've just had the update from Ma'am Holmans . . .' She turned slightly, that bemused look back on her face, to look across at Eileen. 'And now she's waiting for you. There's not much.' The superintendent started to move away. 'Which means I'm counting on you. I suggested the old cells as a place to crash — you know, if you fancy going old school!' She winked — specifically for Harry — then she spun to make good her escape. Superintendent Helen Banks was a bundle of energy, a whirlwind, the sort you couldn't help but like. Maddie was aware that she and Harry had worked together in the past and even he seemed to like her, which was a long way from a given. Maddie couldn't resist.

'What exactly does *going old school* with Ma'am Banks mean for you, Inspector Blaker?'

'Falling asleep in a prison cell after an eighteen-hour day,' Harry grumbled. There was to be no time for any more explanation; Eileen Holmans had seen them and crossed the floor faster than an elderly woman in a pair of backless slippers had any right to do. The slippers were navy today, almost black, with a lighter blue piping and brown leather tassel that shook with every step. Out of them stretched tights that matched in with the skirt and cardigan. Her glasses looked new, different at least, but as always, cut aggressively straight along the top as if designed to give her eyes a stage on which to perch. 'Mr Blaker . . . Ma'am Ives . . .'

Maddie caught her tongue. She'd spent months asking Eileen to use her first name — or at least something a little less formal but was now resigned that this was never going to happen.

'Eileen,' Harry grumbled.

'I have prepared a side room.' She spun away, her movement silent on a carpet that was host to patches of threadbare and dubious stains in equal measure. The smaller room was bare entirely, save a fifty-inch television on an industrial looking stand. 'I'll be arranging for more furniture,' Eileen said, as if the room needed some explanation. 'Bums on seats are the priority right now — it's a bit make-do.'

'What do you have?' Harry said.

Eileen lifted her hands to reveal a television remote. She gestured with it and the television clunked then paused another second before revealing a still image.

'Jesus!' Maddie exhaled. It was of their fallen colleague. 'A word of warning might have been nice.'

'Police Constable Philip Jones,' Eileen started, oblivious. 'Fifty-six years old, twenty-nine years a police officer and a career beat officer. Based out of Tonbridge. Frant Village Hall is very much on his patch. He used this building regularly, too.'

The screen changed to a photo of three people: two men and a woman. The two men were both dressed in police dress uniform and shaking hands. Maddie recognised a former Chief Constable as one of them; the other was Philip Jones. 'This is PC Jones receiving his long service award for twenty years, though it was three years—'

'Eileen . . .' There was a warning in Harry's tone.

Eileen cleared her throat as if to show her annoyance. 'The woman by his side is—'

'We just met Mrs Jones,' Harry said tersely.

'Jillian Jones. His wife. Correct.'

'Can we stick to today?' Harry said.

This prompted an image of Frant Village Hall, pictured from the front.

'This evening at 17.45 hours, a call was received in the Force Control Room. It was a 999 call, a male voice reporting a group of youths throwing stones at the village hall. The caller stated that he believed they had gained entry.'

29

There was another change to the screen. This time it showed just a flat, white line that started a shiver in time with the voice that came through the speakers. Eileen was playing the call she had just described.

'The voice sounds odd?' Harry said, the moment the seventeen second call had finished. 'Artificial.' Maddie nodded her agreement.

'The superintendent was of the same opinion. It wasn't noted by the call-taker at the time, but the more you play it back, the more it does seem to have an . . . artificial quality. There are apps these days that can change your voice on a call. Most of them are entirely free.'

'Of course there are.' Harry sighed.

'I think the idea is to utilise them as a novelty item, to phone your gran and sound like an alien or a ghost, not to conceal your identity with criminal intentions.'

'The phone number?' barked Harry.

Eileen just shook her head to confirm it as a dead end. 'They didn't offer any details either, which the call-taker didn't make much of. That's not unusual. Another thing to add . . . the hall is in constant use for a variety of reasons. It's the home of a bowls club for one thing, but there are regular coffee mornings, the Scouts meet there, the Girl Guides on another night—'

'Eileen . . .' Harry's growl was now heavy with impatience.

'Today is one of the very few evenings when there is nothing planned. The keyholder lives nearby, a volunteer, and she closed it up at 17.30.'

'You think that Philip Jones was lured to the location? And by someone who knew a little bit about its use?' Maddie said. 'Its schedule, at least?'

'It's just something of note,' Eileen said. 'House-to-house in the immediate area has been all but completed and there is nothing of relevance. The officers knocking the doors were aware to check for doorbell cameras or any home CCTV, as you requested, and I'm afraid it would appear to be a negative result on that one. There's no coverage of the hall at all and very little coverage of roads leading in and out.'

'And the dashcam appeal?'

'The superintendent has that as an action point. She will make that appeal as part of the press conference, which looks likely to be scheduled for 9 a.m. tomorrow morning.'

'We still need to see the scene,' Harry said. 'We should have been out there already.'

Maddie agreed. They had been on their way until a call from the Superintendent had diverted them to Jillian Jones, explaining how she needed to know that this death message was one that was "delivered right". Whatever that meant.

'Forensics are on scene,' said Eileen. 'They intend on working all the while there is daylight and then it will be locked down. There's a search team outside with the same idea. They're doing a fingertip search of the car park for now, but it will extend into tomorrow. There's already a very large cordon in place.'

'Anything yet?'

'No . . . and I tend not to chase our CSI colleagues in the early stages . . .'

Eileen was right. In any job like this, CSI were the most likely to kick an investigation into gear, to give it a sense of direction at the very least and detectives did little more than get in the way. But Maddie wanted to see it too. An early look at a crime scene offered a part of a story that could never be repeated. 'They might talk to us when we arrive,' she said, thinking aloud. 'I'll see if I can pick Charley up a coffee from somewhere.'

'There's a place that's walking distance from the scene,' said Eileen. 'It's called Daisy's Kitchen on the Green. I called her direct. She closes at 2 p.m., but seems to have made herself available to police resources. She seemed very happy to accept two detectives knocking at her door for refreshments on their arrival.'

'What would we do without you, Eileen?' Maddie said.

Her colleague's smile broadened. 'Did the superintendent talk about how we're managing the risk to other officers?' Harry said.

'She's requested all patrols be double-crewed where possible, with at least one of the pairings to be carrying a taser. Firearms will be responding to any calls that come in from a public phone with no details given by the caller.'

'They're going to be busy,' Harry mused.

'They are. All across the country. Neighbouring forces have taken up the same precautions — the MET too, in case this is part of something bigger.'

'Makes sense,' Maddie said.

'We should go,' Harry said. 'Stop this before it *does* become anything bigger.'

'Do you think that's likely?' There was a touch of something approaching fear in Eileen's voice.

'We should assume the worst,' Harry said stoically. 'Have we started looking into Philip Jones for anything to suggest this was directed at him personally?'

'I've made a start, but . . .' She huffed. 'Well, it's a big job. That's not a reflection on PC Jones. I challenge you to look at any police officer with a view to picking out grudges. It's literally your job to upset people. We'll need to go through every call he's attended in recent times — every historic crime report, complaint . . . every outstanding investigation . . . certainly every arrest. It will be very protracted.'

'There might be an answer in the protracted.' Harry's growl had a scolding element that Maddie didn't like.

'One thing we know about Eileen,' Maddy said later, 'is her determination when it comes to pushing through the tedious. She's tireless.' She felt her cheeks burn a little.

'I'm talking about every one of us,' Harry said. 'We lost Philip Jones and it came from nowhere. Now we should assume we're all working to prevent the need to go out to another scene like Frant Village Hall.'

## CHAPTER 9

'I want to hurt another one.'

I said those words without looking up, my eyes locked on the point of the zombie knife and its hypnotic beauty. Inanimate objects can really catch you out sometimes.

We had driven to a block of garages, disused and forgotten, somewhere I'd already identified as a good place to stash a car while any heat died down. Admittedly, that was when I was considering the heat that would follow the report of a smashed-up police car, not the slaughter of its driver, but that didn't change anything. The game was still going to be the same, just the police might turn out with a few more players.

I had a smile that I hoped was reassuring for the man leaning against the bonnet of the parked car. I had rolled it two thirds of the way into one of the garages, one that had been left with its door jammed up and we were sat in the space that was left.

'You want to do what? Are you crazy?' His grin was laced with uncertainty. 'In fact, don't bother answering that.'

'Why is that crazy?'

'We were supposed to put his windows in, teach the old bastard a lesson, show that they're not untouchable. That was what you said and we did that. Then you hit him . . .'

'Once.' There was nothing I could do about the glee in my voice. 'And did you see it? Did you see how fast he went down?'

'Of course, I saw it,' he said. 'That was fucked up.' He shook his head, his focus dropping to his feet. Then the car rocked a little on its haunches as he pushed off. I was sitting on the floor, cross-legged with my back to the wall, my seat more comfortable than it had any right to be. He took a step towards me, kicking a clump of grit that I felt flick up against the part of my shin that was exposed. He stopped close enough to loom over me. 'You would really do that again?'

'We wanted to give them a black eye, right? The police? We wanted to teach them a lesson. We did that.'

'You killed one!'

'*We* killed one.' I stared up at him. 'And it was one hit, one moment and he was down. He might have been dead before he even hit the floor. It was too good for him — too good for any of them. So now I want to do it properly. We've come this far, it's not like it will make a difference.'

'You think killing someone doesn't make a difference?'

'I think killing another one doesn't. There was a line and we stepped over it. There's no going back, so we might as well go forward.'

'Or, just thinking out loud here, we could, you know, hide! I mean, what are we doing here? If we get away with this — and that's a pretty big *if*—then we should count ourselves lucky, never mention this again and stay the hell away from all things police, right?'

'No,' I said. I stood up, taking a step towards him and, to my absolute delight, he flinched. It was subtle, almost invisible. A far more visible reaction came when his two steps backward prompted a jerked response when the car's rear nudged into his buttock. There was a mischief in his eyes that had been a constant, but it was temporarily doused, the self-assuredness too. I had done that. He might even have been a little scared of me, scared of what I had done, scared of what I was capable of.

I hadn't expected to enjoy that so much.

# CHAPTER 10

It was the middle of the evening and, with the sun slipping away, the search teams had called it a day to head back to their vans by the time Maddie made it to the scene. Harry was alongside her. The team were bunched up by the sliding door on the side of the van, each of them holding an assortment of dainty teacups in their sweaty clutches, cups that may never have looked more out of place. They matched with those that Maddie and Harry were carrying. All of them were bone china and all were adorned with a floral theme. "Daisy" of Daisy's Kitchen was utterly insistent: She wouldn't have a police officer arriving on the scene and refusing a hot refreshment any more than she would have an officer drinking out of a "ghastly" takeaway cup. Maddie had needed to be firm to ensure they hadn't been lumbered with matching saucers.

'Ma'am . . . boss . . .' A member of the search team in sergeant's stripes unmerged himself from the gaggle to greet them individually. Maddie recognised him as Alan Day. 'Daisy?' He gestured with his bone china at theirs. 'She's been good to us.'

'Anything?' Harry said, instantly.

Alan shook his head. 'We've done a fingertip of the hardstanding that makes up the car park. I've set the cordon big. I reckon a village green like this floods with dog walkers come the morning so I've taped the whole thing for now. CSI are still inside. I want to do another run of the car park and the bowling green in the morning and then we'll spread out from there. We'll be in first thing to make a start. We would stay all night, to be honest, but . . .'

Maddie nodded knowingly. 'Can't do much in the dark. Back first thing with a fresh team makes sense.'

'We really want to find something for you.'

Maddie peered over at the hall, specifically at the hard standing on the left side. The police car was gone but its position was still marked out by an outline of shattered glass and broken plastic. The sergeant read her mind.

'Couple of mine organised the forensic lift of the car. CSI did their pictures *in situ* but they want it under cover for the close-up stuff. They weren't too hopeful, though. Seems there are ways you can beat up a car that's good for forensic traces and there are ways that are bad. Got the impression this was done the bad way.'

'I guess it would be too much to ask for an offender to slice their hand up real good on a shard of glass,' Maddie said.

'I guess it would.'

'Can we nab a couple of paper suits off you? Before we go in, I mean?'

'Sure, but there's a bag of them around the back. The Common Approach Path is through the back door. Takes you into a short hall and then the kitchen. They think Phil went in through the side door.'

'You work with CSI enough, you learn that turning up kitted out makes them much keener to talk. Far better than turning up and that being the first thing they have to tell you.'

'I'll try and remember that.'

'Phil . . .' Maddie said. 'You knew him?'

Alan shrugged. 'I did, yeah. Did a couple of Public Order deployments with him, but I actually saw him a bit more out of work. He lives in the same village I do, less than two miles from here. Means he was in the pub or the shop at times. I knew him to say hello . . . small talk. Enough to know him as a decent bloke. You get the measure of someone.'

'You do,' Maddie agreed.

'All of the team knew him. One of the faces. Been around forever.'

'As I understand,' Maddie said.

'Wasn't due to be a face too much longer, I hear. Less than a year left.'

'I heard that too,' Maddie said. 'And what have we got over there?' She referred to a small group of people huddled together over to the left. A Police Community Support Officer was standing close by, close enough to keep an eye, not quite close enough to engage.

'Fucking ghouls,' the sergeant said, then checked himself. 'Sorry!' he said, looking at Harry.

'Ghouls is right,' Harry said, dismissively. It was a known term among police officers, assigned to people who liked to turn up at cordons or car accidents to see what they could see of someone else's misery. In this case they looked mostly old, the demographic of the locals. There were people in the distance hurrying towards the group as word was spreading, concerned perhaps that they might miss something juicy.

Maddie got dressed in a fast-disappearing patch of sunshine. The white paper suit was far too big; big enough to cover the clothes she was already in and then to tie down tight at the sleeves and ankles to billow out like some sort of fancy-dress snowman. Next, she added shoe covers, gloves, a mask and a hairnet under a hood pulled up. These additions were all in a bright colour blue. The ghouls watched on in silence, captivated it would seem, by this part of the show. Maddie didn't even look their way as she walked towards the hall, keeping as far left as possible before looping around until she found the back door.

Charley Mace, the county's most senior Crime Scene Investigator, was there to greet her.

'Normally a far closer race between us, I was surprised to have beat you here.' Despite the mask over her face, the smile was clear in Charley's voice. 'And by quite some time.'

'We got held up,' Maddie explained. 'The widow.'

'Ah, I see. You're welcome to that. Mr Blaker . . .' She nodded. 'Long time no see.'

'I was hoping that would continue,' he growled back.

'None taken.' Charley's unseen smile was very much back. 'But I think I know what you mean.'

They went inside. The rear entrance took them straight into a hallway with Charley leading the way. The first door off the hall was to the toilet and it was ajar, the room behind it dripped water in a constant pattern and smelled of over-zealously applied cleaning products. The next was to the kitchen, which had a similar theme. The kitchen units looked old and simple in design but everything was scrubbed down and immaculate. Three different types of cloth hung over an upturned washing-up bowl.

The main hall was next. It was packed up, the chairs stacked in equal piles at points around the outside. The focal point seemed to be a wooden lectern at the far end. The last of the daylight gushed in via high windows to make bright spots in the middle of the floor that thickened the shadow against the walls. The room contained numerous religious notes, one of the pitched roofs had a circular window at its highest point with stained-glass and there were crosses dotted around the walls, the largest of which was mounted near to the main entrance door and bore an effigy of Jesus Christ.

Police Constable Philip Jones lay under His gaze with a stillness that never failed to leave an impression on Maddie. She had accepted some time ago that the dead was something she was never going to get used to.

Philip was on his back, his legs straight out with toes pointed towards the main door. His arms were by his side with tight fists turned inwards. His head too was back, the one eye that was open was fixed in their general direction while his mouth was contorted into an expression that could be read as anything from shock to pain. It was probably both.

'I can't move you much closer, not yet. I'm still working towards him,' Charley said and Maddie could see that was true. The floor was littered with yellow signs, about the size of an espresso cup, individually numbered and triangular in shape to be self-supporting. The numbers were well into the twenties, getting higher as they crept towards the body. The biggest concentration was at the head end, here they were really starting to swarm.

'It's all blood,' Charley said, as if reading Maddie's mind. 'Nothing more exciting than that, I'm afraid. It's what you'd expect from blunt force. You've got a strike to the front, across the forehead which would have caused some damage, enough to put Philip in trouble. But the fall . . .'

'You think that was what killed him?' Maddie said.

Charley shrugged. You never got a commitment from a crime scene investigator; their field was science, the direct opposite of speculation. 'He died from his head injuries. I'd put my mortgage on that. He was hit by something solid to the front and then he took a very solid fall to the back. We'll get a lot more when we can open him up and have a closer look. His head has lost much of its structural integrity, I could feel it.'

'What does that mean?' Maddie said.

'It's mush,' Charley said, matter-of-fact. 'Easter wasn't so long ago. Think of those big chocolate eggs you get all wrapped up in foil. I like to give them a punch while they're still wrapped up, breaks them up nice. Keep it wrapped in foil after you've hit it and it will hold its shape, but it's still in bits. That's what I mean by a loss of structural integrity.'

'So his head is just being held together by what, skin?'

'His forehead and brow. His eye sockets are all popped. The back of the head will be worse. You see the posturing, the fists, the pointed feet, the arching of the neck?'

'I do.' Maddie could hardly have missed it.

'There are two types of posturing . . . decerebrate and decorticate. I can never remember which is which. I just know that both are sure signs of a serious brain trauma. And both are bad news.'

'Decerebrate,' Harry said, though it sounded like he was using the word to clear his throat. 'That's what we have. Normally you see them at RTCs, catastrophic ones. Somebody hit him hard. You don't pop a skull easily.'

'You don't,' Charley agreed.

'Did you find a weapon?' asked Maddie.

'Not the sort that can do this.'

'Something heavy, but agile,' Harry said. 'Something you could carry in then swing around in a place like this. The sort of thing that stayed together when it hit, too. Steel, weighted, slim — a tool of some sort.'

'Go on.' Charley's voice was smiling again.

'A cosh, knuckledusters or something like a police asp, that's not going to be enough. Too small and light to get the momentum. Something like a hammer, something weighted right to cause damage.'

'I would like to hear of any finds of a hammer,' Charley said, nodding. 'The damage to the back of the head suggests he was literally taken off his feet by the blow.'

'So, something bigger,' Harry said. 'At least the part that impacted would have been bigger. A skull collapses around a hammer point, this is something with a flatter head to knock him off his feet.'

'A lump hammer would be an option,' Charley said, 'but we won't be dismissing anything. Force is a difficult thing to predict, so I'd suggest you're deliberately vague with your search teams. Anything with a reasonable weight that you can swing at someone.'

'One hit?' Harry said.

'You know my answer to that, Harry.' There was the hint of a warning in Charley's tone. It softened for the next part. 'But that's my instinct.'

'If it's one hit,' Maddie said, 'it's likely something carried in by the offender. Another marker for premeditated.'

'Premeditated in so much as they lured Philip here for a reason,' said Harry. 'I don't think we should assume it was to murder him.' His eyes searched all around, including up the pitched ceilings.

'What makes you say that?' Maddie said.

'I'm not sure you would plan to beat someone to death. Too unreliable. And if you did, you don't hit them once.'

'I agree,' said Charley. 'I've seen victims who had survived very nasty beatings.' Her voice was low, almost a sigh, and Maddie was sure she saw her lifting her eyes to Christ and his vantage point on the wall. 'You have to be very precise with blunt force trauma.'

'Or lucky,' Harry said.

'I also think your offender may have had another option, something that makes even less sense of the beating.'

'Go on?' Harry said.

'The side door was held shut by a bungee cord, tied off against a wheelie bin. That will be how they trapped him in here. The bin was pulled up against the side of its shelter so it was never going anywhere. The other end was stretched over the handle.'

'The door opens inwards,' Harry said.

'The cord was left. One end on the handle, the other on the bin. It was cut and it was cut clean, no fraying. We're talking sharp.'

'By our offender?' Maddie said.

'I spoke to the search team who made some calls. Phil was found by a local who said the door was swinging open.'

'So, our offender had an incredibly sharp knife and a steel bar in their armoury and they opted for the steel bar,' Harry said.

'Looks that way. And then they took both away with them. And quite possibly a keepsake, too.'

'Keepsake?' Maddie snapped back.

'Phil's missing his handcuffs. I've not done a proper search of him yet, but you can see the pouch from here—'

'Do the search team know?' Harry cut in.

'They do. The skipper seems quite switched on out there. He said he would call Phil's team — see if it can be accounted for back at the nick. I can't imagine a copper leaving the building without his cuffs, but if anyone was going to, seems it might be our friend here.'

'A keepsake would not be good news,' Maddie said.

'It means we should not expect this to be over,' Harry agreed. 'Right then . . .' He had obviously seen enough. 'I need to check back in with Eileen. I want to know if that search through Phil's recent police work has started. We'll need to go speak to his wife again, too. It's not ideal — sooner than we should — but we need to ask questions about his life outside of the Job.'

'What are you thinking Harry?' Maddie said.

'This was personal. *Very* personal. If this was directed at Phil specifically, she should know. This is someone very upset. Someone athletic — strong for sure. And incredibly angry.'

# CHAPTER 11

I couldn't help myself.

I came back to watch. It was all over social media . . . people speculating about something they so obviously knew nothing about. The chat centred around a gang of kids beating up a police officer in a quiet village. Some local rag had put a picture out of the hall. The angle and distance of the picture was such that I could see that a group of people had gathered on one side. So, I went and joined them.

I went on my own and without any explanation. There wasn't one, if I was honest. Curiosity perhaps? More like a desire to see a group of police officers scratching their heads and venting their anger with no idea where to start.

I walked the last mile. I had left the BMW face first in that garage and taken a different car, another one of his, some old Volvo that had a cracked leather driving seat with the instant feel of a favourite armchair. I left it just off a fire road in an area of forest that was popular with dog walkers. So, it appeared, were Volvos.

The group of locals had swelled larger still since the photo. They were huddled together like some impromptu vigil and all managed to look suitably upset. I must have looked just like them as I was welcomed like an old friend

43

with nods and graces. One woman was quick to tell me about a nearby tea shop that was staying open for the community. I could see a couple of people had taken advantage, drinking from highly unsuitable china. Another woman singled me out to tell me how it was okay to be upset, to feel scared even, how things like this just don't happen in nice places like Frant.

But that wasn't true now, was it?

In those first two minutes, having been welcomed, soothed and offered a hot drink, one thing became very clear to me: there had been no witnesses. If two people had been seen beating on a car and following a police officer into a village hall it would have been the tale on everyone's lips by now.

No one had any idea.

Someone had a spare tea. They insisted I take it and I was sure to thank them with just the right amount of sadness. The group fell back to a respectful silence, the only sound the occasional tut, sigh or murmur of 'it's just so terrible'.

Over the rim of my teacup, I looked over at a police van parked up against their blue and white tape. The hall was over to the left and a group of officers wearing navy overalls but still with "POLICE" across their backs were moving on their hands and knees away from it in a scattered line. One of them had called out to me when I had walked over, telling me to walk around the tape as if it wasn't obvious, his tone like he was talking to a child or someone stupid. He wasn't part of the line and had stripes on his shoulders that marked him out as different to the rest, a sergeant. That officer was now back at the van. But my attention was back on the line, on two officers in particular who had reached the area where we had hidden. I watched as they brushed the undergrowth at the foot of the tree, their gloved hands worked quickly — and then, one of them stopped.

Then stood up.

The other followed suit and suddenly there looked to be a hurried conversation. A moment later and hands were thrown in the air like in celebration. I held a mouthful of tea

44

in my mouth, unable to swallow, considering that we must have dropped something, something significant, that this might be the moment when everything started to unravel.

But they weren't looking down and that didn't make sense. They were looking away and both in the same direction, back across the field, shielding their eyes against the low sun. It was towards a uniformed officer, one I couldn't see at first, who appeared with a tray laden with a stack of cups and an ornate teapot. He lifted the whole thing to acknowledge more hands thrown in the air from further along the line. They were celebrating the return of the teaboy.

Jokers.

This was the signal for the entire team to abandon their posts and regroup at the van, each having left a brightly coloured triangle to mark their progress. It was a few minutes later that two murder detectives walked into view. I could tell that's what they were. They might as well have had it written across their backs like their uniformed colleagues.

I wasn't the only member of the community group to notice. The excited chatter started in real earnest when the stern looking older man took a moment to peer over. He wore a waxed jacket, undone to flare behind his walk as if with purpose, like a cape on a villain. His colleague was a woman, sharply dressed and, even looking from a distance, sharp in features. I got a feeling of efficiency from them both, of seniority too.

The officer with the sergeant stripes made a beeline for them, his body language stiffer, having hurriedly brushed away the crumbs of whatever he had been eating. Somehow, the two detectives were also carrying cups. They made short work of the contents then pulled on white suits made of a material light enough to billow in the breeze and blue gloves and shoes.

Then they set off towards Frant Village Hall.

And what I had left inside.

Those in overalls seemed to snigger at just about the moment the two detectives disappeared out of sight behind the building, like they had been holding it in. Someone slapped the sergeant on the arm to pinpoint him as the source and I flared angry. I can't explain the logic of why that resonated with me the way it did, why that man disgusted me so much in that moment. One of his colleagues was dead. It had happened just a short distance from where he stood now, and he was laughing and joking, playing the clown, having talked to me as if I was stupid. I knew his type, the sort of man who liked the sound of his own voice, who liked to stand out, to be noticed.

I noticed him.

# CHAPTER 12

It seemed like there were just a few moments between Maddie noticing how low the sun had got, to it being sucked beneath the curvature of the earth to lay a blanket of total darkness. They hadn't stayed at the scene long, enough to ask a few questions, to look around as much as was possible. They left when CSI had needed to start setting up their own specialist lighting rig. Maddie had become very aware that they were in the way. They had made the call to continue working — inside, at least — into the night.

It was just gone eight thirty in the evening — thirty minutes before PC Philip Jones's late shift was due to finish — when they arrived at his home for the second time that day.

Maddie could smell his dinner.

She could hear the oven too, a low hum telling the tale of a woman who had been told the hardest truth but was still waiting for the moment when there would be nothing left to do but to believe it. It might be the end of his shift that did it, or an hour later, when he still hadn't pulled up on their drive or called to say that he would be late.

They shouldn't be here.

That was Maddie's overriding feeling and it worsened the cramps still lingering in her stomach. They needed to speak to Jillian Jones again, but this wasn't the time, not so soon after giving their message.

Mrs Jones was the picture of a woman operating on auto-pilot as she ushered them in. Maddie's cramps flared brighter as she walked past the downstairs toilet, almost convincing herself that she could still smell the sickly-sweet odour of vomit from her previous visit.

'Mrs Jones, I am so sorry to be disturbing you again.' Harry's voice bursting out of a thick silence was enough to make his subject jump. She took a moment, steeled herself by standing straighter and brushing the front of her trousers like she might be able to dust the day off.

'Jill,' she said with a definitive nod. 'I'm already getting a little fed up of the Mrs Jones, that quickly becomes oppressive. It's Jill.'

'Harry,' he said, 'and Maddie of course.' Maddie nodded and got a blink in return. 'I am sorry to be back so soon, but we have very important work to do. For Phil. We want to know what happened and we want to know who was responsible.'

'And you think I can help with that?' she said, with no feeling or expression.

'We're thorough, Mrs . . . Jill.' Harry corrected himself with another flash of a smile. 'And that means we have to consider all options, no matter how unlikely. Then discount them, until all we have left is the truth.'

'I don't . . . The officer who was here earlier, he said that Phil took a call to a group of youths and he was . . . he was set upon. Why are you not out looking for some vicious group of kids? That's what happened, that's what he said!' She was a little panicked now. She'd had her explanation of what happened, it might even have made sense to her, been a comfort. And now the police officers who had arrived to toss every piece of her life in the air earlier in the day, were back to do it all over again.

'That's one line of enquiry, Jill,' Maddie had sensed that she might benefit from a different voice. 'And let me tell you, there are a lot of officers out looking into just that. The whole area is swamped. We've had officers turn up on their rest days, working for free, just wanting to be involved.' Maddie gave her a moment, letting the words have time to breathe, to then come back softer. 'Phil was well liked, everyone knew him and even for those that didn't, it doesn't matter. The police are a family, a big one that we're all part of, you included, Jill. And this is a family that's hurting.'

'I don't know . . .' Jill stammered, reeling enough to need to take a step backwards, 'I don't know what to do. What do I do now?'

Harry stepped in to reach for Jill's hand once again. She allowed her hands to be lifted for Harry to gather them up and make a warm pile at chest height. Her watery eyes met with his and she flickered a smile as if grateful for the comfort, her shoulders lost some of their tension.

'You don't need to do anything,' Harry said. 'I know you want to. I know you've got the energy inside of you to run a marathon right now and a tiredness that feels like it will bring you to your knees — all at the same time. I know it so well. I remember . . .' He hesitated, the hard exterior Maddie took as permanent, was crumbling a little at the edges. 'I remember the first night.' He fixed intently on Jill. 'It is hard, and it will get harder. When we leave, when the early hours come and you're still pacing and banging on the walls and it's like time has abandoned you, stopped still to leave you wallowing and in pain, I want you to remember something. Can you do that for me?' The intensity was ratcheted even more. Maddie felt like she should step in, say something, at least. She just didn't know what.

Jill nodded her head.

'You need to remember that it only gets better from that point. Whatever happens tonight, in the next few hours, you're strong enough to cope with it and then, when you come through and when that sun comes up tomorrow, you will know that you're strong enough to cope with anything.'

Jill nodded again, her fingers curled tighter. 'Okay,' she said, sounding as if she believed it.

'Do you have anyone who can stay with you tonight?' Harry said.

'I sent her away.' Jill finally broke away from Harry, her eyes shuffling side to side and losing their focus. 'My best friend, but I didn't . . . I don't want anyone here. I just need . . .'

'It's okay,' Harry said. 'Breakfast . . .' The word prompted eye contact again. 'I'll bring it round in the morning, first thing. If you're up and you would like a breakfast delivery, open the curtains in the living room. If they're drawn, I won't even knock.' He took his right hand back, using it to reach inside his waxed jacket for a business card. She took it. 'But if you need anything, any time, if beating the walls and wearing out your lovely carpets isn't holding you, call me.'

Jill gave another jerked nod and still held her hands at chest height when Harry broke away.

'I'm here,' he said, 'and I will be whenever you need me. We're going to find who did this and they're going to realise just what it means when you mess with the police family, okay?'

She nodded again. Maddie took a step back, caught out by Harry who spun away and into a determined march for the door. Maddie managed a curt nod, then almost had to jog to catch up. She only managed it when Harry was already halfway down the path, disturbing the bright pink blossom that was making its best effort to stand out against the dark night.

'What was that?' Maddie hissed and got no answer until they were both sealed back in the car.

'What was what?' Harry said, irritated.

'We had questions.'

'She's upset.'

'We knew that before we came here to ask them. We were going to ask them anyway!'

'It wasn't the right time, we shouldn't have . . . It wasn't the right time.'

'I agree, I thought the same when we walked back in there, but once we did . . . Are we not just prolonging this, now we've gotta go back in the morning.'

'Not you,' Harry snapped, then softened visibly. 'I want to see her in the morning. I want to see . . . I want to see that she's made it.'

'Jesus,' Maddie said. 'She's a grown woman. I know it's a shock but she's gonna be okay.' Then she held her hands up when Harry turned on her.

'She won't, not for a long time. Things won't ever be the same again. Not for her.'

'And not for you,' Maddie said, quickly.

'This isn't about me. I'll go back in the morning and I'll get what we need.' He shifted his attention back on driving as he pulled the car away.

*And I'll get on with the investigation.* Maddie bit her lip to stop the words tumbling out. The rest of the journey was in silence. Harry was already working alone.

# CHAPTER 13

The evening was a pleasant one and it had Louise Day lingering at her front door for longer than she otherwise might have in the winter months. Her evening routine always finished the same, starting at around 10 p.m. with the television off and the kettle on for a cup of tea that would accompany a bedtime book.

Before those few moments of peace and silence were the final checks, including that her front door was locked. Part of that would always be to open it up so their elderly cat could come in. He was a little black and white beast that was affectionately known by most of the street as *bin cat* due to his penchant for kipping on the top of plastic bins where the lids retained the heat. For him, old age had come with some sort of memory malfunction, meaning he had stopped using the perfectly good cat flap at the back as an entrance, to spend his life waiting by the front.

'Hey Kevin.' Louise said as the cat strolled in, one ear bent out of shape from one of the many veterinary procedures dotted throughout his past. 'Which bin took your fancy tonight?'

The cat squeaked, timed like it might have been a reply and then sauntered through the house, his memory sharp enough for him to be able to find his biscuits with no problem.

Louise stared back out into the darkened street. They lived in a typical estate, the sort that had a lot of families packed into a relatively small area and all would fall quiet soon after dinner. Nothing was moving bar the air that shifted the delicious scents of spring. It was Louise's favourite time of the year, the sudden eruption of colours from every-where, the return of the sun's warmth and a general feeling that the world was a better place. She cast a final glance, this one over to the empty part of their drive that would soon be filled. Her husband was working a late shift.

She pushed the door closed and locked it. The next part of the routine was to check on their two children. They were aged eleven and nine, old enough to have established their own structure to bedtime. The eldest was sitting in her *nature tent*, which was really just a sheet between two chairs with two long daisy chains draped over the top. There was a night light inside it, barely powerful enough for Louise to see her daughter's head lift from her book as a silhouette when she pushed the door open.

'Don't be too late, Emmy.' Louise said. She should probably be telling an eleven-year-old that 10 p.m. was late enough, but she could never stop her when she was reading. Their youngest was asleep, at least; she'd been training with a new gymnast troupe and it was effective at wiping her out.

The tea was ready. Decaffeinated and milky, perfect bedtime fodder. She carried it back through the house for a last check of all the doors. Her phone was charging by her bedside, it lit up with a missed call when nudged by her cup: *Alan Sexy Man.*

Her bedside light and her phone screen combined to illuminate her smile. Her husband had been into her phone settings again.

'Sorry, who is this?' she said, the moment the call con-nected after calling him back.

'What do you mean, who is this?'

'Oh . . . sorry, it's you! I thought I was calling a *different* Alan. imagine my disappointment.'

There was a snort down the other end of the phone that turned into a giggle. 'Charming.'

'What do you want?'

'Well, a ten-o'clock tea in my bed with my wife would be lovely right about now.'

'Oh, are you going to be late?' Louise was well used to the life of being married to a search team sergeant. His working day could be long, long enough sometimes for one to run into another.

'No, early. We're just getting off now because we need to be back in for seven. We've got a murder search on. We had a few hours at it earlier but it's not enough. Means I can't do the school run in the morning.'

'I can cover it,' Louise said, though she didn't quite know how. She was due in a 9 a.m. meeting herself. 'You okay? Is it a horrible search?' Alan didn't talk details with her, not often, but she knew of past searches that had included searching a refuse site four days in a row, a sewer pipe for remains and a commercial freezer with sealed bags containing what her husband had described as "mystery meat". Some of the conditions he worked in would test the strongest of stomachs.

'It's just one we want to get right and get back to as soon as.' All his humour dropped away. Alan wasn't often serious.

'No problem. See you soon, then.'

'See you soon.' He seemed to brighten. 'Keep the bed warm, yeah.' And she was sure she detected the sound of a car door closing in the background.

'And you keep your cold, filthy hands off me.' She laughed.

# CHAPTER 14

They came out together. That posed a real challenge, and my first thought was how it was something I had not considered. I was a long way from being any good at surveillance, from even knowing what *being good at surveillance* might mean. I instinctively moved lower in the car seat, watching as the gaggle of officers came out of a side entrance to the police station and then split, each making for different cars. I counted five — all men. Of course they were. The police is nothing but a boy's club.

I was too close. In the movies, when someone is watching someone unawares, waiting to follow, they do it from close, pulling out the moment their target does. But I felt vulnerable, exposed, despite being still in a row of dark cars and mine being the darkest of them all. It was my second time using the old Volvo. The BMW was still abandoned nose-first in a ramshackle garage, tainted with the violence for which it had been a conveyance.

The sergeant was parked close. I couldn't have known, but his car was in the back row of the car park, and it meant that the only thing between us was a wide pavement and a chain link fence. There was a moment when I had been concerned that he wasn't walking to his car at all, that he was making straight for me, that I'd been made already and he was waiting to get close enough to burst into life and wrench open my door, to demand to know what the hell I was doing.

But none of his attention was on me. There was the sudden intrusion of a ringing phone that forced him to juggle the items in his hands, then his cheek lit up bright, his lips too, where they curled into a wide smile. It was perfect timing; it forced his eyes down and delayed him at the same time. The rest of his team spilled out of the car park.

Until it was just me and him.

His phone call was short. He managed to get into his seat with his phone still trapped in place by a head tilted down to meet with his shoulder. He spoke while sat under his interior light, his smile never falling away. A lover, I guessed. His wife, perhaps — I could see a wedding band glinting under that same light, not that that meant anything. Not to men. The fact he was smiling so much made it more likely to me that he was talking to a mistress, and I considered that my plan to follow him home could end up being via a deviation to the address of some part-time lover.

His car started, the interior light dimming away to nothing a moment later and the headlights arced out. I threw myself onto the passenger seat, pushing my cheek down with such force that it squeaked against the soft leather. His headlights were so bright they made a solid square through my window, a square that increased in size, then slid along the roof-lining like a searchlight. Only when I was plunged back into darkness again did I reach out, daring to drop the window, listening for the sound of him moving away where I was still too nervous to sit back up. I heard the car pull up to the barrier that was positioned behind me. The gate had a clunk as it fell back down. The sergeant's car then moved away rather than past, meaning he had turned left.

I sat up. His red lights glared at me in the rear-view mirror — accusatory, getting smaller. Then an indicator blinked to show an intention to turn left. The police station was in the middle of a block, with a main road running parallel to the one I was on. It should mean that if I drove forward and took a right, we would meet again.

I gunned the engine, my body flooded with an excitement that caught me out, then increased as I pulled out into the dark, empty street and surged forward to the junction line. I turned right, the tyre squeal through my open window made me jump. The wind rushed in, buffeting my hair to flail against my cheek and neck as I made for the next junction. I forced myself to slow, conscious that my driving was erratic — that *I* was being erratic. I flicked the window switch to closed as I made the next junction. A quick glance right and I was back under the watchful glare of those same tail lights, their suspicion now justified. Once again, they were moving away.

I pulled out. There were no other cars on the road, which was good and bad at the same time: good, because I could hang back and not be too concerned about keeping him in sight; bad, because there were no other cars for cover. I could only hope that the sergeant wouldn't be taking much notice of anything else out on the road, not enough, at least, to note a car matching his every turn.

He made a mini-roundabout and I could see he was signalling right. There was no need for any indication, I was too far back for it to make a difference and there was nothing else coming. I hoped this meant he was a man on autopilot, maybe tired after his shift and content just to roll a familiar route home without paying the world outside of the car too much attention. I felt buoyed. I was doing this. The surge of excitement this time actually made me gasp. I was tailing a police officer, finding out where he lived. And I was doing it well.

The calmness that was about me was odd, inexplicable. I had no history of violence, no history of anything at all on the wrong side of the law, but I knew what I was there for, what the end game was in tailing that man. It was part of making a plan to murder him in cold blood. I was already dreaming up methods and scenarios where I made him suffer.

I was not without doubts, not unaware that it would be a leap. Swinging an iron bar at a uniform in a moment of lost control had been easy, the urge overwhelming even, one of those moments when the escalation was so natural that you just knew it was meant to be. But premeditating a murder? That was shifting to a whole new level.

We turned into a housing estate and I could sense that his journey was close to an end. I hung further back, distant enough for him to pull off the road and park, then I held my breath as I rolled past the driveway filled with his car.

He was out and walking towards the door, taking no notice of the sound of an engine behind him, only stopping when a black and white cat rubbed against his shins. Beyond the sergeant was a soft light in a top window, adding to the overall impression of a family home. His home with his cat. The smile on my face grew so wide I could feel it, and my breath ran shallow with excitement.

I took the next turn and then had to pull over and just take a moment to sit in silence. I waited almost forty minutes before turning around to make another pass. By then the house was in darkness, the lights off and the house asleep. This was no deviation for a mistress; this was a man who had finished work and been smiling at the thought of returning home to his wife.

And now I was smiling.

Because I knew where that was.

# CHAPTER 15

All the curtains were open.

The ones downstairs were still impeccably neat in their hourglass shape, just like the previous evening, and Harry Blaker was pretty sure that none of them had been closed at all. He had predicted a night of her pacing the house like a tiger walking its cage and he saw nothing that changed his mind.

It wasn't long gone 6 a.m., far too early to be appropriate, but Harry had taken a punt. He remembered vividly the version of himself that existed at 6 a.m. the day after his wife had died — or the day after he had lost his daughter, for that matter — and he considered how he would have reacted to someone knocking on the door as a way of declaring his night of hell was over.

Jillian Jones collapsed to one knee on a coarse welcome mat, her head lolled low, and she had to shift to both knees to stop her falling flat on her face. Harry reached down to hold her lightly by the shoulder, acutely aware of his professional boundaries. Sobs wracked her body for a few moments before she snapped back to her feet and wrapped herself in Harry, both arms strong around him, tight across his back. Boundaries or not, he dropped the bag of breakfast to squeeze her back.

'It's okay,' he said, feeling his own emotion building, his throat the epicentre. 'That's as bad as it gets.'

She buried her head. The sobbing intensified to a painful wail and Harry could do nothing more than to hold on, to ride it out. When it was over, she seemed embarrassed. She backed away, fixing on the damp spot on Harry's white shirt that he ignored. They ate breakfast outside, Jill making small talk about how she was suddenly hungrier than she realised. Neither of them made any reference to the meal that had still been laid out on the kitchen table, a once cold beer with the lid off, still full, sitting in a puddle of its own condensation. Untouched.

The rear garden was neat, hemmed in by flowerbeds that were well kept. The flowers were a good choice, types that bloomed big and bright but didn't need too much fuss. They sat at a glass-topped patio set with a view out over the early birds who were busy at a selection of hanging feeders.

'It was just like you said.' Jill Jones said her first meaningful sentence down towards the ground, then stared after it. Harry didn't feel the need to reply. 'Last night . . . it was like time stood still. And when you turned up with breakfast, like you said you would, I knew it was over. That was why . . . I'm sorry. I don't act like that.'

'Don't be sorry.'

'This happened to you? That's what you said. That's how you knew how this would be?'

'Yes.'

'And that's why you did this. That's why you told me you would come here this morning, isn't it? So, I could have a moment when I realised that this night was over?'

'Yes.'

'What time is it? I feel like the sun only just came up.'

'Not far past six.'

'Six?' She lifted her hands to run through her hair. It was still styled the same and her dress was the same she had worn the night before. Everything was the same.

Everything was also entirely different.

60

'You shouldn't be on shift yet,' she said, her watery eyes fidgeting to fix on him.

'I don't sleep so well.' He shrugged as though it wasn't becoming a problem so large he was starting to consider he was beyond being able to solve it.

'Since . . . since you lost your wife. It was your wife, wasn't it?'

'My wife, yes. A daughter too.'

'Goodness.' It was Jill who reached out for Harry's hand this time, the warmth of the sun matched by the warmth in her hands. 'It sounds like you've had your share. Sleeping is one thing. I think we're lucky you're still functioning at all.'

'There was a time, soon after, when I didn't think I was. When I didn't think I ever would again. But we're strong. People, I mean. Good people with good hearts, they can see beyond the dark times. People like you.'

'And like you. Thank you.' She gave a squeeze of her hand that she then took back. There was a moment of silence between them, then both had their attention dragged towards the plinking sound of spilling seeds. 'Damned pigeons,' she said. 'They're so clumsy!' Jill broke out in a tired smile. Harry did too.

'I like them,' he said. 'And now I should get back to work.'

'At just gone six in the morning? I was just thinking of coffee. Phil has some good stuff in the cupboard. He used to like bringing it out for guests. I think he would love the idea of us shaking off a bad night with a cup?'

'I should go. But next time for sure, I can't say no to good coffee twice.'

Jill stood, brushing her front again as seemed to be a habit. This time she lingered a little. 'Goodness, I don't think I've changed! I should shower. Get myself ready for the day, too.' When she looked up, there was another tired smile. 'Thank you, again. For breakfast. For everything.'

'No problem.'

'And you won't be a stranger?'

'I won't. I'll need to talk to you again, when you're feeling up to it. A few questions, nothing that will take long.'

'You can ask me questions. Go ahead.'

'Another time. Perhaps after you've had some sleep.'

'Nonsense, DI Blaker. What have you got?' She lifted her hands to her hips, the tiredness dropping away for a moment and Harry was delighted to see it.

'Is there any reason you can think of that Philip might have been targeted?'

'He's a police officer. Kids these days . . . not just kids, the things people think of the police.'

'Outside of his job.'

'Outside . . . Oh!' Her hands slipped to fall back by her side. 'Absolutely not!' Her right foot lifted and then fell in what was almost a stomp. Her hair, a little messed up but only at the edges, had a little shake as she did so. 'I don't think he ever upset another person in his life. I don't think he has it in him! Even his ex-wife — his son's mother — they're still friends.'

'That's it then,' Harry said, dusting his hands. 'I'm sorry to have to ask these questions, that isn't why I came this morning.'

'I know why you came. I already thanked you for that,' she said, softening all the time. 'I can't tell you how much it means.'

'I'm at the end of the phone,' Harry said. 'No matter the time of day. Chances are I won't be asleep. You can call anytime.'

'Even if it's just for a breakfast delivery?' She brightened further.

'*Especially* if you want a breakfast delivery.'

'Noted,' she said, and Harry showed himself out.

# CHAPTER 16

Sergeant Alan Day peeled off his blue gloves with some relief, wrinkling his nose to match wrinkled hands that ran with sweat. He lifted his eyes to movement, to the emergence of two people clumped together where the sun was low behind them.

'Sergeant . . .' It was the woman who spoke. DI Maddie Ives was someone he knew by reputation but hadn't met until her appearance the previous day on that exact same green. Harry Blaker had returned too, though he was a step behind, his attention away, his eyes searching the area as if he expected to see something his search team had missed. Alan took the opportunity to get a good gawp at the scar that ran along Blaker's right cheek, part-concealed by a beard, but visible enough. Blaker was someone else he only knew by reputation — a legend really, the stuff of tales so extraordinary that you could build him up in your mind to then be disappointed on meeting.

Alan hadn't been disappointed. Harry Blaker was a thick-limbed brute, no doubt about that, but there was something else about him. Authority perhaps, a charisma that made you want to please him. Alan was rarely impressed by anyone, the pool even smaller when it came to senior officers, but there was something impressive about Blaker, about this pairing in fact, and it made it all the more disappointing that he didn't have anything positive to share.

'Ma'am,' he said.

'Long day?' she said, instead of asking if they had found anything of significance. She looked him up and down, too. His hands weren't the only parts that were sweaty, his whole torso was sticking to his polo shirt and he could feel that his waistband was damp. When deployed as a search team, the tactical team had a specific uniform. It was a long sleeve polo shirt and ripstop trousers with pads sewn into the knees, topped off by steel toecaps in their boots. Hardy, tougher materials than the patrol uniform and a reflection on some of the environments they would have to search, but tougher meant thicker and heavier, which also meant warmer. At least they had been excused the full overalls of the previous day.

'Long day for us all.' Alan replied. 'Early days for the investigation, but we're going to catch this bastard, right?' He noted how Harry Blaker's attention locked onto him in an instant and he suddenly felt the need to explain. 'I know we're all doing what we can . . . We helped earlier . . . when the coroner's officer arrived to bag him up . . . Jonesy. We helped.' There was a softening from Blaker — not much, just a subtle change in his expression, a pursed mouth that loosened a little.

'That can't have been pleasant.' It was still DI Ives doing the talking. 'Are you and your lot okay?'

Alan nodded. 'Perks of the job.' His teeth gritted as his mind flashed with images of stepping into that hall, where the sound seemed to have been sucked out entirely, dumbly following instructions as they heaved their fallen colleague awkwardly into a body bag.

It had been a minor interruption in a long day of search-ing. The team had been on scene from 07.20 hours and the searching had started straight away. They'd been in from 06.00, but the first part had been consumed with poring over maps and divvying up areas to make sure every inch was covered. Then, when the vans had arrived and the teams had spilled out, it had been straight to work, not the usual delay for an attack on the tea urns. Everyone had ideas of being the officer who found something, that one item that moved this investigation on.

It hadn't happened.

'I just wish we could have found you something to work with.' Alan added.

'We appreciate your efforts, you and your team.' DI Ives said. 'And don't think of this as a waste either. The fact we're not finding anything still tells us something.'

'That you're looking for someone who knew what they were doing?' Alan chanced.

'Someone aware, someone organised. And it makes it all the more likely that it was premeditated.'

'Someone with cold blood in their veins.' Alan said, 'Phil . . . I mean the fella might just be the most inoffensive bloke I ever met!' He tried laughter that came out as a nervy snort. 'He was an old-school rural bobby, you know what I mean? Filled his days with tea and biscuits, a word in the ear where there was dog-fouling and wagging a finger at the cars parked like idiots to drop their kids off at the school. That's not a man upsetting someone enough to get a club round the head . . .'

'It doesn't always take a lot,' DI Ives said.

'I've been thinking about it. I even got to thinking that maybe he was OTS, you know? That he might have upset some fella that way. But ask about and anyone will tell you . . . Phil Jones was loved up and proper. Just . . . happy.' OTS stood for *Over The Side*: police speak for someone being unfaithful to a partner. Infidelity was so common in policing, perhaps, that their own label was needed.

'We're still working on the reason why.' DI Ives said.

'Maybe it was just that he was wearing that badge.' Alan offered, getting to the question he had wanted to ask all along. 'Maybe it could have been any one of us. I mean, we roll around as a team of eight a lot of the time, never on our own, but there's plenty out there that do. Do you know if anything's being done about that?'

'Response have been briefed already,' she said. 'There's to be no single-crewing for the foreseeable. That was a decision taken a lot higher up than me and it seems to make sense. I can't tell you that someone targeted PC Jones because he was a police officer—'

'But you can't say that wasn't why, either?' Alan cut back in, immediately wishing he hadn't. Even more so when DI Blaker stepped closer.

'We're all working as hard as we can.' His words were deep, growled almost, like he was using them to clear his throat on their way out. 'If you have any ideas on how we can solve this quicker, I'm all ears.'

'Sorry, boss,' said Alan. 'I'm not having a pop. Far from it. We all just want . . . we all saw Phil. They really meant it, whoever did this has got a real problem and we all want to be the ones bringing him in for it.'

'I'm going to bring them in.' Harry Blaker's growl was deeper still.

'I'm sure. Thank you, sir.' Alan silently cussed himself. *Thank you* felt like such a stupid thing to say.

'Your team are due off, right?' DI Ives stepped in like she meant to save him.

'We are, but we can stay.'

'No need,' she said. 'We have two more search teams on the late shift. The PolSA wants to keep the teams fresh. He recognises how tiring searching wide areas on hands and knees is, especially in the heat.'

'We're supposed to be lates. We changed our shift to get going on this. The team are well prepared to stay on.'

'There'll still be more searching tomorrow. Get your team home, maybe you can take advantage of a sunny afternoon.'

'Thank you, ma'am.' Alan felt suddenly brighter. 'I might do just that. My daughters are at an after-school club. I could make it in time to pick them up.'

'They won't be expecting you then.' DI Ives's smile had warmed.

'No. And they know that a dad pick-up is a guaranteed milkshake.'

'You make sure you get one yourself.' The smile was warmer still — pretty too, just like a couple of the lads on his team had commented the previous day, the moment she had gone out of sight.

'Well . . . if that's a lawful order from a senior officer . . .'

'It's exactly that. Pass on our thanks to your team and go and see your daughters.'

The van was rolling towards the nick within fifteen minutes of that lawful order. Alan occupied the passenger seat, his ear on the police radio for any updating on tasks assigned to the murder investigation. It was quiet. There was to be no breakthrough.

Alan's job leading a search team meant that he had been involved in a good number of murder investigations, enough to get a feel for a job where an offender was close.

This one didn't have that feel at all.

# CHAPTER 17

His car was parked in the exact same parking space, nosed in again too, like a photocopy of the night before, only this time the backdrop was broad daylight.

My choice of where to park was a little different. Not as close as before, but close enough. There was no need for me to be there, in truth; I had some errands to run but there were closer shops that would have sufficed. I think I just liked the idea of being close, of no one having a clue to who I was or what I was planning. There was something extra in my walk when I moved away from the parked Volvo, peering over at the mirrored offices of the police station. I found myself imagining rooms taken up by officers tasked solely with finding the Frant Village Hall Killer. With finding me. Maybe even a whole floor! I was still smiling when the station was long out of sight.

My chores were done at a stroll, enjoying taking my time where normal life was at a hundred miles an hour. There was an independent bookshop tied in with a coffee shop, a gem of a find, one that actually prompted a little squeal of delight as I stepped through its doors. The proprietor beamed a response, I hadn't even realised she was there. She told me to take my time and *enjoy*.

And I would.

I picked something out, attracted by its sinister front-age and title. When I read a little of the blurb to find it was all about vengeance, I knew it was the one for me. Next, I moved to the seating for a barista coffee. It came with a chocolatey musk that mixed in with the smell of new books to create the perfect scent. The perfect afternoon.

I stayed for a second cup and some ginger cake, consumed while lost in fiction. There was real anger in those pages, and I flashed through them, feeling like they were speaking to me directly, as if the words were being whispered in my ears as part of a rousing speech. A call to arms.

It was the only reason I left that place. I was pumped, swamped with a sort of anxiety, an energy more like, a need to stand, to move, to *do something*.

That something was a return to the parked Volvo and the strongest sign yet — as if I needed any more — that the path I was on was the right one.

The sergeant appeared.

He was leaving work. He looked to be in a hurry, still zipping up a hooded top that did a poor job of concealing his uniform underneath. He was still in his big boots and black, cargo trousers and I damned near clapped my hands together. Instead, I thrust them in my pocket, feeling them shake with excitement through the material.

I would follow him again. There was no real reason in my mind, I didn't feel like I needed to, but there was surely a reason that fate had turfed him out of the police station just as I was making my way past with my mind full of vengeance and my veins crackling with energy. My whole day had felt like it was passing me by with no reason, but that wasn't the case at all. I was fast learning that nothing happened for *no reason* — like carrying a zombie knife to a place where the plan was to break windows.

I had the knife with me too. I settled back into the Volvo's driver's seat and waited for the sergeant to make his move. There was time to lean forward and open the glove compartment. The knife was there. I knew it would be, but it was a comfort to see it, somehow, to know that if there was an escalation, then I was prepared, that I had a blade that could stop anything.

The sergeant moved off in the same direction: left at the barrier. Again, I was parked facing in the opposite direction, but I knew it wouldn't matter. The traffic was heavier during the day and it was the fifth car that let me out. I was then held up at the junction to turn right, the sergeant long since disappeared in my mirrors.

But it didn't matter and I never considered that it might. There was no anxiety, no concern. I wound the windows down and turned up a song on the radio that I liked, even singing along to the uplifting chorus as I waited my turn. I took the turn right, then right again, the traffic still sticky. Here I approached the roundabout where I took a right and the sergeant's car came into sight.

Fate was still leading me by the hand.

He was held at a crossing; a family skipped and giggled their way over. The mother held a hand up in thanks while the other hung under the weight of a child's scooter. They were still smiling when I passed, their faces lit by the sun. The sergeant revved off the line, lurching forward, giving the impression of a man in a hurry. I was seven cars behind, seven cars that dawdled by comparison and the sergeant zipped off around a corner that took him out of sight.

I rounded the corner to another roundabout, this one slightly larger and with a grassy middle that hosted a sign telling me to *bee-kind*. He was back in my sight and took the first exit, slowing to the back of a queue of cars behind a bus letting off passengers.

I actually chuckled out loud. Had I lost sight of him, I would have taken the second exit, since I knew that was his route home. But he had something else in mind, something he was in a rush to do, and I now had a purpose in finding out just what it was.

The bus pulled away and then turned off and the traffic flow became a little more fluid. I was four cars behind and the spacing was good, the sun bright in my eyes, my right arm dripping out over the door sill with my fingers splayed to the warm air. The song changed on the radio. It must have been a pop channel and with a playlist that was bright and cheery to match the weather. I knew the words to this one and they tumbled out of me with carefree abandon. Now on autopilot, I flicked the indicator stalk when I saw the sergeant do the same.

He turned off and by then I was two cars behind. I took my time making the turn, increasing the gap, noting the signs that told me to drive with care, that there was a school ahead. The sergeant was already indicating to pull into its frontage. I didn't want to do that; following him in there was a fine way to stand out. I sat straighter, pulling my arm in to put both hands on the wheel, aware that I had switched off, that I was close to making a mistake.

I passed the turning. There was a grassy bank on the left that was a mess of cars, but a gap cleared in front of me and I swung in and stopped. The song on the radio changed again, the cheery theme remained, a Madonna song from an era I remembered only too well and I couldn't help but join in.

Then came a tedious string of advertisements, some inane chat and two more songs before the sergeant appeared again — his car, at least. He turned right, back the way he came, away from the direction I was facing.

The traffic was choked, increasing all the time. School pick-up was in full flow, despite it being four thirty. Schools finish earlier than that; there must have been something going on after. It was a primary school, kids up to age eleven. I'd had a strong feeling of a man with children when I'd sat outside his home — something else I had been right about.

I followed the sergeant to the roundabout, still a couple of cars back. I even indicated left before the sergeant did. I knew where he was going. I knew this was the way home.

Then he surprised me at the very next turn, the one he was due to take but sailed past, though not without incident. His car fishtailed and I thought he might have been getting impatient with a slow-moving car in front. He swerved for the turn, then stayed on that road like it was a last-minute change of mind. Then he straightened up and backed off until we came to an industrial estate on the edge of town.

And then I made a mistake.

This time the sergeant did turn, only it was once again an erratic move. It was late, the car suddenly veering off, and I reacted. I was two cars back and travelling too quick to have time to think. I swung off too, braking hard as I entered a road that split into two lanes and I needed to swerve into the right lane to avoid a collision.

It brought me up directly alongside the sergeant.

All of my good feeling, my arrogance . . . it all dissipated. I must have been spotted, why else would he start driving so erratically? It was a clear anti-surveillance technique, something I'd read up on a little from Google searches.

He was onto me.

* * *

Emmy came out of school first. She was Alan's eldest daughter and in her final year in a primary school. Hell, it was damned near her final term. She was in her summer uniform and she would never wear the winter one again. They'd just had a parents' evening, their last one ever and the following week she would take her SATs as her last meaningful action at primary school. So much was happening, so much was never going to happen again and the rate his children were changing made Alan's head spin.

Emmy burst into a huge smile when she saw it was her dad waiting for her and he was aware not to take that for granted. That might be the next thing to change.

His youngest had far less of a reaction. Dani was the polar opposite, a little colder even, just as loving but more like her mother in that she would make you work a little harder for it. She followed a few steps behind, walking and talking with her friends until the last minute; two years below her sister but already acting like she was in charge of the whole place. Both girls unloaded their bags onto him. Both girls had the same opening demand: *Can we get milkshakes?*

'Definitely not!' he said, but there would be no disguising the twinkle in his eye.

'Oh, okay then, Dad!' Emmy's voice was laden with an awareness that made him want to play a trick. They got back to the car and the radio came to life, a pop classic that Alan did his best to sing badly over, then turned up louder when a second reference was made to milkshakes. This started a wrestling match between father and elder daughter with the volume button as the epicentre: Emmy turning it down only for him to twist it back up again. They moved away from the school but it started all over again when stuck behind a bus. That lovely sound of his daughter's giggles filled the car.

'But it's Madonna! She's a legend!' Alan insisted.

'I don't even know who that is.' Emmy said, matter-of-fact and more hurtful than she intended.

'Am I really that old?'

They were heading for home. Everyone in the car knew the way, which meant that they knew it was straight on for milkshakes and a left turn for home. As the junction approached, Alan made a bigger deal of singing, swaying the car a little side to side in time, then suddenly exclaimed, 'Oh no! I missed my turn! Why didn't you girls tell me!'

'Yeah Dad, you missed your turn.' Emmy said, the knowing even heavier in her tone and said against the backdrop of Dani's cheering from the back. 'Now you happen to be heading towards the milkshakes . . .'

Alan ignored her. Another pop classic assaulted them from the speakers. He slid his window down to enjoy the fresh air and Emmy again turned the volume down, now looking embarrassed as they again came to a stop, ensnarled in more slow-moving traffic. With the sun straight ahead, Alan dropped his visor. They were on the edge of an industrial estate, the next turning on their left was for McDonald's and the holy grail of milkshakes. He sped up deliberately.

'Just left up here.' Emmy said, as Alan sung over her, singing louder still so she would know she was drowned out. He left it to the last moment, until he got a reaction even from the back, the ever-cool Dani squealing for him to *turn here!* and he grabbed at the steering wheel, yanking them off the main route and into the drive-through.

'What did you shout that for!' he said, bringing them to a rough stop in the left-hand lane where the drive-through split into two. Both girls giggled while Alan made a show of looking around. 'How do I get out of here? Oh no! There's a car behind me now!' They rolled forward, Alan still pretending to look for a way out, stopping by a bright screen that was constantly scrolling through pictures of mocked up food.

*'Good afternoon, what can I get you?'* A voice like a teenager holding her nose wafted in through his open window. Alan was still winding up his daughters, looking backwards, still mumbling about getting out of there.

'Dad!' Emmy pointed furiously. 'Dad, you have to answer!' The same nasal voice, only this time there was an element of panic. Clearly the training didn't cover a customer hesitating.

'Sorry . . . If I get two milkshakes, will you let me out?'

There was more cheering. Emmy slid her own window down to allow the breeze freedom to move through. It was pleasant, his body still overheated from his day's work, but it also served to blow away the horrors of that day, images he would rather not have seen. The breeze also carried the sound of squealing brakes as a car pulled up a bit rough in the next lane over.

'Actually, make it three!' he said. 'I think I've earned a nice treat.' The speakers mumbled something back that Alan assumed to be a request for flavours. By the time he answered and they had rolled to the next window, Emmy was tickling him in the side and he wasn't paying enough attention. After the order screens, the two lanes merged again and a car cut across him, forcing him to brake.

It was his fault entirely and he lifted his hand to apologise, before filing in behind on his way to the next window and the treats for all.

* * *

He damn near drove into me! I needed to be more careful. Smarter. I scolded myself, flushing hot where I had wound my window up as a way of trying to feel a little less on show, a little less vulnerable. I had been rash, lurching the car forward when it seemed to be the only way I might prevent the sergeant looking across at me when we were side by side.

I don't know why I was so rattled. My mistake had put me just a few metres away from the sergeant and with a view directly across to where he was laughing and fooling around while ordering. Those weren't the actions of a man who thought he was being followed, who had considered for a moment that he or his daughters were in danger and was making manoeuvres so he could see who the hell I was. This was a man messing about, being tickled, singing and playing.

And he was still acting the exact same way when I cut him up and he then pulled up behind me. I had found some sunglasses while I was hurriedly ordering a burger meal, whichever one was on the screen at the time. I don't even eat meat; I just needed to get through and ordered the first thing I was presented with. The glasses meant I could watch him still, my confidence returning in spades.

He had no idea.

The sergeant only had eyes for his children. He was still bucking in his seat, leaning sideways and laughing like someone was jabbing him in the side. The young girl next to him wore a big smile, wide and carefree, and another child leaned forward from the back. She was smaller, younger, her hair blonder.

I edged forward to pay and retrieve my meal. I had to really focus to make sure I was smooth when I pulled away and then I turned in the opposite direction to the sergeant's family home.

I didn't look back. I drove half a mile away and then pulled up on the side of the road. I picked at the chips that were part of the meal, the car idling. I'd pulled over somewhere easily visible. I wanted to be sure that the sergeant hadn't just given an incredible performance, that he hadn't actually been onto me and had called it in, me and my car details. I stayed there for all of those chips and most of the fizzy drink, easily long enough for any police patrol out looking for me to find me.

No one came.

# CHAPTER 18

It was a strange feeling to consistently walk into a building you once deemed a home and for it to heighten feelings of anxiety. Home was supposed to be a refuge, a place of peace and comfort — not for him. Not for Harry Blaker. He sighed in the darkness of his own hallway, taking a moment to consider turning back around and walking straight back out.

It wouldn't be the first time and it was an urge that was getting stronger. He had been leaving for periods of time, removing himself from the ghosts that waited behind the doors. A nearby pub had offered him refuge the first few times, then he had gone further afield to a hotel bar where sitting in the corner with a soft drink drew less attention, though still too much for him to be able to do it habitually. He dismissed the idea of booking a room, fearing a one-night stay might evolve into a situation where he never left.

A twenty-four-hour fast-food joint as part of a motorway services still ranked as the best solution he had found. Its custom was transient and the glass-eyed employees either knew better or had no inclination to ask.

He dumped his bag, his mind made up: he would turn straight back out, at least for a walk. The weather was nice, the village quiet and he had a spaniel that he had somehow managed to avoid waking so far, but would burst to life at the mere jangle of his lead.

The night air was delicious, the smell a combination of the nearby rapeseed on the breeze and impending rain. He set off with Jock trotting beside him, the skittering of his claws on the pavement the only real sound. There was no sense of time, no sense of direction and no plan.

Just anywhere but home.

# CHAPTER 19

10 p.m. was quiet. Urban quiet, at least, which is the sort of quiet that is made up of noise. White noise. The hum of a nearby major road combined with the whisper of a densely populated town to make something soporific. There was the occasional specific noise that broke out: a fox's bark, a skittering bat or the scuffing, lumbering walk of a late dog walker with a tickly cough.

The darkness came in layers, the night adding more of them as the house windows lit up and the street lights came on. The darker it got, the more confidence I gathered, the more excited I became. There was something about sitting in a darkened car, about watching someone who didn't know they were being watched.

A new light burst front and centre. The front door to the sergeant's house pushed open to reveal a bright, framing rectangle with a black centre shaped like a woman. The wife. It had to be. She leaned on the door surround, her voice gentle like the breeze that brought it to me through my open window.

'Kevin . . . Kevin, it's that time of night. You coming in, mate?'

There was movement — enough to set off the security light above the garage to the right of the door. It had a reach that drenched the entire drive, the two cars parked on it and the cat making for the door.

'Did you get old and forget about the cat flap! Every night, Kevin. Well, I guess you're not going to be changing now.'

Behind her, the internal door had stayed open and my angle was good to see all the way through to a set of windows at the back that were stained black by the night. The wife lingered, even after the cat had moved in behind her. Her attention was out into the night but her body language was still relaxed, no suggestion of suspecting anything untoward. Maybe she was taking a moment to inhale the air tinged with the scent of cut grass or to listen and enjoy the stillness. Whatever it was, she had her fill and the door closed, the handle lifted and the door clicked and clacked where locks found their place. The security light flicked off after a count of thirty.

A cat. No sign of a dog. A family of four with neighbours whose houses were already in darkness. A wife who seemingly had a routine that involved opening the front door for a useable period and a sergeant who worked shifts, some of which had him home late.

It was perfect.

# CHAPTER 20

Maddie Ives waded into the makeshift Major Crime office first thing in the morning as if she was knee-high in water. The energy was gone, an incident room would fizz and hum as if electrically charged when leads were being pursued or new information bundling in. In such times, relevant lines of enquiry could easily outnumber detectives two or three to one and there was a real need to prioritise. And the buzz of a breakthrough? It was like nothing else. It was a euphoria that was tangible, a room full of people suddenly given a single point of focus.

But this was an incident room just about as flat as they could be, a slack tide while waiting for something to happen. It was only the second full day and already the momentum was lost. Forensics had already warned that they were unlikely to add anything significant. House-to-house was complete and work around the victim had produced nothing that stood out. The press conference and the subsequent public appeal had been delayed too, a decision made higher up. Someone paid a lot to know a little had decided that the investigation didn't "need the distraction right now".

But it needed something.

This was turning into one of the most difficult of investigations, the type where the victim had been targeted for no real reason; opportunistic at best, entirely random at worst.

'No such thing as random,' Harry said when Maddie made the mistake of vocalising her internal dialogue. 'Not when it comes to murder.'

She bit back her first reaction, taking a moment to study the grumbling form in front of her. Harry looked every bit as tired as she felt. When an investigation lost its fizz, there were always some characters that could be relied on to continue to drive the room forward, and Harry was so often that force. People listened to him. Fear, respect, whatever the reason, they listened. But that day's version of Harry Blaker was as sullen as he was silent.

'You okay, Harry?'

'Just super. You?'

'A little jaded.' She hoped that might start a conversation. 'Bit of a later night than I should on a school night. Sometimes I wish I could be more like you and in bed by nine with my cocoa.'

'I was in the cinema with a Fanta at 11 p.m., as it happens. Late night showing.' He shrugged out a *doesn't even matter* type shrug, as if regretting that follow-up questions were now inevitable.

'You were at the cinema? Last night?'

'Got home around two.' He shrugged again. 'I'm an adult, I can do what the hell I want.'

'You are and you can, but you don't!' she teased. 'You don't do things like that! What was it . . . like a month ago you were moaning about how you can't even go to the cinema without booking it on your phone in advance, these days? You told me that was it, that they'd lost a customer.' She sucked in a breath so she could let it out with her very best Harry Blaker voice: 'I remember the days when you got a proper ticket, something to show, something to touch. And they put a little rip in it and gave it right back . . .' Her breath was gone, her ability to keep a straight face with it. Harry had broken off to look away, his head down, his pen steady and, Maddie reckoned, desperate to have something to write. Then she noticed something that she was not expecting: a curling of lips — Harry's lips — into something like a smile. It quickly turned into a chuckle.

'What?' Maddie said, egging him on. 'What is it? Did you kick off? Make a scene and demand a proper ticket?' His lips moved again, the smile this time unmistakable. 'You did, didn't you? Oh my God!'

Harry's lips bumped together; he was a man tripping over words, over whether to say them or not. 'I printed my own,' he said. 'The booking gives you the option, so I did. So what?' His smile dropped away in exchange for something more like defiance, but Maddie couldn't help herself. She put her hand over her mouth to try and catch the laughter but she needn't have bothered. Even the miserable bastard who seemed even more miserable than normal, seemed about to get the giggles.

'You printed it out . . . you printed out your own ticket and then . . .' Maddie could barely speak for laughing now. 'Please tell me you bullied someone there to rip it for you!'

'I didn't,' Harry said, seemingly to get control of himself before losing it completely with his next few words. 'I ripped it myself!' He howled. It was a strange noise, not so much like a laugh as something from a man losing his grip on a lot of emotions all at once. Maddie laughed with him, most of her humour now was a reflection of his.

'What on earth could be so funny at a time like this?' Eileen Holmans swept in as fast as that day's slippers — lemon yellow with white tassels — would allow her. She fixed them both with a glare that was a good match for her hand-on-hips stance.

Maddie ignored her while Harry took another minute to get himself under some sort of control. 'Hang on, hang on! What did they say? When you showed that to get in, when everyone else was scanning their phones!' Maddie's laughter died out just a little; she was intent on an answer.

Suddenly, Harry was too. His smile dropped away a little, though not entirely. It lingered while shaping the words that followed. 'Our first date was the cinema, me and Robin. It was the only thing that lasted too. You get older and the things you do for fun change. But date night was always the cinema. That first date she snuck out. Her mum helped. Her dad, see . . . he would have killed me where I stood.'

'Really? I can't imagine you being intimidated, even by an angry father!'

'I was seventeen and nine stone wet through. He didn't like me then and it turned out he never would. His daughter was sixteen. We had a good time and she said she was going to keep the ticket — put it in her memory box.'

'I just can't imagine you were ever anything below forty! And let me guess . . . you still have that ticket? You're really a soppy old fool and I bet it's still on you, right here and now!' Maddie had been joking, but the laughter fell away at Harry's reaction. 'No way! Am I right?'

'Robin's mum panicked. We were back later than she thought. She got hold of the ticket, ripped it up into tiny pieces and buried them all in the bin the moment I dropped her off. Her dad was at the pub but expected home any minute. She didn't want any evidence. It was an overreaction, to say the least. And I was kicked out.'

'Seems like she was a good judge of character.'

'I waited outside, hidden up. Her mum was so frantic that I knew she was going to put the rubbish out. She did. Then she got back into the house just as Robin's dad made it back. I got the ticket. Spent the next morning sifting through that sack of rubbish, finding every last piece. In those days, you dumped everything in one — it wasn't pleasant. I taped the ticket back together and brought it along to our next date.'

Maddie had her hand over her mouth. She didn't quite know what to say. 'Just when you think you know someone!' was what she opted for.

'Robin told me years later that the moment I gave her that ticket back, was when she knew she was going to marry me.' Harry's eyes were glazed.

Maddie still had her hand over her mouth, but it wasn't humour she was hiding. She couldn't recall sharing a more intimate moment with Harry Blaker. He really had to be tired.

Harry reached for his wallet, his hands smooth as he opened it, pulling out a ticket that had obviously been torn into shreds and then meticulously put back together between two layers of tape. 'She always kept it with her. I said she was silly, called it sentimental nonsense. And then when she couldn't carry it anymore . . .'

'Well then . . .' Maddie exchanged a glance with a hovering Eileen then chose her next words carefully. 'That ticket was the start of something quite incredible. A lot of happiness.'

'Dammit.' Harry's eyes flicking back to focus, a sparkle still prominent. 'What I used to think about her, you're now thinking about me!' He folded the ticket back up, overly gentle, making a show of it, his tired eyes forming crow's feet with the concentration as he slipped it back into his wallet. Then he met eyes with Maddie again and said the most un-Harry expression to ignite their laughter all over again.

'I'm still cool, though, right?'

# CHAPTER 21

The best solutions to problems seem to come when you're not even thinking about them. That's the case for me, at least. It certainly was on that morning. I was in a doctor's waiting room, my head down, desperate not to make eye contact with anyone who might want a conversation, praying that my name was the one called next. I only needed a repeat prescription, but the receptionist had insisted that the doctor needed to see me every couple of months. I told her it was a waste of time. The conversation would be the same as the last time:

*Are you still feeling anxious, low in energy with depression that can come from nowhere to knock you sideways?*

*Yes.*

*Still having trouble sleeping without medication?*

*Yes.*

*'Did you try and take your own life, out of nowhere and damned near succeeded this time?'*

*'Yes.'*

*You need your regular pills?*

That last question didn't actually come up, but maybe I should have prompted it. It sounds awful. It *was* awful, but out of that darkness came light. Realisation, more like. The realisation that something had to change. It had been a long while since my last episode, since the black dog of depression had walked back into my life to keep me company, to drag me so low that getting out of bed took more strength than I could summon. And then that was so nearly it. What doesn't kill you, makes you stronger and it did. I got stronger.

That was when I started planning for better, that was when everything started to fall into place. It seemed so logical. I've no idea why I hadn't thought about it before. There was a root cause to all of my problems and it wore a uniform. They paraded around the streets with flashing lights and sirens and they served to remind me every single day of just how my spiral had begun. I had always known what the root cause of my suffering was and I'd tried to move on, to accept it even. It hadn't worked. My realisation was that it never would, that the only way I could deal with it was to find a way to defeat it, to kill it.

And I had found it.

The pills were my backup plan. I knew the pattern of my life well enough by now. There had been false dawns before and the black dog had always found a way. I couldn't have that happen again and not have my pills; I didn't like to think how that might end. But I wasn't taking them, not anymore. I just needed to know I had access to them, that they were there. I never would have considered that my life would come to the point where my two comfort blankets were a pack of pills and a zombie knife.

But that morning was not about medication, it was about an idea . . . *leaflets*. My eyes must have fallen on the stack of them clinging to the edge of a messy table in that doctor's waiting room. They were offering the services of a mobile gutter cleaner. I read the bold claims over twice. It was on the second lap that the idea struck.

My name was called. A thick Asian accent mumbled it over tinny speakers and I shuffled down a stuffy hall. The conversation that followed was as expected: short, sweet and without the need for any cognitive thought, which was just as well, as my mind was very much elsewhere.

When I made it back to the waiting area it was as busy as I had left it. Most of the seats were taken but all of the occupants had their eyes down to the floor or to their phone screens. No one noticed or could care less when I scooped up that whole pack of leaflets and made for the door.

The sun was still pleasant. It had been a few weeks since I could last remember rainfall in the day. I drove for twenty minutes then parked the Volvo under the shade of a tree. When I stepped out, I stood for a while. The streets were quiet, a couple of elderly walkers in the distance, the whirr of a strimmer. I knew I was around half a mile short of where the sergeant lived, on the far edge of his estate.

I lingered under a cherry tree, whose roots were visible in an uneven front garden and were also lifting some of the path. Beneath my feet was a carpet of pink and white petals that was deep enough to make tracks with dragged feet. I was on a junction. The next house on my left was the first on the road that would eventually lead to the sergeant's family home.

The perfect place to start.

The gate had a squeak and the gravel path a crunch. The front door was old-fashioned with a heavy, brass letterbox. I pushed one of the guttering leaflets through, keeping my eyes down and spinning away in one movement. The next house got a leaflet too, but the next I passed by. Doorbell cameras are bulky, easily visible from the pavement and I was sure to stay side-on, hidden behind my hair as I passed.

The sergeant's house was Number 28 and it came quicker than I expected. There was no doorbell camera here — I'd already checked from a distance but I was sure to check again. I also surveyed all of the windows for any sign of a camera lens, considering that a police officer might be more security conscious than most. There was nothing.

Here, the path up to the door was smooth and firm, made up of poured concrete with clear joins. It ran on the left side, the fence marking the edge of the house was a little further left, over an area that was the same size as the path again but filled with chunks of flat, grey flint. The front lawn was all to the right, stopping abruptly to make way for the drive.

The front door was partly enclosed by an arch running over the top. There was a coarse mat on the floor that had some real give under my feet and stated *Welcome*. It made me smile.

I posted my leaflet. The front door to the sergeant's house was more modern in style than most of his neighbours. Its UPVC finish was in anthracite grey to match with the window surrounds and the garage door. It had one long window, off-centre-right, and the letterbox was polished chrome. I lingered, the fingertips on my right hand resting against that glass panel. But there was to be no looking through, so heavy was the frosting that it was only light I could see, no other detail. I felt sure I would have seen movement, had there been any, say an angry reaction from a protective dog or Kevin the cat. But there was nothing but a lark in full song somewhere behind me and the lazy hum of a curious bee.

I turned my back to the door to check for movement and there was none. The white noise of daytime suburbia was barely louder than in the middle of the night. The gate that would lead around to the back was a few paces away and was closed.

But the handle lifted.

The gate creaked inwards but was silent when pushed shut. The fencing behind that gate was taller, the whole rear was shaped into a rectangle, enclosed by eight-foot panels. It was mostly lawn, save for a patio area with a swing chair and a BBQ under their respective covers. The back of the house was flat, broken up by windows and a set of patio doors that were full-length glass.

I was tentative. I half expected to peer through those doors only to make eye contact with someone on the other side: the wife or the sergeant, perhaps both together, their heads turned by the movement at the back door. It didn't happen. I was as sure as I could be that there was no one at home, but it didn't stop me breathing out a little in relief.

I remained on edge, my anxiety made up of that familiar feeling of excitement and of the sense that I was once again pushing my own boundaries.

A phrase was rolling around in my mind, over and over: *I'm really doing this.*

I took a moment, just breathing, just grounding myself, taking a moment to remember that I couldn't afford mistakes. It had me back thinking clearly, checking that I wasn't being overlooked. I could see the backs of houses opposite but they were some way in the distance, too far to be of concern. The direct neighbours were no issue either, the fencing had put paid to that. There was still no sign of any cameras and only one way to access the garden — which of course meant only one way out.

I turned my attention to the inside of the house. There was no dog, something all but confirmed by the pristine white kitchen — white units, white countertops and even white tiles on the floor, though they were speckled with glitter that caught in the spring sunshine. There were three pairs of crocs lined up at the back door in size order. A fourth pair, and the smallest, was a little further away and they were strewn as if changed out of last minute as part of the madness of a school run.

Now that I was looking closer, I noticed that the fruit bowl was skewed too, with a knuckle of bananas clinging on as if they had frozen mid-escape attempt. On the far wall was a calendar, oversized and topped with various pictures of the same black and white cat. Kevin, it had to be. There was writing on it as well, the black marker used was clipped to the side.

*I wonder* . . . I said to myself. I took out my phone to operate the camera, zooming in as far as I could. I got the picture and spun my phone around to inspect it. I did a little more pinching and zooming until the calendar filled the screen. It wasn't great, but it was enough. There was a pattern. The calendar cascaded downwards, the start of the month at the top. I could make out where single numbers turned to double. I couldn't see the numbers specifically but it didn't matter. The days of the week were white, the weekends shaded grey. That thick black pen had been used meticulously to make its mark on every day. The first three days were marked the same: *7-3*. Then the next two days were labelled: *RD*. The next four: *2-10*, then a gap filled with *RD* before *9-7* was scrawled for three in a row. And so, it continued, a pattern that repeated all of the way down.

The sergeant's shift pattern.

I checked my watch for the date. Next week would be the last of the month. I pinched and zoomed the photo I had taken to focus on the third week, having to stop for a moment for breath when my excitement had me fumbling so much that I could barely hold my phone.

*2-10*. That was his shift today. And then the sergeant was *RD* for two days before he was back on an early shift.

'It has to be tonight.' My own words were loud enough to make me jump; I was so close to the patio glass that it bounced back for my own breath to caress my cheek. I moved the photo around, double-checking that I was right. Something else caught my eyes as I did. It was a line of nonsense: numbers and letters, capitals and lower case written in the same black marker and along the bottom of the calendar.

'Wi-fi code,' I said, again out loud against that glass.

And then I had to step back, to reach out for the brick where it met with the door as a way of holding myself up, so overwhelming was my realisation. The best ideas really did come when you weren't looking for them at all.

'Wi-fi code!' I sang, backing away a step or two, overwhelmed a little at how this was escalating and how it was happening so fast.

It could be that night. It had to be that night.

But I would need to work fast.

## CHAPTER 22

Phil Jones's patrol sergeant worked out of Maidstone Police Station according to the resource sheet, but Maddie knew better than to just turn up without calling ahead. She was still late for the time they had agreed.

When Sergeant Sharon Ennis did return, she brought her whole team back with her. The officers sat at the tables of the refs' room with fresh cups of tea, seemingly tasked with staring silently at the two detectives who were investigating the murder of their colleague.

'I just need to grab a tea,' the sergeant explained, having led them into the middle of the room to a space seemingly cleared for their presence. Even the battered sofa had been turned inwards, away from the equally battered television that was muted in the corner, wearing its antenna like a lop-sided party hat.

Maddie considered making some sort of address to her silent audience, maybe put out for questions. She dismissed it as a bad idea and Harry seemed to communicate agreement in the look he gave.

'Want one?' the sergeant added and Maddie turned to where Sharon was standing with a steaming teabag draped over a spoon.

'No, thank you.' Maddie spluttered, 'Just had one, ta.' She grimaced, aware of how that might sound: *No thanks, just been up there drinking tea rather than spending every waking minute trying to find out who killed your mate.*

'First one for me,' said Sharon. 'Run off my feet.' The words travelled over her shoulder, to where she had turned away. Then she turned back to speak again. 'Shall we?'

The corridor had somehow filled with more officers, these just as still and just as silent, their eyes the only thing to move as the group of three strode past. The office was the last internal door on the left before they would have headed back outside. Maddie was asked to close it behind them, which proved to be an effective way to turn a small office into a cramped one. The room was long and thin, quite possibly built as a cupboard originally. Both detectives waited patiently as their host took her time taking off her fleece and cracking open a tiny window at the back. She took a seat pulled out from a desk against the left wall. There were other seats that she didn't offer.

'Thank you for taking the time to see us,' Harry started and Sharon Ennis gritted her teeth as if bottling her initial reaction. 'How are the team doing?'

'It was three days ago. I was hoping Major Crime would have made contact with me much earlier than this.' Sharon said, ignoring the question.

'And what part of the investigation would you have had us sacrifice, in order to touch base?' Harry flashed back.

Sharon sneered a little, then hid it behind her mug as she noisily slurped the top off. 'How do you think they're doing?'

'I've seen it before,' Harry said, 'what it does to a team. Phil's not their colleague, not even their mate, this job makes us family.'

'All of us.' Maddie added. 'We want to talk to you about Phil in general, about what he was like and how he policed—'

'If there was any reason to beat him about the head until he was dead, you mean?' The sergeant cut in and Maddie reacted with a sigh. Then she moved forward, pulling out the seat she hadn't been invited to take.

93

'You know why we're here, Sharon. And you also know why we haven't been able to get here any earlier. Frant is on your patch and, I reckon, it's pretty quiet most of the time. But it's not right now, is it? These last two days there've been coppers on every corner. Every inch has been searched, every door has been knocked and I reckon just about every resident has been spoken to. Those are what we call fast-track actions, something you know all about, seeing as FTAs are used for everything from livestock getting loose, right through to a police officer being beaten to death.'

'We don't just deal with sheep in the road, you know.'

'I do know that. And we don't just sit upstairs waiting for the solution to the most devastating of jobs to pop up and bite us in the arse, either.' There was a stand-off, it was barely a few moments but Maddie would have stretched it out as long as it took for Sharon to speak next. She shifted her position, leaned back a little like she might be relaxing, she brought her arms up to rest on the table.

'What is it that you need? We want to help. The whole team are out there asking. What more they can do. I've got people refusing to go home at the end of their shift. If you need bodies . . . any job, any—'

'Tell us about Phil.' Maddie brought the conversation back where she wanted it.

'Phil . . .' Sharon exhaled, almost wistfully. 'I mean Phil was Phil. Every station needs one, right!?' She chuckled, though it never really took hold. 'Old school, if you were after a two-word summary. Popular. There, I can get it down to one. He wasn't the most dynamic officer, never was going to be, but I found a role that suited him out in villages as the Rural Communities Officer and he thrived.'

'That was his title?' Maddie said.

Sharon grinned.

'Not according to anyone else in the world, nothing official, but Phil could be a bit of an arse to handle, to manage, at least. Like I said, the man was old school and that meant he wasn't the most responsive to change. But dress it up with

94

a new title and give him time to realise that it's mainly tea-stops and noise complaints and Phil's putty in your hands. Early retirement the rest of the team called it, but no one begrudged him that. I've got a young team, a lot of inexperience but a lot of enthusiasm, still got cops out there who think they're going to spend their shifts on car chases and drug busts. Not for me to tell 'em that ain't the life anymore.'

'I guess not.' Maddie agreed.

'But officers like Phil know the deal. All of their thrills are behind them. The soggy middle, right?'

'Soggy middle?' This was an expression Maddie hadn't heard before, Sharon seemed to enjoy this fact.

'Must be a uniform thing. Work response your whole career and there's a pattern. You're excited at the start, excited for it to finish, but the bit in-between is a bit . . .'

'Soggy,' Maddie said, prompting another smile.

'Can't think of a better way to describe it, personally. Phil was starting to get excited for the end, but the middle of his time had caused some problems. He did a good job for me, even if it was between tea-stops with little old ladies.'

'It can't just be little old ladies,' said Harry. 'What about the younger generation out there? Phil was responding to a nuisance youths call. Was there a problem out there with youths?'

'Have you been to the village?' Sharon had another smile.

'In the last few days, a lot. But I bet a village like that will look very different the day after something like this than it did the day before.'

'I've already been back through his calls — everything he's attended in the last couple of weeks. I started out with his pocketbooks but . . . he wasn't big on detail, at least not on writing it down. He hasn't been sent to a nuisance youth call for quite some time. There hasn't been one in the village at all since last summer. There's only one lad under twenty in that area that Phil's dealt with and he's more into nicking from his nan's purse than throwing stones at a hall.'

'What do we know about him?'

'Everything I know about him I've already sent through. I had an email request with a form attached, then a chase up all of three minutes later. Irene, or someone? I assume she's in charge of you lot. She didn't give her rank?'

'Eileen,' Maddie said.

Sharon picked up on her knowing smile. 'A good boss, is she?'

'She's the sort of person we all want working this, that's for sure,' said Maddie. 'What can you tell me now? Is there anything we need to know, anything you've seen or heard from talking to Phil about his patrolling? Anyone he might have upset, anyone with a history of assaulting police, anything about that hall or the people that run it?' Maddie could go on but she shut herself down, reading her colleague's change in body language and aware that she might be leaning into the teaching-how-to-suck-eggs category.

'No. You're talking about a sleepy little village where decent people go to retire and a decent copper who should soon be doing the same. Phil wasn't the sort to upset people, I would go as far as to say that he made a career out of avoiding doing just that.'

'You don't go with the nuisance youths theory?'

'Do you? The idea that a group of kids were stoning the village hall, then beat a police officer *to death* when he arrived . . . that's not even a theory, is it?' Sharon looked at them both in turn.

'We have to keep our minds open,' Maddie said.

'And what about his handcuffs? Are your minds open enough to consider some sick fuck killing a man, then taking a little trophy to jack off to at home?'

'We're considering a similar version of that theory.' Maddie managed, before Harry offered his own response. She moved on quickly. 'What about Phil's life at home, Sharon? Did he talk about his personal life?'

'He has a wife, an ex-wife that he gave a house to, so she wouldn't steal half his pension — his words, not mine — and he has two grown up boys who . . . who must be going through hell right now. He was close to his boys. They're all season ticket holders at Charlton and Phil would go whenever his shifts allowed and sometimes when it didn't. He was always trying to swap out a Saturday afternoon and a good few midweeks — caused a bit of friction, to be honest. I had a chat with him about it and he put me right.'

'Put you right?' Maddie said.

'In this room. Sat in that same chair. He said to me that he was going to keep being a pain in the arse, that he would do whatever it took to get to the games with his boys. Said it just like that. He told me that there was going to be a game that would be his last, said he might not even know it at the time, so all the time he could . . .' She broke off, emotion clear on her face. Her jaw gave a little judder, as if tears might break out. But then she sniffed hard and it was all gone. Restrained. Buried deep for another time.

'You seem very switched on,' Harry said. 'A good investigator would go back over Phil's calls, but there are plenty that wouldn't even consider it. What else would you be doing? Just in case you've thought of something we haven't.'

Sharon seemed a little surprised by this. 'I'm sure you have it all in hand. There's nothing more I can tell you, really. Phil was a creature of habit. He liked things just so and he would pretty much come in and do the same thing over and over. He had a set route, set locations and people he would go and see under the premise of patrolling. Tea-stops, like I said. But that's what rural policing is all about. Checking in on the vulnerable and the isolated, being seen, but also frequenting a bakery and a couple of farms that are often good for something home-cooked. Then he went home to his wife. I met her at a social. Most don't bring their partners out but Phil always would. She seemed nice. Quiet, but nice. Phil talked highly of her. He didn't eat much at work because he liked to eat with his wife, even on a late shift they would sit down together when he got in. She would just have a cuppa, but they would still talk about their days while he ate. I could just tell that he cherished that. She was a big part of his excitement about retirement.'

'He earned his time with her,' Maddie said, wistfully.

'You get a lot of talk about retirement — the dinosaurs talking about what holidays they'll go on and the lie-ins. But Phil . . . he just wanted to go to the football with his boys and share dinner with his wife at a reasonable time.' Sharon had held it together well, but those emotions she had pushed back down for another time were starting to get insistent. She sucked in a breath. 'You're going to find them, right? The bastards that did this?'

'We always do,' Maddie said, and then somewhat regretted it.

'So we hear. You two come with big reputations, you know.' Sharon's smile had returned, though there was an edge to it. 'I'm sure you know what you're doing. My team out there, they were all asking about the press coverage, asking me what the thinking was and I said that you people know what you're doing.'

'Do you have a question about that?' Maddie said.

Sharon shrugged. 'We've all seen it. The press are reporting a death on duty, a fifty-six year old officer found dead at the scene, but that's it. Where's the national uproar? Where are the details about how he was beaten to death in cold blood? The appeal for witnesses? The response to that would be huge!'

'It would,' Harry cut in and Maddie was happy to let him answer. 'But we don't want that from Day One. I've been involved in enough of these to know what we do, why we do it and that it works. If we put out the theory that a police officer was lured to a location to be murdered, the traction in the press will go huge, for sure. We might want that later on, we might want the flood of responses that comes with that and we *might* be able to allocate the resources needed to sift through every one for the one per cent that is relevant. Right now, we need to be playing it down. I know how that looks, to you and your team, but my team need to be agile. I need to be able to turn all of them towards a lead when we get it and that means protecting them.'

'And if that doesn't get you anywhere, then you go public?'

'We do. Talk to your team. Tell them what we're doing. Tell them why and make sure they understand how important it is to keep this under control.'

'I get it.' Sharon said with a raised palm. 'Is there anything else you need to ask of me?'

Maddie shook her head. She'd covered what she needed.

'You said that Phil had a set route,' Harry said. 'Stops that he used to make whenever he was on shift?'

'Yes. I mean, it wasn't like you could set your watch by him, but there were places he would go and a route he would drive.'

'Eileen, the lady who emailed you, could you share his route and all the stops with her? Just send her an email and copy me in. I would like it driven, anyone mentioned spoken to.'

'Do you think any of those people might have something to do with what happened?'

'No, but they might have something relevant to say.'

'Whoever you send, can you ask them to be sensitive. He was the village bobby and he was well liked. Those people were his friends, as much as anything else.'

'Do they know?' Maddie said.

'They'll know, for sure. The rural is a far bigger place than our towns, but it's a far smaller place when something happens.'

'Sounds like the sort of thing I should be doing myself then,' Harry said.

'And you will be sensitive?' Sharon seemed to be taking a moment to eye Harry's hulking frame and scarred face.

'You wouldn't believe how sensitive I can be,' Harry said and Maddie had to hide her grin behind her hand.

## CHAPTER 23

'Am I going to be able to rely on you!?' I snapped at him, seemingly catching him by surprise. He had no response at first, not in any way. It was as if I was speaking to a sack of potatoes or a propped-up pillow with googly eyes drawn on.

'You know you can rely on me,' he said, eventually. But there was a dullness to his voice, something non-committal about it.

Outside, the transition from light to dark was just about complete, the death throes of daylight visible as a faint glow on the horizon. It was close to 8 p.m.

'We've got the time to go over this again . . .'

'No!' he whined, 'I got it. I'm not stupid, I just . . .'

'What?' I said.

'I'm not sure I can do this . . . Do you really think you can?'

I leaned in, close enough for my breath to shift his fringe. 'Just you fucking watch me.' And then I pushed the car door. The interior light punctured the darkness between us like a strip of lightning — cackle and all — to light him up brightly and I felt a pang of guilt. He looked scared. I cursed myself for feeling that way. I couldn't afford to hurt him. But I couldn't afford for him to let me down, either.

'Are you going to be a problem?' I had stepped out of the car but I leaned back in to ask the question and was sure to look him dead in the eye.

'No.' He shook his head.

'You just have to do what I say, that's all.'

'I know.' He spoke now like a man resigned.

'Good then,' I said. 'Because you know what happens otherwise. If you let me down, you let us both down and then we both get caught and we both go away. And I'm not talking like before — a few years at a doss house. I'm talking life. Every last minute of it pacing between two walls in a concrete hell. Cop killers don't get to breathe free air again.'

'I know that, that's my point. Isn't that what makes this . . . stupid?'

I was suddenly struggling not to lash out. I took a moment. 'I told you, once this is done, you'll see . . . you'll feel better. This is how we move on.' I was aware that my efforts to stay calm had me talking through gritted teeth.

'So what do we do now?'

'A recce,' I said. The word felt good in my mouth. *Recce* was a word I had seen in the movies: war movies, cop movies, action movies. Always said at a point when a mission was just starting, the plot always one where the hero wins out in the end.

The evening was chilly. Chillier than the previous few for sure. The metal of the car's door frame shocked my fingers when I pushed it closed, careful to do it quietly. The interior light disappeared, the vision of the man sat inside, staring out with pleading in his eyes disappeared too. And I was glad of it.

I walked away, along the same pavements I trod earlier in the day, past the house with the disruptive roots and through its carpet of blossom.

There was someone else: a dog walker on the other side of the pavement, coming towards me having just stepped out of a house.

'Evening.' The greeting was forced, reluctant from the man with the lead, as if he hadn't wanted to be seen either but now etiquette demanded acknowledgment. I lifted a hand in response. My mind swirled with reasons as to why that was the right thing to do: *your voice reveals your gender; an accent tells him something about you; ignoring him completely means you stick in his mind as rude.*

'Fuck! I'm good at this!' I muttered but it was barely audible, nothing more than a vibration in my throat. I walked on and the dog walker did the same. We moved in opposite directions. I counted out twenty paces before shoulder checking, observing a man who might have been caught out by the drop in temperature too. His fleece didn't seem quite enough; he'd plunged his hands in the pockets and his chin into his collar. He took the next turning, his head not even lifting. There was no chance he had noticed the parked car or the full-grown man scared of his own shadow who was ducked down in the passenger seat.

I walked on, approaching the sergeant's house and I checked my pace. It was certainly no chore. I liked walking urban areas at night. I would choose a different area: somewhere with blocks of flats or terraced streets, the sort with their front doors butted right up against the pavement. The people living in those areas seemed to use their curtains less, accepting perhaps, that they were effectively on show. It meant that those walks were peppered with little snippets of the lives lived within: old men in comfy sofas, their many chins lit up by the silver light of their television, a takeaway wrapper balanced on the arm of the chair; a family sitting in two rows, the youngest two having to sit on the floor; an old lady with a paperback open, working around the cat on her lap.

Snippets of life, other peoples. Snippets of what we are, of the moments that make us human.

But there was no such thing on the estate where I walked. The windows were too far away, the use of blinds far more stringent, those inside far more hidden.

If I wanted to see anything of the lives behind the blinds and curtains, I was going to have to force my way in.

\* \* \*

Another slam of the lockers was enough to prompt Alan Day into a slump back in his chair, rubbing at his temples. His tactical team had their own area of the police station and they were damned lucky to have it, truth be known. A team such as his came with a lot of kit and each officer had a locker that was oversized in space, which meant oversized doors, too. And Tactical Teams didn't seem to attract the types of officers who could close a locker door quietly.

The clamour was always worse when they were being released early. It might have only been twenty minutes early, but the news had been greeted like a significant win and a starting gun for them to clear the building.

Alan took another ten minutes to write his update, cursing the fact that he didn't feel he had anything positive to add.

'Tomorrow's another day,' he muttered, then scooped up his car keys and took a moment to revel in the silence. He opened up his phone to let his wife know that he was leaving, giving her a chance to have a cup of tea ready for him when he got in.

But he changed his mind. He would surprise her instead, make tea for them both.

In the room next door, some of the lockers still hung open. Bits of uniform were forcing their way out of one and a pile of unused evidence bags dripped out of another. Alan changed his top, ditching the POLICE-marked fleece for a deep red hoody, not bothering to change out of his rip-stop trousers or search boots. Half-blues, it was called, and officers were constantly reminded not to, that the trousers and boots were just as distinctive to a criminal as a solid 'POLICE' written across their chest. Alan knew he should do better, now more than ever, but he was spurred on by the thought of that cup of tea with his wife. His home was only a fifteen-minute drive. He had no intention of stopping; no intention of doing anything that would put him on show to the public, save for walking across a moonlit car park.

He surveyed his own locker before closing it, checking it was up to the required standard before he raised the state of the locker room as a point of order with his team the next day. No one would be going early in the future if their locker was in disarray. That would sort it.

He swept out of the room, needing to step over a pair of discarded flip- flops that were so far out into the middle of the room that he couldn't even tell which locker they matched with. He turned to take a picture of them, he now had the image that would accompany his first email when he next sat at his desk, the one requiring a team meeting to discuss *standards*.

He could already see how that was going to go. The important message about standards was going to get lost among a group session of light mickey-taking and, if previous experiences were anything to go by, a game of match-the-flip-flop.

He left the police station already smiling about the start of the next working day.

* * *

'Jesus!' he said, and I knew I had surprised him. He had dropped the window on the passenger side of the Volvo since I had left for my recce and I could see his head hanging out as I approached, his fingers gripping the sill while he gulped at the fresh air. I wasn't even quiet. I just changed my angle slightly to come in from his blind spot.

He should have been more aware. He shouldn't have had a blind spot in the first place and he shouldn't have been hanging out of the car, breaking the silhouette — standing out. For all the planning, for everything that had got me this far, he was the clear weak spot.

'One car on the drive, lights on in the living room and a smaller room upstairs. Might be more lights at the back, but . . .' I had to pause, check my breathing and curtail the excitement still coursing through me. 'But it's just like I said. The sergeant is at work, his shift pattern has him there until ten. It's a fifteen-minute journey home. The wife lets the cat in at ten—'

'Once!' The answer started with some power but dwindled down to a shake of his head. 'You saw her put the cat out once. That's what you said.'

'She does it every night and at the same sort of time,' I said calmly. Why would I not be calm? I knew I was right. There was not a doubt in my mind, not even a consideration that I had seen anything other than a set pattern, though I wasn't about to waste my time explaining how I knew. 'Are you ready?'

He wasn't. He nodded, but he wasn't. I knew him too well. It didn't matter. I would keep my instructions bold, clear and simple. That wasn't the first time I found myself wishing I didn't need him, but there was no getting around the fact that I couldn't do this alone.

I stepped away from the car, hearing the door clunk shut and then the scuffle of a man stumbling as he got out. Everything was heightened to me. I could feel the gentle movement of the breeze and hear the trees shuffling their reaction. I could feel every contour of the tarmac under my feet. The street lights too, were crisp and bright, stark against a night that was now complete. There was no moonlight, the nights had been cloudy, a pattern of early morning showers had set in for the sun to then emerge and steam all of the moisture away. The air felt like rain, smelt like it too. It was delicious and added to my overall feeling of being switched on, plugged into my surroundings, of really being *alive*.

I was ready.

I led the way, not checking if he was following, knowing that he would. Confirmation came in the form of a stone kicked from behind that clattered over a drain grate. As I led him under the cherry tree with the overhang, the breeze met me head on to caress my face and run through my fingers as I walked. I could feel the petals crunch even through the soles of my shoes. They seemed drier even than just a short time earlier. I heard him drag his feet through those same petals a few paces behind. He seemed to be slowing up, aware perhaps that we were approaching the point where he was going to have to start operating on his own.

This point was at our arrival at another tree. It was bigger than the cherry and leafy — ideal, since the leaves projected a firm block of shadow against a solid wall. This was the hiding place we had discussed. He stopped and slunk backwards to become engulfed in that shadow. His movement was jerky, his heels clattered against the wall, but the result was pleasing. He was gone. There was a small flash of white where the shadow didn't quite cover his feet — I'd told him to wear black trainers — but you would have to be coming down here slow and looking for someone hiding, to pick him out.

'Perfect,' I said. 'Now you just need to wait until that phone in your pocket shakes. You'll know from your watch that it's from me so no need to get your big, bright phone out. And then you move. Clear?'

'I know . . . I know what I'm doing.'

'Good to hear. You know what happens if you leave me here on my own. If you don't turn up when I call. I get caught and then you get caught.'

'I know—' he said, but I stepped in on instinct, moving into his shadow so we were both wrapped up — just two pairs of trainers left out on the street — then I kissed him before he could say anything else, in the way I had done before when he seemed to need something more to put him at ease.

'I wouldn't trust anyone else to be here,' I said. 'This is me trusting you with my *life!* You know what this means to me, how much this means to me, but if you don't want to do this . . . if you would rather walk away, I will listen. I would do it. For you.' I waited, staring into eyes that had a white surround, a reflection from a distant light.

'You know I won't let you down.' He said it and that was it, his last chance to stand up and tell me what he really thought, what he really wanted to do and he didn't.

The coward.

'I know you won't,' I said, and then I moved away before there was any chance he might reverse that. I was a good ten paces away before I checked back.

All I could see was an empty street.

* * *

Alan Day made his way across the car park and, as expected, all traces of his team and their vehicles had long since disappeared into the night. The streets beyond were quiet too, it was the middle of the week in an area that was mostly dwellings. There was a row of shops nearby, but they were all daytime businesses.

He always parked in the same spot and the same way: the outer limit of the car park where it met with the pavement and nose in, to face out over the street and away from the station. He'd had a tough start when joining the team at this station, damned near quit just a few weeks in but he had clung on, found a way to cope. It was a lot of little things really, like parking in a way that left him facing back out over the normal world. He could then take a moment, after parking for work, to remind himself that policing was just a bubble he worked in, a bubble that he would step back out of again at the end of the shift. Eleven years on and in a far better place in his career, he still started every shift the same way. He would take a breath, focus on the lawn, the pavement beyond, the cars passing with people going about their business and then, when he was ready, he would step out and turn to face his work. It was stupid really, a clumsy mind trick that had somehow lasted to become a routine.

The recent images of a fallen colleague had brought some of those doubts back and he wasn't sad at all to be leaving his work bubble with another set of shifts done.

He was going home.

* * *

The sergeant's house had less lights on than when I had left it. The living room was still glowing but the upstairs light was gone. *Or was it?* I got closer, strained my eyes a little and felt sure I could pick out the faintest of glows along the bottom of the window where curtains blocked the rest. A night light perhaps? That would certainly make sense if it was one of the children's rooms.

I crossed over, to where there were more trees rupturing the pavement, the tarmac bursting around them. There were more of them at this end, close enough that they might make ideal goalposts for the local kids and between them was only shadow, every bit as deep as the one I had just left. It was the ideal spot.

The front door opened just a few minutes later. It was just like before, like a landed spaceship in a movie, opening its doors for first contact, the form of an adult woman in its middle who took a step out to call for her cat.

It was time to move.

'Hello!' I exclaimed the moment I stepped out of the shadow, then gave the woman in her doorway a moment to react, to adjust to the fact that an empty street was no longer empty at all. I was smiling, broad enough for the smile to be seen from a distance, my hands up, palms forward, the right one filled with my lit mobile phone. 'I'm so sorry!' I said, tutting, 'would you be able to assist at all? We've not long moved to the area, my husband and I . . . goodness, I feel so silly! I'm actually lost. There, I said it!' I giggled, now crossing the road, moving closer. The sergeant's wife straightened, a black and white cat flitted between her legs to be absorbed into the light behind. She crossed her arms, which I took to mean that her defences were up, but then she shivered. It seemed to loosen up a smile. That chilly breeze I mentioned, though I was no longer feeling it.

'Easily done. Where do you need to be?'

'You've lived here a while then?'

She nodded, taking a single step out of her house. 'I have, but I was an out-of-towner once, I remember when this estate all looked the same.'

'Northbourne Road. We're at number twenty-two. I should know it by now — I've walked it enough. When we were waiting for the sale to go through, we would come down and just walk around the area. So silly . . . I learned a good lesson tonight.' I tapped the phone. 'Don't rely on phones to get you home. They run out of data.'

The woman smiled. 'You're a few streets away is all. It's . . . oh!' she chuckled, 'I was going to say it's easy if you know it, but of course it is! I'm just trying to think of the best way to . . .'

'There's an alley right, a shortcut, or am I completely going mad?' I was still smiling.

The sergeant's wife had uncrossed her arms for them to fall by her side. She now pushed one of her hands into her pocket. 'There *is* an alley!' she said. 'See, you do know the area! I don't have my phone. It would definitely be easier for me to show you on that. Just let me grab it.'

'That would be great, thank you!' I sang, suddenly aware that I might be overdoing it. She was already walking back into her house, that was all I needed.

I moved after her. I moved fast, despite being up on my toes to be quiet. I had already fired off the text message that would summon my backup. There was time for a quick look around, over at the next door that was already in darkness, down the street that was empty in both directions. No one saw me step in through the open front door, still moving silently, lifting my T-shirt to expose the handle of a zombie knife.

No one saw anything.

* * *

Alan turned into his estate and a little sigh of satisfaction dropped from his lips. His wife, Louise, was a DFL, Down From London, but he had grown up nearby and never dreamed he would ever be able to live in a place like this. It was a good estate, perfect for a family.

He must have been early, there were still lights on downstairs. No doubt Louise would be watching the last of her TV shows, something light and romantic, the sort of slush she never admitted to actually liking but always seemed to have on.

He swung into the drive, his headlight beams shrinking in against the rear of his wife's car. It was a chilly night breeze that he stepped into. His kit bag was in the boot with hinges that creaked so much he found himself looking over with concern at his neighbour's windows. They were such lovely people, the sort that would check his shifts before they mowed their lawn. There was no sign of movement at their windows, no sign of movement anywhere.

He glanced up at Emmy's window, seeing if her reading light was still on. Of course it was. He should scold her for that, it was over an hour past her bedtime, but there was no way he would; it meant she might still be awake and she would always tiptoe down the stairs for a bedtime cuddle.

The front door pushed in with a twist of his key. There was an internal door too, straight after. It was half glass; the stairs were visible, as well as the living room door and a view straight through to the kitchen, where they had extended it to make it as wide as the whole house at the back. He put down his kit bags as softly as he could, then used the bottom step on the stairs to take his boots off, a sigh tumbled out with the first of them.

That was the moment he was grabbed from behind.

Emmy.

He stood up to spin around, one foot in a boot, the other out, grabbing her up in a cuddle that lifted her off the stairs, their cheeks firmly pushed together and a little tickling in her side. Emmy did her best to stifle her laughter, to not make a noise, both of them clicking into the pretence that they would be in trouble if her mother heard.

'Right then,' he said, softly, putting his daughter back on the stairs. 'Get back to bed. Don't you go getting me in trouble now!' Then he pointed with two fingers at his own two eyes, before turning those fingers to point at Emmy. The standard *I'm watching you* symbol, one that they used a lot, something that was theirs. He did watch her too, all the way as she spun on the stairs and made her way up them, still giggling and not very quietly. He could track her progress on the first floor too, across creaking floorboards and onto bedsprings that squeaked.

Dani would be asleep. Alan would often describe their youngest as a little firework, either lit and screeching across the sky, shedding colour in bursts of energy or laid out and silent. There was no in-between. She was all or nothing and he adored her for it.

Now in his socks, he walked along the hall. The living room light was on, the television too, paused on a scene that looked very intense. Louise wasn't in there, which meant she could well be making that tea he had promised himself.

But the kettle was silent. So was Louise. She was sitting at their dining table looking like she had been waiting for him and his gut twisted, his instincts telling him that something terrible had happened.

# CHAPTER 24

'What is it?' he said.

'Sit down, Alan,' said his wife.

'Lou, what's going on?' He moved closer, into the kitchen.

'You can't make a noise. Not a *single* noise! If Emmy hears — if either of the kids come down — they said they'll have no choice but to hurt them.'

'Hurt?'

'And no one needs to be hurt.' A different voice swept in from behind him, from his periphery. There was a solid jab in his back, too, something with a sharp point. The sensation was enough to override his instinct to turn towards it. He stayed staring ahead, still locked on his wife, her expression was enough to hold him still, to tighten the knot that had his stomach gripped. A figure appeared behind her: a tall white male in a creased white T-shirt with the sleeves rolled up so it was almost a vest, enough to show a full sleeve of tattoos up his right arm and numerous bands on his left. He looked tense, scared and determined. None of those things were good. There was another tattoo that crawled up the left side of his neck until it was lost under a shaggy crop of hair that fell untidily over his ears. Long sideburns merged into a couple of days stubble and the tattoos continued on his face.

His left cheek showed a thick, black tear. Alan knew the significance of that particular one, depending on the wearer. It either signified someone who had served significant prison time or someone who had committed murder. It could mean both. More things that were not good.

Alan lifted his hands slowly, his palms open and outward to communicate that he was no threat, that they had his attention and his compliance.

'Okay, so we're just going to do what you say.' Alan said. 'You can take what you want and we're all going to be calm.' He looked at his wife for the last part. She nodded but it was so fast it was more like the reaction to a jab.

'Sit down,' commanded the voice from behind him. He twisted his head slowly to the left but managed less than a quarter turn before the pointed object was pushed firmer between his shoulder blades, enough for the pain to make him gasp. 'Don't,' the voice warned. 'Do as I say. *Exactly* as I say. Nothing else.' He felt a hand against his hip, it felt for the shape of his phone in his right pocket then plunged in to retrieve it. 'Now . . . sit down.'

Alan snapped back to face forward. He pulled out a dining chair that left him sitting opposite his wife; each occupying one end of the long table. Alan calmed himself by thinking like a cop. There were two intruders — that he knew of — he couldn't be certain there weren't more. The one behind him seemed to be in charge and was holding a weapon. Access to his children was via the hall that was now behind him, over his left shoulder. His wife was straight ahead and access to her was now obstructed by the table.

'Push your chair right in,' the voice spoke again. It was as if his mind was being read. The point had moved with him, the sensation on the nape of his neck always there. There was a breathiness to that voice, something that Alan had heard before in high-stress situations: a mixture of excitement and fear. He was detecting something else in there too. Anger.

When Alan budged his chair forward, the wooden legs caught on the tiled floor with a loud screech. His head jerked instinctively to his left shoulder, towards the stairs, and the increased pressure in the back of his neck got deeper, enough that he leaned his head away from it and hissed. The voice, when it came back, was closer. His assailant leaned in enough for him to feel each word against his ear.

'That's right, you keep it quiet, *sergeant*. If you make enough noise that your kids hear and they come down to investigate . . . well, then we have ourselves some more witnesses to add to our little party down here.'

The point dug in as if the offender had used it to push off, to straighten back up. The table was now so tight in Alan's midriff that it was uncomfortable. He tried to quell his rising panic, desperate to stay detached, to treat it like a live job, but the mention of his children was making it impossible.

His first reaction had been that he had walked in on a burglary, but he was no longer sure what this was. He could feel a rage building, it filled the void as his initial shock ebbed away. He knew anger wasn't going to help. He surveyed what he could. The blinds were down over the back doors in what was probably the first time they had been used since their installation. That meant the offenders had closed them, despite the fact that the rear of the house wasn't overlooked. They were being careful. The blinds had a little movement too, a gentle sucking in and out with the breeze that told him the doors were open behind. They were never open. Louise always locked up when she was here on her own and the darkness set in.

He also knew that these people had gained access without the children knowing. His wife must have let them in. She was street-smart, more risk averse than he was, which meant she had been duped somehow, something carefully constructed and believable. The back door would have been opened by the two offenders as a means of quick escape.

They knew about his job and about the kids too — that there were two of them. *If either of the kids come down* . . . Louise had said that, but he didn't think she would give something up they didn't already know. They must have been watching.

There were other details. The offender he could see, the man with the tattoo marking him out as someone who could be well used to violence, wore gloves — blue nitrile gloves, the exact same type that had wrinkled Alan's hands earlier that day. He knew them as gloves with only one purpose: to limit the possibility of leaving a forensic trace. Another detail occurred to him, taking its place as the most significant yet. He had been positioned so he was able to stare straight at one of the offenders and his wife was positioned where she could stare at the other.

The people invading his home had been careful and they were smart, they seemed intent on not leaving any trace that might identify them. But they were not covering their faces. All of this together pointed to one outcome: they weren't planning on leaving any witnesses.

## CHAPTER 25

Harry Blaker's garden was dark, the long grass damp where spring nights always seemed to come with a layer of moisture. He was in slippers and they were not up to the task, soaked in a moment. Though the sensation was far from pleasant, he was quickly numb to it — numb to everything.

This garden had been his everything once. *Their* everything.

It was his wife, Robin, who had got him into it in the first place. She had talked about how a garden was a blank canvas on which to create something. Living art, she called it. Pretentious nonsense, Harry had said, but with a grin lurking just beneath the surface. She always had an artist's eye, saw beauty and meaning where others couldn't — where he couldn't. Just one of the many reasons he loved her so.

Initially, he had only been there for the manual labour, a bit of digging, some lifting and carrying while Robin did anything that required skill or vision. It was the spring that followed those efforts that had ensnared him. From bleak soil and flat green erupted a canvas of colour and life that grew from his drops of sweat and her gentle hands. A shared passion grew with it.

The garden became their place: quality time, good conversation, hard work and clear rewards. It was their sanctuary. It was supposed to be forever.

When Robin died, the garden was the part of her that Harry clung onto for the longest. Still, it wasn't letting him go, the unkempt and spindly ends of the bushes had grown long enough to reach the kitchen window, to scratch against it in the breeze and tug at his heart strings.

He had stopped going out at all. Days turned into weeks. The neglected tasks piled up until it didn't bear thinking about. Harry had become accustomed to not looking, let alone stepping out of his back door.

But something brought him out that night.

He had already been out of the front door, Jock's lead trailing in his hand, his dog knowing the pavements well enough that he didn't need to apply it. When they returned home, he had left the lights off like he always did, then he had walked right through, until his hand rested against the back door. His other hand spun the key and he had pushed the door open to be rushed by all the familiar smells at once, as if they had all been waiting for the opportunity to swamp him.

In the centre of the garden was a bench. It overlooked a pond that seemed always in the right position to catch the moon. He stared at its reflection and considered that this felt like something positive, being back out in a place that he had written off as a part of his history. Maybe he would be able to go out there when the sun was up, when he could clearly see the ornate, wooden Robin Red Breast he had carved for his wife in those early days.

In that moment, he thought about the first few nights that followed his own wife's murder and how he had sat in this very spot. It was never called that . . . *murder*. That was the thing with drink-drivers. They could commit the most horrific acts and they'd only ever be labelled as *drink-drivers*, but Harry knew what it was. The nights had been the hardest then and they still were now, when it felt like everyone else was in a contented and deep sleep while you suffered alone. It was inevitable, perhaps, that his mind turned to Jillian Jones. He wondered how she was getting on, what she was doing at that very minute, whether she was coping.

He stood up. He would go for a drive. Philip Jones's patrol sergeant had been true to her word. She'd sent the route and the regular stops to Eileen, who had shared it with him in turn. The route ran through a number of villages, including Philip's own. Harry would just see if there were lights on, any sign that everything was okay inside.

He told himself that wasn't why he was going. There were other reasons: maybe someone had been watching for a while, learning Phil's pattern, biding their time. If that was the case there might be obvious places to sit, some useful CCTV coverage on a farm or industrial unit that might show Phil's movements and, more importantly, the movement of someone following. Harry almost convinced himself that this was important police work, work that couldn't wait, that had to be done right then.

It wasn't just a man running away from the ghosts that had taken over his sanctuary.

## CHAPTER 26

'So, this is how this goes. You're going to get on the floor . . .'
Alan grimaced as that solid point was pushed firmly into his
neck to emphasise the words. 'And then it's the turn of the
good wife. Do it now.'

Then the sensation was gone, the point removed completely and he heard a step back behind him. Alan was gentler
with his chair this time, using his hands underneath the seat
to lift it slightly, to move in silence. When he stepped away
from the table he felt a push, this one from a flat hand in
his back that led him past his wife, to the open part of the
kitchen. His shoulder was grabbed and 'Here!' was hissed
into his ear. He hesitated, but only for a moment, as long as
it took for the sharp point to find his lower back.

He dropped to one knee first, delaying, trying to think.
His wife was now over his right shoulder, still seated and
facing away. His children were over his left shoulder — or
at least the way to them was. Dani's room was just about
directly above where he was at that point and he stole a glance
up before lying on the floor. There was no option, nothing
that guaranteed the safety of his family in that moment. All
he could do was keep this room calm.

119

'Don't you fucking move!' The faceless offender spoke again, the voice just above a whisper, directed downwards. The next words were directed at the man with the tattoos. 'If he moves, stab him until he stops moving.' The footfalls behind Alan then moved away, around the other side of the kitchen island in the middle of the room. Two drawers rolled open, the sound of their mechanism something that Alan knew well. Then came the rattle of dinner plates, picked up as a stack, still rattling as they were carried. Closer.

'Stay very still.' The next sounds were of a cracking knee joint, a deeper breath and still that shivering stack of plates. Then came the sensation of weight on his upper back, directly between his shoulder blades, weight that spread out to push through to his chest and restrict his breathing, to make him gasp a little deeper. 'Don't be breathing too hard now.' The voice was different again, excitement taking over. 'No moving at all, if I were you. Move an inch and these are gonna go. I reckon smashing plates is the sort of noise that'll wake a child. Have them coming down to see what's going on. There can't be witnesses.'

*There can't be witnesses.*

Alan screwed his eyes shut and cursed silently. He had known that already but the confirmation made it strike home. He had lain down and been compliant, waiting for his opportunity. But it was getting more hopeless with every moment that passed. He had sleepwalked into a position that he hadn't foreseen. The plates shifted slightly; he was having to concentrate to keep them up. It was all he could do.

'Now, you . . .' The voice was directed away from him. At Louise. He couldn't see her; he had been left facing in the wrong direction. He heard her chair scrape, the noise close to his ear and he could feel it through his chest. 'Next to your sergeant — but not too close.'

'You don't have to do this!' Alan blurted. 'We're no threat, okay? We know who's in charge. We just want you to go. Just take what you want and go. We're not trying to stop you . . . we just want you to go . . .' Alan was aware that his voice was breaking for the last part, that he was pleading.

'Next to him.' The voice said, as if Alan hadn't spoken at all. He sucked in another breath, it came with the scent of bleach tinged with strawberry, his wife's choice of floor cleaner when he would always buy the lemon variant.

'No!' said Louise. 'I won't. I won't lie down there so you can do whatever you want to my children!'

There was a strong slap then a scuffle of feet as if the blow had knocked her off balance. Then came a shocked sob — just one. From his wife.

'Go and get one!' the voice snapped. 'Use the torch. No lights. There's no need to be waking them both up. We'll start with one.'

Alan felt a nausea so strong he could barely get his words out. 'No!' He croaked as a spot of white light from a torch flashed across the ceiling.

'No!' his wife whined, voice thick with panic. 'Okay, okay, I'll do what you ask. Okay, I'm doing it, look!' The footsteps had got some distance away, but they stopped in response.

Alan needed to be facing the other way, even though it meant lifting his whole body off the floor. He needed to move slowly, his focus on keeping his back flat no matter what. The stack shifted, he felt it tip away from his head, the plates rattled and clinked. He adjusted in time — *just* in time — spreading his arms out and ducking back down, his cheek pressed against the tiles. It wasn't going to be easy.

He would try again. He planted his hands down firmly and turned his feet in for his toes to take his weight. Then he heaved himself into the slowest press-up of all time.

The plates on his back shook and clacked again, then they shifted. Their movement was larger than before, towards his head, and he had to adjust quickly, pushing harder through his hands. The strain of the additional weight became a shake in his chest that spread out to his arms.

He made it high enough to turn his head, banging his chin in his haste.

He could see Louise. She was on her knees next to him, her hands up like she was appealing for calm. The man with the tattoos had made it down the hall, the torch still lit in his hand. But Alan's attention wasn't on him, it was on the ugly looking zombie-style knife that was pressed firmly into the side of his wife's throat to stop her in her tracks.

'It doesn't need to be her too . . . please . . .' Alan inhaled hard and fast, catching a sob before it could form. The action caused a jerk through his body and the plates shifted again. They slipped to the right, probably only a few millimetres, but it felt like the start of a disaster, the first tremor of a killer earthquake. He countered it with a subtle raise of his shoulder blade, but it wasn't enough and he scrunched his eyes shut, waiting for the inevitable sound of smashing crockery, readying himself to leap to his feet.

In the milliseconds that passed, a sort of plan formed. The crashing plates would give him a moment to react, his focus would be solely on getting to his feet and pushing past. They would be expecting him to protect his wife, but his only chance was to surprise them, to charge past her, past the knife at her throat and hit the man with the torch with everything he had.

Then he would turn and he would form a barrier to the stairs that no one would pass all the while he was breathing. He would do anything to protect his children and, even in the briefest of moments, he knew that meant sacrificing their mother.

# CHAPTER 27

Violence was out of place here.

This was a sentence that seemed to be on repeat, running through Harry Blaker's mind as he rolled over single-track country lanes, past beautiful homes made from a hodgepodge of brick and exposed beams. Some were topped in thatch, some with roofs that pointed up at the dark sky in the shape of a wizard's hat, where their original use had been as oast houses.

Even in the dark, there was a warmth to the area, a quaintness that was personified by cosy looking pubs and the passing of a sleeping cricket pitch. The quintessential British existence.

The older, traditional country piles came to an end, their final hurrah was a row of cottages, the countryside version of a terrace. Their exteriors were adorned with mismatched windows and front doors that looked like you'd need to stoop. These had thatched roofs too, only here they wore them like individual hair pieces tied down; a row of gossiping old women sitting side by side in the salon.

Violence was out of place here.

The scenery changed to larger, far newer builds; modern takes on country living. There were slabs of glass to refract his headlights, block-paved drives straining under the weight

123

of Range Rovers and raised flowerbeds with tulips nodding in unison. Then he came to the outskirts of the village that Philip Jones had called home. Harry was less than two miles from Frant Village Hall and the feel changed again.

It was sobering. The homes that flashed past his window were now semi-detached, obviously built in batches, using a template that repeated itself like the backdrop of an early cartoon. It was a far cheaper part of the housing market than much of what he had passed, but it was a nice estate, decent people like Phil, just trying to—

There was a flash of light.

Harry slowed and checked his mirror, picking out at least three streetlights. He considered that one of them had surged and reflected in the living room window of a house, the angle just right. But his instinct had been a torchlight from the inside and Harry had learned some time ago to trust his instincts. He knew of only one type of person that used torches rather than house lights in the dead of night: burglars.

He pulled his car up, trying to make it smooth, satisfied that he had rolled far enough for any lookout to be unaware. He had his own torch stashed in the centre console. It was heavy, purposefully so, to double as something firm to swing. He kept it off for now, finding the pavement and pacing back in the direction from which he'd come. Despite the street lights, the darkness still seemed thick under gathered clouds. The air was still. Any breeze he had detected earlier was all but gone. His footfalls sounded heavy, clumsy almost, and he was careful to pick his feet up to try and watch where he put them. The air smelled like woodfires . . . sweet chestnut. Someone's evening burning still hung in the air. A hedgerow on the other side shook where he'd startled something small and quick, the noise merging with a water feature that had a pleasant gurgle in a front garden.

Violence was out of place here.

So was a burglar.

He made it back to where he had seen the flash of light. His eyes were adjusted enough and he took a moment to work out its house number, in case there turned out to be anything worth calling in. One next door bin was daubed in white with the number 26. The one on the other side had a shiny number big enough to see: 30.

'Number twenty-eight, then,' Harry murmured as a way of committing it to memory. The property was flat fronted with four windows, the longest of which was on the ground floor. The front door was on the left-hand side and concealed in thick shadow cast by an overhanging arch. There were two cars on the drive, parked in an obedient line. Harry lifted his eyes to the first floor where the smaller of the two windows had the faintest of glows.

Harry walked up the drive, then pushed himself against the garage. His attention remained on the windows for more flashes but there was nothing. He moved left, daring to stay his full height as he moved across the biggest window for a clear view into a living room. It was in darkness. The internal door was in the back left corner and so Harry could tell that there was a light on at the back of the house. He needed to get around there.

He lingered at the front door for a moment. There was frosted glass and that light was visible again. There was a flicker, someone walking between him and the source of light.

Movement.

Harry quickened his pace to the gate. The latch was clumsy, the sound of it lifting like a dropped pan and he paused, his thumb still holding the cold metal down to see if he got any sort of reaction. There was nothing he could detect, nothing audible, at least.

The gate swung in with a subtle creak. He could see down the side of the house now, far enough to see another area of lawn, only this one had a white block of light projected out from the rear.

Harry moved towards it.

# CHAPTER 28

The sound of crashing didn't come. The plates rattled — their loudest yet — but then they settled. Alan's breathing quickened, deepened too, enough to feel like his whole body was rising and falling with it. He might not have brought the stack down, but he had found its limit.

His wife lay on the floor next to him, having fallen onto it as if she had been pushed. Her bloodshot eyes were just a few inches from his; they shuffled in watery surrounds as if she was trying to focus. Her nose was running and her hair fell over her face to shiver when she exhaled a frightened little whine.

Alan tried out a smile. It might not have seemed like the time or the place but it was all he could do to keep her calm. He needed to play for time. He needed to think again. He could hear another stack of crockery being lifted from a cupboard. It would be for her. The only thing Alan Day could do now was to keep those plates up, to keep quiet, to let this play out and to pray that there would be another opportunity. Or he would have to fashion one.

'Please . . .' Alan said. 'You don't have to do this. It's not too late. You may think you've gone too far, but this is nothing right now. You don't have to make it something. You can still just leave. Take some things if you want, but you can leave. We won't even call it in.' Alan knew he was talking to an audience that would never believe him. A police officer, attacked in his own home and then *not* calling it in. It was preposterous. A foot was planted between him and his wife and it made him recoil enough for the plates to rattle on his back. It was his wife's shoe. Her Croc, at least, last seen at the back door, a white background with a daisy motif. The foot inside was wrapped in a plastic bag, which rustled as a knee came down next to it. Alan sensed an assailant leaning over him, getting as close as possible to his ear.

'You still don't have any idea, do you? I know you saw what we did to that other copper. I know you were there after. I was too.'

Alan's moment of clarity took a beat, then it came all at once. He hadn't been thinking about Philip Jones, about the crime scene, about what he had seen. Now he was. The people who had done that . . . they were here. In his home. With his family.

A crowbar slipped directly between them, the hooked end thumping the white kitchen tile with such force that it cracked into a spider-web pattern beneath it. It stayed resting on its nose, so close that it took a moment for Alan's eyes to be able to adjust, to make out any detail. Then they did, one detail in particular: a patch stained a copper orange. Blood. This was the weapon that Alan had spent the last two shifts looking for. This was the weapon that had disfigured Phil Jones to the point where he was almost unrecognisable.

The sound of that breaking tile travelled out of the kitchen and up their stairs, it reached far enough to prompt a voice to call out from halfway down those stairs. It was a child's voice . . . inquisitive . . . uncertain.

'Dad? Is everything okay?'

## CHAPTER 29

A finger shot across lips, though Alan didn't need the instruction. He froze in panic, stayed silent, prayed that his wife did the same.

'Mum?' The question changed where he hadn't answered. The anxiety was clear; Emmy spoke as if through a tightening throat. Alan couldn't have answered, even if he was permitted. He was too scared — terrified. Then came a noise that only increased his terror: a dulled thud and a creak. The top step always creaked when weight was shifted. Emmy was coming down.

'What was that?' Emmy called again. It was clear that she wasn't going away without an answer. She was going to need reassurance.

'I need to talk to her,' Alan whispered — barely audible, breathy. 'I can just tell her that everything is okay. I'll tell her to go back to bed.' He could see just enough of his wife to see that she was starting to squirm, perhaps trying to turn her head to face the stairs. It could bring those plates down, which would bring Emmy running. 'Please!' He added, but every word was a struggle. The weight on his back was pinning his torso to the ground, crushing his chest into the floor. It was difficult to breathe, let alone talk.

'Shout to her,' said the voice. 'Tell her everything's fine. Tell her to go back to bed.'

'I can't!' Alan hissed. 'I'll sound crushed, stressed . . . different.' Alan was simply being honest. He wasn't sure he could manage louder without bringing the plates down. He knew his daughter too; he knew she would keep coming unless she saw him to tell her everything was okay.

There was a pause. Not just from his captor, it seemed, but time itself. It resumed when an ugly knife appeared in front of his eyes with a casual swing to it.

'You need to listen now, sergeant. Closer than ever.' The excitement had built up again in that voice. 'I'm going to let you up. I'm going to take these off you and I'm going to let you walk out there and deal with your daughter. And I'm going to wait right here, with this knife at your wife's throat. You tell the kid to go to bed, you keep both your feet on the ground floor at all times and you stay in my sight. You take a single step on those stairs, make a movement I don't like or do anything that makes me think you're fucking me about, and I start stabbing and sawing at her neck. And when she's done, it's the rest of you. Do you understand?'

The excitement was still there but there was a coldness too, as detectable as the determination. Alan didn't answer, he couldn't. There was movement above him and the stack lifted. The difference was crazy, a sudden feeling of lightness.

'Where are you?' Emmy called out, then there was another dulled thump of a hesitant child walking down carpeted stairs.

'Hold on!' Alan called out, his voice strained where he was trying to get to his feet. His legs had a shake, he felt a little dizzy and his vision blurred as he tried to move forward. 'It's okay, honey? Just coming. Stay there!' Alan put in extra effort to sound light and cheery, looking away from his wife and the figure stooped over her with a blade to her neck. When he made it out into the hallway, he could see a pair of legs out of a white nightie. She was halfway.

'Hey!' Alan said, 'what are you doing! No coming down. It's bedtime now. You're supposed to be in bed. Long day tomorrow!'

129

'I heard a noise!' Emmy tilted her head slightly to one side.

'Yeah, you did!' Alan rolled his eyes. 'Dad's an idiot, see. Dropped something in the kitchen. I think I might have cracked a tile. Mum doesn't mind, she said it's not like I do it a lot.'

'You're always breaking something!' Emmy's uncertainty seemed to leave with her giggle.

'Fine. Your mum isn't happy and she said that I'm *always* breaking something.' He had to rush the words out where his bottom lip had a shake at the sound of his daughter's glee.

'Can I have a cuddle?' Emmy said and took another step down. She was tall for her age, her eyeline still above where she would have a clear view into the kitchen, to where her mother was laid out with a stack of crockery on her back and a knife to her throat. But one more step might do it. One more step and she was a witness.

*There can't be witnesses.*

There couldn't be a hug either. That would mean him going up to meet her, that would mean stepping off the ground floor and his instructions had been explicit.

'No, Emmy!' Alan's fear, his desperation, made him out as angry and he felt bad. 'No! How many times have we told you? Bedtime is bedtime. We can't have this every night. Now come on . . .' He softened as her expression changed. The smile she'd been wearing dropped like a crowbar onto a tiled floor. She welled up a little.

Emmy had never been much of a crier, always way too old for her years and nothing seemed to faze her. He'd noticed a change in her recently, she was growing up, her emotional intelligence growing with it and her ability to cope with the changes to herself was becoming more and more difficult. But she moved back up the stairs, made two steps before Alan called her back, despite knowing that he shouldn't.

'Emmy . . . I'm sorry! I shouldn't snap at you like that. I shouldn't be so mean!' She stopped, half-turned. 'I broke something because I'm clumsy and I'm annoyed at myself,

130

not at you. You do need to go to bed, so no cuddles, but . . .'
He choked back his next words, welling up himself. He could
see movement in his periphery, someone in the kitchen took
a few steps towards him. Alan was pushing his luck, but the
desire to say something to his daughter that might stick, that
might outlast this moment, was too much. He couldn't be
out of character. He couldn't let on that he was upset or
Emmy would be back for that cuddle.

'I'm watching you!' he said. 'I always will be, don't you
forget that!'

And then Alan Day pointed at his eyes with two fingers,
before spinning his hand around to point at his daughter
with those same two fingers. A gesture that she repeated right
back, just as he knew that she would, like so many carefree
times in the past.

Alan exhaled his relief when she spun on her heels,
jogged the top few stairs and then went into her room, closing the door behind her. She was giggling again and, as he
peered up into the darkness of the landing, he found himself
yearning for the same interaction with Dani, for both his
daughters to giggle with him.

He was being beckoned from the kitchen, by a free hand
where the other held a knife to his wife's neck. He was supposed to return to where a stack of plates was ready to render
him immobile, to take away all chances of protecting his
children. Returning would, of course, protect his wife.

But for how long?

Sergeant Alan Day had a decision to make.

## CHAPTER 30

The back garden was a featureless square, the lawn pushing right up against new-looking fencing. Everything looked new to Harry. Even the lawn showed as strips of recently laid turf that ran the full length across him.

The back door was open. Ajar, at least, the gap it created lit up like a lightsabre stood up on its end. Bright white. There was a light shushing noise where the full-length blinds had found enough of a breeze to shuffle. They were closed, made of a thin material so they were still letting out light, but Harry couldn't see in.

He edged closer, turning so his chest was against the brick, reaching out with one finger to make a gap in the blinds, his view a thin slice of the room. He could hear something, a voice — words indistinguishable — then a moan, like someone in pain. He took another step to the left, slowly making the slice wider. The next moan was louder than the last.

The back door was a slider and Harry edged it away, its runners were smooth and quiet. His next movement was all at once. He pushed the blinds aside and moved over the threshold and into a kitchen made bright by downlights reflecting off any number of white surfaces. His attention was drawn to the floor, to a bundle of long dark material that had a face at one end and slippers at the other. The face was turned up, screwed into a plethora of wrinkles. It was an elderly man, pain written all over his face.

'Hey! You okay?' Harry took a moment to check if there was anyone else in the room.

'Who are you? Get out of my house!' The man erupted, his wrinkles ironing out for a moment before collapsing inward, even tighter still, as he emitted a long hiss — as if his pain was excruciating. 'I fell!' he said. A free hand appeared to reach down for his hip. He sounded hopeless, but only for a moment. 'I fell,' he snarled through gritted teeth and with a combination of pain and rage. 'But when I get up from here, I'll still be a match for you! I'll tear you limb from limb. Now, get the hell out of my house!'

Harry lifted one of his hands to show his palm, with the other he replaced the heavy torch with a warrant card lifted from his back pocket.

'You're alright, I'm a police officer. I saw a torchlight. I thought you were being burgled! What happened?' Harry dropped to one knee.

The man had stiffened, but he slumped the moment Harry's words struck home. The wrinkles now formed an expression of relief.

'Torch was me. I got it here somewhere. I try not to wake the wife with the big light. I'm always up for a wee in the dead of night. I use the toilet down here for the same reason. But this old hip . . .' He grimaced again and Harry reached for him.

'Take it easy there, I'll get someone here to help.'

'They don't do nothing. I lay four hours last time — out on the flower bed. Wife was worried at first. Didn't know what to do with herself. Soon got used to it, though. She was stepping around me by the end. That was the final straw.'

'You got rid of her?' Harry smiled.

The man coughed a laugh. 'Got rid of the flower bed. Not sure it was the right choice! I couldn't manage it no more — the garden I mean. I was only clipping some bits back — nothing really. She been saying it's too much for me for a while. Dunno what I hate more . . . that she got rid of my flowerbeds or that she was right all along.'

Harry's smile held. He could relate. 'What can I do?' he said.

'Throw me on the scrap heap with my prize roses, probably be best! Saving that, best put the kettle on. No doubt the wife will be down shortly. I'm weak and white, but I guess you can see that. She's stronger but needs a sweetener. My dad it was who said that we become the tea we drink.'

'That I can do. If I get it wrong, though, you promise not to tear me limb from limb?' Harry grinned.

'Once upon a time I woulda been a match for the likes of you.'

'I bet. Anything I can do to make you more comfortable? I'll make the call, get an ambulance here.'

'Nothing that'll make me comfortable for a four hour wait.'

'It won't be four hours, not with me calling.' Harry was already working his phone. Just as he was about to dial, it burst into life. 'Seems we're in luck,' he said to the stricken man. 'This is the control room calling me.'

'Is it though? You must really be someone.' The old man found a chuckle that mingled seamlessly with his pain. His expression changed as Harry's did, the dynamic of their conversation with it. Somehow, it was the old man who looked concerned by the end. 'Everything okay, son?'

'No.' Harry's hand was a little shaky as he put his phone back in his pocket. 'I will sort that ambulance for you, it'll be right round. But I've got to go.' He was already making for the door, but turned for a last look down.

'Sorry,' he said.

'S'alright son. That's the problem with being someone, see? Everyone needs a someone.'

134

# CHAPTER 31

The sergeant's death was carried out in almost complete silence. It was a marvel, just like I had read. Get it right, the internet had said, and it will be just like when you snip a balloon at the neck for a controlled deflation. That might have been a perfect description of a man who had jolted his eyes open in surprise, then hissed out his last breath with just a few jerks, flinches and a kicking out of his legs to deal with. We caught the plates between us, lifting them off to put them gently to one side in a stack.

And then his wife was just the same.

It wasn't just air, of course. There was plenty of blood too, warm and wet, even through my gloves. I saw my accomplice turn his palms up to inspect the blood he had on his hands, his expression so unmoved it was as if he was wearing a mask. I found myself lingering too, but for me it was on the sergeant and his wife, taking something from the fact that they had died facing each other, that one had been able to watch the other.

I wasn't expecting that. I think *satisfaction* is the right word. You hear about revenge and you hear how, when it comes down to it, it doesn't actually scratch the itch, that when the big moment comes and all the pieces are supposed to fall into place to fill the hole that has been left, well . . . it just doesn't.

They're wrong. Or maybe they're not doing their version of revenge right.

Then there was just the need to finish, to enact the final part of the plan. I looked right at him before I did it. He was still flicking between looking down at the two bodies laid out on the floor and inspecting the blood on his own hands, still murmuring something under his own breath as he did, but he sensed that I was staring at him, that there was more to come, something he didn't know about.

'What is it?' he said.

I didn't reply. I just picked the first plate off the top of the nearest stack and I brought it down firmly onto the kitchen floor, watching as the pieces shattered, skidding off in different directions.

'What are you doing!' he hissed. The sound seemed to bring him back into the moment. 'The kids!' And his eyes now lifted to the ceiling, to where a floorboard groaned. He lifted his hands too, both of them to rest against his head.

I didn't hesitate and I had thought that I might. I thought the gravity of what it all meant would slow me down. But it didn't.

I stepped around the bodies, clearing my throat as I did, a deliberate sound so he would know I was coming, so he would turn into my momentum. This meant my first stab met him on the half turn. I was bending forward, my aim for his thigh, and I got a direct hit, the landing more solid than I had expected, the knife still pushed in up to the hilt. He roared in surprise and pain, his hand shot out for the wound, exposing a bare patch of his wrist above his gloves and out of his sleeve.

No hesitation.

This time my attack was with a slashing motion. He went down to the floor and I used my weight to pin his arm, to roll it over so I could slash at the wrist. I lost count of how many times. I was expecting an explosion of blood, like in

136

the movies, the sort that hits the ceiling. There was blood for sure, but it bubbled and frothed more than spurted. I stabbed him in the thigh again, this time higher, close to the groin and that one was much more like I was expecting. He pushed himself away and found a sitting position, propped up against the wall, eyes wide, losing focus quickly while his blood arched out in a rhythm.

I stepped away. He was still moving but it was in on himself, as if he was deflating, his head falling forward into his lap. The arcs of blood were smaller every time.

'What's going on down there? Mum?' The voice of a child again, but the fear was thicker. She was back on the stairs, they creaked as she took a step down, but stopped when a second, younger voice, called out, this one from further away.

'Emmy,' it said, 'what's going on?'

## CHAPTER 32

Harry got a startled expression and a single word in response from the male officer in uniform who answered his hammering on the front door.

'Boss!'

'What have we got?' Harry said, despite the rushed briefing he'd had from the control room in the time it had taken him to run to the address.

The uniform barring his way looked like he was trying to form words, to offer some sort of explanation. 'It's the skipper's house . . . Alan Day . . . Jesus . . .' was all he could manage.

Harry moved into a hallway. The layout was the same as for the house he had left just a few roads over, meaning the kitchen was at the other end but lit so brightly that it seared into his eyes. The next thing he saw seared into his memory.

There was a child.

She was in a long nightie, white with frilly ends to catch in the breeze that came from front and back doors both being wide open. Harry got closer, close enough to see that it was actually two children wrapped up in each other, like two sheets of paper screwed up together, impossible to tell where one ended and the other started. Both stood still and silent over the bodies of three adults.

And then he saw the blood.

It was vivid in a white room and it was everywhere. It still seemed to be expanding in slow motion, like lava slowly consuming a mountainside. It was a lighter shade on the kitchen sides and worktops, speckled in some places, running in others.

'Girls . . .' The word caught in his throat.

They didn't move, didn't react — it was as if they hadn't heard him. The breeze that toyed with the nightdress also ruffled long, untidy hair. He reached out, placing his hands on the taller girl's shoulder, increasing the force so he could turn them, move them away. 'Girls, let's move away from here, shall we?'

There was no reaction, no nothing.

'We need to move away.' Harry was firmer, enough to get them moving. He locked eyes with the police officer who had let him in. 'What the hell!?' He growled and the officer just shook his head.

'I'm sorry . . . I didn't . . . it's just me. You got here fast!'

'We need everyone here. Everyone you've got.'

'I put the call out . . . I did that already.' The officer's mask of shock was barely slipping.

'Do it again,' Harry said. 'Everyone you have. And I want Major Crime called in — everyone turfed out of bed on my say-so. CSI will put you off until the morning but I want them here *now*.' Harry checked himself. He could feel the emotion, could feel tears building as a burning sensation. He couldn't remember the last time he'd cried, nor the last time he'd felt much of anything. It was sudden and it was overwhelming.

The officer moved away, leaving Harry with the two children, his hand still on the shoulder of the taller girl. He could feel how small she was. He guessed at ten or eleven years old. She was a little more willing to be led, which meant they both were. Harry cajoled them to the stairs, his emotion growing with each step. By the time they reached the top, he couldn't hold back those tears any longer.

## CHAPTER 33

I stepped out of the Crocs that were not mine.

I took off my gloves and the bags over my feet.

I took off my jeans, the same ones I had worn to Frant Village Hall.

I took off my T-shirt, my socks and my underwear and still I felt no chill in the breeze.

I bundled them all into the dark belly of a metal bin and I tipped in fluid that glugged, then cascaded against the metal sides.

Then I struck a match, lingering on its flame, watching it fizz and shiver, bright yellow and beautiful.

I watched it all go up like a beacon, I was forced to take a step backwards.

I watched it all burn.

I felt the heat from the fire, I felt the smoke in my throat and the light in my eyes.

I felt happy.

I felt full, somehow. I felt finished.

# CHAPTER 34

'Hey.' Maddie Ives appeared backlit in a doorway and it took a moment for Harry's eyes to adjust, to make out more than just her outline. She was leaning on the door surround, her voice a whisper so as not to disturb the two kids laid out in their parents' bed behind him. He didn't know if they were asleep. He didn't know if they would ever sleep again. 'Oh, Harry . . . are you okay?' The change in her voice was distinct, she'd taken one look at him, summoned all the warmth she could and it damned near had him sobbing again.

'Shit night.' It was all he could manage.

'I can't even . . . I got here as soon as I could.'

He waved her away and swallowed hard, summoning what he needed. 'Everyone's here. Not like there's much you can do. I overreacted. I got here, saw what there was and I think I just wanted the whole world here with me.'

'I would have done the same.' In a pause that thickened, Harry ventured to stand up from where he was sitting on the edge of the bed. He'd tried a couple of times already and the eldest girl had complained, demanded he stay. That was between asking if her mum and dad were going to be okay.

'Emmy,' he said to Maddie, peering back at the outlines under the covers. 'And Dani. Eleven and nine. Alan Day's

141

kids. We sent him home early yesterday so they could get milkshakes.'

'I'm sorry.' There was nothing else she could say.

'Me too.' He stepped away, out into the hallway that was lit by a dimmer switch. He twisted it to bring the lux down to almost nothing, then pulled the door to.

'Are there plans?' Maddie gestured back at the darkened room.

'Besides making sure I'm still here when they wake up? No.'

'You want to be the one . . .'

'That tells them this wasn't just the worst of all nightmares and it's all true? Not at all. But they've seen enough strangers tonight. I can't hand this over to another one.'

She sat down heavily at the top stairs, her legs trailing down. 'We got him,' she said. 'I know it won't mean anything right now, not to them, but one day I think there will be some comfort in knowing that their dad put up a hell of a fight, that the bastard didn't walk away from this one. He's still downstairs.'

'He?' Harry said.

'He. Ryan Archer. He's the one sat up against the kitchen wall with stab wounds in all the right places. Not long out of prison for aggravated burglary, among other things. He's a man who knows how to get into houses.'

'This wasn't a burglary,' Harry said, 'aggravated or not.'

'It wasn't.' Maddie agreed. 'Archer's a career criminal. His last conviction was woolly. He proclaimed his innocence the whole way, gave his probation officer hell to the point where that same officer put numerous intelligence briefings in about how he's got a problem with the justice system. Some direct threats in there too, about what he would do to the police if he could.'

'And you think he could.'

'I think he did. His car's outside. It's not registered to him but the keys are in his pocket. I had a cursory look. Enough to see a bloodstained crowbar in the boot.'

'And you're thinking that is PC Philip Jones's blood?'

'It was just a few miles from here. There's a knife missing too, from that scene. Something sharp that was used to cut a bungee cord. And downstairs—'

'I get it.' Harry ran his coarse hands over his face, lingering on the eyes to see if he could work some life back into them. 'There will be work to do — to make sure.'

'Lots.' Maddie smiled. 'Seems it was worth calling us all out, after all.'

'Maybe.'

'I've put a call into Social Services, but it's just a recorded message at this time of night. I got the FCR to wake someone up from HR, someone with access to Alan's records, someone who might have details about close family. You're right with what you said about strangers. We need to get a friendly face here.'

'That would be ideal,' Harry agreed.

'Then maybe you can get some sleep.' She eyed him as if she had more to say.

'It doesn't matter who they get here, I'll still be the next person they see. I need to be the one telling them.'

'You don't. If we can get a close family friend, or an aunt—'

'I've been given news before, a message just like what they have waiting for them . . .' He swallowed a couple of times until the pressure behind his eyes relented. 'I still remember every single detail about it. I still remember the officers who told me. I see them about sometimes and I make it my business to avoid them, but it doesn't matter. The moment I see their faces I'm taken back to the worst time of my life. If these kids are ever going to have anything like a normal life . . . it needs to be me. It needs to be someone who isn't part of picking up the pieces.'

Maddie stood back up, stretching out a little as she did. 'Okay then. I need to get back down there. CSI are on their way and they'll go spare. I should at least hand out some token shoe covers.'

143

'They won't be happy, no matter what.' Harry forced a smile for Maddie to force one back.

'But we got him, Harry. I know that won't mean much right now. The skipper down there . . . he got some good hits in, enough for the piece of shit to bleed out before he could get out. He got him for us all. This is over.'

Harry's anger bubbled up like a geyser that he was barely able to slam a lid over. He couldn't speak; it would only give it an outlet. He knew what she was doing. She was trying to make him feel better, to put some positive spin on things. She was half right: Ryan Archer had received a form of justice, administered on behalf of Philip Jones and the whole police family. But his wasn't the only body down there. And in this family home, for the two survivors, the children who had found a troubled sleep in their parents' bed, this night was never going to be over.

# CHAPTER 35

Eileen Holmans was lacking the pomp and ceremony that was a standard part of everything that she did. She was still going through the motions, still standing at the front of the room and still leading the daily briefing, but the sharpness was gone. Even her choice of footwear was sombre. The slippers that day were navy blue, no piping, no tassels or details, no contrasting colours. They could almost be mistaken for normal footwear if viewed from a distance.

'Good morning,' she said and was barely right. It was eleven thirty. Harry hadn't long handed the children over to Social Services. An uncle had been found: Alan's brother, John Day, someone the girls could go to. Despite the family connection, despite John and his wife presenting as decent people, it still hadn't gone smoothly.

Harry had been the one to tell the uncle what had become of his brother. Social Services had loitered in the background while he did, which meant they then bore witness to John Day's reaction. It was the raw emotion, the hurt and the pain that Harry expected. As was the inevitable twist into anger and promises of vengeance. Harry watched it play out, waiting for it to pass, for the most powerful and lasting of all the emotions, sadness, to throw its blanket over and douse those flames.

Social Services however, had a different interpretation and had immediately started with noises about how John's might not be the most suitable place for Emmy and Dani, not with all that anger, and how they would make some calls about emergency foster care.

But John was allowed a reaction. He was allowed to be angry and then he and his wife were allowed to hold those girls so tightly that they became four pieces of paper screwed up together. Harry made that point to his Social Services colleagues at a time when his own anger was still close to the surface. Social Services had experienced a rethink and Harry had un-balled his fists. Raw emotion was just about all that he had left fuelling him, and even that was running low by the time he made it to the briefing.

'Ryan Archer . . .' Eileen started, the name puncturing Harry's musing. She would normally make the effort to create her own amphitheatre out of positioned chairs but, on that day, she hadn't seen the need. Most of Major Crime were out of the building, already tasked, leaving Harry and Maddie flanked by just five DCs. A couple of others would flit in and out during. There were plenty of chairs but Harry still opted for a lean on the edge of a desk. Exhaustion or not, it didn't seem right to be sitting down.

'A mobile fingerprint device was used at the scene and we were also able to use previous custody pictures as confirmation that Mr Archer was one of the deceased at Number 28 Elm Road. Preliminary investigations suggest that Archer died from puncture wounds to his thighs and a slash wound to his wrist, both of which contributed to a catastrophic loss of blood. Two early theories exist: Ryan Archer murdered Alan and Louise Day and then turned the knife on himself.' Eileen paused here, as if she might be expecting a show of hands as part of a vote. 'The second being that Alan or Louise Day inflicted those fatal wounds to Ryan Archer as part of the overall incident. The scene is a busy one . . .' Eileen paused. The large television on wheels that had been in one of the side rooms was now pulled out into the main office and she clicked it on. Harry knew it would be a photo of the scene and he dropped his eyes to insert a moment's delay.

The angle was wide, enough that it included all three of the dead. The husband and wife were on their side and facing each other. Ryan Archer was behind them, propped up against the wall, the door that led out to the hallway was close to his left elbow. His left hand was in his lap, upturned to show the part of his wrist that was cut. He looked like any number of suicide victims Harry had seen. It was a theory made all the stronger by the fact that he was holding a vicious looking knife in his other hand.

'Gloves,' Harry said, a thought that was so sudden it erupted as a word.

'Sir?' Eileen stopped mid-flow.

'He's wearing gloves.'

'He is.' Eileen said.

'A man intending on gaining entry, on murdering the occupants and then taking his own life . . . Why would he wear gloves to do that?'

'Backup, maybe?' Maddie said. 'Maybe he didn't go there intending to do himself in. You can see how it would have escalated. Maybe the wife wasn't part of his plans. We didn't find any traces at Phil Jones' scene either.'

'Ah yes. PC Philip Jones . . .' Eileen cut back in, seemingly keen to keep control. 'Murdered forty-eight hours earlier. Last night, as part of the initial scene inquiries, searches were conducted of a vehicle outside where a potential blunt force weapon was found. This is being tested, but the weapon, in the form of a crowbar, contains staining that is suspected at this time to be blood.'

'Phil's blood,' Maddie said.

'Not confirmed.'

'Two miles apart. Victims linked and a common motivation.'

'It's a working theory, ma'am, of course it is. At this time the two investigations have been formally linked, but it's only proximity that has allowed us to do so. They are fast-tracking that element through, however. There could be a result as soon as today.'

Eileen was always the devil's advocate and she was right to be, though Harry didn't say so — he tried to avoid encouraging the woman too much. But Major Crime was not the place where things should be taken for granted.

'There's other forensic work, too,' Eileen continued. 'Fragments of glass were taken from the same vehicle, including from the footwell on the driver's side and then from the soles of Ryan Archer's boots. They will be compared to each other, with fragments seized from outside Frant Village Hall and from the damaged police vehicle.'

'Now we have a name, can we make a link between Archer and Phil Jones? Or Alan Day?' Harry said.

'Nothing in regard to Phil Jones. In April of 2019, Alan Day was the sergeant leading a search team when they executed a Theft Act Warrant at a vehicle breaker's yard on the outskirts of Maidstone. This was believed to be a location that a number of car thieves were using. Ryan Archer was suspected to be one of them.'

'Was that part of what he went down for?'

'No. The Theft Act Warrant was a negative. Some items seized but nothing was ever linked to any vehicle crime. Archer wasn't there at the time, the only link to him and that warrant is the intel that lists him as one of the thieves that used it. It was never proven.'

'So, he never met Alan Day?'

'I can find nothing that concludes that they ever met, no.'

'It was just police officers,' Maddie said, her tone matter-of-fact. 'It didn't matter who. Archer was angry at the system that put him away — at the police, and he went out for his revenge. It could have been any of us. How long did he do in prison?'

'His last spell wasn't his longest,' said Eileen. 'Not even close. He pleaded not guilty, which went against him when it came to sentencing, but it was only three and a half years.'

'The term won't matter if he was innocent,' said Maddie. 'Let's assume that he was . . . that's three years the police stole from him. Three years to stew, three years to consider what he was going to do when he was released.'

'What else do we know about his offending?' Harry said, trying to build a picture.

'He was a juvenile offender— theft offences of varying types — and then he further committed violent offences in a juvenile prison. He was then tried as an adult for an aggravated burglary that he committed at seventeen, but he turned eighteen soon after. He was sentenced to nine years for that, serving just over four. Since then, he's been in and out.'

'What sort of violence?' Harry said.

'Sir?' Eileen said.

'Aggravated burglary is burglary with violence. What happened?'

'It was blunt force. He got disturbed and picked up the nearest thing to hand and struck the homeowner. Turns out that was a fire poker. It did some damage.'

'Awfully similar to beating someone with a crowbar,' Maddie said.

'Indeed. And I think the prison assault could be relevant too . . .' Eileen took a moment. 'I believe you would call it a *shank?* A makeshift and sharpened comb. Enough to break the skin of his victim in what was described as a stab wound.'

'So, he's beaten someone before with a steel poker in one incident and stabbed someone in another.'

'In the throat,' said Eileen. 'Quite a serious injury.'

Maddie rocked back on the desk, the same one that Harry was sat on and he felt it shift under them. 'Well!' she said, though she didn't need to. She was convinced, Harry knew it. He could see why. All logic pointed at Ryan Archer and he was pretty sure that, by the end of the day, a lot of the evidence would too. He felt the exhaustion inside him grow as the crushing pressure and constant anxiety from this case abated just a little.

They had their man.

## CHAPTER 36

Harry heard the doorbell, but waited until it went again to get up. He knew it would, just like he knew it was Maddie ringing it in the first place. You didn't need one of those fancy video doorbells that were so widespread these days, not when you're an experienced detective.

'Maddie!' he called out from his gate to where his front door was. He'd been sitting in his garden and the moment she reacted to the sound of his voice he turned away to go and sit in it again. He left the gate open for her, the breeze was stronger, as strong as it had been for a while, and he heard it toss the gate against the garage wall three times before Maddie reached it. He grimaced at each one.

'Don't come over here and make yourself comfortable!' he called out again, a few moments after he heard the bolt on his gate slide into place. 'Not if you're going to want a hot drink.'

'I'll go and make it, shall I?' Maddie looked incredulous but she did divert into his kitchen.

Harry hitched up a little when she reappeared. Both remained silent when she took her seat next to him, the water feature in the pond in front of them provided the backdrop — that and the birds.

'I see you mowed the lawn,' Maddie said, at last. The mower was still out, its engine still making an occasional *tick* where it was cooling. The lawn was also criss-crossed in neat lines and the breeze was saturated with the scent of cut grass.

'I reckon you should go for detective with an eye like that.'

'Learnt from the best.' After a further silence, she patted the bench they were sitting on. 'Robin's seat.'

'It was once,' Harry said and immediately wished he hadn't. He wasn't intending on making Maddie feel bad but she flushed a little and he knew that he had. 'I mean, yeah, it's still in her memory. I appreciate you remembering.'

'Two things to say to you . . .' Maddie said, the warmth and some humour returning to her voice. 'Three actually,' she added, looking around.

'One at a time,' Harry said. 'Do I need to brace myself?'

'Number One . . . where's Jock?'

'Okay, so that one's easy. Young Jock spends the day with a lady in the village. She's ex-MET — got a long way up the greasy pole. Worked Counter Terrorism at the end. She's got some good stories. She's also got a soft spot for stupid spaniels and she insists on having him for the days when I've got a job on. Suits me. Our days can be long.'

'Fine. Good answer.'

'One down, two to go.'

'You went home sick,' Maddie said. 'That's Number Two. If I checked with personnel, what would they tell me? Is this the first time ever?'

'I've had some time on the ol' Tom Dick, as it happens. I remember a good chunk was just after I met you for the first time.'

'When you were shot?'

'Yeah.'

'I don't think *getting shot* counts as being off sick, Harry.'

'I wasn't well enough to work, I tell you that much.'

'You were shot in the face.'

'I was. Your point?'

151

'You don't do sick.'

'I thought we just agreed that I did and that this is my second time. Now I think about it, both instances came at the time I was crewed with you. Must just be a coincidence.'

'Must be,' Maddie said. 'But you're okay? I mean you're not actually sick, are you?'

'Are you accusing me of skiving?'

'No. Maybe taking some time after a shit call. Sounds sensible to me. You didn't have to go sick, though. You worked all night. You could have just called it a day rather than call the Resource Unit. And this wouldn't have appeared on your Bradford Score.'

'You think I'm worried about my Bradford Score?'

'I'm pretty sure you don't know what one of those is.'

'You would be surprised what I know.'

'Would I?'

'You said you had three things to say.'

'You moved?' she said, quick as a flash. 'That was the other. Or, at least, you moved back. Last time I came out to see you, you were two hundred metres up the road at a totally different house, surrounded by your dickweed.'

'Tickseed. Which you know only too well.'

'Fine, I knew it was Tickseed. But I don't know why you're back here.'

'I never moved — not officially.'

'HR said you did. That was the address you updated them with.'

'So, I moved back.'

'From the address you shared with Karen McAdam? At least according to Voters.'

'Karen . . .' The words that were due to follow died in his mind and then on his lips. 'You're right.' He gathered himself a little. 'I forget how good you are at this detective lark. Didn't work out.'

'With Karen?'

'With me. I guess that's what happens when you move for the wrong reasons. You end up moving straight back.'

152

'Was it the pull of the Dickweed? Was that why you moved?'

'It was getting away from here.' He gestured at the back of his own house. 'I didn't want to be here, didn't have the guts to sell it, still don't have the guts to open at least two of the doors in there. I guess there was someone the next road over who came up with a solution. I'm not sure that was what she was offering. I think she thought it was something else entirely, but I saw a solution. I probably didn't treat her very well.'

'I'm sure that's not true.'

'I'm sure it is.'

'Did you tell her that, what you just told me?'

Harry took a moment to look at Maddie and it seemed to be all the answer she needed.

'Of course you didn't. Have you any idea how much easier life would be if you just spoke to people sometimes!?'

'No.'

'So, begs the question again as to why you'd be calling in sick. You don't want to be here and work's a decent excuse not to be — and yet here you are, moping in the garden.'

'Not moping. Mowing.'

'It still looks like shit, by the way.'

Harry didn't have the strength to protest at the language or to argue. He certainly didn't have the energy to explain.

'The Boss would have given you the day, like I said. You just needed to ask. I checked in with the superintendent and she didn't even know you'd gone.'

'She'll live.'

'I guess if you'd called her then it would mean questions about why you wanted a day off. And you don't want that.'

'Still don't.' Harry was gruff enough to stop her in full flow.

'I should just leave you alone then.' The bench flexed as Maddie stood. She hesitated for his reply; it wasn't what she was expecting.

'You were sick in Jill Jones's toilet.'

153

'And I still made it into work,' Maddie said, dismissively. 'I came here to talk about you.'

'That's not how life works. Does Vince know?'

He'd rattled her. She was trying to hide it, but he knew her too well.

'I know you and Vince aren't talking so much, I know you've been through a lot and I know you, Maddie.'

'What does that mean?'

'It means that you might be thinking that Vince can't handle something else, that he's a man with enough on his plate right now. But maybe someone else is what brings him back?'

'Not my job to bring him back.' She was clearly agitated, angry even.

'I agree.'

'There's nothing to tell him.' Maddie was giving a show of defiance. She turned to face him, doing her best to back up her words. It had the opposite effect.

'Okay then.' Harry slapped his thighs. 'Then we should get back to work. Eileen said that Archer's dad has refused to speak to the police. I told her we would give it another try.'

'What do you mean? When?'

'About ten minutes before you turned up.'

'After you called in sick?'

'Who do you think I called in sick to?'

Maddie took a moment. 'It was Eileen who told me.'

'I imagine it was.'

'You knew I would come. All this was just so I would come here? You were sat here waiting for me.'

'You would find an excuse not to talk about yourself at work and I needed to mow my lawn. Did you want to sit back down?'

'Really?' Harry considered that she might be about to explode. 'That arrogance of yours becomes something different entirely when it steps over the line!'

'Concern?'

Maddie took a moment to consider her response. 'There's nothing to say, nothing for us to talk about.'

'But if there was, you know that you could talk to me about it. Anywhere and anytime.'

'I do.'

'So, I won't need to coax you somewhere you can't run away from.'

'Who says I can't run away?'

'This is my garden. You have to do what I say in my garden.'

Maddie smiled. It took a while, a moment of eye contact before it broke out. 'I'm fine, Harry. I think you might have the wrong end of the stick. I was sick. It happens. Something I ate.'

'Must have been.' Harry was a long way from convinced and unabashed in showing it. 'Let's go see this witness then, shall we? I'm making a day of talking to people who would rather be anywhere else.'

## CHAPTER 37

There was no doubt that the man hammering on the door was the most interesting thing about the block of flats that Maddie was certain was hiding Neil Archer, Ryan Archer's dad. It was a thick, square building with the individual dwellings marked by a single door and a square window to break up the off-white rendering. Each bled into the next, the homes utterly featureless and unapologetic with it. The inspiration for the design seemed to be: *how to merge the poor effectively into the background.*

Maddie had called Eileen on the way over for an update and had quickly regretted it. Eileen wasn't good at succinct and they had sat through every detail on the attempts that had already taken place at this address. Four DCs — she named each one — had been here already over two separate visits. The first of those had succeeded in prompting an appearance from the occupant, but only for long enough for an exchange where he had refused them entry, been told of his son's demise and then slammed the door. The second visit had been nothing more than hammering on the door. The third visit was now going the same way.

The activity was attracting attention from elsewhere. The neighbour to the immediate right appeared, wrapped

156

tight in a faded dressing gown, taking a moment to light the rolled-up cigarette between her pursed lips.

'He's ignoring yous,' she said, the moment it took. Her words were delivered in a good-humoured drawl, the smoke expelled through yellowed teeth that then formed into a grin. 'I tried too, but I only got so much patience in me. Thought I'd come out here where it's quieter.'

'He's in then?' Maddie said.

'I mean, I ain't his keeper. Makes no odds. In or not, he ain't gonna answer.' She slipped back through her door, but only to retrieve a stool. She set it up clumsily on the walkway where its height was far from ideal as it brought her hips level with the iron handrail between her and the five-storey drop she sat facing away from. She preferred to watch the live show that was DI Harry Blaker and his fists.

'NEIL!' Harry had now changed tack, simply roaring a name into a letterbox. He looked awkward, dropped into a squat, his back rounded to push out against the waxed jacket that had him sweating. Maddie was far enough behind him to lean on the handrail, her role to watch for movement. There was none. The neighbour was right: Neil Archer was never going to answer that door. Maddie knew a thing or two about people and how they reacted to bad news and it was common for them to remove themselves entirely. Some people needed the time to process, to get to the point where they had questions and needed to resurface for the answers.

'YOUR SON'S A MURDERER!' Harry stood up to bellow at the slab-sided UPVC door. 'IN COLD BLOOD! UNLESS YOU WANNA TELL US ANY DIFFERENT.' He lashed out again, a palm strike that flexed the door from every edge.

'Jesus!' Maddie pushed off the handrail, aware that the woman to her right had jerked up so suddenly as to almost tip herself over the side. If she did, she would have followed the cigarette she'd just spat out.

'Is that what we should think? IS THAT WHAT RYAN WAS?' Harry roared.

Maddie put her hand on his shoulder but he shrugged her off. 'We should come back,' she said softly. 'Eileen might have a phone number by now, or something else we can use.'

'He's in there,' Harry growled, his chest puffed up like he was ready for another assault.

It wasn't going to be necessary.

Neil Archer's door scraped, then was pulled open so hastily that it caught violently on a security chain, then on the toes of the man standing on the other side when he took it off. The pain mixed in with his fury.

'What the hell?' he spat.

'Let's do this in private, shall we?' Harry bundled forward, giving the man no choice but to back away. Maddie followed and they scuffed clumsily into a tiny hall. Maddie pushed the door firmly shut behind her before he had any chance to protest.

'What the hell do you think you're doing?' Neil Archer said. He wasn't entirely what Maddie had been expecting. She had seen pictures of his boy, showing a young man with a thick build and solid features.

His dad was nothing like it. Neil Archer was emaciated, his face sucked in at the cheeks, his shoulders a spindly coat hanger for a denim shirt forcibly tucked into a tiny waist. He was tall, at least, like Ryan, with long limbs leading to long fingers that now fiddled with a tobacco tin pulled from his shirt pocket. His hair was long enough to fall over his ears, though cut into a style rather than unkempt. His shirt sleeves were rolled up to show a stack of leather bracelets on his right wrist, one of which had a guitar pick attached.

Even Eileen, with all her resources, had admitted to knowing nothing about this man. Just a couple of steps into his hallway and Maddie knew three things for sure: he was submissive, he was anxious and he lived alone.

Neil took a seat on the bottom step of a set of stairs that rose up at the end of the hall. This caught Maddie out a little, since there'd been no signs of this being a duplex from the outside. Harry wasn't having the meeting in a dark hall, he made that quite clear, marching through into a living room where the no-frills theme of the outside was very much continued.

There were curtains where they were needed to restrict sunlight, two sofas and a small television angled towards them. A low, glass table was the only other piece of furniture. It held an ashtray that had been shaken out and an oversized Crystal Palace FC mug with an inch of tea staining from the bottom up.

They weren't offered to sit.

'Mr Archer . . .' Harry paused until the man got a little more control of his wild eyes. He was clean-shaven, and his face had a rash that suggested a recent shaving nick under his jawline. Perhaps his mind had been elsewhere for it. 'I know my colleagues have already been out to give you some bad news, but that's not enough. You can't slam your door on it, not on what happened and not on what has to happen next.'

'Next?' Neil's nose twitched in his anger. 'What does *next* mean? What does it even matter? My son is dead. He's gone! There is no next.'

'There is for you.' Harry's tone took a clear step down. 'We don't like giving a message like that and then having to leave. Sometimes . . . sometimes there might be things we can do to help, things we can arrange, questions we can answer.'

'That's why you're here, is it? That's why you're hammering on my door, shouting nonsense out for my neighbours to hear? People around here—'

'I needed you to open that door. I can't help you from the other side.'

'Help me! Are you going to bring him back? Is that what you mean?'

'No, Mr Archer.' Harry paused for longer this time, enough for the man to start leaking a little confusion, to look from Harry to Maddie as if anticipating more. 'But now we're dealing with his legacy. That's all he has left now. That's all you have left.'

'And you've already made your mind up about that! You made that quite clear!'

159

'That's the problem with having one side of the story, you can make your mind up pretty quick. But it can be wrong. I need to understand what happened. I need to know if what I saw was right.'

'You lot are all the same. You know his history. You know he's been in trouble for most of his life and that's enough.'

'It's quite a leap from what he was according to our records to what he did.'

'Or what he didn't do.'

'So, let's start again. We have something in common, you and I — like it or not, Mr Archer. We both want to understand what the hell was going on with Ryan. We can only do that together.' Harry held out his hand to shake. Neil stared at it as if he was being offered a rattlesnake. 'I'm Detective Inspector Harry Blaker and this is Detective Inspector Maddie Ives, and we're here as part of the investigation into your son's death.'

'He's not a murderer.' Neil's eyes flicked again between Harry and Maddie.

'If we can start again, I can tell you our side.' Harry nodded his head towards his extended hand. Neil took it up, the shake brief and lacking any real conviction, but it was enough for the dynamic to shift, for Neil's posture to open up a little.

'So, tell me,' he said.

# CHAPTER 38

'Ryan's body was found in the kitchen of a family home. A police officer's home' Harry began. 'It would appear that Ryan gained entry via an insecure back door with the intention of causing that police officer harm. He murdered two adults — husband and wife — and he was fatally wounded himself.' Harry was talking fast, matter-of-fact and each fact was hitting Neil Archer direct in the chest. It was a tactic Maddie knew: give information like a machine gun, no time for retorts, no time for questions on specifics.

'Holy sh—'

'The police were called by two very young children who had been upstairs throughout.' Harry had delivered the firmest strike yet. 'They would have heard everything. They were beside themselves with fear . . .' Harry finally stopped, recognising, perhaps, that Neil Archer needed to take a breath. His eyes had grown so wide they might burst. 'And they got to find what was left.'

'No.' Neil's head shook on stiff shoulders. 'No, that's not . . . not my boy.'

Harry had him where he wanted him: saturation. So much information, so much horror that he couldn't form questions, he could only listen to theirs.

'I want to talk to you about Ryan, about where his mind has been these last few days and weeks, about how he ended up where he did.'

'Not with kids . . . and a woman too? No.' The denial was getting stronger. Neil's conviction was getting stronger.

'We only have what we can see,' Maddie said. 'What was left.' Neil's eyes shifted to her. 'The aftermath. But we need to know a little bit about Ryan before and that's why we came here.'

Neil Archer deflated with a long sigh that took him all the way off his feet, into the battered sofa behind him. Harry sat too.

'He's been living with me since he got out,' Neil began. 'Living right here. Two nights ago he was sat in the same place you are, telling me all what was wrong at the Palace. I was a season ticket holder once, back in the days when they were priced for the working man. Now it's all corporate back slapping and city twats who don't even go to most of the games — certainly don't go away. Used to be a whole load of us go up together, sit together, few drinks after . . .' His eyes lost their focus, the flicker of a smile from whatever he was seeing as a memory. 'I only know of one who still goes, scrapes and borrows every season to keep hold of his seat. I tell you this, he can keep it!'

'Did you take Ryan with you?'

There was still no real focus to Neil. His smile grew. 'First when he was three years old. The boy had no idea of what was going on. It was standing then and I could put him up on my shoulders. He spent an entire season up there. But he got big — too big too quick. That's what happens, right? Every parent you speak to will say it. They get too big, too fast. They grow up . . .'

'They do.' Harry sounded wistful; genuine, and Maddie watched the two men share a glance that felt like a moment of knowing. Bonding. Grief would do that, leave scars like calling cards that two people can match.

'He went off the rails, I know that as well as anyone, but he was a good lad and just recently he'd been showing it. He's been different. A year ago, one of you lot knocking on that door to tell me Ryan was . . . to tell me he'd done something stupid, got himself hurt or worse, woulda had me admitting that I'd been waiting for the call. This time you coulda knocked me down with a feather.'

'Different how?' Harry said.

'Straight. I know you hear that a lot, right? But I could see it in him. I know that boy. I got ill, see, while he was in prison. Prostate cancer. They caught it early and the prognosis was always good but I played on it a little bit — judge me if you want, but I needed to scare him. I needed to make him see that time is not something you should be wasting behind bars.'

'Serious illness or not, that sounds like good advice,' Harry said.

'It worked. He came out there more determined than I ever saw him to play it straight.'

'What about his feelings toward the police when he came out of prison?'

'Come on now!' Neil snarled and Maddie sat back a little, waiting this part out. The two men shared another moment, this one more like they were sizing each other up. 'If you came here to pretend to be sad then to fuel your own fantasies then I'll tell you this now . . . you're wasting your time.'

'I came here to understand your son, to hear from the person who knew him best. We only have the opinion of a probation officer so far who's saying that Ryan wasn't a big fan of the police.'

'Is that right.'

'If he was the only person I listened to, then Ryan was a young man who spent the whole of his last stretch moaning it was for something he didn't do.'

'He didn't!' Neil snapped. 'I know what you're thinking. I know you must hear it all the time but it wasn't him out breaking into those houses, nicking them cars. He always fessed up when he did something wrong, Lord knows he'd done it enough for me to know that. But this time he was insistent. This time he looked me right in the eye and he told me it wasn't him.'

'So, he was angry? He lost three years of his life that he shouldn't have. Three years of his prime. That would make anyone angry.'

'No.' Neil's long hair shook as one. 'I mean he was angry, no doubt, but it was all at himself. He went to prison because of what he is, not what he did. He didn't do what he got nicked for, the spate that got him inside, but he said bold as brass that he was a thief — said it to me. Said there was plenty he *hadn't* been caught for. Strange to say that I was actually a little proud of him, the way he was talking. He reacted right. Reacted like a man finally taking responsibility for what he done. Like a man who realised there was no point looking for someone else to blame when he needed to be looking at himself.'

'You're saying he didn't blame the police?'

'No. He talked his solicitor down a lot. I don't think he could understand how he still went down for something he didn't do, not when he'd got away with stuff before that he did. I don't think they got on so well. I told him to get someone else but he didn't have that option. She was just what the state provided and it was like or lump it. It was complicated.'

'Complicated?'

'Complicated. From the off he was saying that he didn't do what he was accused of and from the off she was telling him to say that he did, how it was in his interest. She said a guilty plea could avoid time behind bars. She was wrong about that.'

'He listened to her?'

'In the end. He's easily manipulated, especially when they got a good set of tits.' Neil's eyes shot to meet with Maddie's. 'Sorry, I don't mean to be so coarse.'

Maddie shrugged. 'Why do you think Ryan ended up dead in a serving police officer's house?' she said.

Neil reacted as if her words were a physical assault. 'I don't know.' There was a little whine to his voice.

'There's another murder,' Harry was keeping the strikes coming. 'Another police officer who was targeted, who was killed. We can link your boy to that scene too.'

'Two?' Neil Archer wore shock well — and wore it genuinely. Harry broke away to make eye contact with Maddie. 'You've got something wrong, here. Ryan was a lot of things but he weren't no murderer. He weren't petty either, or stupid. He was *laissez faire*. He's always been into cars, posters up on his wall to fuel his dreams. Head in the clouds like we all are when we're kids. Then he got old enough to realise that people like us, we don't get to drive the cars we dream about, or pick our solicitors. We don't get to watch our football team no more. He was angry, sure, but at the world and his place in it. Angry enough to get the idea that he would just go out and take what he wanted. You know I got him the job?'

'We do,' Maddie said. Ryan's ability as a burglar had taken a huge jolt in the arm the moment his dad had somehow convinced the window-fitting firm he was working for that they should take on his son. He lasted less than eighteen months, but that was easily long enough to get to know his way around double-glazed windows and doors, long enough to know how to get through one entirely undetected.

'I fitted windows for two decades. Not once did it cross my mind that I could use that for breaking into other folk's homes.'

'Working for a living is hard graft,' Maddie offered. 'I guess he saw an easy way out.'

Neil shook his head vigorously. 'He had a record already, before that. He stole his first something or other young. It was a mistake, sure, but it was one you lot would never let him forget. Followed him around everywhere he went, scuppered every job interview before it even started. I had to practically beg my boss to give him a chance. Staked my own reputation on it.'

'You don't fit windows anymore,' Maddie guessed.

'Now I sweep up. A maintenance man — but that's pushing it. I was a skilled labourer once. Got paid like one

165

too. It was strained with me and my boy when I had to leave that job, but we made our peace. Needed to do that more than once. But ain't that the way with the relationships that matter?'

Maddie exchanged a quick glance with Harry. Neil must have picked up on it. 'You two are close, right? I can tell.'

'We've worked together a while now,' Maddie said. 'Been through a lot. I guess that's part of what makes a relationship matter. What about Ryan, Mr Archer? Did he have someone else in his life he was close to?'

'You mean a girlfriend?' Neil's expression changed, hardened.

'Did he?'

'He was seeing someone, sure. He never said it out loud, not to me, but he didn't have to. Wears his heart on his sleeve that boy and he's always been the same with the women. When he falls, he goes like a dropped boulder. That was always the reason he got back into taking other people's cars. A good woman needs good money.' Neil turned to Maddie. 'Not what I think, you understand, something Ryan said. I know what he meant. We all want to give them the world at first, not until you get older and wiser that you realise what the world actually is.'

'So, you had no clue who this woman is?' Maddie said. 'It would be very helpful for us if we were able to speak with her?'

Neil took a moment and then shrugged. 'She might not even be real.'

'What does that mean?'

'Means he meets women on the internet and some of them stay there, if you know what I mean.'

'I don't think I do.'

'They might be real people but they sure ain't local. In my day you picked someone up at a local bar, down the pub or from where you worked. These days you talk to someone on another continent, you fall in love, even . . .' Neil stopped himself. 'And you don't never leave your place. Don't never meet.'

'Is that what Ryan was doing? Was he seeing someone over the internet?'

'He has, that's all I'm saying. But he's been going out a lot more. I figure he had something going on. There's been this girl before . . . Chloe, that's all I know. Dark haired little thing — dark to go with her soul if you ask me. You know how some women are just trouble? I could tell that the moment she stepped foot in here.'

'And you think he was still seeing Chloe?'

'They've been together off and on for a good ten years, feels like longer. You wanna talk about anger? That's a girl with a whole lot of anger in her heart. My boy was like a little puppet on a string around her too. Pathetic it was. Said he was in love.' Neil huffed so hard it dislodged something from his nose. 'That boy fell in love with every girl who ever wrote him back!'

'When did you see her last?'

'Oh, she only ever came here once. I told him I didn't like her. Meant it too. Said she was trouble. We would fall out about it and then, on one of their off moments he would tell me how right I was. Said he couldn't help it. I think maybe that was what he liked so much about her. Maybe she was exciting.'

'Did he have any pictures of her? Anything that might be here?'

'No.'

'So, he was on dating apps. Social media, too?'

'Ain't they all?'

Maddie stared down the response. 'What about passwords? I just want to understand. Kids these days . . . their social media is their social life and it might give us a bit of balance. I want to be sure we're right about Ryan.'

'All on his phone. I assume you have that? I ain't ever seen him leave a room without it, let alone the house.'

'He didn't have the phone on him,' Maddie said. 'Not when we found him.'

'Well then, that ain't right.'

'If you're planning something major and you're savvy, you leave your phone somewhere else,' Harry said. 'But we can check his social media from a computer, we just need an idea of his passwords.'

Neil only took a moment to consider. 'He got me one of those streams, not sure it's too legal but you can take it for all I care.'

'Streams?'

'Plugs into the telly there, means I can watch the Palace, all the football to be honest. Sometimes you get a bit of foreign commentary but beggars and choosers an' all that. He set it up with a password, reeled it off like it was one he used . . .'

Maddie took out her pocketbook while he paused again. 'It was his mum's name but jumbled up a bit with symbols an' that. Here?' He reached out for Maddie's pocketbook and pen. She handed it over, watched as he wrote something in scratchy handwriting.

'Janet.' Maddie read the first part when he handed it back.

'Where is Ryan's mother,' Harry chanced.

Neil chewed his bottom lip for just a moment. 'She didn't make it.'

'She's dead.' Harry's usual tact was still in place.

'She is.' Neil lifted eyes that seemed heavy all of a sudden.

'How old was Ryan?' Maddie said.

'Six. Old enough to understand a mother's love, young enough to miss her like crazy when she went.'

'I'm sorry, Mr Archer. Can I ask what happened? You said she didn't make it?'

'The sickness. It gets called depression. Wasn't even treated like a medical thing back then, I barely believed it myself at the time. I know better now.'

'Did she take her own life?'

'Not here. She made a decision one day that she didn't want to be here and she upped and left, just like that. I was working all the hours and she was here sleeping. I don't blame her. Don't think me bitter, I know that's part of how depression gets you. I don't like it as a word; it don't come anywhere near doing it justice. It's a sickness like no other, leaves nothing but the shell. I wouldn't see her for days, despite us living in a small place then, too. She would just be hiding out under the bedcovers.'

'I can't imagine how difficult that was.'

'Hit Ryan pretty hard. I think something like that's worse when they're young. When he got a bit older, we talked about it, then he would get older still and have more questions. Feels like I broke the news to him five times or more and every time he seemed to take it worse. It messed him up. Even now, a grown man, he would still tell you that his mum's passing was all his fault.'

'Was it postnatal depression?'

'Does it matter?' Neil's eyes glassed over. The sadness that must have filled his home in the time he was describing seemed to have been summoned back to fill the shadows.

'No,' Maddie said, not wanting to push that button any further.

'She took herself away and did it. I think she was trying to protect us, in her own way. She wasn't thinking straight, that's what the sickness does to a person.' Neil sniffed, for a moment it seemed like it might become more. 'There was a time when he was older, mid-to-late teens, a mess of a time for any boy becoming a man. He didn't believe me, that she was dead. Went looking for his mum. Broke my heart.'

'That must have been tough on you both,' Harry said.

'We survived. You have to, I certainly had. I was all that he had.'

'There are no siblings?'

'No . . . he was all I had, too.'

'What was Ryan doing for his money? You said you didn't think he was back stealing cars.'

'He was still working with cars, I know that. But it was honest work. He's got an eye for a good one at a good price. He'd use these websites, buy a car and spin it for profit. I lent him the money for the first one and he'd paid me back by the end of that month. I think he turned over five cars in four weeks. He's got a few people at spray joints, knew what to focus on to turn a quick profit. Like I said . . .' Neil was still on the verge of breaking, his strength sapping away in front of them. 'He'd turned a corner. Figured out that you can get what you want without taking it. He was a good lad.' His tone almost pleading. 'He was a good lad who could be led astray. If he was back with that Chloe, if she was in his ear then, honestly, I don't know what he wouldn't do for her. That's all I can say, that musta been what happened. Ryan would do anything for a woman.'

It was time to go. They made their excuses and left their details. When they made it back outside, the woman in the gown was still in her front row seat. She was still smoking too, no telling how many that was in a row.

'You alright, Neil love?' she said to her neighbour, who ignored her, closing the door firmly to prompt a shrug. 'I'll keep an eye on him. He'll be alright' she said, second guessing what they might say next. Maddie nodded and they hurried away, desperate to avoid a conversation.

'What do you think?' Maddie said, when they were back in the car.

'Sad old man. Been wallowing since his wife left. Now he gets to wallow some more.'

'I don't mean about him. I mean his boy. Dad seemed pretty convinced that it was out of character.'

'No parents think their kid capable of what I was describing. But what he said about this Chloe was interesting . . . the things a boy will do for a girl.'

'Murder?' Maddie said.

'We've all seen it before. Things can escalate, get out of control pretty easy when you're only following the small part of your brain.'

'I think I know the part you're talking about.'

'Ryan's background, his childhood, sounds like someone who could be influenced by the right woman.'

170

'We need to find her. Do you think she was involved?'

'Despite what we just said to Neil in there, it will be the girlfriend that really knows him best.'

'I'll give Eileen a bell, set her off on it. Knowing her, she'll have something for us by the time we get back in.'

# CHAPTER 39

Upon their return, the office had a definite aura of smug, at least Eileen did. She couldn't help herself. 'Chloe Falconer!' she sang.

'That's our Chloe?' Maddie said, a question that only served to heighten the smugness.

'Why of course it is. I have to say, you two make it all rather easy with a first name and a password. Suffice to say I was able to do the rest in the time it took you to get back here.'

'The password worked?'

'Like a charm. Can't say I'm surprised. I never met a man who had more than one password, have you?' Eileen clucked and then both women looked at Harry. He waved them away, but there was the start of a grin for sure.

'Local?' he grunted.

Eileen snapped to attention then spun on her heels, searching the table tops while striding away as fast as her slippers would take her. She scooped up a bunch of A4 papers that were stapled together. 'No fixed abode, but there's a couple of addresses worth trying. I've put the most likely on top—'

Harry snatched the papers, an action that only stopped Eileen for a breath.

'Known for petty theft and some illicit substances, also a rather nasty theft from an elderly woman when she was supposed to be working as her carer.'

'Any violence?' Maddie nodded to where Harry had taken the papers with all the answers.

'Minor. Some street brawls where alcohol was a factor. The dishonesty offences are what makes up her most recent behaviour.'

'Let's go then,' Harry growled. 'I'll do the knocking.'

* * *

117 Alexandra Place was another address contained in a block of flats but nothing like the solid, featureless square they had just been to. This one was a mess, built around existing shops and buildings in a commercial centre, like they'd poured the concrete in any gaps, then carved windows where it had set. Roughly speaking, it was horseshoe shaped, with much of it concealed behind other buildings entirely. Harry's first thought was how there was no clear way to cover all of the exits.

'Do you think we need some others here?' he said.

'If it were an arrest request, yeah?' Maddie shrugged, 'but it isn't, is it?'

'We don't know what it is yet,' Harry said.

'Maybe, but we're only here for a chat. My guess? Someone answers the door to tell us she isn't here. We'll end up sitting up on the place for a while and we might get lucky, she might get spooked and walk out or turn up to go in.'

'I want to talk to her today,' Harry said.

'In that case, best let me do the knocking,' Maddie said.

Harry moved to the panel next to the main entrance that was littered with the flat numbers. He pressed the button marked "T" for Trades and the door shuddered, released from its magnetic lock. The flat was up a short flight of stairs and Harry continued past a front door displaying 117. He signalled for Maddie to wait. The corridor was long, sweeping left and out of sight. He followed it until another exit came into sight. It was at the far end and he could see through it to people walking past at a steep angle. This was an exit that would come out at street level where the rear of the building pushed into a cobbled hill. He made it onto the street, wedging the door so he could get back in. He walked down a little until there was a break in the shops, from there he had an obstructed view through a tall, padlocked gate to the back of the block. Specifically, he could see a row of windows and he reckoned the first one was the address Maddie was knocking on.

There was activity almost immediately.

A window burst open. Harry's eyes were dragged to it by the change in light. It was the next one over from the one he had been expecting. A leg appeared, wrapped in black, a second leg, then a bare stomach where someone was being lowered out for a white T-shirt to ride up. It was someone petite, a woman who dropped like it wasn't her first time, then straightened her T-shirt over black leggings, lifting her hands to push back her dark hair.

Chloe.

Harry resisted the urge to pile back through the door, knowing he would lose sight. Instead, he pushed himself against the gate, trying to get a better view, a sense of her next move. She'd dropped into a lawned area where numerous rotary washing lines stood in formation. She swiped at one, grabbing something bright red, and then broke into a sprint, left to right as he watched and out of sight.

Harry spun right, pacing further down the hill. There were shops packed either side. Chloe was somewhere behind the left-hand row and, he reckoned, contained. His phone lit up as he walked and he resisted the urge to break into a run. He had a strong sense that he and his prey were moving towards each other and that there would be an advantage in not standing out.

'Harry! I got in, but she's gone out the back. I saw her go!' Maddie's voice was hard to make out over shrieking in the background.

'I know. Are you okay in there?'

'Yeah, just not popular. I can't see where she's gone. No one's helping.'

'Call up and get someone there with you,' Harry said. And then he cut the call, thrusting his hands into the deep pockets of his waxed jacket. He bent his head a little too, slowing his pace and moving out into the middle of the cobbles.

Someone was coming towards him. A female . . . petite build . . . long black hair . . . black leggings . . . a bright red top hanging open to show flashes of white underneath. She was agitated, walking fast, checking behind herself, reaching to put up her red hood.

Harry was able to get almost right on top of her before he reached out to grab a hold.

When he did, all hell broke loose.

# CHAPTER 40

She lashed out. Harry hadn't been expecting that, nor could he have expected the accuracy. Her fist was firm into the groove of his cheek to rattle his teeth together and blur his view. The effects lasted just a moment, but it was enough for her to flash past him and up the hill in a blur of red.

Harry needed to steady himself before he set off after her. The cobbles underfoot were loose, not ideal when running uphill. Nor was a heavy jacket, a beating sun and an officer some way past his prime. It was no surprise that by the time he made it to the top of the hill, Chloe Falconer was gone.

Harry cussed, turning on the spot to take in the three streets that led off from that point. There were also plenty of shops — maybe an alleyway or a wall she could jump, the sort that any criminal worth their salt would know. By contrast, Harry had never been here before in his life.

She was lost.

He ignored his ringing phone to take a lean on a glass fronted shop. The phone persisted and he knew it was Maddie. He also knew she wouldn't stop until he answered.

'You okay?' she said, instantly.

'Yeah, great. You?'

'Did you get her?'

'The twenty-something with the jet heels making off up a steep hill? I just strolled right after her until she got tired.'

'That's a no, then?'

'That's a no, Maddie. I said we needed to have others here, I knew she was going to give us problems.'

'That's not exactly what you said.'

'Who have you got there?'

'No one,' Maddie said, 'unless they gave me their correct details. In which case I just left Daffy Duck, Mickey Smith and Jessica Rabbit.'

'Is there anything there of hers? Anything that gives us a clue where she might be going?'

'Not that I saw.'

'We need to get back in there. We need to search it.'

'We can ask . . .' Maddie's words faded out.

'I'm a little beyond asking!' Harry raged, already stomping back towards the address. He cut the phone too, switching to his radio, calling up control to see if the local CCTV was monitored. It wasn't. There was a time when all towns had someone sat watching, a police radio in a cradle for a direct talk-through, but between police funding cuts and council funding cuts, they were long gone.

Harry gave the description anyway, as part of a request for the area to be flooded with whatever police patrols were available. He called Eileen too, for her to direct any available DCs.

It was a waste of time. Harry knew that. Chloe Falconer would go to ground, possibly in one of the twenty addresses they already had listed for her or, just as likely, she would now know that she needed to be hiding in one that they didn't.

# CHAPTER 41

It would be another four hours before Harry left the area. It might have felt like a waste of time from the moment the search had begun, but waste or not, there were a lot of tasks to be done. He set about directing the house-to-house, identifying CCTV on numerous routes away from where Chloe was last seen and using his foul mood to gain entry back into the address he had seen her leap out of.

Mickey Smith and Daffy Duck were still there, while Jessica Rabbit had reportedly gone looking for a Roger. That was the only wisecrack after Harry's entrance, they got a glare from him, a closer look at his swollen face and seemed to decide it was in their interest to offer up their correct details. Mickey Smith was actually Michael Sires and 117 Alexandra Place was his address. His police record was far more extensive than his imagination. Daffy Duck — Stuart Masters — was similar, both petty criminals, their offending histories merging into each other's. In theft, violence and drug involvement, they were often co-conspirators, often with Chloe. As was Jessica Rabbit — Jess Lawrence — who confessed to being Chloe's cousin, having picked her phone up on the first ring when Harry used Michael's phone.

Despite these shared experiences, it would appear that none of them knew anything at all about the woman who had jumped out of their window. According to each of them in turn, she was a real anomaly who didn't live anywhere, spoke no words and knew no people. No matter how threatening Harry got, this didn't change.

Which meant that Harry was still agitated when he made it back to Cranbrook Police Station. He tore through the building, palming open doors, well aware that Maddie, who had accompanied him back in silence, was catching them behind him. Eileen looked up as he entered, then formed a confused expression when he slapped down some stapled papers on the desk in front of her.

'Chloe Lily Falconer!' Harry spat. 'The address you gave for us.'

'Sorry, sir, I'm not sure I—'

'Run the address!' Harry pushed the papers roughly towards her, his weight shifting so he could lean on the desk. Eileen took a moment, managing to break away from the intensity of her inspector for her eyes to flick around the room for help. Maddie completed the first syllable of something but Harry was ready, his hand shooting up to silence her.

Eileen reached out for the papers and made a show of placing her index finger beneath what she needed and typing it into her terminal. The office was still running on a skeleton crew. The few scattered DCs who had been busy with tasks were now still and silent to watch.

'Okay.' Eileen said, clearing her throat.

'The intel linked to it,' he growled.

Eileen clicked her mouse. 'Okay.'

'Read it out.'

'Harry . . .' Maddie said, but Harry silenced her again. 'Read . . . it . . . out.'

Eileen shifted in her seat, her lips pursed, then un-pursed, her eyes flickered where she was reading ahead. Then she cleared her throat. 'There is an intel report dated March

2022.' She cleared her throat again. *'Attending officers should be aware that one, one, seven Alexandra Place is located in a part of the block where visibility allows an approach to be seen from three angles. It is not possible to enter the building from three of the four sides without being seen. Movement is constantly monitored from the windows and wanted persons have previously made off out of the window. This address is believed to be the home address of Michael Sires, though it is registered with the council to his mother. It is a general doss house, used by any number of criminals and any attendance should be carried out by a minimum of four officers to ensure cover and officer safety.'* Eileen had read through her glasses, she lifted her eyes now so she was peeking over them to look at Harry.

'That's the third intel report down,' said Harry. 'Hardly a deep dive.'

'I thought . . .' Eileen cleared her throat again, then she stiffened, bristled even. 'Did you just want to put me out of my misery here? If you have something to say to me, let's hear it.' Then she stood up, forcing Harry back to his height for a stand-off.

'This is Major Crime, Eileen. This is the big league now, not some book-club crusade against littering. Your job is *attention to detail*. Your job is to assist us so we can do our job and to keep us safe while we do it and THIS!' He thumped a fist down on the table. 'This is how you do that?'

'I—' Eileen started, but Harry wasn't finished yet.

'Two of us are dead!' He stepped away, now aware of his audience and a distant inner voice telling him that he needed to be calmer. 'We can't get lax. we can't start thinking that this is over just because we have a body. Do you think Ryan Archer is the only person out there who would take out a copper if they could?'

'Well, no, absolutely not.' Eileen said, brusquely. 'This was a mistake. This was my mistake and I cannot promise I won't make another, either. If you feel that means that this is not the department for me, then I'll respect that decision. For now, Working Time Directive suggests that I am entitled to a break and I think I will take a moment to step away.'

Harry reached back for the table, his weight again taken through palms that were now slippery. He closed his eyes, scrunching them tightly as some of his own words replayed themselves alongside the last image of Eileen Holmans trying to hold it together as she gathered her bag before sidling away.

'Harry, do you have a moment?' The voice was off to his right, it was one he recognised: Superintendent Helen Banks. There had been no footsteps preceding them, she must have been in the room the whole time. 'I could do with an update.' She raised her voice slightly for the benefit of the gawking onlookers. 'And these people could do with getting back to work, I think.'

Harry opened his eyes in time to see the office reanimate.

Then he followed the superintendent into his office.

# CHAPTER 42

'Are you okay?' The superintendent started with the obvious.

Harry slumped in the chair directly opposite the questioner, leaving him on the wrong side of his own desk. He closed his eyes again, though this time it was to rub them firmly, then slumped forward, his elbows sharp against his thighs.

'I'll apologise . . . to Eileen. I didn't handle that very well.'

'I asked if *you* were okay?'

'I'm fine.'

'Those were the actions of a man who is fine?'

'We can't afford mistakes.' Harry sensed that the superintendent was waiting for him to look up. He relented. She had also steepled her fingers.

'We can't. The stakes are high in here, we all know it. And Eileen knows it. You're not wrong to reprimand her for that error, but that isn't how you do it.'

'I know.'

'Anyone else and this would be a lecture on how we don't destroy each other in public, on how the culture we want is one where people learn and grow. But you don't need any of that, Harry, you're a fine leader, a natural one. So that

182

out there . . .' She gestured at the window. 'Was that just because she got you a smack in the face? Because she made you run?' There was a little humour in her voice, just a spark and Harry knew that any telling off was over.

'I do hate running,' he said, matching it. He pressed at his cheek. It was tender to the touch, warm too. 'Not as much as I hate losing key witnesses.'

'It happens. And to us all. You're calling her a *key witness*, I note. You don't fancy her as a suspect?'

'She's a witness. What Ryan Archer did was extraordinary, a spiral into madness. I'll need convincing that he was able to take someone down there with him. But she knew what was going on, something of it, at least, and she sure as hell knows how serious this is. You should have seen how she reacted to me.'

Harry was aware that the superintendent was back staring at his cheek. 'I think I can see what her reaction was.'

'She lashed out the moment I had her cornered, it was desperation. To get away. Whatever Archer told her, I bet she never thought it would get this far.'

The superintendent rubbed at her chin thoughtfully. 'I've read up on her a little. The intel we have describes a young woman who is good at hiding. From the police, at least.'

'I read the same,' Harry said.

'But she's been hiding for low-level stuff previously, helped out by any number of cronies. Nothing like this. We already have a press conference scheduled for later today and I'll use it to turn the screw. We can put her face out everywhere, there won't be anywhere to hide once—'

'Ma'am, I wouldn't do that.'

The superintendent moved through a number of expressions, bemusement was her last. '*Ma'am?* Since when have I been ma'am?'

'I messed up. I got Chloe Falconer all riled up and scared and then she got away. If she gets a special mention on national television, we just drive her further underground than ever.'

'So how do we find her?'

'Subtleties. We task the source handlers to go out and speak to their grasses. They'll have some that know Chloe, no doubt. We give a good incentive to tell us who's giving her a sofa and then we pick her up.'

'Harry Blaker pushing subtlety as a police tactic?' There was still humour in the room.

'If we go all out, we risk pushing her deeper, like I said. But maybe she escalates too, gets inspired by her dead boy-friend and someone else gets hurt.'

'You think she's capable on her own?'

'I'm not talking anywhere near the extent of what Archer did, but she could cause some trouble. She's certainly got a decent right hook.'

'So I see. But, just so I'm clear, we're not talking Billy the Kid and the last stand here?' Now the humour was leaking away.

'We're talking the unknown, the unpredictable and I always want to do what I can to limit that.'

The superintendent took a moment where it looked like she was considering his words. 'You're the one leading the hunt on the ground. How do you feel about sitting out in front of the cameras with me? That way, you can control the narrative.'

'You want me to do the press? People have always tended to keep me away from cameras, certainly ones that have the reputation of Kent Police attached.'

'I'm not people. And I think you're right. But if you're too bruised and too ugly, then I'm sure Maddie would be a far better face for the corporate image anyway—'

'You can't put Maddie out there. She was undercover once. Worked with some very nasty people, the sort who'd be very interested in seeing her outed as a police guv'nor on their TV set.'

'Then it's the old man with the bitch-slapped face. Maybe you can tidy yourself up a little on the way. It's at headquarters and we're leaving now. We have a phone meeting on the way to talk scripts.'

'Who with?'

'Someone from the senior leadership team. The Chief himself might dial in, someone from PR for sure and legal services to make sure we're sticking to the straight and narrow.'

'My specialty,' Harry said, the sarcasm thick.

'Cheer up, Blaker, at least it's not a video call.'

Not for the first time that day, Harry Blaker had a sense of humour failure.

# CHAPTER 43

I had a cup of tea that shook in my hand so much that I put it down on the bare boards that ran under the chair. I was in the bedroom, but I can't say I'd done much sleeping in it. It was a sparse room with the bed and a dining chair discarded in the corner that I had spun out to face the small television screen mounted up on the wall. The room as a whole was small, enough that the end of the bed provided a constant shove in the back.

I had pulled the curtains. The window had a busy view, or at least it took in a busy part of the town. It wasn't that I was concerned about being disturbed or overlooked, more that I wanted to block out the idea of a world out there at all.

This would just be me and those about to speak at the live police press conference. BBC News had promised a start time of 1 p.m. It was four minutes past and the newsreader was filling time, talking about *the community* and the shock-waves that had passed through it. They'd spent the last half-hour boring us all with loops of the same footage over and over, while talking head locals argued that they lived in a *quiet* and *peaceful* village. Old women with stupid little dogs were now having to lock their doors at night, apparently.

Good.

The screen changed, the newsreader suddenly hurried, her words the backdrop to an image of three empty chairs that filled quickly. A man and a woman were first, both dressed smart. The man was someone I had seen up close very recently and I smiled broadly at the idea that I might actually get to know who he was. His cheek had swollen up, no doubt of that, though I didn't think that was the only reason he looked so uncomfortable in a shirt and tie.

The woman I had never seen before. She took the middle chair. The third and final participant was a second man, he was young, looked instantly nervous and sat much further away to the woman's right. The woman spoke first.

*'I'm Superintendent Helen Banks and I am joined by Detective Inspector Harry Blaker and our Head of Communications, Johnathon Hutchins.'*

The Detective Inspector made no reaction to his own name. There was a real air of displeasure about him as he stared the camera down like he had been accosted by a homeless person holding out a polystyrene cup. Now, with High Definition cameras aimed on him, I could get a far better look at him. On the opposite side to his swollen cheek was an obvious scar. This was a man who was used to being in the wars.

The screen filled with a close-up of Helen Banks and she was instantly better, more human, despite reading from a script. She spoke of a terrible few days for the police family, for the community as a whole, following two separate incidents that were being treated as linked. She used the word *murder* and her demeanour became all the more serious. She gave scant details, just the overall number of victims, their gender and their ages.

Then Harry Blaker was introduced as the officer leading the day-to-day investigation and the camera panned in closer. It emphasised the swelling and I could see that the colouring to his face was off too, one side different to the other, a sign he had done his best to conceal it. I delighted in the fact that the swelling was the reason he came across as so angry. He hadn't liked that hit.

He mainly talked in figures. He gave the number of work hours and resources that had been diverted, a thinly-veiled way of saying *we are doing what we can.* It came across as defensive, his demeanour overall was of someone gruff and unpleasant.

When he was done, the superintendent handed over to questions. The very first one was perfection, almost like I had worded it myself and I found myself shifting forwards for the answer, the movement so sudden that the tea I had gathered back up now slopped out onto my thighs. The burning sensation was intermittent at best, like background noise.

*'Are you looking for anyone else in connection with these murders?'*

The journalist asking the question did so with a brash confidence so typical of their profession. There was a silent exchange between the two and then Harry Blaker gave a response.

'As stated, we believe that the main offender for these horrific incidents died at the scene. But we are still looking to speak to those people out there who knew him. That is the reason for this appeal today.'

The screen changed to show the torso of a man labelled as RYAN ARCHER. He was pictured in happier times, a sweaty smile with his shirt undone and a background that might have been a pub or nightclub. Harry Blaker continued.

*'You should be seeing a picture of a male we now know to be Ryan Archer. If you know this man or if you have seen him recently, then we would like to hear from you. We are trying to piece together his movements in the days and weeks leading up to these terrible incidents that we are still trying to understand. So, please, if you can help us with that, do get in touch.'*

Contact details appeared next, then the superintendent took her turn to repeat the same appeal.

I flicked the television off, expelling a lungful of air through lips shaped like a smile. It was perfect, like a press conference had been called just to put my mind at rest. They weren't looking for me. They weren't really looking for anyone — not for murder, at least. Though I reckoned Harry Blaker was going to be pretty determined to catch up with whoever had given him a nasty hit to the face.

That smile of mine was quick to turn into gurgling laughter.

# CHAPTER 44

Dawn. A warm start, a still sea and the sun adding a little magic to its surface. Maddie had never taken this view for granted, nor the fact that her apartment was so close to the beach that she could basically run straight out onto it.

It was a view she had missed. Moving in with Vince had seen it change to a far more rural setting, where nature still surrounded her, but in the form of subtle changes of seasons, rather than the high drama of a moody ocean. Maybe it was a reflection on her personality, but she much preferred the drama.

She walked her usual loop, her return home giving her a long view of the communal entrance to her block. The sun was on her back, causing the man sitting on the railings to have an arm raised to the sunlight, shading his eyes to watch her approach. He stood, straightening his back like he might have been sitting there a while, his other hand holding a brown paper bag that he swung out like the first word in a conversation.

'You lose your key?' she said, referencing the fact that he should still have a key to her place somewhere.

'Didn't feel right.' Vince Arnold said, his stance as awkward as his expression.

'Is that why you brought me breakfast?'

He grinned. 'Who said it was for you?'

'No way you're getting in here unless most of the contents of that bag is for me.' Maddie pushed the communal door and moved up two flights of stairs. Outside her apartment door she reached down for the key she had left under the mat.

'The old doormat gag? Really?' Vince said, eyeing her closely. 'You ever do the door-to-door campaigns where we tell the old dears not to leave spare keys under doormats or hidden in plant pots?'

'Can't say I did.'

'Where we used to tell them that even the dumb wrong-uns will look there first.'

'Can't say I did,' Maddie said again, her tone now with an edge. 'No pockets,' she said. 'And this is a town that sleeps in. I reckon I've seen three people in total out walking at this time of day and not one of them looked like a wrong-un.'

'Ah, but what does a wrong-un look like?'

Maddie lifted her hands to her hips. 'Heavyset male, white skinned, shaved head, carrying a bag and sitting out on people's doorsteps.'

Vince grinned again. 'Very good.'

Maddie opened the door and made straight for the kettle. 'Still hot?' She said, gesturing at the bag hanging from his hand.

'Fuck yeah, Mads. I get people telling me that all the time.'

'Outstanding, Vince. I see you've been working on some new material.' He chuckled, Maddie did too but it was still different, awkward even. The problem with being a close couple, the sort entirely comfortable in each other's company, is that the moment that changes, it's impossible for either to ignore. Maddie busied herself making the tea while Vince took a seat at the table, the scraping of his chair seemed louder than a close pass from a jumbo.

'So, what's going on?' He said, so obviously casual that it was clear it had taken some effort.

'You tell me, Vince. Seeing as that's why you're here.'

Vince looked hurt, enough to stop him chewing where he had ripped into his sausage and egg muffin. 'Peace offering,' he said, his mouth full, his knuckles now dripping plastic cheese. 'I come in peace, just to talk.'

'Where's the boy?' she said. Jake Arnold was his sister's boy really, but they'd lost her to illness recently, enough for it still to be raw, and they had taken him in. Jake was a good kid but he had made a difference. Dependants came with pressures, things you couldn't know or plan for. They hadn't known or planned for Vince losing his career either, or a pause at the very least. He was suspended from duty, a full investigation ongoing into his conduct on the day he had lost his sister, then lost his mind.

Maddie wasn't convinced he had got it back just yet.

'He stayed at his mate's house last night.'

'He's staying away now?'

'First time overnight. I spent the first few hours checking in so much he told me to piss off! I think he's doing good — a lot better, that's for sure.'

'Resilient — kids are, I mean.'

'He's doing alright.'

'And you?'

'You know me!'

'I do, that's why I'm asking.'

'I'm just missing you,' Vince said, again with his mouth full. This time the errant cheese was on his lip and he chose that moment to stare at her longingly, puppy-dog eyes and all. Maddie laughed. 'What the hell, Mads!' he said, then grinned himself. 'That was my big line. I practised that fucker on the way over!'

'Did you have a face full of muffin for your trial runs?'

'I'm starving! I came this close to nibbling it in the car, truth be told.'

'I have to get a shower and get to work.'

'Is that your way of saying that you miss me too?' He pushed the last of his breakfast into his gob, his chewing slowing for the answer.

'You know I miss you. That isn't the problem,' she said, then regretted it instantly.

'I get that. I'm the problem.' There was nothing detectable in his words or expression other than acceptance.

'Right now, *we're* the problem. And I don't have time to talk about it.'

'How's the investigation going? I saw the boss on the TV, sounds like you're already onto the mop-up?'

'We should be past any more scenes like the one from the other night.'

'Did sound nasty . . . with the kids . . .'

There were echoes between this job and the last one that Vince had attended, a sight that had started his downward spiral. She didn't know if she should reference that or not. 'It was nasty. Never seen a murder scene that isn't.' What she'd opted for was a cop-out at best.

'I get it, you don't wanna talk about it. I just wanted to know that you're okay, to see if there was anything you needed. Other than breakfast, obviously.' He grinned that big, dopey grin that she had fallen so hard for. He'd brought her breakfast that she had ignored, sat down for a tea she wasn't going to finish and was asking for an assurance she was keeping from him. She exhaled her pang of guilt as a sigh.

'Thanks for the breakfast. I'm okay, we're all okay. Harry's taken the brunt. He was out sleepwalking right around the corner when the call came in. Then — you know what he's like — he took it upon himself to make sure everything was going to be alright for the kids that he found. When of course everything isn't going to be alright. Not ever. So, then he takes that with him, loads it up on top of everything else that he seems to be feeling guilty about . . .' She realised that she was in danger of digging herself deeper.

'Just like me.' Vince's smile still held its shape but none of its warmth.

'The men in my life.' Maddie shrugged. 'They're all so complicated.'

'Hence the crack-of-dawn sea-air walk. I get it,' he said again and Maddie just nodded, preferring that explanation to the reality of morning sickness at 4 a.m. The first few times she had gone out in her running shoes, refusing to accept any limitations. *It's not a sickness!* she had told herself but had only made half a mile when the jogging motion had been very much a sickness, some of which was still visible as specks on those running shoes.

'Hence the walk,' she repeated. 'I imagine Harry did the same.'

'Is he okay? What's that about him being out sleepwalking?'

'He's Harry,' Maddie said, thoughtfully. 'And I used to know what that meant.'

'Problems?'

'Not at all. I dunno. Harry, when he was talking with the widow, with this job in general, he's just been . . . different. I think he just spends his nights driving country lanes in the dark these days or sitting in an empty cinema when he should be getting the rest we all need.'

'Different?'

Maddie waved him away. 'The problem with him is he's like a rock. The exterior might weather a bit but it never really changes. You can easily forget what's happened to him, what he's been through. I get so wrapped up in my own stuff, I guess . . .'

'Easy done,' Vince said.

'It doesn't mean I don't care.' She took a step closer to where Vince had stood up. Mercifully, he'd wiped his face too. He opened his big arms and Maddie accepted the hug. It felt good . . . safe. Her lips were close to his ears and they moved, forming the words where she told him she was pregnant, *they* were pregnant and how it was going to fix everything and that it was going to be okay from here on, in. But it was just the silent movement of her lips; there was no voice, no sound at all.

Once she said those words to Vince she'd lose control of them, lose control of this whole situation, of her own body and the decisions around it. There was an even bigger truth, one that she couldn't even admit to herself yet.

She wasn't sure she was going to be able to do this.

She wasn't sure she wanted to.

# CHAPTER 45

There was no sense that anyone else was in the building. Harry had walked through a car park that was empty, save for the row of cookie-cutter pool cars. He progressed towards the early morning sun that was positioned perfectly to show up the dusty windows of Cranbrook Police Station. The feeling of a lonely walk while the rest of the world still slept was a familiar one and it seemed a natural follow-up to another restless night. He'd taken Jock out on a midnight walk, even pushed into the woods for a reasonable way until the thickening darkness and the uneven ground had conspired to turn his ankle and he'd limped back the way he had come.

Even a filthy black wood had seemed better than the alternative that was his own home.

It caught Harry out a little to see Eileen Holmans at her desk. The weak morning light was being assisted by a lamp she had brought in from home. Its bulb reflected in her glasses when she peered over the top at his arrival.

'Sir . . . There's a fresh pot of coffee. I'm just about to pour.'

'Allow me,' Harry grumbled, withdrawing to a room the size of a large cupboard used as a makeshift kitchenette. It had running water in the form of the smallest sink in known history and little room for anything else. The coffee smelled good. Harry wasn't a big drinker of the stuff, but he poured himself a sweet and black. He paused with a second cup readied, cussed under his breath, then leaned back out with a full lungful of air ready to shout. He didn't need to: Eileen hovered just outside of the door, her arms crossed.

'White with one,' she said.

'I should know that . . . I should make it more,' Harry said awkwardly. 'I should apologise too.' He poured her drink in the silence that followed, then made sure he was facing her so he could say it again, but better. 'I'm sorry, Eileen. I have a lot more respect for you than I demonstrated yesterday. I was hoping to talk to you sooner, but I got dragged off to do something and . . . I thought about calling, but . . . I'm sorry.' He reached back in for her drink and handed it over.

'I appreciate that.'

'You'll be pleased to know that Maddie tore a strip off me. She was right to. She said that the part about your attention to detail hurt you the most. For the record, you have an attention to detail like I've never seen and that's only one reason why you're such a huge asset. To me, to this department.'

'I did miss the relevant part of that intel report.' Eileen's eyes seemed to lose focus for a moment. 'And you were assaulted.'

'We all make mistakes. I wasn't . . . it wasn't . . .'

'Are you okay, sir?' Eileen's focus was back, her eyes narrowed a little as she took in the inspector. 'That respect goes both ways. I've always found you to be very level. I like people like that. It's a good trait in a leader. It means you always know where you stand. What annoys you today, annoys you tomorrow. I can work for someone like that, no problem.'

'I appreciate the same.'

'But what annoyed you yesterday—'

'I know. This case . . .' He stopped himself, unsure what to say next.

'Ma'am Ives might have told you off, but it's because she's worried about you. I think she knows you better than anyone, so if she's worried . . .'

'She said that?'

'She didn't have to.'

'I'm fine. I'll tell her the same.'

'She was worried before this case came in. You're not sleeping, right?'

'I've never been much of a sleeper.'

'Perhaps not sleeping isn't the concern. Perhaps it's what is keeping you awake that you should address.'

'I'll keep that in mind.' Harry supped at his coffee. 'And what is it that has you here at the crack of dawn?'

'I always wake early. Then I can either lie listening to a ticking clock until the hour becomes more reasonable or I can get up and do something productive with my time.'

'You mean come to work?'

'Yes, but I take my time. I like to park up a few miles short for a nice walk in. I like walking. It's when I think best.'

'Anything in particular?'

'Yes, actually. Seems a few miles to think gave me the space for an idea or two. Around this case of ours, actually.'

'Oh?'

Eileen walked back to her desk. It was clear to Harry that he was supposed to follow. She opened up her screen to a site that was familiar, even to Harry: Facebook. Another click and an image appeared, still bordered with the distinctive branding. The image was of a car, an old-style BMW coupe, olive coloured, shown at an angle with the wheels turned.

'What am I looking at here?' Harry said.

'A post by Ryan Archer. Facebook has a marketplace where users can buy and sell and he was selling.'

'Cars. We know that. His dad told us.'

'This one's on here too.' Eileen clicked for another image to appear. 'A black Volvo S60 D2—'

'The car from outside Alan's house.'

197

'The very same. Up for £4,000. Listed three days ago . . .' Eileen lingered on him as if he was supposed to say something.

'And that seems odd to you?'

'Does it not to you?'

'Which part?' Harry said.

'The part where Ryan Archer seems to be getting on with his life. Buying and selling cars to make a little bit of money . . .'

'And then attacking and murdering police officers on his time off, slashing his wrists as part of the second one.'

Eileen gestured at the Volvo on the screen and sighed. 'It's not registered to him, still to the last owner. There's no discernible way to link that Volvo with Ryan Archer, at least there wasn't until he put it up on his own Facebook site.'

'You have a theory. Let's hear it.'

'I mean, I'm just the civilian analyst, barely above making the tea—'

'Eileen . . .' Harry growled, but he kept the humour in there too.

'Okay, so there are theories out there. The first is that this was a murder-suicide, that Ryan Archer went to Sergeant Day's family home with the intention of committing murder and with no intention of coming out alive, having already murdered PC Jones a few days earlier.'

'From the evidence we have . . .' Harry took a moment to put his thoughts in order. 'Archer has motive. His life hasn't exactly turned out a fairy-tale. And there's a history of mental health — depression on his mother's side.'

'So why go to the bother of putting a car up for sale on social media if you know you're going to die before you ever get to sell it.'

'Maybe Alan Day's murder was opportunistic?' Harry said. 'Or Phil Jones was the opportunity that presented itself. This could be something Archer had been considering for a while that suddenly escalated, even catching him out?'

'Possible.' Eileen said. 'The other theory is that Ryan Archer went to Sergeant Day's address in order to murder him and with the intention of getting away with his crime, like with PC Jones.'

'He might not have got away with that,' Harry said.

'No, you would have caught him in the end, I'm sure. But we can both agree that he took measures and that these were the measures of a man who was intent on not getting caught.'

'We can.'

'So why, with Alan Day, would you park a car directly outside that is linked to you so prominently after a quick social media search?' Eileen pushed.

'So, you're saying the murder-suicide theory is the more likely of the two to be right?'

'The most likely, from two that seem wholly unlikely.'

'Okay, so what's left?'

'Left?'

'What other explanations?'

'That I don't know. I don't even have a guess, but finding these pictures had me considering that I might be able to dig a little deeper into Archer. I might be able to get a lead on that. I know the focus will be on finding Chloe Falconer, but I provided the relevant package for her yester—'

'Lead?' Harry cut over her.

'These cars . . .' Eileen's attention moved back to the screen as she flicked between the two photos a couple of times. 'What do you notice about the backgrounds?'

'Looks like a row of garages,' Harry said.

'The same row of garages. And they don't look in the best state. He's used a camera mode that takes the background out of focus but these blurs on the ground look like piles of rubbish to me, patches of weeds too and I can't see any other cars. Overall, I would say that these garages are unused.'

'Okay . . .'

'In a previous life, I worked for the council. On the fly-tipping investigation team.'

'I think you've mentioned it,' Harry grumbled.

'Old garage sites were often targeted. A housing block gets condemned you see, or there's a change of use to the land but the garages are separate, sometimes under a different agreement or even owned by someone else entirely. It used to be common for landlords to own a block of flats but for the council to own the garages. The rent would be separate, the—'

'Eileen, I get it,' Harry said. 'Why is this relevant?'

'There aren't many left.' Eileen bristled a little. 'As I was just about to say. I worked for the County Council and there's a database with all the sites where fly-tipping has taken place. I know that, because I set it up. So, I could ask for increased patrolling or apply for funding for preventative action . . .' Eileen must have felt Harry's stare. 'When 9 a.m. comes, I'm going to call the old team for a list of sites still left with garages. From there I can whittle it down to sites local to Archer. I think I can find where this is, where Ryan Archer took those photos.'

Harry nodded. 'Worth a drive out.' He would go himself. Even if he was far from convinced that it would do any good, this would be his way of making it up to her. It was working already; Eileen beamed.

'Okay then. Just as soon as we're in office hours . . .'

'The plates on the BMW?' Harry said.

'I ran them, sir. First thing I did. Previous keeper details only. The DVLA were notified three months ago. It was declared off-road prior to that.'

'Okay. Keep an eye on it in case it gets re-registered. Maybe he sold it just before and we can find someone to talk to, someone who can tell us about his state of mind.'

'Will do. I'm going to see if I can find older posts, too. See if there's anyone who communicated with him in the comments that might be worth speaking to.'

'Great.' Harry now felt like he could break away and go and hide in his office.

'I'm not really sure what I'm looking for here,' she said. 'This might all be a waste of time.'

'Most of the time spent on a major investigation is time wasted. My old boss always used to say that we're just panning for gold.'

'Seems like a good analogy.' Eileen said. 'But this . . . I don't really know what can come of it, but it doesn't *feel* like a waste of time.'

'Nor did panning for gold,' Harry mumbled to himself.

# CHAPTER 46

It was seven minutes after nine when Eileen stood over Harry's desk to once again emanate with smugness. Harry knew the time specifically because she was sure to tell him, before adding *and guess what I have for you already?*

It was an address, a location, at least: a block of garages clinging to the edge of a brand-new housing estate that she believed Ryan Archer had been using as a backdrop for his car sales. Harry snuck out, taking Maddie with him, leaving Eileen to brief the rest of the team with all the outstanding actions in the hunt for Chloe Falconer. That search now belonged to his detectives and to uniform.

Why pan for gold when you had people who could do it for you?

Any trace of the original building the garages might have served was entirely gone, swamped by traffic islands and white weatherboarded contemporary homes. The site was fenced off by a thick chain running through chain link gates, an eyesore on the rump of a pristine new estate. The first newbuild on the estate was a show home that flew the flag of the estate agents tasked with shifting the units. Harry used its car park, the opening and closing of their doors like a fly agitating a web. The front door burst open with a flash

202

of bright white teeth and an even brighter orange tie. Even without the flag, Harry could tell an estate agent a mile off, as, it seemed, could Maddie.

'No thanks.' She dismissed him with enough gusto for his smile to drop away.

'Are you in the market for a new home?' he said.

'Not with your prices. We were just gonna look at the garages, just about all we can afford around here.'

'This parking is for customers only!' The estate agent called after them both with faux cheer.

'I'll bear that in mind!' she called back.

Harry was ahead as they both walked across newly laid, pristine grass onto a strip of tarmac that acted as the dividing line. The other side was a step up onto a rough bank then an expanse of broken concrete that led up to those gates, the piles of rubbish evident behind.

The heavy chain came off in Harry's hand. His eye was already caught by something of interest. There were three rows of garages, most were shut. Some looked as if they'd been bust open. Some had the door missing entirely. But only one had something sticking out of it, something olive green, and Harry was already wagering with himself that it was a BMW coupe.

'Archer's car,' Maddie said when they were close enough for confirmation.

'One of them,' Harry said against the backdrop of his phone ringing. 'Eileen . . .' he growled, aware that he was going to have to praise her for more good work.

'Sir, are you at the location yet?' She sounded agitated, excited.

'Still on our way,' Harry lied, turning away from Maddie with her hands on her hips. 'Why's that?'

'I went back through the CCTV taskings after PC Jones's murder. Seems these video doorbells things really are all the rage—'

'Eileen . . .' Harry sighed.

'Sorry. There's a house in the next village over from Frant. It's on a very quiet road and their doorbell caught a car passing at just after three in the afternoon. It slowed right down — the road isn't wide enough for two. The car was olive green. Looks like the one from the photo to me. And the window was down, which meant you could see the man clearly enough.'

'Archer?' Harry said. 'So, this car was used for Philip Jones's murder. We have just arrived, Eileen, I can see the car is here. I'll arrange for a forensic seizure.'

'I think that's wise sir, you see . . .'

'Eileen, is there something you need to spit out?'

'Sir . . . Ryan Archer was in the passenger seat.'

# CHAPTER 47

Harry bristled, his whole body involved, a shake that started at his fingertips and spread out to cover him entirely. He had walked a few paces away, far enough that Maddie couldn't have heard his side of the conversation. He stole a glance back over, to where she was still at the open garage, up on tiptoes as if trying to get a view through the back window of the abandoned car.

'Sir?' Eileen was still there, still talking through the phone that he had pushed so hard against his ear it had gone numb.

'That's fine work.' Harry managed in words laced with gravel. 'Have we got a view of the driver?'

'We have an unfortunate flaring of the sun, but it does allow a glimpse of dark hair. Long, dark hair.'

'Chloe . . .' Harry sighed, lifting his hand to a cheek that was tender no more, but with purple bruising that had come out under his eye. 'I had her, Eileen . . . right in front of me. We'll be back soon.' He hung up, plunged his phone into his pocket and stayed facing away for a few more moments while his breath remained shallow. There was an anger in him, but it was more than that, mixed up with something else.

'You okay?' Maddie had come back to him and was just off his shoulder. 'I can't see anything else in the garage. Looks like this was just a place to abandon it. I've put a call in for a full forensic lift. We can search it when it's back at—'

'There was someone else,' Harry cut in. 'Someone driving. Eileen just called. There's CCTV of that car on the way to where Phil Jones was murdered. Ryan Archer was in the passenger seat.'

'Passenger seat?' Maddie looked over at the car, as if picturing the occupants. 'And Chloe Falconer driving?'

'Can't be certain.' Harry had more to say but his breath escaped him, his insides still in turmoil.

'I'll get a patrol out to oversee the seizure of the car. It might be worth CSI coming out to have a look at the garage first. They might think it's worth giving it the treatment.' Maddie seemed to be thinking out loud, while Harry was struggling to get his own thoughts in order. His mind swirled. A moment later, the loose ground around him did the same. The next sensation was an impact through his kneecap — something sharp, the pain enough to penetrate where a fog had descended. Then came Maddie's voice.

'Harry?' He felt her too, her hand on his shoulder, her grip tightening as if she was keeping him steady and he let her, leaning into her a little, the only thing steady where everything else seemed to be moving. His ears felt blocked then popped to leave a loud whistle that increased in pitch rather than dying away. The pain was next, erupting like a lit match from the fingers on his left hand, a flame that raced for his chest. Instinctively he slumped to a sit, his left arm shooting out to support him, his hand now pins and needles that flared hot on impact.

And then he passed out.

# CHAPTER 48

Daylight. Maddie Ives. A warm breeze.

Harry's awareness returned in that order. He sat up. Maddie was complaining. His ears still had a whistle. He missed the first few words but got the gist. She was complaining that he wasn't staying laid down, then she complained that he had scared the shit out of her.

Sharp ground. Garages. People approaching.

More details emerged out of the fug: those approaching were jogging, dressed head to toe in green, their bags matching, only with a chartreuse yellow strip that was brighter than the sun itself.

It was an ambulance crew and they arrived with questions, lots of them. They were mainly for Maddie, it seemed. He could only make out some of what she was giving as answers. She described a man who had suddenly lost all pallor in his face, who had dropped a phone from his left hand and then been unable to function correctly to pick it back up again, who had then collapsed trying. Then she described a man laid out with a racing pulse and shallow breathing.

The paramedics were looking at him the whole time and nodding a lot, their expressions knowing. The one asking the bulk of the questions moved closer so that Harry could make him out. He asked about medical history, about a date of birth and medication. Maddie was still giving the answers. Then she talked about sleep and how she didn't think this man she was describing was getting any. The paramedic followed that up with a question about any recent stresses and their nodding became more and more emphatic as she spoke.

Harry's pain was back. This time it wasn't a striking match, this time it was a slower burn that started at the chest to spread from there. The sensation was of someone crushing his entire torso like a drinks can in a fist. He wanted to speak, to let them know that he was in trouble, but nothing happened, nothing would come. He couldn't see; he might have shut his eyes, but his vision seemed to have been lost from the sides, like curtains pulled. He could still feel the sun on his face and he could hear voices, Maddie's voice. She was talking to him. She was back to sounding urgent. He replied, though he couldn't be sure the words made it past his lips.

'It's okay. I'm in trouble, but it's okay.'

He didn't want her to worry, he didn't want anyone to worry. This was going to be okay. This was what he wanted.

# CHAPTER 49

Two press conferences in two days. The difference was clear even before a word was spoken: Detective Inspector Harry Blaker was missing.

Superintendent Helen Banks sat still and expressionless, like a sombre statue. She delivered her script and there were to be no questions, at times it looked like she was struggling to hold it together.

I hadn't made a drink for this one and I soon realised this to be a mistake. My mouth was dry, my whole body wracked with an energy that could not be contained in a pokey bedroom. It was a constant battle with my own instincts not to simply get up and run away.

Something was different, something was wrong. The superintendent got straight to the point.

*We are here today to make a further appeal. To ask members of the public who live in the area marked on the map now appearing on your screen to consider if they can help us. Did you see this vehicle? Did you capture this vehicle on your home CCTV system, on your doorbell device or on your car's dashcam. For those that do not live in the area but were travelling through, or visiting on Tuesday the sixteenth of May, do you have dashcam? Did you take a picture or a video on your phone and happen to capture this vehicle in the background? Maybe you saw it while it was moving, or when it was parked up and looked out of place. Maybe you saw the occupants in the car when they drove towards you or past you. If you did . . .'*

Occupants. *Plural.*

That was what she said. She was still talking but I stood up, feeling the coarse floorboard nip at my bare feet. I moved around the bed to watch from the doorway, scared to be any closer, as if the television was a window through which those officers were drinking in my reaction.

No, not scared. There was something else . . . *anger.* This had been over. Finished. They had hurt me and I had hurt them back and we were even. It had been a long time coming, but it was finished. The aching void that had consumed my days and nights had gone, the anxiety too. But not now. Now it was back in spades.

They were looking for someone else, someone else responsible. They were looking for me. I watched as the superintendent stared straight down the camera to urge the public to respond — she stared straight at *me.*

I spun away from the screen, from her face, taking a moment to catch myself, fearing I might whirl out of control. I couldn't afford that.

'They're looking for me,' I said out to the room in a voice that didn't sound like mine. My throat was drier than ever. Swallowing made a sound like a retch. 'That's a mistake,' I said, still in someone else's voice.

The superintendent was still talking and was now off script, appealing directly to the person they were looking for. Appealing directly to me.

*'The person who was in that car will see this, I'm sure. They might even be watching now. If you are then we need to talk to you. Maybe you just dropped someone off. Maybe you didn't know who your passenger was and what they were planning and now you're worried — scared. Whatever the reason you were in this car at that time, with that person, we need to hear from you and we can help you. Please call us. We need to talk. We need to remove you from our investigation and we need the information you have — information that could bring closure to many grieving people. Thank you.'*

She was done; they both were. The man from the background of the day before had managed to stay in the background for this one, too. They both stood up, the action like a starting gun for a barrage of questions. None of them were answered.

The television clunked off, the silence that followed did nothing to calm my raging mind. I needed to think. I set about pacing boards that creaked and groaned, extending it by going out onto the landing.

The police were desperate. The whole appeal stank of it — the refusal at the end to take questions that would show up just how little they knew, that had to be why.

Not to mention the no-show from the man leading the investigation. They hadn't broached that, how he had collapsed, maybe even died — it looked like he might have to me. The thought of that was enough to spark a smile. Then, in that silence, after taking a moment to think, my smile started to grow.

There was still a way out of this, a way of stopping them looking for me. Part of me had been hoping it would come to this.

I was going to have to hurt another one.

# CHAPTER 50

'I'm not allowed visitors.' Harry sounded gruff, even more so than usual. Every word felt like its origins involved a razor blade and the inside of his throat.

'The nurse told me you had asked her to say that,' Eileen Holmans replied, flatly.

'Why would she tell you that?'

'Because it's the truth and I made it clear that she should be telling members of Kent Police the truth.'

'Did you bully my nurse, Eileen?'

'You could sit there and lash out at someone else for being a bully or you could look inward, at a person that forced another to lie.'

'I'm supposed to be resting,' Harry groaned.

'You called me, sir.'

'Not for a visit, certainly not for small talk. Words hurt like hell.'

'They certainly do, you would do well to remember that.' Eileen huffed and Harry couldn't help but smile. He was being told off. In a previous life and before her time as a litter detective, Eileen had been a secondary school teacher. She'd had a long career honing the skills required to manipulate and control difficult adolescents forced to attend a place

212

they would rather not be. Perfect fodder for the policing environment.

'Point taken,' Harry said. He reached out for his water, pushing his hand through any number of wires to get it, gasping as he did, his breath suddenly taken away where his heart raced. Eileen watched him closely, her expression changing like she might be satisfied enough with his suffering. She lifted a magazine into view to drop it on the same bedside trolley as his water.

'*Gardeners' World*?' Harry said.

'I went in for a newspaper but, goodness me, the things they're trying to palm off as journalism these days. I thought you might appreciate something to read.'

'I would appreciate a lift home.'

'The nurse suggested that might be some time coming.'

'They can't keep me here.'

'I'm not sure it's about what they can do, sir. it's more about what they should do.'

'Thank you, Eileen. Is that why you came? To interrogate the nursing staff and then to lecture me on what I should be doing?'

'No, like I said, I came because you called me—'

'And you didn't pick up.'

'I did not, sir. I have been told specifically not to pick up the phone to you.'

'So, your presence here doesn't break that rule?'

Eileen allowed a subtle smile. 'And there lies the grey area in which I am currently operating.'

'I left you a voicemail.'

'You did, in which you asked me for reading material.' Eileen lifted *Gardeners' World* up for another moment.

'That isn't what I meant, Eileen, and you know that.'

'Well maybe you should be clearer, sir.'

'I couldn't say it. Not over the phone. Not in a message anyway.'

'This is the only sort of reading material you should be concerned with. Ma'am Ives was going to bring you something similar, but—'

'But she called ahead and was told I wasn't allowed visitors.'

'She did. She said she would let you rest anyway, said that you hadn't replied to her messages so you must still be sleeping it off.'

'I haven't replied to anyone. People tend to turn up if you do.'

'You don't seem very surprised to see me.' Eileen lifted her hands to her hips.

'I am surprised to see you in shoes.'

'Special occasion.' She shrugged. 'Plus, if you wear slippers in a place like this someone will try and take you back to your ward. Where are they with the tests? Do they know what happened, yet?'

'I know what it was. I don't need their tests.' Harry was well aware that he wasn't sounding convincing. 'I also know that I have an investigation to get back to.'

Eileen took a moment, her eyes running along his form, all the way along to where his feet were pushing up the thin, white sheet. She sniffed like she was a long way from impressed. 'If I may, sir, the most important investigation right now is with those doctors, the ones who are trying to work out why you collapsed on a patch of wasteland in the middle of the day. You know better than anyone that you need to understand why something happened to stop it happening again.'

'I ran for the first time in years, then got a sharp right hook and some news that made me angry. I'm not as young as I used to be, I certainly don't sleep like I used to and it all added up to bring me down. I know better, now. Won't happen again.'

'So, it's rest that you need?' Eileen said.

Harry gave her a look that he hoped would stand her down. It might have worked on anyone else.

'I need to know where we are,' Harry snapped. 'We had a big appeal go out, that means there will be information coming in, potential leads. Did we find Chloe Falconer yet?'

'Against your advice, according to the superintendent.' Eileen looked like she was waiting to judge his reaction.

Harry did his best to shrug. 'Who's to say when is the best time to go public. I assume it hasn't had the desired result? That she hasn't called up to assist us with our enquiries?'

'No. The response has been strong in general, however. The FCR have been swamped. We've got student constables on the phones just to make sure we're answering the calls.'

'So, you need all the hands you can get.'

'And most of it is rubbish. Cranks, or people that just want to help and are doing nothing of the sort.'

'Most isn't all,' Harry said.

'There will always be leads.'

'What have you got?'

'Nothing to share with you, sir. I think I told you already that I was told not to pick up the phone to you.'

'We're not on the phone.'

'I just wanted to come and see that you're alright. I'm glad that you are.' Eileen seemed satisfied with herself and made movements to leave.

'There's more to it than that. You've been sizing me up this whole time. You came here with something, you just wanted to see if I was fit enough before you gave it to me.' Eileen was clutching a bag, it was over her shoulder, her arm through the strap. She clutched it a little tighter.

'You're fit enough to read *Gardeners' World*.' She moved a little closer to the door.

'I'll just get hold of someone else. Only I won't waste my time on calls. I'll discharge myself from here and turn up at police stations — houses if I need to. I know a lot of people — it could be a lot of houses. A lot of driving when I shouldn't be, but I'll do it.'

Eileen seemed to consider this. 'I'll make you a deal, sir. I do have some more reading material that might help you fill the time and I'll leave some of it today and you can call me when you're done for the rest.'

'Eileen . . .' His voice carried a warning tone, the effort required raising his pulse. He wasn't into playing games.

'And when you call me, make it a video call and if I see a hospital bed, some machinery, maybe a scratched jug of water and a scowling nurse in the background, then we can talk about the rest and how else I might be able to help you. But, if you call me from anywhere other than here, you should expect me to start following orders a lot more closely.' She opened her bag to plunge a hand in. There was some shuffling of papers that she then lifted out. She tucked them in the *Readers' Letters* section of *Gardeners' World* before making her way back to the door. Harry resisted the temptation to snatch them up immediately.

'They could officially discharge me, Eileen. I could be free to go at any time. They certainly won't be calling you to let you know I've been released.'

'You say that . . .' Eileen made a subtle movement that had her glancing out into the corridor.

'The nurse . . . you've got her reporting on me, haven't you?'

'I'm an intelligence analyst, sir. My job is to consider every and any source.'

Harry peered over at *Gardeners' World*. 'Sometimes I wish you weren't quite so good at it.' But his protestations were to himself.

Eileen Holmans had left the building.

# CHAPTER 51

There wasn't the need to linger. It had taken just a few minutes to do what I needed to do. I never lingered, not at this stage, but something strong was holding me there. A morbid fascination perhaps, a sudden desire to get to know the man I was about to wipe off the face of the earth.

Detective Inspector Harry Blaker.

It was dusk. I had planned on coming here after dark but my nervous energy had got the better of me and I just couldn't wait. I was in a different car. Another that Ryan had secured in the last few weeks. He had been happy with it, said he wouldn't need to do much to it at all to make a couple of hundred quid on what he had paid. I couldn't imagine paying a couple of hundred quid on the thing in the first place. Every part of the damned thing made a noise. If it wasn't a mystery rattle it was the engine that wheezed or the exhaust that blared. I wouldn't mind if there was performance from all of that noise but the speedo needle had all the energy of a movie death where the victim pointed out his killer.

I parked some way short, giving myself a two-mile walk that was pleasant through muggy air that smelt like rain. I let myself in via a small window on the side of the porch, the side that was hidden from the road. It was easier than I ever imagined, easier than I would ever have believed it if I hadn't been shown. Just a few tools and ten minutes alone with it — though I had seen it done faster. Putting it back was easier still. I wasn't quite as efficient at that and it wouldn't look quite right under scrutiny, but I was a long way from being concerned about scrutiny.

The only greeting was a clock ticking down the end of the far hall.

I walked through to the kitchen at the back, taking a moment to take in my surroundings, to enjoy the excitement flooding my body just from being there. I tried to imagine the life that was lived there, pulling open the fridge door that was hiding a light that was bright in a gathering gloom. It accentuated the colours of some cheese, butter, a few eggs and then a packed salad tray at the bottom. No beer, no meat. No personality. I sniggered as I spoke out into his kitchen, 'I'm gonna be doing this fella a favour!'

I spent longest in the kitchen. It's the room that people always seem to go to first, the focal point, centre of the house. When I was out of there I sauntered around the room, the next longest visit was in a bedroom that felt like the master. This was the only other room that had real signs of habitation, even if the contents did nothing to add personality. There were gardening books, biographies of cricketers, an address book with neat handwriting and a smartwatch still in its box. The box had something written on it and I pulled it into the light. *Dad, surprise us both and use it! Mel and Faye.*

It seemed Detective Inspector Harry Blaker had done no such thing.

When I made it back to the front porch, I ran my mind back over the route I had taken and the things I had touched until I was satisfied that I had left no trace. The way out was via the front door, the keys hanging on a peg next to it. The paper suit I was wearing ruffled a little in the breeze that I met when I opened it and my hands suddenly felt damp in two pairs of blue nitrile gloves. Two pairs, just like the police used. They were supposed to be an effective barrier against shedding any fluids. The plastic overshoes were for the same reason.

The darkness, the porch overhang and the high hedge-row along the front of the house offered the perfect place to strip down. I was still careful, slow and meticulous, bagging everything as I went.

When I finally left, there was time for a last glance back at the house merging with the darkness. There was something about that house that meant the darkness just seemed to suit it.

'I'll be doing you a favour,' I said again, this time my voice was missing the earlier glee, to be replaced with a cold determination.

# CHAPTER 52

'It's eleven at night, sir.' Eileen Holmans didn't sound sleepy. Agitated, for sure, but not sleepy.

'And you answered.'

'More fool me.'

Harry ignored the disapproving tone. 'I've been going through the stuff you gave me.'

'Of course you have. I am now going to hang up, sir, with the greatest of respect. I believe we set some ground rules earlier to which you don't appear to be adhering.'

The phone beeped three times in a dead tone and he was left to cuss at himself. 'That bloody woman.' He worked his phone to call her back, this time selecting the option for a video call.

'There, that's better, isn't it?' Eileen's smugness was so much worse when it was visible.

It was most definitely not better.

Eileen sat in a high-backed chair, white with a floral pattern, her hair in a tight mesh net and her face sullen and dimpled. Harry could see himself too, mercifully smaller than his colleague and boxed up in the corner of the screen, but it was enough to be reminded of classic vampire films. He looked as pale as a ghost, his eyes grey and listless, the only colour to his face provided by the ugly scar on his cheek where it peeked out from under a greying beard.

'Now then, would you kindly show me around?' Eileen said.

Harry harrumphed. He may not be up for playing games, but it didn't matter, Eileen was in her usual position of power. He lifted his phone, relieved, at least, to be taking it off his face and moved the lens like a lighthouse to prove he was still in the same wretched hospital.

'Very good. How are you settling in?'

Harry spun the phone back to scowl into it. 'Very good, Eileen. I read the material you left. There's not much there.'

'I told you there wasn't.'

'You said there were some leads.'

'There are.'

'I counted ten sightings of an olive BMW. They all need to be followed up on—'

'Twelve. But we can't be certain of any of them. One looks promising, a carpenter who was at the back of his van for some tools. His van was causing an obstruction while he unloaded, and he reckons an olive BMW was held up and first in the queue.'

'Did he give a description? What did he say?'

'I had a brief conversation on the phone. A detective is going out to see him tomorrow. He did say that he didn't take much notice but it was definitely a man and a woman. Both with dark hair, the woman driving.'

'And?'

'And that's it for now. He doesn't tell us anything new, but a few probing questions could change that.'

'There's more. More than what you left me. I knew it from how you were acting.'

'There isn't. There might be soon. We have a lot of CCTV coming in . . . dashcam footage . . . doorbells . . . privately owned—'

'Straight to the DMS?' Harry knew the process. The DMS or Digital Media Service was a recent introduction and one that had felt like a huge leap forward. It was a new system that gave members of the public the ability to upload their own footage via the police website. No more was there the need for officers to attend every shoplifting or burglary with a data stick; it could be sent by the victim, appearing for officers to view it without even leaving their desk. It was touted as something that would save hours of work but the reality was proving to be very different. The system had taken away any sort of a filter and members of the public were merrily uploading hours of footage with no idea of its relevance and no motivation to check. Any major investigation now had the added drain on their resources that came from sifting through far more material than ever before. And that was before the uplift in home CCTV and video doorbells was taken into account.

It was a huge undertaking.

'Yes. We have four officers working twelve-hour days assessing it, but—'

'What was the time window?'

'Twelve hours, six hours either side of the 999 call that summoned PC Jones to Frant Village Hall.'

'Twelve hours!'

'It's proving to be a large job.' Eileen mumbled.

'If I had my laptop, I could help. I could take some of that work. Do it right from here.'

'From your hospital bed?'

'Not necessarily. From here or from home. I'm only here because you won't let me leave.'

'It is your own well-being that is keeping you there, sir. Which is also what is keeping me from providing you with access to your laptop.'

Harry huffed. The computer Eileen was using was placed on her lap, the screen and camera clearly angled upwards. Perfect to capture the sudden appearance of a ginger kitten calmly pacing along the back of her chair, its entrance perfectly timed. Not so much the walk as the sniff of the old woman's ear.

'Eileen, I was assuming this was a private conversation,' Harry said and Eileen lifted her hand for the kitten to nudge with its head.

'Don't you worry about Ted. He's even better at secrets than I am.'

'No way such a being exists.' Harry forced a grin, waiting for the reply, the next part of his plan ready to go. Eileen was to see right through him.

'Is this the part where you challenge me on that? Where you have me provide you with your laptop and promise to keep it a secret after loosening me up with a conversation about a kitten?'

The thing with video calls is that you get to see your own reactions live. Harry watched his own smile drop away. 'It was my last play,' he admitted. 'I considered a lawful order, but right now I'm not sure it would be.'

'It wouldn't.' Eileen said. 'That was another thing that was made quite clear. And any attempts made by you, to make lawful orders or otherwise, should be reported direct to the superintendent.'

'And you've decided to.' Harry was resigned to his fate.

'No.' She surprised him with a sudden stand and a statement off camera, where the screen looked to have tipped off. 'I'm going to pop out to drop off a laptop.'

'Eileen?' His screen was now just showing a wall with some shelving that looked busy with ornamental owls. He could still hear that Eileen was replying, he even found himself wishing for her to pick her screen back up. Owls could look very accusing when frozen in porcelain.

'I'll be right with you, sir. Perhaps you would tip off that lovely nurse.'

'You're coming here?' Harry said, disbelieving.

'I know what will happen if I don't.' Her reply sounded even more distant. 'I'll come in tomorrow and there you'll be, sat at your desk, wires hanging off you, maybe even a backless gown, God forbid.' Harry saw his own eyebrows lift at this. Then he heard a huff and some mumbling far enough away to make it indiscernible. Then a kitten meowed before the screen lifted from wherever it had been discarded. Eileen's voice came back louder than ever. 'My husband was the same. Kept putting off his rest and then he died. Well, now he has all the rest he needs, the flaming idiot.'

The screen went blank, Harry's phone announced it was over.

Eileen Holmans had left the conversation.

# CHAPTER 53

When Maddie left her home early in the morning, she was cussing and hurrying in equal measure. Sleep had taken a while to come, her mind a constant battle of everything she had done in the investigation versus what she hadn't. For Maddie, periods of poor sleep were a regular part of the work. Being a detective was very little about celebrating the capture of an offender or the solving of a crime, most of the time was spent kicking yourself for not having done it sooner.

She emerged still putting her jacket on, her bag too, while trying to operate the phone jammed between her shoulder and her ear. It was her second attempt that morning at calling Harry Blaker and the second to go straight to voice-mail. She didn't see the point in leaving another message.

She bundled into her car. It was a job car, to be precise. Her own had given up the ghost. There were perks to her job, even if this particular perk smelt like a McDonald's restaurant discovered after a decade of being sealed shut. It was also reluctant to start up. It was ten years old, a decade of mistreatment from stressed out coppers with no time for mechanical sympathy. Maddie wasn't so far off a decade in Major Crime herself and she was finding her own start-ups could be just as reluctant.

'Eileen,' Maddie said, the moment the call connected to the Bluetooth, 'I overslept.'

'Morning, ma'am. I don't think you're due on duty until 0800 hours, officially. I'm not sure we can class you as late just yet.'

'I wanted to be early. What have we got going on in there? Are the digital team in?'

'I would assume so, ma'am. They were given strict instructions to commence at 07.00 hours.'

'Are you not in with them?' Maddie was confused. The latest she had known Eileen arrive at her post, no matter where they were in the county, was 7 a.m.

'I am walking the last mile. Maybe ten minutes away. I can call you with an update when I arrive?'

'Okay . . .' Maddie had a question, but no right to ask it. Eileen helped her out.

'I slept in myself, ma'am. Quite deliberately, you understand. I had a late night, so I set my alarm for a little later accordingly. Eight hours is very important to me.'

'Working late?'

'No, no. A little socialising, that's all.'

Maddie was moving now, the sea twinkled through her open window and Maddie smiled out at it. She had conjured an image in her mind of Eileen Holmans dating — definitely wearing slippers — and how that might play out. She was desperate to know more.

'Yes then, give me a call when you get in if there's anything to talk about. I'm not heading straight in, I want to go and speak to Ryan Archer's dad again, see if he has remembered anything that might help us find Chloe. I'm also hoping to speak to Ryan's probation officer and his solicitor today.'

'Still with Chloe Falconer in mind, ma'am?'

'Yes, but I still don't think we know enough about Archer. I'm still not set on his motivation.'

'Understood. I have already constructed a list of all Ryan Archer's known associates and split them down into sections.

The two you mention you will find in the professional section. The spreadsheet has all of their details, but I will call ahead so they know you are coming and you don't waste a trip.'

'Of course you have! And thanks, that would be great.' Maddie paused for a moment of dead air, where Eileen might have been expecting the call to end, but Maddie couldn't help herself. 'I'm glad you had a good night.' She felt like a schoolgirl teasing her mate at the back of the bus.

Eileen thanked her, seemed in a hurry to get off the phone and Maddie's grin widened.

# CHAPTER 54

Maddie chose to go to the solicitor first, but it would be far from straightforward.

'She's gone out.' The receptionist blurted the words with some satisfaction and before Maddie could offer any introductions. Then he moved back behind an aggressively positioned display of leaflets with titles like *You've Been Arrested, What Next?* and *Your Rights and How They Will Be Protected.*

'I need to see someone called Megan Vrana,' Maddie said, calmly. 'My colleague called ahead to save either of us wasting any time.' She moved so she could see him. He was sitting behind a corner desk that was built around him; it reminded Maddie of the front counter at a police station, which made sense, seeing as it was often the same people they served.

'I took the call,' he said, helpfully.

'Excellent. So, she's aware.'

'It's literally my job to pass on her phone messages.' He sighed. 'But calling ahead is no guarantee of anything.'

'So, she went out anyway?'

'She has a busy diary.'

'As do I. My diary is full with a murder investigation that—'

'Oh, you know how diaries work, then?' He huffed. 'Only I did explain to your rather rude colleague about our system here. I offered her the next available appointment, which is the end of the week, 4 p.m., but—'

'Does Mrs Vrana have a mobile number? Other than the one advertised. I mean, she doesn't seem keen to pick that one up.'

'Almost like she's busy. And it's *Ms* Vrana.'

Maddie bit back her initial reaction. This was the first time she found herself really missing Harry Blaker. He would be growling by now, might even have bypassed the blockage completely to start opening the doors up to the rooms behind.

Bypass the blockage.

Maddie's mind was made up so quickly that she caught a number of people out, herself included. The man behind the desk was caught out too when she sidestepped him to make for the nearest door, wrenching it open to surprise the third person in the sequence.

Megan Vrana.

Maddie knew it was her, and not just because she was the only person in the room, though part-obscured behind a desk, a computer monitor and a fruit bowl. There were also a number of framed certificates high up on the wall behind her; each was awarded to *Ms Megan Vrana*.

'I was trying to get some breakfast,' she said, after her surprise fell away. She spoke through a mouthful of something, a delicate finger lifted to brush her lip. She wasn't speaking to Maddie, her eyes, darkened by liner, were lifted to pierce the man who had bundled in after her. He stayed filling the doorway while Maddie made herself comfortable in the seat opposite, reaching out to take a grape from the fruit bowl.

'She just pushed through!' he whined. Maddie waited for Megan Vrana to finally make eye contact.

'It's okay, Julian, you can leave us to it.' Megan then scooped up a spoonful of something that was heaped enough to bulge her cheeks. She took her time chewing. With the door closed, the room filled quickly with the scent of strong perfume.

'If he's the face of your business, you might want to consider how it could be a little more welcoming,' Maddie said, when she'd finished with her grape.

'We're a legal service, inspector. Which means we work on one side of an ongoing argument and not everyone will be welcome.'

'And this is a murder investigation, which means I couldn't care less.'

Megan Vrana took another large scoop of what was probably yoghurt. Again, there was a forced pause while she chewed it down. It seemed to be the last of it. She followed it up with a small mirror and an application of a purple lipstick, the shade of which reminded Maddie of the dead. The lips were always the first part to discolour.

'I fail to see how I can be of any use in a murder investigation,' Miss Vrana said, eventually. 'So, what is this? I assume you wish to talk to me about one of my clients, past or present, who is now a suspect in your murder enquiry and you're here to ask for information on this person. A current address perhaps? And, let me guess . . . by giving you this information I am effectively helping this person help themselves. Am I close?'

'That's what happens when you make yourself unavailable. You end up guessing. You know who I am, then?'

'I was expecting a Detective Inspector Maddie Ives.'

'To what? To wait out front until you were done with your yoghurt?'

Megan Varna eyed Maddie closely. 'You have a reputation. You know that right?'

'I put bad people away for a living. As far as defence solicitors go, I hope I'm utterly reviled.'

'Because they're all criminals, right? Which makes defence solicitors a part of the problem?' Ms Vrana pushed the yoghurt pot away to steeple her manicured fingers on the desk.

'I'm not here to talk about the politics of the legal system.'

'No, you're here to talk to me about one of my clients, one of the people you would label as guilty before the luxury of a trial.'

'Oh, but this one's special.'

'Go on . . .' Megan leaned forward a little to feign interest.

'This one's dead.'

There was a flicker of a response — blink and you'd miss it. 'Ryan Archer.' Megan shrugged as she sat back. 'I saw the news. We have worked together previously but I'm not sure how talking to me can be of any assistance.'

'He didn't like you, did he?' Maddie bit into a second grape, exaggerating her reaction. 'Bit sour.'

'I spend my life telling people what they do not want to hear. It's rarely the basis for a strong friendship.'

'He murdered three people,' Maddie said. 'Two of them police officers. Then there was a wife murdered in front of her two children. No matter what you thought of him, no matter what you think of me, no matter what you think comes under client confidentiality, this is bigger than all of that.'

'He never talked to me about killing people, I can tell you that much.'

'Did he talk to you?'

'Not really.'

'At first?'

'They all talk at first.'

'Give me a clue here, Megan.'

She huffed. Maddie had used her first name to try and make this a little more personable but it had definitely pissed her off. Megan Vrana was an easy read. She had sharp features made more prominent by a slim build. Her long nose was pointed to meet with those thin lips in their shade of corpse purple. Her eyes were piercing, an intensity about them that no doubt served her well when directed at some poor sap in a witness box. But she had met her match, something she might have realised as her bony shoulders slumped a little.

'Ryan Archer is — *was* — a thief. One of life's losers and that's not me speaking ill of the dead, he would tell you that himself.'

'His dad said as much.' Maddie shrugged.

'Quite. I had some rather frank conversations with his dad, too. The legal system doesn't work so well for people like Ryan, uneducated young men who start out in a life of crime as a juvenile, but manage to keep it up into adulthood. That's the turning point. I've seen it so many times. Get yourself tried as an adult and that's a criminal record that will go before you in anything you try to do from that point. And these people, the men in particular, they're still boys at eighteen.'

'I see it too,' Maddie said. 'Some still make it out the other side, though. I've seen young men like that go on to have good careers, a family life, a part in decent society.'

'Decent society?' Megan actually laughed. 'Are you new to your career? I don't meet too many of your lot who still believe in something like that.'

'The eternal optimist,' Maddie said, her smile frosting over. 'I have also seen men like Ryan go onto become career criminals, their violence increasing with their frustration. I've seen some despicable acts, but this . . . this feels like an escalation too far. Ryan Archer does not have the record of a man who might go from stealing cars to triple murder. There's a significant piece of this puzzle missing.'

'Frustration can be a very powerful thing.'

'You think he's capable of murder?'

Megan took her time to give an answer that was emphatic. 'Yes.'

'What makes you say that?'

'He didn't have to be quite such a loser. He was smart, actually. Smarter than most. And if he hadn't got off to a false start, he could have been someone. I think he knew that.'

'So, he murdered police officers because he didn't get the career he deserved?'

'His past pushed him in a certain direction and the police played a big role in his past. He became quite determined to be good at what he did, to outwit you lot. He did for a time too.'

'You mean a good thief?' Maddie said.

'And he was. He made mistakes when he was starting out, but he learned. That's why I say he was smart. We all make mistakes. It's the fool who makes the same one again.'

'That's lovely. Still quite a leap from stealing luxury cars to murdering in cold blood?'

Megan hesitated. Her lips twisted as if she was chewing it over. 'I would agree . . .'

'But?' Maddie probed.

'But in his modus operandi, or at least what it evolved into, there are echoes of the most dangerous people in our society.'

Megan Vrana was loosening up, dropping her guard a little. She was thinking, at least.

'His MO was identifying victims with multiple cars,' said Maddie. 'At least one of the cars would be something exotic, the type that was generally left at home. He would burgle the home for the keys and he had contacts who could make the car disappear before it was missed. What am I missing in there that makes him a killer?'

Megan still looked like someone considering her options. 'I mean burglary is a link. A lot of the worst killers in history started out breaking and entering. It's thrilling. I've been told that by enough burglars to know it must be true. Being inside someone else's house as a trespasser, watching them sleep, taking what you want. It's quite the power dynamic.'

'Is that what Ryan did? I have the impression of a man who got a job fitting windows and realised that he could use those skills to go after car keys when the victims were down the shops?'

'There was more to it than that. More to *him*.' Those corpse lips flickered into a sort of snarl.

'Go on . . .' Maddie said.

'Ryan Archer gained entry without the homeowner even knowing someone had been in. He would take a window out,

233

then put it right back in again as if it had never happened. The first entry was all for preparation, he would use what he could find, like a calendar hanging on the wall with a week's holiday listed or a long weekend away at a wedding. We all do it. Then he would go back with all the time he needed to relieve them of their exotic sports car. By the time it was even discovered, the vehicle was long gone.'

'You almost sound impressed,' Maddie said.

'You make it sound like we can't be. You've never dealt with a criminal that you had a grudging respect for?'

'No.' Maddie hoped that she sounded convincing. 'And this all sounds like a man putting a lot of work into avoiding people — avoiding the need to be near anyone at all. I still don't see a link to violence.'

'But there was violence. One of his victims had employed a house-sitter. Mr Archer couldn't have known, and he got spooked. He lashed out for his first taste of prison life.'

'You're still not telling me anything I don't already know.'

'He made a mistake and he changed, evolved.'

'Evolved how?'

'You really don't know this?'

'Was it in the court papers? Did you divulge to the court how your client was evolving into the master burglar or did you give the bare minimum that is required for a guilty plea?'

'Everything was divulged that was required.'

'That wasn't the question,' Maddie said. 'So maybe you'll divulge it now.'

'It's not just holiday dates and social occasions written up on calendars for all to see. It's wi-fi codes too.'

'Wi-fi codes?'

'Every house needs one. And the big houses now, the vast majority, they'll have a smart security system. Just a doorbell in some cases, but some have a whole network of cameras.'

'He hacked into that network?' Maddie was thinking out loud.

'He didn't hack into anything. He set up his own.'

'I don't follow.'

Vrana sighed like it was oh-so-obvious. 'Mr Archer went in through the patio doors at a place that had a rather exotic car parked up in a barn. He noted a trip away, just like before, so he knew to return when the house was empty. He stole their spare house key. We all have one, right? And we would all just assume we had misplaced it if we even noticed it was gone at all.'

'So, he could let himself in whenever he wanted.'

'When he knew the house to be empty. Only, he needed to make sure it was *really* empty after his earlier experience. So, he started leaving cameras.'

'Cameras?'

'His own. The sort that link to the wi-fi, that activate on motion, that record sound and vision if you want. That are no larger than a matchbox — smaller even. Designed to blend into their surroundings with a battery that lasts a month or more.'

'He told you all of this? Why?'

Ms Vrana smiled and leaned back, stepping out of raconteur mode to bask in the aftermath. 'You know what men are like. They can't do something clever without someone knowing.'

'He was boasting.'

'He was very pleased with himself — and I tell you something else . . . he soon found himself *enjoying* the watching. There is your first real link to the worst of humanity out there. It's a power thing, like I said. He was watching those people going about their lives while he was preparing to ruin them. A part of it, at least. He would also put cameras up on the perimeters for comings and goings. He knew their patterns; he knew their *lives!*'

'Seems we did underestimate him,' Maddie said.

'I told you that I saw the news. If you're now telling me that Archer went into a police officer's home to cause harm, all I can tell you is just how much work he put into stealing a car.' She leaned forward, watching for Maddie's reaction.

'Which means we should expect the same MO if he was planning to commit murder.'

Vrana shrugged. 'We'll make a good detective of you yet.'

'A good detective asks you to put what you just said in a statement.'

'A good solicitor considers her reputation at all times. Not a chance.'

'While we're off the record, then, did Ryan Archer have any associates?'

'I wasn't defending his associates.'

'Were you not? There was a girl. Did he mention her?'

'I think I said already that he was a man who liked to boast. If I were to believe everything he said, there were any number.'

'I talked to his dad. He's under the impression there was one of particular significance.'

'If there were, it might be someone who was difficult to impress.'

'What does that mean?'

Ms Vrana took another moment of contemplation, still demonstrating as easy to read. 'He was always desperate to impress and there are some women out there that can make a man all the more desperate.'

'So, he told his girlfriend how clever he was, too?'

'Maybe she was the reason.' Ms Vrana shrugged. 'But I can't tell you about conversations he had with other people.'

'Did she go with him? To walk around in other people's homes, to enjoy the power dynamic you talked about. Maybe it was Ryan's idea, set her up as lookout to show her first-hand how clever he was.'

'Some women are not satisfied with being lookout.' Ms Vrana's eyes twinkled beneath that oppressive eyeliner, her dead lips twitching like they had more to say, more to reveal. She changed her mind. 'Now, if you don't mind, I feel I have offered all that I can.'

'Chloe?' Maddie leaned in for any reaction.

'Nope.'

'Nope? Is that a nope, I have the wrong name?'

'This whole conversation is now at the point of nope, Inspector Maddie Ives. I know the police make a habit of barging their way into places they're not lawfully allowed, but I'm very well versed on my rights. I told you what I know about the dead so that you may close your case and move on. But I do not wish to talk with you about the living.'

'Even if they're an accomplice? A danger to us all?'

Vrana took a moment to hold Maddie's stare. 'No one is anything until it is proven in a court of law, remember? I appreciate how that might be an inconvenience.' Megan Vrana pulled her laptop into view and lifted the lid. All of her attention now moved to its screen as her long fingernails clacked its keys.

'Chloe Lily Falconer.' Maddie persisted, now taking her moment to watch the other woman closely. 'You know her, don't you?' The tapping stopped. Vrana didn't look up straight away, but it came finally, with a very long sigh.

'You will have your own records and they will show that I met a young woman of that name a couple of times when I was doing the slog.'

*The Slog.* It was a reference to what most solicitors find themselves doing when they start out. It's the role of a solicitor called in to represent an arrested person in a custody suite. The role is to provide legal advice for those initial twenty-four hours. It was generally despised, but a necessary evil to get the experience needed to work in the courthouses or for a firm. It could be relentless too, prisoners backed up if you were unlucky — a real slog.

'You represented her?'

'I'm not sure you could call it that. She didn't talk to me anymore than she would have talked to you. That's hardly something I can *represent*. Very few prisoners get under my skin, detective, but she dug herself right in. She might just be the exception.'

'Exception?' Maddie said.

'Proven or not, of what she was accused then, she was guilty.'

'That's why I need to find her. You will have clients, people that might know where she is — might even be putting a roof over her head . . .'

Ms Vrana's snarl now seemed permanent. 'Are you asking *me* to become a police informant? Have you any idea of the legalities behind that? I think you should think a little harder around this subject and I will do you the favour of forgetting your request.'

Ms Vrana went back to her typing and Maddie stood up. The movement seemed to prompt a cramp in her stomach and she took a moment, her hand lifting to it instinctively. When it passed, she dropped her contact card onto the desk. This time there was no response.

'My number. Maybe, when I'm gone, you will think about the victims I described. Two parents and the two young children who found them. And maybe you might consider that we're not two sides of an argument at all, that we all want the same thing.'

'And what is that?' Ms Vrana lifted a snarl that was at its most intense yet. 'And don't you say justice!'

'Is that not what we're all here for?'

'I have your number. My assistant would have written it down.' Her eyes dropped back to her computer screen, the snarl remained.

'And now you have it again.'

Maddie was on the phone before she made it out of the building. Eileen Holmans picked up too fast — the first ring — and Maddie had to stall her until she could make it past the surly looking receptionist. Then she blurted out her needs all at once.

'Eileen, the search teams out at Frant and in Alan Day's house . . . They need to look for cameras. Concealed ones. And they need to scan the wi-fi for connections. I need everything connected accounted for.'

Of all Eileen's positive traits, she now demonstrated the one that Maddie appreciated the most. There were no follow-up questions, no asking why, she just noted the request and the urgency with which it was delivered and gave one word in response.

'Okay.'

# CHAPTER 55

Harry heard the door but didn't turn to it straight away, then he didn't need to turn at all.

'Resting as per orders I see, sir.'

Eileen was plainly in scolding-teacher mode and Harry couldn't help but feel guilty at being caught out of his hospital bed and hunched over scattered pieces of paper laid out on the surface of a locked cabinet.

'I remember a recent conversation, Eileen, where you made a prison for me out of this room. You said I couldn't leave. You didn't say I couldn't stand up.'

'I had to protest really rather strongly to get you this room, made you the subject of a national security concern, laid it on real thick. And they want it back. One word from me and they'll gladly put you out on the ward.'

'Uh-huh,' Harry muttered.

'I told them how you were famous, how you would be a security risk that they would need to deal with.'

'Uh-huh.'

'And I did that because I knew just how much you would despise being out in gen pop. Maybe I should have just left you, how did one of the young detectives put it earlier . . .'

She tutted as if it might assist her recall. 'On a ward among the moaning and the flatulent.'

'Who's famous?' Harry spun on his bare heels to face Eileen, her stance exactly as he expected with hands on hips and head slightly tilted.

'Poor turn of phrase. High profile.' She rocked her head to the other side and eyed him closer. 'Have you ever actually Googled yourself, Inspector Blaker?'

'What the hell does that mean? Are you being foul?'

'No, sir. I can assure you I am not. But thank you for the image . . . You will have used Google in the past, I'm sure. Have you ever taken the opportunity to put in your own name as a search parameter?'

'Why would I do that?'

'To see what comes up. In your case, rather a lot. You were shot on duty as part of the arrest of a serial killer. It was big news. I only clicked through the first few pages of results but the coverage was comprehensive. They even got a photo of you out and about in your bandaging after your release from—'

'What's your point?'

'There isn't really one. It's just something that I used to get you this room. You're welcome by the way.'

'You could be right.' His mind clicked into a new gear and new direction.

'About what, specifically?'

'About officers being targeted.'

'You mean individual officers? I've been through everything we have regarding Ryan Archer. There's nothing that links him to PC Philip Jones and only the very tenuous link to PS Alan Day that I have already shared.'

'And Chloe Falconer?'

'She mostly has the same associations and links as Ryan Archer, which means I can't link her to the victims either. Not yet, at least.'

'Yet?'

'I'm still working through the material. I've got pocket-books and search records coming back from secure storage.

It's taking a little longer than it should. There shouldn't be anything in that material that isn't on a digital system, but it will need going through to be sure.'

'Maybe it doesn't matter, anyway,' Harry said. 'Maybe we already know the job that links them.'

'How do you mean?'

'If the target was the police in general — any one of us — then Phil Jones was an ideal candidate. He works an isolated area on his own and he wasn't exactly switched onto threats.'

'Okay.'

'So, someone got to him, made a scene and then saw who turned up.'

'Alan Day and his search team,' Eileen said.

'The search team, CSI, PCSOs . . . any number of response officers. There was a crowd of ghouls, our missing offender could have been in amongst that crowd looking for someone to pick off.'

'Ghouls, sir?'

'Police term. Anyone who turns out to watch the police clean up something messy.'

'Very apt. Acting Inspector Ives has voiced a similar theory, sir.'

'Did she do anything about it?'

'Yes, actually. The . . . ghouls were the task of a PCSO and—'

'So, you have a list?' Harry cut back in.

'I do not. The PCSO in question . . . Well, he was not able to get names.'

'What happened?'

'He said that he asked the group and there was one woman among them who didn't take too kindly. Started spouting Human Rights legislation at him and blocked anyone else from giving them up. The irony is that she was mouthing off about how the police should be out there looking for the killer, not taking the names of innocent people merely concerned at what their village was turning into. She was really rather aggressive.'

'The PCSO said that?'

'No, no, I saw it myself. The DC tasked with getting the names gave me a summary as to why they hadn't got them, and I deduced that the PCSO might have had the common sense to at least switch their camera on. It's in the training, right? If someone refuses details, at least capture them—'

'And he did?'

'He did and I moved the footage over.'

Harry shook his head. 'Why are you not one of my detectives?' His frustration was real.

'Because I've seen what happens to them. The pressure, the lack of sleep, the falling over and waking up in hospital beds. Not to mention the whole getting shot thing.'

'Is this where you tell me that Chloe Falconer was one of those ghouls?'

'It is not. But I should warn you that it was far from definitive. The PCSO is rather young in service. Young in general, in fact. Once he was told off, he rather retired, stepped away.'

'He said that?'

'He did when I pushed him. He was a little reluctant, but he admitted that a number of people arrived — men and women — after he had recorded those present and he didn't make any further attempts.'

'Outstanding,' Harry growled. 'Can you forward it to me still? The footage.'

'In exchange for you getting back into bed and getting some rest?'

'That won't work anymore. I'm just waiting for the doc to do his rounds and they're kicking me out.'

'They told you that?' Eileen's hands clamped back onto her hips.

'I'll be telling them.'

# CHAPTER 56

The role of Maintenance seemed like a bit of an oxymoron in the surroundings where Maddie Ives' meeting with Neil Archer took place. He worked at a power station, a huge site, half of which was in the process of being decommissioned. The other half would remain functional, but only following a last-ditch reprieve that still wasn't confirmed. The result was a place that had been stumbling for years towards termination with no budget, necessity or appetite for improvements. The walls were faded, peeling and mottled by damp, the sight of which was backed up wholeheartedly by the smell.

It reminded Maddie of much of the police estate.

'I really don't know what you think I can tell you that I didn't already.' Neil seemed even smaller than she remembered, more slight in his build, wrapped as he was in a light blue overall that gathered at the sleeves and ankles. 'I only agreed to meet because I saw on the telly that you're looking for someone else. That makes sense, see. Means it weren't my boy that did what you said. Not for sure.'

'It means there's a big chunk of the story that we're missing,' Maddie admitted.

'I'm not sure what I can tell you.'

'Tell me about his mates. The people that he hung around with.'

'He wasn't . . . Ryan didn't do so well with mates. When he was a lot younger, sure, he had loads of mates. A whole gang of them. But they used him, no other way of saying it. Ryan was looking to impress. You know what it's like when you're young. He did whatever they dared him to do. That was when he first started to get in trouble. He did work out what was going on, but not in time. He left them to it after that.'

'That was it? He must have had people that he went out for a beer with. Who was he calling when he fancied a Saturday night out?'

'He . . . He didn't do so well with going out either. Had a few problems that must have come from his mother's side.'

'Problems? Do you mean her mental health?'

'You were listening then. I thought it was all just that gruff fellow. Thought maybe you were just there as the eye candy, you know, to get in the door. Used to be a bit of a trick for the door-to-door people I worked with on the window fitting.'

'That's a real progressive version of women in policing you have there.'

Neil Archer's expression changed to that of a man caught with his hand in someone else's cookie jar. 'I didn't mean nothing by it. Sorry, love. I know you can't speak like that no more. This is a world that's got away from me — what you can say, what you can't say. Especially when it comes to girls.'

'Yeah, you gotta be real careful around those girls. I wouldn't worry about it.'

'That's why I never really dated. Not since . . . not since she left. It's all on the phone now, right? Apps. Where you gotta put your mug up on there then write something under to explain why you look like you do. I couldn't get into all that.'

'What about Ryan? Did he use those apps?'

'Probably. Sometimes he was good at talking. You could take him out and he'd be talking to everyone. Other times you couldn't get a word out of him. That was how his mother started.'

'Ryan was depressed?'

'Not formally. But you live with something long enough and you know how it looks.'

'But he wasn't on any medication for it?'

'You'd need to go and see a doctor to get medication. Ryan never liked doctors. I told him to go. Begged him on one occasion.'

'It got bad?'

Neil Archer nodded. There was a stainless-steel counter a step to his left and he reached for it, seemingly needing the support. 'Same old story. He would be up and then something would happen, some sort of trigger, and he would come crashing down. Most of the time it was a girl problem.'

'Chloe?' Maddie said.

'She was the damp that you just couldn't fix.' He nodded at the surroundings to illustrate his meaning.

'And you said they were together ten years?'

'Off and on. They were just teenagers. She moved to the area, started hanging out with the group and I reckon he had a thing for her straight away. That was when he started with the showing off, it was all for her.'

'Did she encourage it?'

'I reckon she liked it, for sure.'

'Liked it?'

'Having men do what they might otherwise not, just to impress her. She must've, 'cause he spent the next ten years or more doing just that.'

'What do you mean?'

'She was a bad influence. Bad to the bone, that girl. Did you catch up with her yet? Did you speak? You meet her and you'll know exactly what I mean.'

'My colleague met her. Only briefly, but it was enough to get an impression.'

'If you want to be arresting anyone, it should be her. Like I said, bad to the bone.'

'Bad enough to be involved in murder?'

Neil Archer was stopped in his tracks where he had been in full flow. He had lots to say, then he had nothing. He might even have been holding his breath. His focus was lost, the sign of a man deep in thought. 'I think she could kill someone. At least I think she might want to. Decent people like you and me, it never crosses their mind. My Ryan was a decent person too. I know you won't believe that.'

'Did Ryan ever talk about her being violent?'

'He talked about violence happening around her. They would go out for a drink. Ryan would be sat minding his own business and she would start pecking at people around her, trying to get a wind up. Or she would make a beeline for some lad stood up at the bar, knowing Ryan could see and she would start all the flirting. She knew what Ryan was like, knew it was only going to end one way.'

'Ryan was jealous?'

'Every man is jealous.'

'But he would get violent when he was jealous?'

'Not with anyone else. He came home with bruises, did his ankle good too, one time. He told me how it had gone down, looked right at me and told me that girl was trouble. Of course, I said then that he needed to cut her loose, that it couldn't end well and he knew I was right. He didn't listen though, of course he didn't.'

'You said you met her only once?'

'I met her more than that. I said she only came to my place once. I can't say I knew her well, but that don't mean I didn't know her. It was like a drug to her. And like any drug she was needing a bigger hit every time to get her thrills.'

'She was escalating?'

'They both were.'

'Do you have an example?'

'Not that I want to talk about.' His focus was back; there had been eye contact but he looked away now, like a schoolboy who knew he was about to get into trouble. Maddie shifted, moving to where a table was set up against the mottled wall. The top was Formica, stained with tea rings that overlapped, like a mood board for the creation of the Olympic symbol. It wobbled too, the moment she brushed it as part of taking a seat. Neil Archer stayed where he was, still leaning on the side for support, still with his eyes to the floor. 'There was a touch of his mother in her,' he said, so quietly that Maddie almost missed it.

'How do you mean?'

'The anger she had. You ask me about Ryan hating the police? That was Chloe's trick.'

'Why?'

'That I don't know. I saw it in her, just like I saw it in his mother.'

'Ryan's mother had an issue with the police?'

'She had every reason.' He snapped straighter now, his eyes lifting, their intensity piercing.

'And what was that reason?'

'You done your digging, all about me and my family. You already know.'

'You would be surprised at just how much there is to do on a case like this. I can't say we've looked into Janet too closely. What should we know?'

'Typical police, never turn up with the full story. She was sectioned. Mental Health Act, right?'

'It's a police power,' Maddie confirmed, 'but it's not used lightly and it's for the safety of—'

'DON'T!' The word stood him straight and forced spittle out in a clump, some residue stayed on his lip and his movement to clear it was slow and deliberate via his overalled sleeve. 'We heard it enough. Back then. We heard a lot of lies, too. So many that you could never tell the true bits among them. She could cope, just about, when she was at home. Once you took her out of that house it became much more of a struggle. She used to come back . . . It was like a different person.'

'She was sectioned?'

'A month at a time. Those places . . .'

'I'm sorry, Neil, really I am. That you had to go through that, all of you. The system still isn't great today, but it's better than it was twenty years ago. I can't imagine.'

'It was Ryan that suffered the most. They took his mum away and she would fight, we all would. Then they would try and reassure him, tell him that she hadn't done anything wrong.' He slumped back to take a lean. 'Can you imagine what that did? He was six years old. He loved his mother like any boy would. He sure got a warped idea of the police, of what you are.'

The only sound now was a ticking clock and a dripping urn.

'We're guilty of that sometimes,' Maddie said. 'We deal with what we see but we can't be there for the aftermath.'

'No, you told us that was someone else's job. Never did quite work out who. Then I realised you lot meant me.'

'It must have been hard.'

'For me? Forget about me. Think about Janet. She used to talk about the bond with Ryan, how she never felt it, not the sort you see with mums and their boys that starts strong and only grows stronger. But she used to see his face, used to see how scared he got when she was struggling and the guilt from that ate her alive, sped up her spiral. He was never more scared than when a load of uniforms turned up to cart her away.'

Maddie needed to change the direction. She needed to get some focus back in Neil's eyes.

'I know a little more,' she said, then waited for the words to sink in, for Neil to look at her. 'About how Ryan was operating when he was stealing cars.'

'What does that matter?'

'He did a little more than break into places for keys. He installed cameras in the houses so he would know the right time to go back. He watched his victims for up to a month beforehand and he might have *enjoyed* doing it.'

It was the word *camera* that marked the point when Neil's head started shaking.

'That was her! That was Chloe!'

248

Maddie gestured at the other seat. 'Tell me what that means, Neil.'

Neil dragged his feet for all of three paces. The seat dragged too, catching on the stone floor. His fall was heavy, his head was too, judging by the way he took it in his hands. Maddie gave him a moment to sort his thoughts, to sit back and to start talking again.

'Ryan got caught out. Some fella left in a house that he hadn't been expecting. I didn't know about none of this, okay, not until it was all done and dusted. So then he changed up what he was doing. Used cameras. But it was outside the houses, not in. Just so he could see the people leave, see them packing up their cars for a weekend away and also he would get a notification ping up on his phone if anyone else went in or if they came back.'

'He did put cameras in the house, though, so that isn't all that he did.'

'She did! At least, she told him to. It was Chloe that liked to sit there watching, that liked to see the lives these people were living. She didn't grow up nice. Moved all over the place, housed by the council, no dad, mum a loser and in a household where there was never any money. My Ryan told me how she would just sit there and watch these rich people going about their lives. She would get to know every detail and then she would talk about how best to mess it all up. She especially liked it when it was families, 2.4 children and a picket fence. The more perfect the family, the more she wanted to fuck it all up.'

'By stealing their spare car?'

'That was Ryan's thing. But not for long, he didn't want to be doing that anymore. But Chloe, she wanted more. She wanted to take anything they could, anything and everything. Not like a normal burglar either, not for some cash on the black market. She wanted to mess with their heads.'

'And did they?'

'No. Ryan put the cameras inside these places for the same reason he did anything, to impress her. But when she talked about burglary, about wanting to go with him, about getting involved, he would shut her down. She would still watch the cameras on his laptop, but he would never tell her where they were.'

'So, she was part of it?'

Neil Archer smiled. 'Not if you lot were ever to ask her, she weren't.' And then he stiffened, the chair squalled beneath him. 'That's what happened, isn't it? We had a few beers back home after a Palace game and I knew he wanted to talk about something. It was her, how she was getting out of control. He told me he was stopping, that she was pushing him to do more and he didn't want any part of it. But he didn't stop at all. He changed to what she wanted him to do, just like he always did. She knew him. Better than anyone. Knew all about his mum and what happened. It wouldn't be difficult for someone like that, someone like her, to make him hate the police every bit as much as she did.'

'I . . . we can't know that. Not right now.'

'You have to arrest her. She'll lie, but everyone lies to you, right? You have your ways of getting to the truth.'

'Do you know where she might be, Mr Archer? Did Ryan ever talk about somewhere that she would go to if she was lying low — or someone, perhaps?'

'He . . . no. That one time she came to mine, it was . . . She was hiding then. The police came straight to my place. They knew those two were together and I . . . I lied for them. I said I wouldn't again, but I did that time. I lied for her!'

'It's okay.'

'I lied for that evil bitch! And now look! Look what she did to my son. Look where we are!' Neil Archer was starting to lose it, the transition from angry to sad gradual, but complete. Maddie stood back up, moving to where the dripping urn clung to the wall, rusting from the arse up. Neil had started making them a drink, got as far as dropping two teabags in two cups. She filled one of them to take back over to Neil. The delay was long enough for him to have gathered himself up a little.

'I think I've taken enough of your time,' she said. 'If you think of anything that might help, you have my number.'

He nodded vigorously. 'I'll ask about. I know some of his old friends. I'm not sure it will do us much good, but they'll know who Chloe is. Maybe they're still in touch.' He pulled a phone from his pocket to stare at. It was old, as old as Maddie had seen for a while, the sort that pre-dated smartphones. Its appearance cemented the impression she now had of Neil Archer.

He wasn't going to be of any more use.

# CHAPTER 57

'Do you have any idea how difficult it was to get in here? Most of the police stations in the county are easier to get into than this room.' Maddie spoke while taking in the form of Harry for the first time since bearing witness to his collapse. Just like in that moment, he looked like shit, the right side of death, at least. He was gaunt and pale, his skin waxy under the white lights of the ceiling, an effect that made his cheeks stand out where they were marred by clumps of burst capillaries. His lips contrasted in a dark red.

'Not difficult enough,' Harry growled, then licked those lips. He sounded even gruffer than normal.

'Been busy?' She nodded towards the papers stacked up on top of a laptop bag. 'How did you get that in here?'

'I had it with me the whole time.'

Maddie smiled at the lie. 'Anything useful?'

'Just keeping up to speed.'

'Any thoughts?'

'We're a long way off. Unless you're here to tell me something different.' He eyed her closely.

'I didn't come here to talk to you about work.'

'But if you did, what would you say?' There was still intensity in him, a hunger for answers that belied his physical state.

'I would say that very little has changed and then I would say that you shouldn't really be worrying about it, that you have a very good team working night and day to make progress.'

'Is there progress?'

Maddie broke the stare and took a moment to look around. Harry was in an individual room, a television with wires hanging out like innards and some low cabinets the only real furniture. The walls were white, the floor too and not a single touch of homeliness. Maddie couldn't help thinking that anyone else in that room, in those circumstances, would at least have a smattering of get-well-soon colour.

'You did well getting put in here out of the way.'

'Eileen,' Harry said.

'Of course. I should have brought her with me. I would probably have a hot drink by now. And a biscuit.'

'There's a machine in the family room across the way. A Costa in the foyer.'

'Is that a hint.'

'Seeing as you refused to stay away, you might as well make it worth my while. But when you come back, we'll call it Part Two, where Part One was the small talk.'

* * *

Maddie stepped out of the room, aware of someone shuffling up to her as she pulled the door shut. it was the same nurse she had needed to convince that she should be let in. She was instantly different. She had been surly and obstructive, only wavering when Maddie had laid it on thick, explaining how she had been with Harry when he had collapsed. Now she was awkward, shuffling from one foot to another, her head slightly tilted, her expression that of a motherly smile. 'Are you okay?' she said.

'I'm okay,' Maddie confirmed. 'It's nice to see him.'

'And how is he?'

'Harry Blaker is not the best candidate for hospitalisation. I feel like I should apologise for him. Don't take it to heart, he's like that with everyone.'

'He's been fine, actually. His wife has been keeping him in good order. There's no doubt who's in charge in that relationship!'

'His wife?'

'Eileen?' The nurse's expression was now of someone considering that they had put their foot in something as sticky as it was smelly.

'Oh, very much in charge!' Maddie grinned.

'We thought we would see her today, after . . . after the doctor did his rounds. I suggested to Mr Blaker that he might like to give her a call, but he didn't seem to have the intention. When he agreed to speak to you, I wondered . . . I wondered if you know her well enough to be able to speak with her?'

'I know her well. We'll be speaking later today, actually. She . . . she works away.'

'Ah, that would explain why her visiting times have been a little out of the ordinary.'

'It would. Is there something specific you would like me to pass on? Something he needs?'

The nurse bit her lip, clearly contemplating her next words. 'Well, I can't really be . . . I just wondered if you could pass on that Mr Blaker might need the advice of his family right now. I get the impression that there's children, but he's not . . . he's not exactly an open book.'

'He certainly isn't that and I will pass that on. But I'm sure you can imagine how that would prompt a lot more questions from the family. Can you give me a little more, enough to put their mind at rest, perhaps?'

'Hospitals are not always places where minds are put at rest.' She looked away, her eyes to the floor. 'Just like families are not always there to endorse a decision made by a patient. Sometimes they need to challenge that decision. They need to make their husband or their dad see some sense.'

'I'll make sure I pass that on too.'

'I . . . thank you.' The nurse hurried away, not looking back. Maddie's walk to the foyer was long enough for her to be able to run the conversation back through her mind. She got two teas, Harry's a decaf. She didn't know much about heart conditions, but caffeine seemed like a bad idea.

'What have they said, then,' Maddie asked a moment after she'd kicked Harry's door open with enough force to cause the patient to jerk upright. 'About you going home?'

'No sudden movements,' he croaked. 'That's what the nurses said. And no surprises.'

'You're welcome,' Maddie said, making a show of putting his drink down next to him. 'Well? The nurse said the doctor's done his rounds. I assume he's the guy who can send you home?'

'She,' Harry corrected her.

'Of course it's a woman. Smartest person in the hospital, I'd bet.'

'Seemed to know her stuff.'

'What did she say, then? How long did she remand you for? And can your time served be halved with good behaviour?'

'Very good.' He still avoided any answer.

'I spoke to Faye.' Maddie tried a different angle with the mention of his eldest daughter.

'I know.'

'You spoke to her too?'

'Messaging, but we will speak properly.'

'When?' Maddie said, unperturbed by the look that told her it was none of her damned business. 'Only the nurse out there, she seemed to think you might want your family here?' Maddie stepped in closer so she wouldn't miss a beat of his reaction.

'It's not always about what I want.'

'You don't think she would want to be here?'

'I told you this was Part Two.' Harry made a *cheers* gesture with his tea, then sipped it.

'This isn't small talk, Harry, this is important.'

'Not as important as the case. There might still be a threat out there, we need to make sure it's completely extinguished.'

'I tell you what. I give you the latest update, then we talk about Faye and you actually engage. How does that sound?'

'What's your update?'

Maddie considered for a moment, then took a lean on the units to fold her arms. 'I got hold of Archer's solicitor. I got excited for a moment there, I thought I might have got some sort of breakthrough, but it fell flat.'

'What breakthrough?'

'She told me a little more about Archer and his offending. A lot more, actually. His MO was a lot more specific than we realised. We know he was a car-key burglar. We know he targeted high-end cars, and we know he had contacts who could get rid of them. We also know that he used a previous career in fitting windows to *unfit* them as a way of getting in.'

'We did.'

'We didn't know that he took his preparation so seriously and how it was evolving all the time. He would gain entry to a home and take spy cameras with him, the sort that run off wi-fi. He would set them up in the home or on the perimeter of the home so he could see comings and goings, with the intention of coming back. He even tracked some cars to get a pattern of movement. It was all so he would know the right time to strike, be able to get away clean.'

'That is more than we knew.'

'Neil Archer told us that his son's defence solicitor persuaded him to go guilty, now we know why.'

'Sentencing,' Harry said.

'Exactly. The judge sentenced him as a common burglar, a chancer who broke into houses for a set of car keys. Had he known the premeditation element, the invasion of privacy, the planning and just how much Archer knew about his victims . . .'

'He might still be in.' Harry sat a little straighter. 'So, you fed this back to the search teams, for spy cameras?'

'I only got the info this morning. The search teams have it as part of their tasking today. I also got the techies out to do a full sweep for devices that link to the wi-fi. That's a much faster process, so I already know that they didn't find anything. The early word from the search team isn't positive either.'

'Where? The village hall and Alan Day's place?'

'And Philip Jones' place too. I know he wasn't attacked there, but I thought it best to be safe.'

'And nothing?' Harry's voice was a little more urgent.

'Nothing,' Maddie said. 'Your girlfriend's safe.' Then she held her hands up in response to his expression. 'A joke, just a joke! You had a connection, that's all. I totally understand what it was.'

'Inappropriate,' Harry growled and Maddie kept her palms up until he continued. 'So, Archer has an MO he knows and trusts, one that worked for the most part and then he ditched it for his most serious offending?'

'Doesn't sound likely, does it?'

'No. So we're back to his accomplice, to the other person in that car. It stands to reason that they would know about the cameras, might even have been party to installing them. Which means they would know to remove them.'

'They would. *She* would. Neil Archer talked a little more about Chloe. Ryan told him that Chloe knew all about what he was up to and how excited it made her. She wanted to be involved. She was to a point. Ryan had her watching the cameras when he went back as some sort of a remote lookout.'

'She didn't go with him.'

'I said he was evolving. I think we can assume she was a big part of that. I'm convinced she was going with him, that she went with him when he was intent on murdering police officers, that she might even have been the one driving that idea.'

Harry ran a big hand over his face, it had the effect of pulling the loose skin of his cheeks down, exposing the veins of his tired eyes. 'And we still haven't found her?'

'No. We talked about the source team being our best bet. We've got a strong budget signed off to offer up for information. Source fully mobilised today and they'll be talking to anyone they have with access to Chloe's world. It's a long list. Someone on it will take the money and talk. I'm positive there'll be movement on her soon.'

Harry looked thoughtful for a moment. 'The techies . . . can they see if camera devices had been attached to the wi-fi before?'

'No. I asked the same question. A router doesn't have a memory.'

Harry harrumphed. It turned into a cough, his face contorting like it might have been a painful one. 'Of course it doesn't. I keep hearing how technology is the answer—' He cut off for another grimace that prompted Maddie to take a step forward. He was breathing heavily, like the strain of sitting up was too much.

'Harry?' Maddie said.

'I'm fine.'

'I was good to my word. That's your update. Now we need to talk about you. Did you want me to call Faye and ask her to come down here?'

'No.' Harry's reply was instant. 'She's got her own life — a busy one.'

'Everyone thinks they're busy until something like this happens.'

'Like what? I'm waiting to go home. I would be wasting her time.'

'Would you?' Maddie leaned in, locking onto Harry, sensing there was more to say.

'She wouldn't come, okay. I didn't ask her to, not outright, but she had the opportunity to offer.'

'So, you have spoken to her.'

'We've spoken.'

'And she knows all that she needs to know to make an informed decision?' Maddie picked up on the hesitation in replying. 'I thought not.'

'We're not . . . It's not like it used to be. Her view of me isn't like it used to be. It's my fault. She's mostly right, if I'm honest.'

'Is she? And are you doing anything to change that view?'

'The best thing I can do right now is to leave her alone. She needs space and time.'

'To do what?'

'To come to terms with what I am in her life.'

'What does that mean?'

'It means she had a mother and a sister. She had a family. Now she doesn't. I'm the common denominator in that, that's something I can't deny.'

'And your solution to that is to take away her dad, too? Do you really think that's what she wants? She needs you around more than ever.'

'What she needs is something to blame, someone. Maybe that's how she makes sense of all that has happened to her. I would rather she had that than being driven crazy trying to work out why else the world came for her twice.'

'Wow! A realisation like that could be the sort of thing to keep a person up at night.' Maddie still watched him closely.

'Life isn't always straightforward.'

'Still sounds like a cop-out, to me. Maybe you just don't have the balls to tell her what's really going on here, what that doctor told you earlier today. Maybe because you know it would make all the difference and you would have to be a dad again. And there was me thinking you were braver than that, the bravest man I knew, even. There's nothing more terrifying than the truth.'

'You want to talk to me about bravery?' Harry spat. 'You want to talk to me about keeping the truth from the people we love? Vince doesn't know, does he?'

Maddie had been ready with what she was going to say next, still on the front foot, but this took her right off it, almost right off balance. She gripped the struts at the side of his bed to keep herself steady. Her right hand then lifted to rest against her stomach, a movement that was instinctive.

'Know what?' Her own voice sounded strangled.

'Exactly.' Harry scowled again, gasping a deep breath to come back with a rasp to his voice. 'Nothing more terrifying than the truth?'

## CHAPTER 58

Maddie made her way across the car park, following the directions from her phone that were so detailed, she couldn't help but smile. They were so Eileen.

As instructed, she followed the building line around to the left, away from the overloaded bin ringed by spent cigarettes, away from the car park too and across a paved path that was slicing up a small garden. The instructions took her left at Ante-natal and then she found herself counting her own steps for a walk of twenty paces to an alley between two buildings. It was twenty paces exactly. No doubt Eileen had done some maths to compensate for Maddie's longer stride. At the other end she found a smaller car park, barrier protected. It was for staff only.

And Eileen Holmans.

'How did you even get in here?' Maddie said, as a passenger door was pushed to meet her. She took a seat. The car was small, Eileen's personal one, with a Nissan logo in the middle of the steering wheel and a dated feel. It was immaculate, however. It even smelled nice, an owl shaped air-freshener with oversized eyes doing a fine job. 'Could we not just have sat out in the main car park? Or met along the road?'

'There are some areas that patients can walk, this is the only place you can park that isn't overlooked by any of them. There should be no way for Mr Blaker to see us here.'

'Harry didn't look to me like he was turning out for a stroll any time soon. What does it matter if he sees us talking, anyway?'

Eileen looked horrified. 'I don't want him to think we are in cahoots!'

'We are in cahoots, Eileen. We work on the same team. I told him I needed you to get me in and I told you that you were very welcome to come in with me.'

'Men like Harry Blaker . . .' Eileen paused for thought. 'It's the *linking*, that's what I always found with that type. Things happen around them, things that you do and that's fine, but you should never show them how.'

Maddie was rarely speechless, but it took her a moment or two to think of a response to that. 'There's always a bigger picture with you, isn't there? Just what is the end game for Eileen Holmans?'

Eileen smiled out her next words. 'Oh, just a little world domination. How is he?'

'That's the reason I asked you to come.'

'You think he'll tell me something that he didn't tell you?' Eileen said, her face screwed up by doubt.

'No. But the nurse might. Somehow, she has the impression you're his wife?'

'I know! Never been so offended in all my life. I am quite some way out of that man's league.'

'So, you didn't suggest that for your own advantage? And you put her right, so that the medical staff wouldn't overstep when it came to patient confidentiality?'

'Absolutely not, ma'am. I played on it from the off and I will continue to do so.'

'That is good to hear. I need you to do just that. The nurse in there, she was talking in riddles, but the summary seemed to be that Harry's not following medical advice.'

'I'm not sure I would need a medical expert to tell me that, ma'am.'

'But there's something about Harry's condition, something she wanted to tell me. Something she might tell his wife.'

'And you want to know what it is?'

'I need to know what's going on, just how bad this is. Reading between the lines, Harry isn't helping himself.'

Eileen nodded with vigour. 'There's a team of nurses, but one in particular seems to be most useful. She slips out on occasion for a coffee from the foyer. I'll set up there. The hospital wi-fi isn't the best, but it will be good enough. I can still keep on top of the search for Chloe.'

'If anyone can.' Maddie grinned. 'Your nurse . . . strawberry blonde bob, slim build?'

Eileen nodded. 'Annie.'

'Makes sense. She was the one who suggested I call his *wife*.' Eileen reacted by stepping up out of the car. Maddie did the same, their eyes meeting over the top of the shiny, blue roof. 'Are you leaving your car here?' Maddie said. 'This is a staff car park. They're pretty hot in these places.'

Eileen answered first with a *thunk* of her central locking, then with a dismissive wave. 'I had a word. I'm pretty much on the team.'

# CHAPTER 59

Harry was not a man for regrets, but he regretted the conversation with Maddie. How it had ended, specifically. It was a regret that was to linger for the ninety minutes more he had to wait for the doctor's final visit. She came with the results that were expected and with an attitude that hadn't changed: Harry needed to stay.

She even brought along a surgeon to back up that opinion, who repeated the same warnings and then made an offer to make an immediate space in his diary.

*We just need to get scrubbed up and you can come right down.*

But Harry was to refuse again. Then he thanked them with genuine sincerity when they stopped trying and warned him to expect a call very soon with a date to return, if he could fit it into his busy schedule. This was said with crossed arms, through an expression that was a mix of anger and concern that only doctors could muster.

Then he was told, in no uncertain terms, of his immediate future. He would be lacklustre, tired at the slightest effort, short of breath and often dizzy. He needed to rest, be easy on himself and, more than anything, should be avoiding any element of stress.

Harry actively agreed to it all, but none of the people in that room believed it for a moment.

Despite the stark warning, the exhaustion still caught Harry out. He had expected his strength to return the moment he stepped back out into the sunlight. Instead, it had contrived to take his breath away, to have him falling into the back of a taxi, then breathing so heavily with his destination request that the driver had taken some persuasion to drive him away at all.

There were two destinations. The first was a chip shop. It wasn't one that Harry knew and his expression was as dubious as his driver's when they came to a stop outside the Plaice. Its frontage was made up of glass windows that pushed out like a three-sided box, a poor choice of material if you were not able to commit to a stringent cleaning routine. The glass was condensed and greasy in equal measures, the bottom third yellowed.

'Did you want . . .' Harry started out, but the driver was already shaking his head.

'Got me dinner in the back, mate,' he said, hurriedly. 'You sure you wanna be eating outta here? Not many people leaving hospitals with general advice to head straight for a chippie.'

'Keep it running,' Harry growled, before launching into the effort required to lever himself out.

Harry's second destination was twelve minutes further on. It was just gone 5 p.m. and, despite everything, the paper bag that was hot against his shins was smelling delicious. He had to take a little longer to catch his breath at his second destination, it had been the leaning back in for the chip supper that had done it, rendering him dizzy. When the taxi pulled away, he leaned on a wall for a count of thirty, doing what he could to ensure he didn't look like a man who was ill-advised to walk away from an emergency operation, before knocking on the door.

The house was silent, the curtains drawn at all front facing windows, a house that might be shut up for the night already. And Harry could hardly blame her.

The front door opened while Harry was still gathering himself and he cussed. The point of no return had just lurched forward to catch him out. Jillian Jones was smiling. Harry took a little comfort from that. Her smile broadened too, when he lifted the bag of hot food by way of explanation. By the time he made it up the path to the open front door, she was nowhere to be seen.

'Through here!' she called out and Harry followed the sounds of clacking plates and a sliding patio door. The kettle had a hiss as he walked past it, out into a garden drenched in the sun's last hurrah. There was a sense of déjà vu as Harry sat in the same chair at the same table, sitting opposite Jill who wore the same smile. Even the birds, still frantic at the feeder, seemed to be the same ones. This suddenly didn't feel like such an inappropriate idea.

'I can't say I was expecting to see you.' Jill said, a little stiffly. Awkward, Harry thought.

'No . . . I probably shouldn't be here,' said Harry.

'One of your colleagues said that you were taken ill at work. I got the impression it was rather serious. I'm still waiting for the update he promised.'

'Oh, I didn't mean . . . Well yes, the doctor would definitely say that I shouldn't be here. And that's before taking a look at the fried cholesterol I have wrapped up in there.' He lifted the bag to the table. 'I just meant . . .' He stopped when he realised he wasn't quite sure what he meant. 'You hear of coppers getting themselves in trouble with members of the public, with people who are vulnerable due to circumstance . . . and taking advantage.' Harry stumbled to a finish, 'that isn't what this is!' He knew he was flailing, not having the right words was a little alien to him.

'I know that.'

'I just . . . I had some time to go over stuff, too much time. And I wanted to see how you were doing. I remember with me, the first few days . . . Everyone checks in every five minutes and it was like there wasn't the time to grieve. And then I remember when everyone stopped. It doesn't take long and it can be difficult.'

'Didn't see a soul yesterday.' Jill said through a smile that wasn't about joy. 'I got messages, but I always think a message is a way of someone talking to you without the need for a conversation. So, I appreciate your visit. I see it for what it is and I'm really hoping you went to the Plaice for our dinner!'

'You like it?'

'Oh, it's the best. Looks like shit from the outside, enough that it might scare some people off. But all the best takeaways are a bit . . . slippery.'

'They are,' Harry agreed.

'And the best thing about chips is eating them out of the paper,' she added.

'Sorry!' Harry flapped, handing hers over.

'You're okay, then?' she asked. 'Fit to be back on duty?'

Harry couldn't answer the question immediately. He was trying to catch his breath. It had been getting easier and he had convinced himself that he was getting stronger, but the irony was not lost. 'No, as it happens.' Harry took to unravelling his supper, using it as something to focus on so he wouldn't have to look up.

'No?'

'Dicky heart. It gave me a little warning and the doctors are saying that they could do with doing some work in there, just to be sure it doesn't happen again.'

'And then you went to a chip shop and then you came here?'

'Nothing like a heart attack to make you realise that life is for living.' Harry wasn't very good at jokes, but this one seemed to hit the spot. Unfortunately for Jill, she had a mouthful of chips to contend with.

'A heart attack?' she said, when she'd recovered. 'That's what it was?'

'No, actually. There was a very long, very Latin-sounding word for what it was. The doctor summarised it as the warm-up act.'

'Did the doctor talk about how soon the main performance could be? Phil talked me through the whole CPR thing, but I can't say I was listening too intently.'

'Just don't let me eat this whole portion. And don't tell Maddie.'

'The woman you were with? You two struck me as close.'

'We are.'

'Which is why you haven't told her?'

'I haven't told anyone yet.'

'Because if you did, they would be telling you things you really don't want to hear. You lot are all the same. Phil was just like that. He would look out for the people he came across at work over himself. I take it that's why you discharged yourself? So you can get back to your work?'

'This is a case that needs solving.'

'Solve this and there will be another one straight after. Phil told me that, too.'

'This one's personal. This is someone who came after us, came after police officers.' Harry was aware there was anger building in his voice. He stuffed some chips in his mouth as a way of curbing it.

'Have you worked together long? You and Maddie, I mean.'

'Long enough that she can see right through me.'

'I'm right then. She'd be telling you to get your ass back to that hospital?'

'She would drive me herself.'

'Is she in charge of your investigation while you're away?'

'Effectively,' Harry said.

'Is she not very good?'

'She's incredible. When she first came into the department she was a pain in my arse. I was the miserable old bastard who'd seen it all, who couldn't learn anything from anyone, let alone some mystery woman transferring in from another part of the business.'

'Woman?' Jill still wore a grin.

Harry shrugged. 'I do think that was part of it. Part of why I felt like that and I was wrong to. She turned into the detective I always wanted to be right in front of my eyes and she gets better with every case. I don't know where that woman's ceiling is, but it's somewhere I can't even see, let alone reach.'

'Well then, I'll be sure to tell her.'

'Tell her?' Harry met the mischievous smile that ran under a glint in Jill's eye.

'This is the real reason you came here, right? To tell me the things you can't tell her? Then, if the worst happens, and it would seem to be a little more likely than you're letting on, I get to tell her all the things you wished you had.'

'That's . . . that's not—'

'It's okay.' And her expression told him it really was. 'I'm happy to help. You told me all about the police family, the first time you came here and you were right. We need to look out for each other. And besides, you brought me chips.'

'I did. And now I should go. I'm glad I saw you. I know it's tough and I know you're suffering, but you're doing great.'

'I'll survive.' She gave another tired smile. 'Just promise me you will too.'

* * *

By the time Harry made it home, his exhaustion had him drifting in and out of a half-sleep, brought back to planet earth by the sensations of a car pulling up to a stop.

He opened his eyes to find that the taxi had pulled right up on his drive, positioning him almost by the front door. He was totally out of breath by the time he scratched at its surface with his key. He'd somehow got the same taxi driver back. The man had taken a fare nearby, meaning he was still local when the shout had come out. He said he had wanted to be the one making sure Harry got home. Harry had thanked him for that. He lacked the energy to resist the notion that he was some vulnerable old man being returned to his carer.

There was no carer. There was no one at all. The air in his home had the thickness of a place that had been closed up for a couple of hot days. His first job was to push windows open at the front and in the kitchen at the rear, which was also, happily, the place for the kettle and a high stool on which he could rest a moment.

And a laptop that wasn't his.

Harry stared at it in the silence. The lighting was poor. By that time, dusk was closing in and he reached for the light for the first time in a long time. It seemed brighter than he remembered and his eyes darted around the room to see if there was anything else that was an addition — or missing. There was nothing, besides a layer of dusty cobwebs along the top of the kitchen units. The lighting hurt his eyes enough to affect his concentration and he turned it back off again.

The laptop was on the raised breakfast bar, dead centre. Put there for him to find. Harry did what anyone would.

He lifted the lid.

It powered up in an instant. The screen blinked on. A circular picture appeared of him in its middle with *Det Insp Harry Blaker* written out underneath. The picture was candid, taken side-on to provide a clear view of the white dressing covering a fresh wound. Harry recognised himself in the period after his last hospital release, when he had suffered a gunshot wound to the face.

The laptop had a tracker pad and he used it to move the cursor, clicking on himself. The screen changed and a moment later there was a noise, a sort of ring tone, like you might expect from a child's toy. The centre of the screen changed to a white circle with a torso-shaped silhouette in its middle and one word written out underneath it: *Ringing*. There were two icons, a red phone and a green phone. Harry clicked the green.

*'Detective Inspector Harry Blaker.'* The voice was male, flat and with an artificial twang, like it was playing out through a filter. Instantly, it cast his mind back to the voice that had made the call that had summoned Phil Jones to Frant Village Hall.

'Who is this?'

*'Take your phone out of your pocket and put it face down on the tabletop.'*

'What?'

*'Take your phone out of your pocket, make no attempt to unlock it and put it face down on the tabletop.'*

Harry sniffed, delaying for a moment, then did as he was asked. He placed it behind the open laptop, off camera, leaving his hand pressed down on it.

*'Remove your hand.'* The voice demanded and, when Harry did, it continued. *'How are you feeling, Detective Inspector Harry Blaker?'*

'What do you want?'

*'I saw your collapse. Quite the dramatic fall.'*

Harry was back to searching his own kitchen, his eyes chasing over it like it was a crime scene, where anything could be relevant. Nothing stood out. Nothing was different.

'I'm fine,' Harry said.

*'Press the escape key.'*

Harry hesitated, the instruction taking a moment to make sense in his mind. The laptop's keyboard was backlit, the escape key in the top left. He pressed it. Whatever application he had been communicating through had covered the whole screen and pressing the key shrunk it to a third of the size. Over that, a box appeared that contained a message: *USER "POLICE REAPER" IS ASKING PERMISSION TO JOIN YOUR SESSION. ALLOW?* There were two buttons underneath, *YES* or *NO*. Harry knew which button he should be pressing even before the flat tone instructed him to. He clicked *YES*. A moment later and the cursor drifted across the screen, propelled by an invisible force, a ghost in the room. He'd seen it before, when he had lost patience with a computer at work and the IT helpdesk had been able to do the same. They could take over via remote access to fix the problem. He had watched them work, watched the cursor flick about, watched typed words appear and thought nothing of it. But here, in his darkened kitchen with the laptop the only source of light and accompanied by a strange voice, it was truly disconcerting.

'*Empty your pockets.*'

'Why on earth would I do that?'

'*You know who I am, Detective Inspector Harry Blaker. I know you do.*'

'Police Reaper.' Harry read out the username. 'Gives me a starter for ten.'

'*Good. So, you know what I am capable of.*'

'Or some sick wannabe who watches the news.'

'*Empty your pockets.*'

Harry sighed. He had a wallet in his back pocket, nothing else. He put it out on the table.

The screen changed again and it caused him to suck in a lungful of that stale air. The laptop left in his home was now a portal, through which he had been able to watch the placement of that wallet from an elevated angle. Harry snatched his eyes up for the source. The angle suggested something resting on top of his kitchen units, the lens somewhere among the thick shadow. The image opened out, back to full screen.

'You have a camera in here,' Harry said, keeping his emotions in check.

'*I want you to understand something right from the start.*' The voice was still flat but the artificial twang was more prominent, like it was becoming a struggle to conceal the emotion behind it.

'Go on,' Harry said.

'*Detective Inspector Harry Blaker, you die today.*'

## CHAPTER 60

Maddie was juggling grocery bags, a laptop bag and the fob she would need to gain entry to her own building just as her phone rang. It meant she had needed to force it between her shoulder and her ear. She tutted when she found the communal door had been left open on a wedge.

'Eileen?'

'Ma'am. Sorry to call you out of hours. Are you at home?'

'Just. But I've brought my work home with me, Eileen. I wasn't intending on clocking off just yet. Have you got something?'

'Nothing that you need to come back out for, don't worry. It was just to let you know that Mr Blaker has left the building.'

'When?'

'The nurse couldn't give an exact time. These people are very busy. But I think it took her a couple of hours to call me, at least.'

'Did she say how he was? Did you get anything more?'

'Seems they take this patient-confidentiality thing very seriously. Even more seriously when the patient in question has specifically told them not to give anything up to his busybody of a wife.'

'He called you that?'

'I'm not sure which of those words is the more offensive, ma'am.'

'So, she didn't tell you anything?'

'She's a woman after my heart, is our Annie — able to say what we need her to say without saying anything at all.'

'What on earth does that mean?' Maddie grunted as she shouldered the internal fire door that brought her out onto her floor. The corridor was long and straight, so she could see a bike right down the far end. Her flat was the fourth door on the left. The same door had a figure sat up against it. 'Shit!'

'Are you okay, ma'am?'

'There's someone sat at my door.'

'PC Arnold?' Eileen ventured.

Vince had been Maddie's instant thought, too, but it wasn't him. The figure in her corridor was side-on and dressed in dark clothing, black trainers and white socks, and the closer she got, the dirtier every part of him seemed to get.

'Oh, for . . .' Maddie stopped herself swearing in Eileen's presence. 'We've had a problem with rough sleepers in the halls. Usually in the winter. I have a neighbour who's quite the good Samaritan and will jam the door open for them. Often cooks them a dinner. Looks like one has taken up residence.'

'Did you want me to have a patrol move them on?' Eileen said.

'I'm sure I can manage.'

'Keep me on the line.'

Maddie rolled her eyes at the instruction, then considered it wasn't the worst idea. She had an inside pocket to her blazer and the phone slipped in it neatly, the call still running. The man was at her feet and his position wasn't quite at her door — a metre or so short. He took a few moments to look up, enough for Maddie to note that his long hair was matted in places. His face was as dirty as the rest of him, his eyes a shocking blue against the dirt and brown hair.

'Hey, there. Have you been well looked after?'

'Yes, miss, a nice lady,' he said, a wide smile breaking out.

'Good to hear. You can't stay in the halls, though. Fire hazard.'

'Yeah, I know. Sorry miss.' He started to move, his knees had been pulled up to make a "V" shape of his legs, now she could see they had been covering bags underneath. His whole life was quite possibly inside it.

'Did you want a coffee, or anything?' She pulled open her shopping bag where she had a tube of pringles and a knuckle of bananas. One was for now, one for the morning. She held them out. 'Some snacks?'

'Thank you, miss.' He took the offerings without missing a beat and with that grin returning. 'No need for the coffee, miss. Won't be able to sleep.'

Maddie didn't know how to react. She was pretty sure he was joking, but it still didn't feel like she could laugh. She tried out a smile.

'I'll get off,' he said. 'Just resting the feet.' Totally unprompted, he lifted two bare feet out of trainers tied too loose, as if she might need a visual aid. Somehow, the smell of them beat the sight and Maddie was unable to talk with her breath held in. She gave a thumbs-up instead, then fumbled through her own front door.

# CHAPTER 61

'Is that right?' Harry pulled out a stool. He could feel his strength wavering all the more. He was tired, dog tired, his own weight feeling like it was conspiring against him, pulling him down. The stool scraped. He adjusted the screen to where he was lower. 'And how do I die?'

*'I'm going to cut your head off, Detective Inspector Harry Blaker.'*

'I see,' Harry sniffed. The voice was losing credibility with just about every word. Someone had worked out a way to get a laptop into his home, but that was hardly difficult. His house was unattended most of the time and he lived in a small village. With the right question in the local shop or pub, the chances of being pointed in the right direction for *the copper who got shot* were pretty good. The fake voice thing also struck him as amateurish. If you wanted to strike fear with a threat, you made sure your target could hear every ounce of the intent in your voice. And now there was the method of death, it was too much. Cartoonish.

*'You don't sound too scared, but then, why would you? You're not an easy man to kill, Detective Inspector. Even a bullet to the face couldn't finish the job.'*

'Very good, you've done your research.'

*'More than you know.'*

'A colleague of mine gave me a little precis of this thing called *Google*. Just today, in fact. Seems even the most incompetent amateur would be able to find out a few basics about me. Being shot is the first thing you will see.'

*'You don't sleep — hardly at all. You had two daughters, now only one. They clubbed together to buy you a smartwatch that they knew you would never wear. You work closely with a woman called Maddie Ives. She's worried about you, just like you're worried about her. On your release from hospital, you didn't come straight home. You visited a widow with a bag of chips.'*

Harry shifted to sit straighter. He didn't reply straight away either, he knew he should, he knew he shouldn't hesitate, but he had been caught out. Now they would both know it.

*'At least some of that isn't on Google, would you say?'*

'What do you want?'

*'I already told you what I want from you.'*

'So why all this? Why talk to me about it first?'

*'Because it needs to be a certain way and we need your help.'*

'We?'

*'You think this is just me? Just one person? Of course you do, you were happy to believe it was only Ryan Archer just because I left a knife in his hand. I gave you a chance, I left you clues. I even left wearing the wife's sliders. They're missing from the house you've been searching for days.'*

'We know it wasn't just Ryan.'

*'And now you're talking to Chloe, right? Is that another thing you know?'*

'Who am I talking to?'

*'Here's how this happens. You get up and you walk out of your house. Turn right at your drive and walk the pavement until you come to a red Vauxhall Corsa. It's old — it will stand out in your nice neighbourhood. The keys are on the driver's tyre. Bring the laptop. You can close it up. It doesn't need to be open.'*

'Where am I driving to?'

*'I will contact you again with instructions.'*

'Why would I follow them? You've already told me you want to kill me.'

*'I don't have to, Harry Blaker. What I have to do is kill a police officer. You do have a choice. You can close this laptop and you can choose not to leave your home. You can start making calls, reporting what has happened here to your superiors and our game of chase will continue. But, if you do that, I will have to choose someone else. And they will be dead before you dial your first number.'*

'The next police officer you see? There's never been a specific target, has there?'

*'You are my specific target, but say the word and it will be someone else.'*

The screen changed. The cursor chased to open a web browser, then more windows opened. Whoever was operating the computer knew what they were doing, passwords were auto-filled and starred out, the screen busy with movement.

Then there was just one window left. It was more footage, the quality similar to when Harry had watched himself put his wallet down. But the lighting was better. Much better. The sort you would expect in a communal hallway. He could see doors that marked out individual homes, a bike was leaned up against the wall in the distance, but, much closer, close enough to almost be sat under where the camera was positioned down at a slight angle, was a dark figure. A man, Harry reckoned. He was sitting on the floor with his legs pulled up so he could rest his chin on his knees. He lifted his head as Harry watched, his face away from the camera, looking down the hall where there was movement, someone approaching.

Maddie Ives.

They had an interaction and Harry watched it play out. There was no sound, but he could see an icon on the screen that told him it was muted. The conversation was short, then Maddie gave the seated man something from her bag before moving into her flat. The man looked like he was going to get up, but then he didn't.

The door shut beside him and Maddie was gone. The man reacted like he had been waiting for it, a moment later he looked right up at the camera, then gave a thumbs-up. The screen changed, the source a different camera, back trained on Maddie Ives. This camera was her in her home, the angle lower, waist-height and fixed, with a constant shadow over the top right corner as if it was tucked in behind something.

This one had sound. Maddie took her phone out of her pocket the moment she made it through the door and spoke in a way that suggested the call was already connected. She started out apologising. He saw her drop shopping bags on the kitchen worksurface, slide out a meal and pierce the lid before putting it in the microwave. She was out of shot while it cooked and he could only pick out a few words here and there.

Harry let his head drop. He took a few moments with his eyes closed, a few moments to contemplate what this all meant. There was no way of knowing how long Maddie had been under surveillance — him too. No way of knowing who else and that meant he had to work under the assumption that these people knew a lot and that the threat they posed was very real.

This was Ryan Archer's method. But Ryan Archer was dead, meaning someone had taken it from him. It had been an effective way to steal high-end cars, but Harry could certainly imagine how effective it could be if your mind was more set on murder.

He'd had his update earlier from Maddie, the one that confirmed Chloe Falconer's involvement and her inside knowledge of Ryan's methods, the methods he was now experiencing first-hand in his own kitchen.

'Okay then, you've shown your hand.'

*'We've done no such thing.'*

'Who are you?' Harry said, with no expectations of getting an answer. The screen changed again. This time it was Eileen who appeared and Harry could guess who Maddie was on the phone to. She was holding the phone in one hand and scratching the chin of Ted the kitten with the other. She sat in a high-backed chair in a robe and, of course, slippers. She stood up, getting a little more animated. She was muted but the screen split into two halves to show both his colleagues at once.

*'These are only some of the cards we hold. Just a sample. We have cameras in more houses than you can imagine, more than you can possibly make safe. Your choice is clear. You, Detective Inspector Harry Blaker, or I make the call to my friend sat out in Maddie Ives' hallway. He's very good at what he does.'*

Harry focussed on Maddie. She was smiling down the phone. She had opened a bag of crisps to pick from while the microwave was still alight behind her. She didn't eat one straight away, she lifted her hand to rest flat against her stomach instead.

Harry's stool made another squeal as he got to his feet, catching on a tile join to topple over, the sound like a gunshot in his silent house.

'It's me,' he growled. 'You want a police officer? It's me. But this is it . . . this is where it ends. You want me to help you with this, to do what you want, then I'll play along. But you hand yourself in when it's done.'

Laughter sounded odd with AI suppressing it. *'Do you think this is a negotiation?'*

'I think you need to negotiate. I think you need this to be me. This is my investigation. You're making a statement. I'm right, aren't I?'

*'I make Detective Inspector Maddie Ives the same rank, I make Superintendent Helen Banks higher still.'*

Harry was shaking his head. 'You want me. You can have me, but then it ends, with you in handcuffs.'

*'This ends with you, but I'm not going to your prison. I don't deserve your prison.'* There was another pause as if words were being considered carefully. *'I am going to make a statement with you, with how you die. That's how I know this will be over. Once they see what I did, what happens to those who come after me, there'll be no one left with the will. All I need is to take out Harry Blaker, the legend.'*

'You're wrong. A police force is like an ant's nest. The more you disturb it, the more will come running out to bite you.'

'*You coppers are all the same. You think you know people, that's why you do what you do. That's why you choose who to believe. Not a single thought that you could be wrong. But you are wrong. When you are dead, they will stop. And this is over.*'

'The only way this stops is for you to hand yourself in.'

'*A red Vauxhall Corsa. Leave your phone. Bring the laptop.*' The screen changed again, to a blank desktop. The call had been cut.

Harry slammed the lid shut, sweeping the laptop under his arm and scooping his wallet up to push into his jacket's inside pocket. He made his way back through a quickly darkening house, eyes forward. The only place he lingered was at his front door and the dog lead that hung from the hook. He stopped, running it through his hands, the sensation seemed to prompt the feeling that this was real, that the moment he let it go and stepped out of his door, it was to be for the last time.

When he reached the end of the drive, he was still holding it.

# CHAPTER 62

'So, what do we know?' Maddie said, having retrieved the phone she had stowed in her pocket.

'Know, ma'am?'

'Last I saw, you were heading into the belly of a hospital to find out what there was to know about Harry's situation. Did you get anything from that?'

'Like I said, they were not quite so willing. They were also a lot less inclined to speak to me like I was the wife.'

'You think Harry told them?'

'He said something. Annie was different, there's no doubting that, but she kept her part of the bargain and told me when he was released.'

'Discharged.' Maddie corrected her, the word laden with humour.

'Discharged, of course. She also made it clear that it was against doctor's advice and that they were expecting to see him back very soon.'

'In the same circumstances or for an appointment?'

'She said a heart surgeon tried to convince him to stay. I think we can take a steer from that.'

Maddie huffed. She'd dumped her bags on the table, a microwave meal hurriedly purchased on the way back, spilled out from where she had packed it last on purpose. She turned it over in her hands where it looked far less appealing now she'd got it home. It would have to do. She stabbed it with a fork, the action satisfying, then cracked open a bag of crisps where two minutes was too long to wait for it to cook. Eileen's huffing at the sounds of the crunching only encouraged her more.

'Harry didn't want to, it would seem,' Maddie said.

'He did not. The nurse was just as frustrated — and this was the part where I worked out that the wife charade had fallen apart. She said he'd told them that he was working a case, something very important, so important that his heart would have to wait. She then suggested that I make sure this case was closed sooner rather than later, talking to me as if she knew I was involved, even as if I was in charge of the whole damned thing and it was down to me.'

'So, she went from believing you to be his wife, to being his commanding officer?' Maddie couldn't contain the humour in her voice.

'My own husband would have told you that a woman can be both.'

Maddie smiled, but only for an instant. 'This is all I need. As if we didn't need to find Chloe Falconer enough, now we need to do it before Harry Blaker drops dead in his waxed jacket.'

'He won't be allowed to do any police work, ma'am. You should take some of that pressure off yourself. He'll be forced to rest up at home.'

'This is Harry we're talking about. He woke up in a hospital bed after a suspected heart attack and, by the time I got to see him next, he already had his laptop and some case notes.'

'Yes . . . About that, the circumstances were rather—'

'It doesn't matter, Eileen. If he had asked me, I would have probably done the same.'

'I thought we could find some middle ground . . . keep him informed just enough to feel involved, so he didn't go out looking for his own information.'

'I wonder if keeping him informed makes it more likely he turns up for the juicy bits.'

'Juicy bits, ma'am?'

'If we get a good lead on Falconer, or a break in the case somewhere else. He'll want to be a part of it. He's just the sort to turn up in the middle of a car chase.'

'I see what you mean. Which reminds me of the one other snippet I was able to glean from Annie the nurse.'

'What was that?'

'At all costs, Harry Blaker is to stay away from stressful situations.'

## CHAPTER 63

The car started with a guttural cough that took a few seconds to smooth out, like any old diesel. The lights came on with it, shivering to the sound of that cough, their mustard yellow lux hardly making a difference in the gathering gloom. The car was a manual, a Vauxhall Corsa as promised, the same make and model year that his youngest daughter had learned to drive in. Harry considered this might have been done on purpose, but dismissed it, not wanting to dish out that much credit just yet. One thing he should give credit for was the forensic consideration: the steering wheel was wrapped tight in clingfilm; the seat had a crackle from plastic covers; even the indicators and door handles were wrapped tightly like a butchered turkey. It made the driving sensation odd, detached and unpleasant.

To add to that, the gearbox was soggy, the engine underpowered and the smell akin to something that had been sealed up to baste in its own damp. There was also a piece of something that rattled and Harry traced it to the plastic trim beneath the handle on his driver's door. On closer inspection, there was a foot-sized dent and some splintering, as if someone had lashed out at it from the inside. Harry considered that this was a car that might have been used for darker purposes before.

Everything outside of the car was familiar, at least: the junction that appeared when he took the same route out of

284

the village he had done a million times, then the old railway station that passed on the right, now reduced to a couple of carriages hosting a coffee shop. A smattering of trees appeared on his left that opened up to reveal a church, the stone walls giving way to some houses before the village shop appeared with its lurid green sign that was even more vibrant when uplit in the darkness.

It was all so familiar and yet, everything was so different.

The brow of the hill gave way to a roundabout and Harry pulled into a dormant bus stop. He had been stationary for just a few moments when the darkness was punctured by the muted sound of a ringing phone. It was coming from the glovebox.

'*You moved. You were told to wait for instructions.*' That flat voice that had started to grate on Harry, edged over into infuriating where it was now piped directly into his ear via a cheap feeling phone.

'I moved so you could give me instructions. There's no phone signal until you get to the top of the hill. If you want to do something like this, it's the details that will get you.'

'*You don't think I'm prepared? You're underestimating me.*'

'No one can think of everything. I've made a career out of finding what gets missed.'

'*A clever one, are you? Looks like I made the right choice about who to take out then, doesn't it?*'

'I'm not the best at it. Not by far.'

'*The news reports would suggest that to be a lie. Detective Inspector Harry Blaker, the hero cop.*'

'Heroes are rarely clever.'

'*So, who's a bigger threat then? Maddie Ives? Maybe I should choose differently.*'

'This ends with me. I told you that. I'm making this easy, doing what you say, but that's the only reason.'

'*Because you're in control of this?*' The voice dared Harry to agree. He didn't. '*Like I said, when they find their boss, their hero boss reduced to a bloody mess of nothing, any cop with even an ounce of intelligence will leave me well alone. This is how it ends.*'

'Let's get this done then,' Harry growled, revving the engine for a soundtrack to his discontent. 'Where am I going?'

# CHAPTER 64

'This could be your lucky night, Ms Ives.' Maddie tagged the voice coming down the phone as familiar, but that was all the detail she was getting.

'Is that so?' She stalled while her mind tried to conjure up who the hell she was talking to.

'I don't normally pick up my phone out of hours. In our line of business, you learn very early on that a call at that time only ever goes one way, right?'

*Our line of business* . . . It was Megan Vrana, the solicitor Maddie had spoken to at the start of the day. It already felt like a long time ago.

'I'm out of hours too, Ms Vrana. Are you about to ruin my night?'

'Depends what you would count as ruining your night. You might have to tip back out, assuming you're at home.'

'I'm at home.'

'Off duty? I can call 101 — just leave what I have and we can all get on with our night. I just thought—'

'You thought right. What do you know?'

'I got a call from Chloe.'

'Chloe Falconer?' Maddie's meal was done. She'd been hungry, tearing into it with a gusto that had lasted as many

286

as three bites before the rest had met with the bin. The disappointment in her microwave meal had her overcompensating with crisps in front of rubbish telly. She sat straighter to shift the crumbs from her chest.

'She has my number still, it would seem.'

'You talked to her?'

'I did not. Nor do I want to get your hopes up. Like I said, I don't pick my phone up out of hours, but I will occasionally have a moment of weakness and play a voice message back. Chloe called to ask for my help, my representation. I can't now, of course, seeing as my next course of action was to call you.'

'Call us why? Did she say where she was?'

'That's why I said not to get your hopes up. She left me a phone number and a few words. This might assist you in finding her, or more likely, mean nothing at all.'

'What words?'

'The rules first, Detective Inspector. You will remember we talked about my reputation.'

'This didn't come from you, don't worry.'

'It didn't. And you can't go calling the number she used either, not a few minutes after she called me. Do you understand?'

'I know how this works. You can trust me with information.'

'Okay, then.' Megan Vrana reeled off a number that had Maddie scrabbling for a pen to record it.

'And those words you mentioned?' Maddie prompted, getting a pause as if Ms Vrana was still mulling it over.

'I don't think Chloe is having a nice time on the run. She's very aware that you lot are after her. She's full of piss and wind normally, but that seems to have fallen away quite considerably . . .' Megan's pause had Maddie biting her tongue where she might have challenged the fact that Megan Vrana had denied knowing Chloe at all, let alone knowing what she was like *normally*.

'I can help her with that,' Maddie said.

287

'I'm sure you can. She said she was sleeping rough. I know that's not ideal, but she said it was somewhere you lot had looked at recently. I think she thinks she's being clever.'

'Looked at?'

'Been before, I think. I listened back a few times. She was agitated, talking fast, but I'm sure she said that you had searched it already and that it was a *garage*. Does that mean anything to you?'

'Can't say it does, but we'll have a look into it,' Maddie said — too fast; Megan Vrana would be every bit as good at spotting lies as Maddie.

'I imagine you will.'

'And she was there a few minutes ago?'

'More like half an hour by now. I didn't listen straight away when they came through. She said she was bedding down for the night, then she would be coming into my office half an hour before opening in the morning. She said how clever she was being to avoid capture. The whole tone of the message was that of someone who seems to think we are a team now. I think she sees a future where I assist with sneaking her into my office. Maybe I'm supposed to give her a new identity and a plane ticket to somewhere that has no ability to extradite back to the UK. I do think Mr Archer has given her a rather overinflated impression of what it is that I do.'

'You might be right,' Maddie said, a grin forming. She was now aware of why this call had been made in the first place. The future Ms Vrana was really seeing was one where Chloe Falconer made herself a rather large pain in the arse. The police could stop that before it even started. Maddie could.

'But you need to be smart and I need you to explain to me what that looks like.'

'You mean with how we pick her up? How we protect that reputation of yours?'

'You know I do.'

Maddie was already pacing around her flat, getting what she might need together. 'We'll go now. The seriousness of the offence means we can't be waiting and I think that's best anyway. You don't want us picking her up when she turns up at your office — she'll smell a rat for sure.'

'Agreed.'

'So, we go tonight. I'll have a uniform patrol pick her up. There are some sites that we routinely sweep for fly-tipping. I have a feeling that will be one of them.'

'And you won't be seen? Personally, I mean?'

'Who says I'll be there?'

'Come now!' Megan said, and Maddie couldn't make out if she was amused or annoyed.

'I won't be seen.' Maddie confirmed.

'Okay then. So, a random search of sites for fly-tipping and you happen to find a murder suspect? I guess it's the best I can ask for.'

'Don't worry.' Maddie did her best to sound convincing. 'This will be nice and easy. It's the sort of thing we do all the time.'

# CHAPTER 65

The first thing the monotone voice had Harry do was to flip the laptop back open, then he was instructed to search for a wi-fi signal. He was offered just one word: *CORSA*. He was then told that the car had a hotspot stashed somewhere that would enable him to connect to the internet. He was keeping up, even if he wasn't the most tech-minded. The connection worked but it was slow, enough for a long silence until the controls of the laptop could once again be taken up by a ghostly entity.

The whole facade was purely designed to make the same point all over again. The same programme that had shown an image of Harry dropping his own wallet on the table, then a live stream of Maddie Ives and Eileen Holmans, now showed him sitting in the driver's seat of a car, losing patience.

'I get it.' Harry didn't even bother to look for the camera in the car. 'I got it a while ago. You're watching me and you're watching others.'

*'They're not just others, Detective Inspector Harry Blaker, they are your friends, aren't they?'*

'We're wasting time.'

*'I dictate the times.'* The voice was still flat, still monotone but the distortion, the artificial twang was stronger, as if the

system was working harder to disguise the emotion behind it. Harry was getting under their skin, prodding their anger. Angry people made mistakes.

'Where am I going?'

*'I am recording you, sound and vision as well as tracking GPS. The phone you are holding has a screen mirror, meaning I can see every single action you do with it. It also has a kill switch that I can operate at any time—'*

'I get it. I said that already.'

*'I just want to be really sure that you do. You follow my instructions, that is all you do. You cannot use that phone to signal for help. You cannot divert that car to signal for help. If you so much as flash the lights in a way that I deem suspicious, I will know and I will cut you loose. And then the only kill switch you need to worry about is the one I have sitting outside Maddie Ives's flat. Do you still get it?'*

'Where am I going?' Harry growled.

*'Head out of your precious village, through Coldred and over the A2. You're heading to the A20. Can you manage that?'*

Harry pulled away, one-handed, the other still held the phone to his ear. The laptop, still open, slid across the seat to bump into the passenger door, the screen twisting to face him, the image once again a live stream of Maddie Ives. She was agitated, busy, a look Harry had seen a million times before. She was still on the phone.

'I can,' Harry said, but he was covering the phone's mouthpiece with a tight fist.

*'Good,'* the voice said. *'This will be easy if you keep on doing as you're told. I'll be back in touch soon. I have a garage to prep.'*

The phone call ended and Harry had the confirmation that his movement was indeed being tracked and his audio wasn't just being heard through the phone. He had no choice but to follow the instructions, for now, at least.

He dropped a window for some fresh air on a muggy night.

*Garage?*

## CHAPTER 66

When Maddie bundled out of her front door, the homeless man who had been sat out in the corridor was gone. She'd forgotten about him, but there was a reminder in the form of a stack of carrier bags that had been left by her door. She stepped over them, the phone connecting as she did.

'Ma'am?'

'Eileen, I have a strong lead. I need some logistics. We're going to need a tactical team . . . and can you identify an RVP for a briefing? We'll need to work out where we go after, a forensic strategy, searches . . .' She was thinking out loud, realising in real time that she should have taken a moment to think this through before making her call.

'I assume these are action points for now, ma'am?'

'Yes, Eileen! These are for now!'

'Then I will return to work out of hours. Thank you for checking that first.'

'Oh please . . . You'd have been devastated if I hadn't called.'

'True. But perhaps you could be a little clearer? All I have is the need to summon a tactical team who we will meet at a suitable rendezvous point. I'm sure that is something I can arrange, but I will need to know a little bit more.

Perhaps a reason and a rough area of the county as a starting point?'

Maddie tutted. She was struggling to open her car door, just like she was still struggling to organise her thoughts.

'It can't be Alan Day's tactical team, though. If that's the team on duty then we may need to think again. I want something left that is capable of answering questions.'

'Okay, but ma'am, what is going on?'

'Chloe Falconer. I know where she is.'

# CHAPTER 67

Harry had been told to park up short, then he had been told that every step he took was still being recorded.

He wasn't entirely convinced.

The technology existed that could record in low light, no doubt, but the place where he was instructed to stop felt like another oversight, like it might have been chosen during the day when the sun was up, not in the dead of the night when the huge trees either side cast shadows easily capable of swallowing a Vauxhall Corsa whole.

He kicked his driver's door open, aiming for the already damaged trim, taking some satisfaction when a chunk shattered, spilling bits of plastic. He stepped out into gravel that was now littered with large clumps of dry, fresh mud, that was his fault too. He had pulled over too far, the wheel on the right side had mounted the bank and he'd been too heavy on the throttle to spin the wheel like a disc cutter against the bank. The dim interior light showed a scuff on his boot and he cussed, lifting his foot onto the seat and spitting in his hand before rubbing at the scuff and the sole. Perhaps his shoes were the last thing he should be worrying about, but he was a man who knew he was on camera, who was trying to show that he wasn't rattled.

The phone was ringing. Harry lifted it in his right hand, shaking out his left where it was starting to ache from an old injury. It was the reason he only drove automatics these days.

*There's a path that leads off the right side of the road, it will take you into woodland.'*

'I can't . . .' Harry huffed as the call was cut, then wrenched open the passenger door to finish his sentence where he could still be heard through the laptop. 'I can't see a damned thing!'

He considered leaving the door open, his experience telling him that any passing police patrol would take note of a car roughly pulled over and empty, with a passenger door left to shiver in the breeze. They would investigate further, note the tyre marks in the bank and damaged interior and it would hold their interest. Perhaps they would then follow the path he had been instructed to take and do it all in time to thwart whatever it was that was waiting at the end.

Then again, even if the miracle of a passing police patrol did occur, the more likely outcome would be that his colleagues lumbered down that path in their big boots, radios blaring and flashlights all over the place, to spook whoever was leading this merry dance. The music would then stop for Harry, but he had to believe that he would be enabling it to start for others: Maddie, specifically.

He slammed the door and the darkness closed in.

His left ankle rolled on the second step, his foot twisting over the edge of a pothole. He cussed loudly at the sharp pain, roared his frustration back towards the silent car and those that had brought him here. He limped away, his left foot dragging a little, the darkness so thick that he couldn't even see to the ground.

He woke up the phone from the glovebox, spinning it so the screen was facing down, the light just enough for him to pick out any large shapes that might be a trip hazard and also the path as described. He was breathing heavily; less than ten metres of forward motion and he was already struggling. He felt a little dizzy too, a sensation made worse by trying to follow a tiny pocket of light.

The trail was hard-packed, the results of weeks of being scorched and with very little to drink. It ended with a clearing that, from a distance, looked to be cupping the moonlight. As Harry got closer, the phone rang.

*Follow the path towards the village. Before you make that, there is a block of garages, follow the light.*' The line cut again and Harry had to fight himself not to smash the device on the floor in his frustration. A few more steps and a stile unmerged from the darkness. It was of wooden construction with three steps up and Harry made the other side in such a state that he needed to sit back on it for a minute or more, just to recover.

Inevitably, the phone rang.

'I'm not as fit as I used to be,' Harry said, and the line cut again. He pushed on. The woodland quickly thinned, it was barely a copse and he could see lights of habitation beckoning him to the edge. The hard-packed path became grassland, the near distance a flat expanse with low rows of squared-off shadows.

Garages.

A square of light erupted from the middle, its door up but broken to hang back down lower on one side. A car was parked in front of it, its headlights the source of the eruption.

Harry headed for it.

# CHAPTER 68

The tactical team's sergeant had a nod that contained the enthusiasm of a man whose team had been called away from routine work to lead a murder arrest, and one with an element of the clandestine to it, too. The RVP Eileen had arranged was an area of hardstanding behind a hardware store on an industrial estate that was four miles out from the block of garages where they had found the olive BMW. Eileen had insisted on going herself, hitching a lift with Maddie. She then forced everyone to wait while she made some calls that confirmed that the BMW had indeed been seized earlier in the day and that the scene had been closed a short time after.

It was when Eileen stepped out of the car to confirm this that Maddie considered that Chloe really had been rather clever. This was the last place the police had searched, making it the last place they might think to search again.

The whole team were lined up in a horseshoe, awaiting instruction from their skipper or the inspector, a sense of direction at least for the operation. With Eileen's appearance, they waited for an explanation of who this woman was and why she had appeared in a pair of deep ruby slippers.

Maddie didn't have the time.

'We are good to go then, sergeant.'

His eyes snatched up from the ground. 'Okay then. Nessy . . . KitKat . . . I want you in a response uniform. You've gotta look like a regular Joe, out on patrol. KitKat, take your fags. I want you sparking up and out of your car for a stroll, that's how we find her. Nessy, you're walking with him. Stay close and chat. I want the approach casual, surprised to start with. Boris and Chalky . . . You're in the unmarked and in the area first. I want you in plain clothes and out early. Use the night vision for an exact location. I also want an update on the layout from you. I want to hear the best way to get KitKat close without it looking like he was trying. Understood?'

'Sarge.' Four answers came in unison.

'The rest of us are in the van. Once Nessy and KitKat have our target under arrest they'll call up for conveyance. I want her in the back with you lot, lit up and watched like a hawk. We know her history, Chloe Falconer can be a shit if you give her a chance. We don't give her a chance. What have I missed?'

The team exchanged glances.

'What about NPAS? They got night vision that'll cover the whole area.' NPAS stood for National Police Air Support in full terms, the copper chopper in shorthand.

'Can't put a chopper up. They're big and bright and they're fucking noisy. Falconer needs to think KitKat stumbled over her with a fag on the go, not as part of an operation.'

'What about dogs?' This was the woman he had called Nessy offering up. 'If she makes off.'

'We've got a handler on the way. There's only two covering the whole county so he got a bit of a JT; too long to wait. He said it's a still night and we're rural so if she disappears into the night, he should still be able to get a scent. But what is *not* going to happen tonight, ladies and gentlemen?'

'She ain't disappearing into the night.' The man he had been referring to as KitKat offered up.

'She is not. We all do our job right and this is a piece of piss. Chloe Falconer in some shit-covered garage floor, subdued by a bright torch in the face, few questions chucked in and then cuffed up before she can say *I didn't do nothing*. Any questions?'

There were none. Everyone understood what they were there to do. Everyone seemed to have understood the seriousness.

Everyone took a last glance at Eileen and her footwear.

# CHAPTER 69

The car's headlights shivered, then dipped to just sidelights as Harry got closer. The driver's door opened and closed, a rear door the same, then the passenger side.

'In the garage.' A voice — a real one this time — called out towards him. It was female and it was choked in a combination of excitement and tension.

Harry kept walking. The car was silver to catch in the moonlight and he trailed the fingers of his left hand along its haunch as he walked past. The gap where the car ended and the garage opened up was just big enough for him to squeeze through, it meant lifting his legs a little higher, then he stumbled on the other side, his breathing laboured.

The lights burst back on.

Harry turned to them, instinctively raising his hands to shield his eyes from the full beams. There was a movement, a single shape moved around to the front of the car to flicker the lights, then it stopped to lean on the car, positioned directly between the headlights. It was too bright for Harry to make out anything more than a petite silhouette with long hair tied back into a ponytail.

'You seem to be struggling a little, Detective Inspector.' Now there was glee in the voice and Harry found himself wishing he had at least forced a word or two from Chloe Falconer before she had disappeared out of sight. As sure as he was, he couldn't positively ID a silhouette. 'Have a seat. And I assume you know how to put those on?'

Harry turned where she was pointing beyond him. A wooden chair had been pulled out into an otherwise bare space. A pair of rigid handcuffs lay on top and Harry knew instantly who they had belonged to: Phil Jones. His handcuffs still remained unaccounted for. Beneath them, the concrete had the dusty pattern of a space that had been brushed recently, the air smelled of it too, enough to tickle the back of his throat. There was shelving down the right wall, a solitary tin of paint with a rust-coloured blob, long since dried into a tear-drop shape from the lip. The shelving along the back wall was a little more cluttered with various sized tubs, most wounded to spill their contents.

Harry sat heavily enough for the chair to creak. He swept up the handcuffs to just hold onto them for now.

'Have we met?' he said.

'How's the face? I think I see a little bit of swelling there.'

'Least of my problems, apparently.'

'Ah yes, I watched your collapse. For a moment there I thought nature might have beaten me to it, that I might need to make another choice.'

'You still have a choice.' Harry shifted in the seat to try and assist his breathing. He could feel his pulse racing, the oxygen depleting as a result. 'You can still call this off. End this now. Give yourself up and I'll take you in.'

The woman laughed. 'Why would I do that?'

'Or go back on the run. You've shown yourself quite adept. You might last another week, maybe two.'

The figure pushed off a car that had a creak of its own. 'Two weeks? Even now, that's all you give me?'

'Continue with this tonight and you only bring that forward.'

'And who is taking me into custody? Detective Inspector Maddie Ives? That foul woman Eileen? Or the dead sergeant's team perhaps? Even among that lot, there won't be anyone stupid enough to go after me, not after tonight.'

'Maybe Ryan Archer's dad will get a hold of you.'

'Neil!' There was forced laughter. 'I watched that whole interaction you had with him, which means I saw your face. You respect that man about as much as I do.'

'You have cameras in there too?'

'Had.' The woman corrected him. 'Everywhere was covered. Everywhere and everyone.' She was proud, arrogant. 'How do you think I knew you were still alive?'

'You really did think of everything.' Harry shifted again. 'Or, at least, you really did copy everything Ryan Archer did. Before you double-crossed him, obviously.'

She stepped back, one hand out to find the bonnet of the car. 'He knew where this was going. At least he could have, if he wasn't so damned stupid.'

'You killed him without leaving a trace of yourself at the scene.'

'I was careful.' That arrogance was still front and centre.

'The fact you were able to do that, that tells me a lot. You weren't just careful. Ryan never saw it coming, did he?'

Her answers had been fast, self-assured but there was a pause for this one, then a slight shake to it when it came.

'It was necessary.'

'Perhaps. But you seem a little sad about it all the same. I saw what happened at that house, in front of children. It had me thinking that it would take some sort of monster to do that. But monsters don't get sad. Maybe I'm wrong about you?'

'And maybe you were right.' She moved forward a little more, the movement jerky, like a decision made on instinct. She brought her hands round from behind her back, revealing a large knife. Its blade caught in the light to dazzle, the point pushed in so close to Harry's forehead that it was just a blur he looked beyond.

'I've been threatened by worse,' he growled.

'I had better,' She retorted, quick as a flash. 'I had to leave it with Ryan. The handcuffs . . . put them on.'

'Or what?' Harry scoffed. 'You'll kill me?'

'This can be quick and simple or I can just start slicing off small bits. Don't think I haven't got anything to barter with, that's a state of mind I can change very quickly. If you're smart, you'll do as I say and then you'll beg me for mercy.'

'You and Ryan?' Harry watched closely for a reaction. 'He trusted you, didn't he? But it was more than that. There had to be more for him to do what he did. He was only doing it for you, wasn't he? Did he love you?'

'Nice try,' she replied.

'When you killed him, was that the moment that you realised that this had all gone too far? The moment when you thought there was no turning back? That's not true, you know. You can still end this. You can stop, face up to what happened and start—'

'The CUFFS!' She spat. 'Behind your back and through the backrest.'

Harry sized her up for a moment, the point of the knife more specifically. He picked the cuffs up, turning them over in his hands and noting the scuffs and wear that gave them the look of a pair that had almost had a full career.

'The moment I put these handcuffs on, Phil's handcuffs, I know this really is over.' Harry still held them as he fixed back on her. 'You could at least tell me what's really going on here, how you did what you did, how you eluded me. Seeing as you were the only one who ever did.'

'Are you trying to delay me, Harry Blaker? Are you still hoping for a rescue?' She was laughing now, carefree, perhaps the most disturbing noise she had made to that point. 'I mean, you never know, maybe there is a flashing blue wall of rescuers hurtling across the county towards you!' More laughter. 'Fine, seeing as I've been dying to tell someone, I guess it might as well be you. If nothing else, I might enjoy the look on your face when you realise that none of this is quite what you thought it was. The great Harry Blaker . . . wrong and then wrong again.'

## CHAPTER 70

'Why do you call him KitKat?' Maddie said, the moment the man in question was out of earshot. He had changed into his response uniform as requested, the cigarette that was to form a big part of his ruse already tucked behind his ear, visible as he walked away from them.

The sergeant shrugged. 'Silly team banter.' But Maddie fixed him with a look that told him she still wanted to know. 'He has a bit of a reputation, see. He's always on a break.'

Maddie smiled. 'I can see why you picked him for this role.'

'He's the only smoker we got. Actually, don't get me wrong. He's no chump. Him and Nessy are pretty formidable.'

'Nessy. Also not her real name?' Maddie guessed.

The sergeant looked a little bashful. 'Scottish.' He shrugged again. 'Teams like this don't really do names.'

'So, I see.'

The police radio sparked into life. The two sent ahead in the plain car were reporting in with "eyes-on". They clarified that this was only on the garage block, not the suspect.

'All received, any signs of any persons?' said the sergeant into his radio. Maddie and Eileen were pinned to their own radio to listen in.

*'We've done a sweep. It's a bit of a strange one. We have one garage lit up like a beacon. We can't get an angle to see in, but it's the excuse we needed for KitKat to have a wander over.'*

'Only one lit?' the sergeant said.

*'Only one. Bang in the middle of the blocks and like a Christmas tree.'*

'Sounds like the garage we searched,' said Maddie. 'It has to be her.'

'Why would she light it up if she's supposed to be hiding?' The sergeant frowned then raised his radio. 'Alpha three, receiving?' Alpha Three was the uniform patrol Maddie had just watched drive away.

*'Go ahead.'* A woman's voice: Nessy.

'Slight change. No need for the break ruse. You can both tip out. We have a garage lit up in the middle of nowhere. Makes sense that you would check it out. Routine search. Remember, when you get hold of her you don't know her. Radio through to me for checks. She has previous for false details. She has visible tattoos, so we'll get her easy enough. It just needs to play out as a stop-check and it needs to be believable, understood?' The radio beeped to confirm the transmission over. The sergeant held eye contact with Maddie for a response that didn't come. 'Alpha Three, did you receive my last?' he prompted. Another beat passed. Then came a noise that confirmed someone was coming back. It was KitKat.

*'Yeah . . . we received your last . . .'* He sounded hesitant.

The sergeant picked up on it too. 'KitKat, are you all in order?'

'Yes, yes . . . it's just . . . can I still have the fag?'

Maddie stepped away. Despite the tension and what was at stake, even Eileen Holmans was smiling.

'Nine minutes.' Maddie referenced the time it should take Alpha Three to drive from their location to the garage block.

Eileen nodded. 'Fifteen minutes or so and we'll have her in custody. One step closer to closure on this one, ma'am.'

'This has to go smooth,' Maddie said.

'We're going to move a little closer with the van,' the sergeant said. 'We know she's a slippery one. She might fancy a little run. We should have it covered, but it can't harm to be closer.'

'We'll move with you,' Maddie said, then cut back in quick when it looked like the sergeant had something to say. 'We'll stay out of sight.'

They edged closer, parking up just a few minutes away in a woodland car park well worn by dog walkers. Maddie stepped back out into a muggy evening, narrowing her eyes as a bright light tore through the darkness where the side of the police van slid open. Then she tutted where her phone was buzzing in her jeans pocket. She had left a voice message for Superintendent Helen Banks with the briefest of updates. This would be her calling back for a little more.

It wasn't.

# CHAPTER 71

'So now you know.' She was back to a silhouette, though a little different from how she had first presented. She had removed something from the boot, he had thought it a hoody at first, but when she had pulled it on it had formed a curious shape. Squared off.

She was still resting on the sloped bonnet of a car, her legs crossed at the ankles as if she was chatting with a mate. Harry certainly felt like they knew each other better after her long and narcissistic explanation of how she had outwitted them all. But it was still some way from being mates. For one thing, she had insisted he handcuffed himself to the chair before she would start. Then it became quite apparent as to why.

She was on her own.

There were no *others*, something Harry suspected early on, then noticed how she had stopped saying *we* some time ago and how the doors of the car had all been opened one at a time for no one else to appear. The fact that she was on her own should have meant that he stood a chance, that he could have taken her on, gone for the knife the way he had been trained. But he knew better. He knew his own body. His heart was beating so hard he might even have a visible shake. He was no match for her; no match for anyone. He might not be a match for himself much longer. He needed to move this on.

'Your move, then,' he said. 'Nothing of what you just told me means that I can't help you. It still isn't too late. We don't have to go down this road.'

'I think I'll cut your jacket off first.' She took two steps forward. 'It's too dark. I like the idea of the white shirt underneath. I want the impact from the blood soaking into that. In this light, that'll be perfect.' The zeal was back and Harry knew that she had made up her mind.

'You don't get to take my jacket off!' he snapped. 'You don't cut it.' His sudden anger mixed with his fear as his chest beat even harder.

She chuckled. 'You seem to think you're in a position to tell me what I can and can't do!'

'You brought me here to kill me. We're now at the point where I either fight you with every ounce of strength I have or I sit quietly and you get what you want.' Harry allowed a gap for her to reply, all he got were lips curling into a snarl. 'So, I'll die in this jacket and I have some things on me that I'll be holding onto. For the end.'

'Well . . . this is cute!' Her chuckle upgraded itself to laughter. It was sudden, manic and just as quick to fall away.

'You may not have mercy, but you can have some compassion. My wallet, inside pocket. There's a picture of my daughters in there and a stub from a cinema. I want to be holding them both.'

'A cinema ticket?'

'Put one in each hand and you can do what you want.'

'Why a cinema ticket?'

'Because I'm a sentimental old fool and it's the closest thing I have to holding hands with my wife. I would like that one last time.'

There was a pause, Harry held eye contact while she seemed to mull it over. Then, she stepped forward, her hand rough as she pulled his waxed jacket apart to get to the pocket. She searched his wallet, pulling out the torn-up and repaired ticket first.

'What the hell happened to this?'

'It's a story that isn't for you.'

She scowled, hooking out the picture of Mel and Faye next, then throwing the wallet to the floor. Her fingers were clumsy in gloves, lacking dexterity as she moved around him to push both items into his clammy palms.

Harry gripped them tight.

'Don't you want them back in your pocket?' There was something different in her voice, it might have been compassion. The volume too, was lower. 'You're going to drop them pretty quick.'

'I won't drop them,' Harry growled. 'I've seen enough violent murder scenes. We call it the death grip, meet a violent end and your hands clamp shut. I've had to break a dead man's fingers before to get something he was holding.'

'Noted.' She moved away, staying out of sight for Harry to hear the sounds of items being moved from up on the shelves. When she reappeared in front of him the weapon she was holding had changed.

Considerably.

Harry was sitting face to face with a jagged bow saw. He tried not to stare.

'Best I make sure this is as violent as possible, then.' She leaned in closer still. 'I'm going to saw at your neck until your head comes off.' She paused for a reaction and got nothing. 'It didn't have to be like this. I tried walking away from this once before. I was done after the sergeant, two miserable coppers was enough to take the feeling away. You should have just taken Ryan as your man and walked.'

'You killed him so he didn't tell us about you. And he would have. It wouldn't have taken much from me and he would have seen right through you. Seen the truth.'

'If only you had got to him first. But you didn't, not in time!' She was delighted with that, with herself, the grin told him so. But it changed in an instant, into a snarl as she stepped back, her free hand pulling out a bundle of white cloth that she pushed at Harry's mouth. He relented, opening his jaw, his head jerked back at her gusto. 'Can't have anyone hearing your screams of agony now, can we?' She lifted her left leg so it rested against his right thigh, steadying the chair. The bow saw caught in the light as it lifted. Beyond it, she licked her lips.

Harry sat tall and proud, determined to do so until he couldn't anymore. He could feel his heart still smashing into his chest, feeling like it might explode out of him at any point, something he had been trying to limit, praying it would last for as long as he needed.

And it had.

His heart was a runaway train. He had been taking deep breaths as a way of applying the brakes, but the solid gag in his mouth meant that there was nothing he could do. He could feel a hot tingle in his left side, he had first noticed it sparking in his fingers on the drive over but it had spread, moved up his arm, and it was at this point that it surged out across his chest. He remembered the sensation. He knew that there would be a lightning bolt of pain, but it would be momentary.

And then it would be over.

His lasting memory from the heart attack just a few days earlier was not the physical sensations that came with it, but the sense of relief when he had realised that his time was up. He was ready, he had known it then and he knew it now. The doctor had made it clear that the next one would be bigger, that there would be no coming back.

There was more than a little comfort in that.

# CHAPTER 72

'Video call incoming?' Maddie read off the screen, turning to make eye contact with Eileen. 'Not a number I recognise.' Maddie swiped to answer. An image appeared, it was video footage, there was some movement but it was pixelated, broken up into big squares that shifted and overlapped as if the signal was poor. It would be a few seconds more until the picture tidied itself up, until she was able to recognise Harry Blaker, sat up in a chair, lit up brightly with a gag stuffed in his mouth. The view was mainly of one side. If Harry was twelve o'clock, the camera pointed at him was positioned at four on a clockface. There was someone else there too, someone standing directly in front of him with a hood up, a hood that was a curious shape — squared off. The shoulders too, as if the figure wore a suit of armour under dark-coloured clothes.

Maddie realised that the shape was an aspect of concealment. She couldn't even tell if it was a man or a woman. The figure was so close it could have been stood on Harry's toes and yet he still didn't react. His hands were pulled behind his back where they had to be trussed. He had to be unable to react. The chair rocked where the figure changed position, lifting a leg. Harry's head moved, his shoulders too, as if they were tensing.

The footage broke up for a split second — more squares, Maddie only able to detect movement. Then it cleared to reveal a large, D-shaped saw resting against Harry Blaker's neck, the side that faced the camera.

The person holding it demonstrated that they were aware of the camera, adjusting their position so the outstretched arm didn't cover Harry's face. His eyes were wide at first, they slammed shut the moment he would have felt those teeth rest against his skin. The background was brick and concrete, shelves with pots.

A garage.

'Eileen . . .' It was just about all Maddie could manage. Then she started moving forward, lifting her radio as she went, holding down the transmit button on the side.

'All units, strike, strike, STRIKE!'

# CHAPTER 73

There wasn't vehicle access, at least not one they could find quick enough. The van pulled up roughly by a cut in the fence and Maddie ditched her car close behind for all doors to burst open.

'Eileen, stay here!' Maddie bellowed, but she was wasting her breath. The ground was instantly uneven, just as Maddie remembered, grit and coarse weeds with larger rocks lurking to bring her down. She was aware of other figures running, mostly they were ahead, having spilled out of the van's side door. Maddie was fixated ahead on the brightly lit garage she had heard described over the radio, still lit up like a flame drawing moths.

She could see a figure, it appeared to stand in the light, then started walking back towards them all, arms raised, movement slow. KitKat.

'It's too late!' he said. Maddie heard the words but didn't stop to challenge them. She fled past, the lit garage still her target.

The first detail she could make out was a wooden chair, set up in the middle of the sparse garage, its seat running with blood. Then the body sprawled out beneath it, laid on its side with long dark hair, darker in patches where it was sodden with blood and falling part over her face.

'It's Falconer, she's been stabbed . . . a lot!' KitKat didn't suit shock. He had been so cool to this point.

'Have you tried?' The sergeant bellowed back. 'We need to try! Get the medics kit, someone get on her chest!' He followed his own instructions, dropping next to the body, rolling it to a position where he could start with chest compressions. The hair fell away, enough for Maddie to make a positive ID. They had found Chloe Falconer.

Her hand had a shake as she lifted her phone back from where she had thrust it in her pocket. What she had seen begin was still going on. It was still on her screen, pixelated at first, then clearing.

'Oh my . . .' Eileen breathed in her ear, where she was close enough to be able to see the screen.

'We were too late!' KitKat said again, pacing aimlessly like walking wounded.

And he was right. Too late for Chloe Falconer and, with Maddie unable to look away from the screen in her hand, too late for Harry Blaker.

Maddie needed to explain, she needed to tell her colleagues what she was seeing, that this wasn't the only site where extreme violence had taken place that night. But she couldn't. A shock of pain flashed through her gut, its strength and veracity enough to take her clean off her feet.

She knew instantly what it was, she just knew.

'Maddie?' Eileen said as Maddie took a knee, her voice thick with concern and confusion.

'Eileen . . .' she managed. 'I'm pregnant.'

CHAPTER 74

It was Sunday morning, early enough that the sun was still a smudge on the horizon, only just starting to gather itself up into a ball.

Two days since . . .

Maddie was back to her rural outlook. This was a view she knew well, out over a steady change of seasons, a dependable pattern that was subtle and slow. She would still have preferred the tumultuous, unpredictable and violent changes of the sea. It would certainly be more fitting.

She was in the top bedroom of the house she shared with Vince, the spare bedroom at the back, the one with the bay window with the sill deep enough to sit on. Vince bundled through the door for the second time that hour, a tea in his mitt, seemingly stuck in his own pattern, a very British one where the only appropriate course of action was to put the kettle on in order to make everything better.

Except it didn't. Nothing could.

'You okay?'

Especially that question.

'I'm good,' she said, for the second time that hour. And she was. The doctor had told her so. Mother and baby had a clean bill of health, but she would need to rest and she would need to significantly amend her job role for the remainder of her term. She didn't just have herself to think about now, the doctor had said — as if she hadn't been spending just about every waking moment thinking about anything but herself.

'A walk perhaps? The sun will be up. Time we get our shoes on.' Vince persisted.

'I'm good,' Maddie said. Third time. She turned away too, away from Vince and his awkward shuffling. She heard the chink of crockery where her empty cup was swapped out, then a dragging sound on the carpet where Vince pulled up a chair. He was staying.

'We need to talk . . .'

'I know,' Maddie said.

'I feel a bit robbed.'

Maddie spun to meet his signature lopsided smile.

'In amongst all of this shit and stress, all this sadness, the happiest moment of my life was kinda lumped in — the happiest moment so far! The announcement. The bit where you tell me we're pregnant. I woulda fucking loved that!'

'I know,' Maddie said, again. She turned back to the window to continue. 'I was at Phil's house when it actually sunk in. His widow was the other side of the door. I was . . . I was sick in her loo. I know that was a couple of days ago now but it feels like everything has been running away from me since. I wanted to go and see a doctor, make sure it was proper, then I wanted to do the announcing bit proper. I didn't just want . . . I wanted us to be fixed.'

'I get that. This fixes us though, right?' he said, with an air of hope — desperation more like. 'I mean, I feel like it fixes me. I don't mean that selfish, just that it's all I can think about. A kid! Our kid! I been in this place mewing and balling, but now . . . I mean . . . I'm gonna be a dad. It's gonna be good for Jake, too. We can be a family. Two-point-four!'

Maddie still stared out of the window, the sensation odd. She felt like she was the other side of that glass, still hearing what he had to say, still aware of the joy gushing from him, but insulated from it by a pane of clear glass. None of it would stick, the joy, the hope, the vision of their future. All she could feel was sadness. Empty. There was another silence. Then the creak of that chair acted as a question: *Maddie?* She needed to respond.

'We're going to be okay,' she said, forcing the smile that went with it. 'You will get your moment, I promise.' He rocked forward to get to his feet then wrapped her up in the latest of any number of hugs, every one somehow less comforting than the last.

There was nothing he could do. It wasn't his fault, but there was no comfort to be had here.

She needed to get back to work.

# CHAPTER 75

Eileen was different. Awkward. It wasn't something Maddie associated with her, to the point where she might almost have believed the woman to be immune to awkwardness of any type, but the awkwardness was clear on their first meeting since the shared experience of Harry Blaker's death.

There was no small talk, no asking after each other, not even a question about Maddie and how she was doing, now that everyone knew. It was a meeting of two women both keen to get to the point. It was carried out in the café that was part of a farm shop near Canterbury. It was the sort of meeting where both coffees would remain untouched.

'They got him not long after we found Chloe. He wasn't far away. I took your phone when you . . . when you were in too much pain to work it. I was going to hand it to digital forensics, but a message came through. It was a postcode. There was nothing else with it. I put it over the air and it was another block of garages. It was only a few miles away.'

Maddie knew this already. Vince had passed on some updates, he'd started with an all-out refusal then swiftly worked out that Maddie was going to need something. He had drip-fed her bits through Saturday, waiting for her discharge from hospital before even mentioning Harry. And then, when he did, Maddie was reminded that he was hurting too.

'Did we pick up Megan Vrana?'

'She came in on her own accord,' Eileen said. 'She didn't add much. She brought her phone that still had the voice message on it. It ties in with what she said to you. She agreed to speak to us under caution . . . she didn't want any legal advice.' Maddie wondered whether Eileen had intended the last bit as a joke.

'So, Chloe called her,' said Maddie, 'and told her where she was at a time that started off an orchestrated chain of events. It was tight too. That call had to be timed perfectly.'

'Duress?' Eileen said, reading Maddie's mind.

'It had to be. But there's so much more that I can't explain. For that to work, someone had to know about my conversation with Vrana. They had to know what reaction I would have to that call and Vrana told me that she doesn't normally pick up her phone out of hours. That call might never have happened in the first place.'

'She shed a little more light on that. There was a text message too, Chloe started it with her name, so when Megan Vrana saw that she was interested enough to listen to her voicemail.'

'Even so,' Maddie said. 'And that's all before we consider Harry. Whoever this was, they would already have needed to have control of him. I can't begin to consider how someone does that. We've checked on his daughter?'

'We have and she's fine. The Police Liaison got in touch with Faye. He broke the news and then spent some time with her. She confirmed that no one's made contact with her at all, let alone issued any sort of threat. It's possible there was a threat against her that she didn't know about, but it would have to have been real enough for Harry to believe it.'

'She's the only thing in Harry's life that could have him turning out on his own, taking those sorts of risks. She's everything he has.'

'We've searched his home,' said Eileen. 'There are some things of note. The front door was open, hanging open. His mobile phone was on the kitchen table and his car was on the drive.'

'He didn't take his own car?'

'No. But he still made it to a location an hour away from his home.'

'Any neighbours that can shed any light on that?'

'Neighbours talk about a man who's barely there. One of them said they'd known him for years, but they thought he lived somewhere else most of the time. Said something about a girlfriend down the road. No one saw anything go on at the house. We do know that he made it home. The nurse told us she called him a taxi, so I spoke to the firm. They picked him up from the hospital, but there was a diversion.'

'Go on.'

'Mr Blaker stopped for a chip supper for two. He then took it to Jillian Jones. We've spoken to her, two detectives from the team. She didn't take the news well—'

'You told her?'

'They were sent with permission to do what they thought was suitable. But yes, they made that decision.'

'They had a connection, Harry and Jill Jones, I could see that from the start. Harry knew exactly what she was going through. I think he was making it better.'

'She said as much.'

'What did he go there for?'

'He turned up under the premise of seeing how she was doing, but she said that she saw through that. She reckoned on a man who wasn't well and wasn't expecting to get better. She said that he didn't stay long but the atmosphere was of someone saying goodbye.'

'Do you think he already knew what was going to happen later that evening?'

'The conversation that Mrs Jones described was one around his health, rather than circumstance. She did get the impression that he was expecting something bad to happen, but it was all centred on the news from the hospital. Mrs Jones . . .' Eileen started to then fade to a stop.

'What?'

'She had a message for you, specifically. She seemed to think that the main reason Mr Blaker attended her address was so he could pass a message on. He told her that he considered you brilliant, that he respected you, to the point that he described you as the detective he always wanted to be . . .'

Maddie took a moment. It wasn't upset. It was something different. 'He could have just told me that.' It was anger, it was building.

'And what would have been your reaction?'

'What do you mean?' Maddie snapped.

'If Harry had discharged himself from hospital hours after collapsing, then turned up to tell you how much he respected you? What would you have thought?'

'Something was badly wrong.'

'You would quite possibly have driven him back to hospital yourself. Mr Blaker would have known that.'

Maddie's anger dissipated just as quickly, pushed out by the exhaustion that seemed to be her default state.

'And now you need to learn from Mr Blaker, from the end, at least, from what he didn't do.' Eileen added.

'Didn't do?'

'Look after himself, ma'am. You're angry at him for that reason, because he didn't listen to the people around him, to medical professionals. Now it's you that's being told to rest and not just for you . . .' Eileen stopped herself. 'You need to go home. I'll keep you informed, just like I said I would. We have an excellent team of detectives already in place and a new SIO in the wings, from what I understand. This offender, this person, this piece of *shit*, they will be caught.'

Maddie couldn't help but smile at the profanity. She was pretty sure she'd never heard anything close from Eileen before.

'Who's the SIO picking this up?'

'We don't know yet.'

'I can't rest. Not in Elham. Vince is . . . he's doing my head in. I'll be back at the flat if you need me.' Maddie was thinking out loud, making up plans on the hoof.

'And Vince . . . when he calls me, desperate to know where his pregnant partner is, having just been released from hospital?' Eileen was a step ahead as ever.

'He won't. I told him I was going to the flat to get some clothes and a few other things. He won't begrudge me a little lie down.'

'And is that all you'll be doing?'

'That's all I have planned,' Maddie said.

'I assume that's as good as I am going to get for assurance?'

'I can't do assurance. Not anymore.'

# CHAPTER 76

Maddie arrived home with anger still battling her exhaustion. It was the anger that had her blurting out at the woman holding the communal door for her, the same woman that Maddie knew to be responsible for leaving the communal door insecure for any waif or stray.

'I had some guy asleep in my doorway!' Maddie snapped, 'I think you made him a dinner?'

The woman stopped. She was older than Maddie, maybe thirty years or more, but she dressed sharper, her hair better cared for, her overall image far cooler. Today she was in an oversized white shirt with sleeves rolled up, the fact it was creased somehow making it cooler still. The bracelet on her exposed arm matching perfectly with the buckle on her slim belt fed through slimmer jeans. This time the insecurity was caused by her holding the door, rather than jamming a chock in the bottom, at least.

'Sorry?' she said, as Maddie took the door.

'The rough sleepers. I know you look after them and I'm sure they appreciate it massively. But maybe consider a takeaway option in the future. Takeaway from the building, that is.'

'Whiff of poverty get up your nose, did it?' The woman snapped back. Maddie might have reared up at the suggestion, but the flare of anger that had pushed out her challenge was just that, a flare, and it was spent.

'Look, I'm glad that you help them out. I'm just asking that you don't leave this door open. We all want to live in a secure building. I don't think that's unreasonable.' Maddie moved into the hall. The door had a creak, it was a heavy fire door, the springs working hard to stop it from slamming. The creak stopped where the woman caught it.

'Someone else let him in, assuming it's the same man. I saw him outside your door and he turned me down for dinner. He said someone else let him in, said they gave him money just to loiter. Some *other bird*, were his exact words, which was the moment I decided not to assist him again. I don't like such terms.' She looked Maddie up and down, biting down on her bottom lip. 'So, you needn't concern yourself with me.'

'A woman?' Maddie said. 'What woman?'

The woman let the door go, timing her answer to ensure there was no way she would hear a reply. 'You're the detective.'

* * *

Maddie's flat felt chilly, despite the pleasant temperature outside. It was always a little cooler in the mornings. The sun would move around to bathe the interior by early afternoon at most times of the year, which meant it was imminent. She still slipped on a hoody, always a little more susceptible to the cold when she was tired.

Her bed smelled fresh. She lay down on top, her head towards the view. The bed was positioned on purpose so she could see the ocean, even if it was a view through iron railings. She barely noticed them. She had coached herself not to see them at all, in truth, but that day they seemed thicker, more intrusive, as if she was peering out of a prison cell.

Closing her eyes was worse. Her mind instantly got to work conjuring images of Harry, the images still there when she opened them again and sat up. It was a memory, the starkest that she had of the man. It was on an earlier case, one that taken her to an abandoned swimming pool with water rushing the back of her legs. All around her had been chaos: people drowning, fighting for their lives, fighting each other and Maddie had suffered a moment like nothing before. She had been overwhelmed, frozen still, terrified.

*I've got you.*

Harry had appeared next to her and said those words, he had been so self-assured that she had known them to be true. He had steadied her, wrapped his arm around her and, in that moment, she had known that everything was going to be alright. Not just then, but always.

And now, as she tried to blink away the prison bars of her own home, it just felt like it wasn't.

Maddie had never felt so alone.

## CHAPTER 77

There was no chance of a nap and the whiff of defeat was thick among the scent of her coffee as Maddie leaned over it, her palms down, head slumped forward. She found herself wondering if this state of suspended exhaustion was what it might have been like for Harry these last few months.

The sun had shifted, the rays bright and strong and her apartment's transition from cool to stuffy was complete. On a whim, she tipped the coffee into a travel mug. She needed some air.

The seafront had a promenade. She turned left, the sea to her right, heading towards the Coastal Park that consisted of well-maintained lawns and a plethora of benches. There was an amphitheatre too, carved into a steep bank, the top half grass, the bottom benches made out of thick wooden sleepers. There was a rough sleeper too. The same man that Maddie had seen in her hall. The first of a couple of coffee places was to the left, a simple hatch in a metal container painted green so that it might blend in.

'Can I get you a coffee?' Maddie said. 'I think they do pastries too.'

The rough sleeper spun to face her. It took a moment but his face lit up in recognition. 'You following me around, lady? I get that a lot. Quite the catch, I've been told.'

'You started it.' She had to force a smile, no doubt the effort showed.

'Four sugars. And they do a cinnamon bun.' He had the grin of a man who knew how to play this game. She was almost all the way to the hatch when he shouted, 'And some crisps!'

Maddie returned with the order, putting it down in an area he had cleared for it. He was now sitting up, rubbing his eyes with fingers dipped in filth.

'How did you get into the building? When I saw you, I mean?'

'What are you, security?' He fixed his gaze on her, his mouth stopping where he had torn a clump from the cinnamon bun. 'Copper?'

'Just a resident. There's been some burglaries in the area—'

'I don't burgle!' He stiffened, genuinely offended.

'I know that,' she said, 'but it's not the time for my friends to be leaving doors insecure for anyone and everyone.'

'Maybe I could be security. What better than someone sat outside all night?' He looked at her closely, sounding her out.

'How did you get in?'

The man smiled, his teeth lined with sugar. 'It was better than ever. I get in there sometimes. Soon as it turns cold, it's a place to go. I usually get a dinner, something hot. But I get a nip of something good too. The lady likes her brandy. This time I got cash.'

'She gave you money?'

His smile got wider. 'Different lady. A bit of a dicky bird, if you know what I mean! I got a twenty just for sitting there.'

'In the hall?'

'Right where you saw me. She gave me a door number, said there was a mark on the wall a little away from it. Said I should sit over that mark. I had to wait outside for an hour, then go and sit for an hour. Gave me a crisp twenty and said that she would know if I moved before my time was up. I never believed her, I mean, I seen her leave, but it didn't matter to me. I weren't busy!' The man's smile turned into a chuckle.

'A mark?'

'X marks the spot!' he chuckled.

'Have you seen her before? In the building?'

'No, no. I ain't ever seen this one before.'

'Describe her for me.'

'I dunno . . . Older than you. Say fifty. Nice dressed . . . skirt. Good legs for her age. Liked a bit of make-up. Gave me some cash with painted nails.'

'White?'

The man shrugged. 'I had her down as a bit Slovak looking. The whole town's full of them. You know that's who they give the flats to first?'

'Tanned?' Maddie tried to ignore everything else.

'Yeah, a dirty tan. Not a darkie — still white, like. Dark hair, though, like they all have.'

'Would you recognise her if you saw her again?'

'You sure you ain't a copper?' He looked a little nervous for a moment; it leaked out where he was still smiling. 'Sort of question a copper might ask.'

'Sounds like someone wanted you sat outside my place for when I got home. That sounds a bit odd, doesn't it? Think I'm right to be a concerned resident about that.'

'I didn't know whose flat it was.'

'What reason did she give you for sitting where you did?'

'She didn't give no reason. She walked me, showed me the mark and walked me back out again. I never asked. I got the impression that the twenty quid didn't come with no questions.'

'Have you got a phone number?' Maddie said.

'You been wanting to ask that the whole time, ain't ya!'

Maddie managed a smile. 'I might wanna talk to you again.'

'Over lunch, yeah?'

'Sure. It's your turn.'

# CHAPTER 78

The mark was still there. It looked like an 'X' as described, marked black biro, but only visible to someone looking for it specifically. It was a metre short of her front door. The rough sleeper, who had given his name as James, had indeed been sitting right there.

Maddie now did the same. She then looked around, right and left where the corridor stretched away in both directions. The main entrance was now to her right, the corridor in the other direction ended in a fire door that had a bike shackled to it. The only other features were assorted doormats and Maddie frowned her confusion.

Then she looked up.

In the next moment she sprung to her feet, lifting her hand to rub her fingertips over a single, drilled hole. There was a circular scuff that surrounded it like an aura, left by whatever it had been holding up, the scuff was deeper at the bottom, suggesting to Maddie that it had been holding something that had been pointed down.

Like a camera.

'Shit!' She stepped back, pushing off the wall as if it might burst into flames. Her eyes dropped to the floor, then she squatted for a closer inspection. This time, her fingertips found wooden shavings shaped like pig's tails. She found white ones that matched the paint on the walls, but brown ones too, where the drill bit had gone through the outside layer.

Eileen was quick to pick up her phone.

'How goes the rest, ma'am?' she said. When Maddie didn't reply she followed it up with, 'Can you hear me, okay? Anyone there?'

'Sorry.' Maddie's reply came with a burst of traffic noise. She had jogged the three flights of stairs to get back to the ground floor and out of the building. 'I couldn't speak for a moment there. I need you to send a search team — the tech guys too.'

'Send them where?'

'My apartment. I think there was a camera outside, there might still be cameras inside.'

'Cameras?'

'Ryan Archer's MO, where he puts cameras in homes, gets into people's lives as part of targeting them. I think maybe someone got into mine — Harry's too. There were cameras used so we could see him die, cameras we never found. It all fits.'

'Okay. Harry's home is still sealed off, they're probably searching it as we speak. If there are cameras, I'm sure they'll—'

'There will be. That has to be how they got to Harry, how they convinced him that he needed to be dealing with this on his own. They were watching him, learned what it was that made him tick. Faye! Her house will need to be searched too!' Maddie was out of breath, marching for her car.

'If you think someone might be watching you, ma'am, may I suggest you come into work until we can establish that one way or another?'

'Just you try and stop me.'

# CHAPTER 79

The Major Crime office hushed the moment Maddie entered. Everyone stopped, their heads bent, some with their arms across their front, all suddenly aware to be sombre, most avoiding eye contact. It was as if she was leading the procession that contained Harry's hearse. Had anyone been wearing a hat, she might have expected them to slip it off.

She had been aware for some time that she was no longer an individual entity in her role, that they came together, they were Harry and Maddie.

And now she was just Maddie.

This shouldn't have been so terrifying. She had been plucked out of a normal career in policing to work exclusively on her own right from the start. She was used to depending on herself, even preferring to do so. But that feeling of being lost rushed back with such a surge that it might have overwhelmed her completely. She had to bite down hard, fight off the urge to sob, close down thoughts of guilt over feeling sorry for herself, for not being stronger, for not being capable of leading this room of people.

All that in a single moment.

And then the next moment it dissolved completely: Eileen. She was there with a reassuring smile and a hand

331

on Maddie's shoulder that led them both into a side room littered with boxes.

'Are you okay, ma'am?' Eileen then looked around and tutted. 'I'll get a chair in here.'

'No!' Maddie took a moment to breathe so she would come back calmer. 'I'm fine.'

Eileen paused and Maddie knew she was being assessed. 'Search team were directed to your apartment first,' Eileen said at last. 'They should be on site by now. I'm resisting chasing for an update.'

'I waited for them to arrive,' Maddie said. 'Handed over the key. They said they would call me direct.'

'Nothing to do but wait, then.'

Maddie wasn't very good at waiting, not in that moment. 'Is there anything else? What have we got coming in?' She was desperate for something else to think about.

'Nothing else significant. CSI are still out at the scene. Charley Mace called me for a rather strange conversation.'

'How so?'

'We have an unwritten agreement that she'll take initial photographs of any murder scene and send them through to me quick-time. It's so I can give you and the team a bit of an edge. This time she chose to call.'

'To ask if you wanted them?'

'Exactly that.'

'What did you say?'

'I said yes, but that I had no intention of looking at them. We have a new SIO. I'll just forward them straight on.'

'Who's the new boss?'

Eileen hesitated.

'I'm not going to like it, am I?'

'Apparently not. DCI Tristan Stepney has taken up the role, at least temporarily.'

Maddie actually laughed. 'I was waiting to see how this day could get any worse! Of all people . . . Was there really no one else?'

'I can't say I was involved in the selection process, ma'am. Nor have I met the man to be able to form any sort of opinion. I have had some tasks but they have come through third hand. I am told he prefers to task warranted constables over a civilian employee. I'm sure I can win him round.'

'And I'm sure it's not worth your effort to do so.'

'There is a bigger picture. I have worked with Little Man Syndrome before. I can certainly work with it again. We need to be finding a killer. nothing else really matters for now.'

'Little Man Syndrome?' Maddie smiled out her question.

'It seems to be how everyone refers to him.'

'It's very apt,' Maddie said. 'And you might be a bigger person than me. A word of warning about him, though . . . I'm not sure I would be forwarding photos obtained outside of the official routes. You probably don't want to shine a light on that agreement with Charley.'

'Yes, I did consider that. His pettiness seems to be as well regaled as his height.'

'Excellent. Seems like you've already had the briefing.'

Maddie and DCI Tristan Stepney had history. He had been Harry Blaker's replacement previously, when Harry made a snap decision to swap Major Crime for a training role to see out his career. It didn't work out well, not for either man and Harry's return was assured when he became part of fixing the mess that Stepney quickly made.

Maddie couldn't think of a worse replacement.

'Did Charley say anything about the photos, any suggestion of anything that might move us on?'

'She said that they were likely to be able to shed some light on the route Harry took. There are some fresh tracks from a car on a grass verge nearby. The verge has damage consistent with a wheelspin. Too dry for a print but they can tell us it was an impression from a fourteen-inch wheel. From that we are pointed towards budget vehicles. Something small. Ford Fiesta sized, I was told. There was some plastic trim found too, photographed *in situ*. Charley is hopeful that they might find something later to compare it to.'

'She'll be able to determine it was the car Harry used?'

'You know Charley, ma'am. She remains the queen of non-committal. But if the trim and the marks are linked, then Harry parked a road over from the garage.'

'A road over?' Maddie had just started to get her hopes up. 'Some tread marks and broken plastic a road over and she's linked that to Harry?'

'Charley was more positive than we are used to. She said that the path walked from where the car had been parked was kicked up, like someone had dragged their feet, disturbing the loose surface.'

'She thinks this was all Harry leaving us a trail?'

'She does. Mainly from a find the search team had, the one that had them working backwards.'

'Find?' Maddie's hope returned all at once.

'The path led through woodland that had a wooden stile at the point where it met with a field. A dog lead was found hanging off the bottom step.'

'Jock's lead?' Maddie said.

'We believe so.'

'And we have Jock? It wasn't a dog walk?'

'He was located at a neighbour's house. A former MET officer, actually. Seems there's an agreement in place. She was most upset.'

'Harry knew he wasn't coming back out.'

'It must have been a consideration.'

'He must have been so scared.' Maddie breathed. 'Is that it? From CSI, I mean, if he was leaving us clues . . .'

'That is all she picked out to tell me but there are a lot of photos apparently . . .'

'I need to look. I need to see what was there.'

'I really don't think that's a good idea.' Eileen said.

'There might be something. If Harry Blaker scuffed his feet, snapped bits of plastic and left Jock's lead for us to follow, that won't be all. No one knew him better than me. If he left a trail then it's a trail for me!'

'Ma'am—'

'Please . . .' Maddie cut in and the two women were locked together in a shared moment.

Eileen's shoulders dropped first, a sign of her intent. 'I want it on record that I think this is a bad idea.' She didn't wait for a reply. She shuffled out to get her laptop, her head bent the whole time. She lifted the lid to tap out her password and the screen opened with the email from Charley Mace still on her screen. Maddie could see the attached file. She could see the message that accompanied it too:

*Eileen,*
*Attached as discussed. I know we already talked this out, but these come with a trigger warning. Maddie will ask. My advice is not to make her aware of their existence. She doesn't need to see this.*
*Charley.*

'I think I will make that tea.' Eileen mumbled, she hesitated at the door, her slippered feet scuffing on the threshold. If there was something she had to say, she thought better of it.

Maddie double-clicked without hesitation, without thinking too much. She didn't want to change her mind. An evidential CSI photo album was a very specific format, one that started with a written piece describing the location, date, attending CSI officers and laid out the circumstances. The pictures would then be presented in an order that made sense, focussing on one element at a time.

This had none of that.

It was pictures uploaded as they had been taken: whatever had caught Charley Mace's eye, whatever she deemed might be relevant and in no particular order. Maddie skipped the first few without even seeing them, her mind registered masses of red, recognising gore before any details, her finger faster to click than her mind was to register. Evidential or not, there were some pictures she was not going to be able to look at.

The first picture she did stop at was of the floor. There were four chair legs visible and a little bit of trouser in the top of the screen, but the focus was down, specifically on a wallet. Harry's wallet. It looked like it had been searched, then thrown. It lay open on its back, some notes lolling out like a tongue.

She clicked to see the next. it was a close-up of the same.

The next image was of a hand. Harry's hand. The focus was on one, she could just make out the other beside it. She could also see a steel band, the handcuffs still applied. They would be their own forensic subject. It would be painstaking and it would be done largely before removal. Even from the picture she could see they were ratcheted too tight, the skin discoloured around them.

Maddie almost skipped it; there was still so much blood. She looked away, took a breath and went back to it, even leaning towards it to take in the detail. It was his left hand, his thick thumb firmly across the middle of a photograph, one that she could just see enough to identify it. It was of his two daughters, Faye and Mel and they were smiling wide. The shot was candid, taken in a booth, but one of those that captured the moments of silliness between the formal shots.

She remembered Harry showing it to her. She remembered the picture, but, more than that, she remembered the look on Harry's face when he held it. Her eyes burned like they yearned to unleash a tear. It would be the first time she had cried, but she scolded herself again and it didn't come. She had to hold it together. She had to be strong. For Harry.

She skipped to the next. Again, the backdrop was the floor and Maddie needed to lean close to the screen to try and work out what it was showing. Little bits of white? Paper perhaps? Torn-up paper? Some of them looked shiny, reflecting the flash.

She clicked again. The next picture was a closer look at some of the ripped-up pieces, it was all she needed. It took her breath away.

It was a torn-up cinema ticket.

It was the entire answer scattered in pieces on a dusty, concrete floor, one that she didn't need to take any time putting back together.

Maddie knew who had killed Harry Blaker.

# CHAPTER 80

'Ma'am?' Eileen's call made Maddie jump as she swept across the carpeted area for the stairs that would take her down and out. She almost dropped the phone she was trying to work.

'Eileen! I'm not feeling well. I think . . . I think this was a mistake after all, like I might have come in too early. Keep me informed, would you?'

'Of course. Are you okay to drive? I can have a patrol—'

'Fine! I'll take it easy. It's just fatigue. I think it's quite common, the things we go through, I think those photos . . . I should have listened to you!' She spun away, her phone still in her hand. She made the bottom of the stairs, then through the door, checking when she was a good way across the car park that Eileen wasn't following, that she wasn't still in ear-shot, that no one was.

Vince picked up quickly, the concern clear in just one word. 'Mads!'

'Vince, I think I understand,' she blurted.

'You okay? Where are you?'

'Cranbrook nick.'

'Cranb— What the hell are you doing? You went to work?' It was hurt now, genuine.

Maddie might have flashed guilty in different circumstances. 'I understand, the way you felt — the anger you felt. When your sister . . . when you were hurting and that little girl was taken. All of that whirled up inside you to the point it was all that mattered — to hell with everything else!' Maddie's volume was rising, but knowing it didn't mean she could do anything about it.

'What's going on, Mads?' The hurt was gone. Now it was concern.

'I understand!' she said.

'Okay. I . . . I mean, yeah, I guess that was pretty much what it was like.'

'That anger, that force that took you over. Do you still have it in you?'

'Do I . . . What's going on?'

'I know who killed Harry. But I can't hand it over. It has to be me.'

'You're crazy, you can't just—'

'Are you in or not?' As she cut him off, her tired pool car spluttered to life on the second attempt.

'Yes,' Vince said, sounding incredulous. 'Where am I going?'

# CHAPTER 81

Vince did have it in him. His anger had bubbled up the moment he understood that Maddie was going anyway, that there was nothing he could do to talk her out of it. Making him understand had the effect of increasing her own anger too, to the point that it ended up being two people winding each other up.

But the journey was long, long enough for a little clarity to appear among the whirl of anger, for Maddie to consider that this was barely a half-formed idea. She hadn't given any consideration at all as to how she might control Vince now that she had whipped him up. It was a more obvious problem the moment they got to their destination, when Vince was first out of the car, propelled by his own frustrations, at the injustice in his own career, the loss of his friend and now with the chance to throw himself head first into a conclusion.

Maddie was suddenly concerned that there wasn't going to be much of Neil Archer left to talk to. She had to run to catch up, just about to utter her first words of calm, when the ultimate damp towel over flames stepped out from behind a concrete post.

Eileen Holmans. She looked odd, not just the fact she was in shoes, but the over-stuffed backpack she wore over both shoulders.

'I saw them too,' she said, as Maddie squeaked to a stop. 'Right after you left. I took a look, seeing as something had you in a bit of a kerfuffle.'

'Saw what?' Maddie said.

'Eileen,' Vince said, 'you need to step out of the way.' His fists were clenched, rising and falling as he breathed in and out.

'And you need to think this through, both of you.' Eileen countered.

'What did you see?' Maddie saw an opportunity to confirm what she already knew.

'The cinema ticket. Ripped up. I was there when Harry was telling you the history of that ticket. The first date with his wife-to-be, how her dad could never know. How her mum ripped it up.'

'Okay then.' Maddie held her breath, fighting off a sob.

'Harry ripped it up all over again, to point us towards Ryan Archer's mother,' Eileen said.

'Neil Archer told me she was dead,' Maddie spluttered, her anger building back.

'He did. I did some checks and there was no confirmation. That's not unusual. Records of death are pretty tight, but there are ways around it. We think that Janet Archer's reasons for leaving centred around protecting her son. Maybe she did what she could to make sure she was never found, to avoid the knock at the door that would bring confirmation.'

'Or maybe she isn't dead. Maybe she's alive and well and taking her revenge on any police officer she can get to. And Harry found that out.'

'Maybe.' Eileen agreed. 'And now you're going to kick your way in there and demand the truth?'

'You have a better idea?' Maddie said.

'More a consideration.' Eileen had that maddening ability to slow everything down. 'Cameras. We should assume the use of them has been extensive, and continues to be.'

'What does that mean?'

Vince stepped a little closer, a sidestep too. Eileen didn't react. She didn't get out of the way either.

'Mr Blaker's death was streamed, to us no less. And your apartment? I have confirmation there was a camera found, positioned on the inside to cover some of your living space.'

'In my house!' Maddie said.

'In your house. We have a find in Mr Blaker's house too so we can assume the use of cameras has been extensive and we should consider that they might cover you kicking a door in, demanding the truth about a suspect, a suspect who could be watching the entire thing play out.'

'You think there are cameras here?' Maddie said. It wasn't so much a question as a realisation.

'If you thought there were, would your approach be different?' Eileen said.

'Eileen . . .' Vince growled, 'either give me a better idea or get out of my way.'

'I have a wi-fi blocker and a device for detecting what is connected.' She tapped the straps on her bag. 'The techies lent me both. They suggested I use them to see if there is anything untoward in my home. We don't know how far this has gone.'

'So what?' Vince was starting to lose his patience again.

'So, it gives us an option here. I just need to get close. Close enough to be able to pick up the network. If I can tell you there are cameras attached to Neil Archer's wi-fi then we know that we cannot kick his door in. At least, not until I block the signal so anyone watching it on a live stream might think that the internet has gone down. It might just give you long enough.'

'How close?' Maddie said.

'Don't worry about that. I have an idea, but it will need to be done slow time. That means you can take PC Arnold away from the area, before his career hiatus becomes a little more permanent. And you can take yourself away too, before you put yourself in a situation you might regret. I will get a whole team here and this will get done. This can still be the breakthrough we want.'

'We *are* the breakthrough,' said Maddie. 'This is where we need to be. Harry was telling us. He was telling *me!*' She was back trying to think, trying to sort the swirl in her mind. 'Neil Archer lied to me, right to my face. He knew more than he was letting on. It needs to be me. He's pathetic, a coward of a man, and the moment he is confronted by the woman he lied to, he won't be able to do it again.'

'Damned right he won't.' Vince spat.

Eileen took a deep breath, her eyes glazed where she looked like she was mulling it over. 'Okay, then . . . this happens now. But I have to go first and you have to give me fifteen minutes.'

'For what? That blocker thing is just pushing a button, right?'

'There's a little more to this than that.' Eileen bristled. 'I need time. Pressing the button is the final part, before that, I need to make a new friend.'

'Friend?' Maddie said. 'What are you talking about?'

'I'm talking about keeping us all in a job.'

# CHAPTER 82

The message came through just eleven minutes later. They had gone back to the car after Maddie had restored her senses enough to recognise that they were standing out. It was a rough area overall, the sort where a well-built, angry man stomping in circles like he was waiting for a fight might not look out of place as such, but the people making up these neighbourhoods knew each other. They knew their own. Which meant they knew when someone wasn't.

Eileen's message confirmed three cameras linked to the wi-fi at the target address. It also confirmed that she could nullify them, but the window would need to be short. It changed the dynamic again, muddied the water, leaving Maddie forced to consider that Neil Archer wasn't as involved as she had thought. But he still knew more than he had told her in their first two meetings.

The third shift in dynamic was a marked change in approach. Once again, Vince and his frustrations led the way. Their progress up the stairs was amplified by the fact that they were constructed of bare concrete. Vince took the last set two at a time, keeping that momentum up as part of his attack on the door.

The door went in on the first boot.

As did Vince.

Maddie followed him in.

Neil Archer met them in the hall. He took one look at Vince and spun on the spot, moving back into the living room, making a dart for the phone that was laid out on the table. Vince knocked an oversized Crystal Palace mug to shatter on the floor as he grabbed Archer's forearm. Archer was leaning forward and off balance. Vince looked effortless as he sent him crashing headfirst into the armchair. The phone spun across the table. Vince loomed over Archer as he tried to straighten himself up.

'You stay in that chair! Try and move and I start pulling bits off, do you understand? DO YOU UNDERSTAND!' Vince roared these last three words into Archer's face. His fists were clenched, the muscle that ran between his shoulders flared, his shoulders were rock solid when Maddie placed her hand on him.

'It's okay.' Her words were for Vince. 'We're just here to talk.'

'You!' Neil Archer managed, his eyes had been full of Vince Arnold's bulk and anger, but now he was able to take in Maddie and he seemed to relax. 'You're police! You can't just come in here like this! You might have broken my phone. You might have broken me! This is assault!'

Maddie didn't reply. The force of his fall into the sofa had pushed it back a little, creating a gap between him and the low table. She used it to sit on, Vince moved to loom over from the side so she could sit right opposite, her knees just about touching Neil's.

'You want to talk about assault?' she said, with a quiet determination. 'Harry Blaker was assaulted. Do you remember him?'

'I—'

'The gruff one that you thought was in charge, remember?'

'Yeah, so what?' Neil switched between the two, staring up at Vince then back at Maddie. He wasn't so relaxed anymore.

'He was assaulted with a bow saw. Someone tried to cut his head right off. That's not as easy as you might think, by the way. It might actually be easier to pull a head off than to saw through the neck.' Maddie leaned in even closer, forcing eye contact and whispering. 'If the next answer you give me is a lie, we're going to test that out.'

Fear. Maddie knew it when she saw it and it was clear in Neil Archer. He was right to feel it too. In that moment, she meant every word.

'We know Ryan was accompanied by a woman. Long, dark hair. We thought it was Chloe.' She paused for a moment, waiting for a reaction. She got nothing, but the man was holding his breath. 'It wasn't Chloe, was it?' Her words were slow and deliberate and she made it clear she was reading every contour of the man's face. He looked defiant at first, as if he'd been expecting this question at some point and had an answer prepared. If that was the case, he abandoned it. His shoulders slumped and his head rocked forward for his chin to meet his chest. Maddie moved even closer, leaning more for their knees to push together so it was almost painful, forcing eye contact, despite his gaze being in his own lap.

'Where is she?' Maddie hissed. Vince moved. His thighs were already against the arm of the chair, the movement pushed it an inch, maybe less. Neil flinched away from him.

'You don't understand . . .'

'Where IS she?' Maddie was louder, her words still through gritted teeth.

'I don't know . . .' He sighed.

'Are you lying to me?'

'I don't know, okay? I really don't.'

'You've been lying to me this whole time.'

'You don't understand, okay?'

'When I was here last, when I stood in this room, when I was telling you about dead police officers, about children stood over their dead parents, about the trail of destruction your boy left . . . You knew it wasn't over and you knew who we should be looking for.'

'I thought it was over!' He whined.

'You could have stopped this. Harry Blaker would still be here.'

'It's not what you think! I—'

'She killed him. You know that, right? She killed Ryan!'

'Please, you don't understand!' Neil's head snatched straight, his lips shuddered as if he was fighting tears. Maddie had hit a nerve, she gave it another moment to really register.

'Then make me.'

'I . . . I can't!' But that was the moment he was to give her more than an explanation. His eyes flicked beyond her, to the ceiling and she spun to it, expecting to see a camera. He wouldn't know that Eileen had disabled them, that they were alone and free to talk.

Except there was no camera, there was just a ceiling separating them from the upstairs.

'She's here, isn't she?'

## CHAPTER 83

Alive. That was what I felt. Never more. I'd been in the upstairs bedroom and in a sort of half-doze, the same state I'd been in since killing Detective Inspector Harry Blaker. I couldn't sleep, such was the excitement from that night, from the misdirection, the police running to the wrong place, then their reactions when they *knew*.

Utterly intoxicating.

But where do you go from there? It was a question that had rattled around my mind when the excitement had cleared, when the adrenaline had ceased pumping behind my eyes with such gusto as to blur my vision.

Then the door had gone in, the sound travelling up the stairs like a gunshot where it was taken right off its hinges. My first reaction was fear, fear that the might of the police force had found me, a SWAT team like you see on those shitty American films, sweeping torches strapped to barrels.

But it was nothing like that. It was Detective Inspector Maddie Ives and some grunt in a hoody. I checked out of the window overlooking the concrete gangway and there was no sign of any backup. I heard the scuffles too. They threw Neil around the bottom floor like a rag doll, breaking furniture and shouting their threats. This wasn't the way the police worked, not those involved in a planned operation, I knew that as well as anyone. It stank of rogue. It stank of desperation, of someone so messed up on grief that they made mistakes.

And coming after me was always going to be a mistake.

I made it halfway down the stairs, a new knife — bigger than the last — plucked from my waistband, before they both appeared. They bundled into the hallway — amateur hour — spinning on the carpet to lurch towards the bottom step. This was what happened when you got a whole police force rattled . . . they get rash.

They came straight for me and I went straight for them, our meeting in the poor light of the hall.

I lashed out and I know I got someone good. The knife stuck somewhere fleshy, somewhere that contracted like it was gripping the blade. Then I was hit, hard and loud, a white flash across my eyes and a roar that filled my ears and mind and rattled my teeth. The next sensation was falling, forwards down the stairs, of someone grabbing me by my shirt so we might fall together.

The ground floor hit me hard too. I took it through my right shoulder, which stung with pain. I wriggled, putting every ounce of strength I had into it, lashing out, with fists this time, where the knife had been wrenched from my hand, still where I had stuck it.

I was just aware of dark shapes, heavy on top of me, of the adrenaline fuelling my grabbing and blocking. I kept lashing out. Neil was there too. I got a glimpse of him, his hand over his mouth, his eyes wide.

The doorway.

It was a bright, white rectangle and its appearance gave me something to fight for. I got a solid hit in, enough to make a gap that I could throw myself at, kicking with both my legs, encouraged by a howl of pain. I got free, scrabbling forward on my hands and knees, a nail ripped off where it caught on the bare boards. I didn't care, didn't stop. I pushed off my hands like a sprinter, my eyes still up, still fixed on the doorway.

And the drop that was on the other side.

They wanted me, they wanted to capture me and put me in their prison cells, but I couldn't do that, I wouldn't do that.

The drop from here was five storeys — more than enough. It would be instant, it would be painless and it would finally be over.

It would deny them one last time.

## CHAPTER 84

Maddie had been in enough fights to know how they went and this was to be no different. It was a blur of confusion, of flailing limbs, of grabbing hands and grunts of exertion.

Vince was in front of her, the equivalent of a wall moving up the stairs to block everything behind, to block her. He met with a shadow coming down, the force of them colliding made a thudding noise, then Vince exhaled a roar that seemed born of anger and surprise.

Then he fell backwards. They both did.

It was like being hit by a cannonball. Maddie's leg was caught under the weight, crushed while pointing up the stairs and, for a horrendous moment, she thought it might snap at the shin. It didn't, though the pain was still excruciating.

Then there was blood to add to her confusion. It covered her thighs and it was thickening. She was panicking, her head down, despite the noise and confusion that came from two people wrestling on top of her. Vince took a blow, his head not far from hers, his cheek making a slapping sound as a fist connected. It rolled him off her. Next, she was trampled by the shadow that had landed the blow, that seemed suddenly determined to move over them both.

As Maddie tried to scrabble to her feet, she bumped into a pair of legs behind and looked up to see Neil Archer standing over her, his hand over his mouth. She spun left, planting her left hand down, staring back at the front door — and the figure now fleeing through it.

'No you DON'T!' She launched forward, stumbling over a door mat that had rucked up, breaking out into the light, horrified to see a figure throw itself at the balcony out front. Now Maddie could see it was a woman, barefoot, a white blouse splattered in red, the back untucked to flail bright in the sun. Her right foot hit the balcony halfway up, the foundation for her next movement, the flipping over of her legs, one hand on the top, the concrete floor a long way down.

Maddie ignored the pain from her shin to lunge at the railing, grabbing a handful of leg, taking the impact through her chest, knocking the air from her lungs. She held on, she only had one leg and it wasn't a good grip, her mouth made a rasping sound but she wasn't taking in any air. Maddie had stopped the woman from falling, but the momentum still slammed her face first into the steel meshed panel. She screamed out, then lashed out with her free leg, desperate to kick herself loose. She wriggled too, like a fish on a hook.

'Let me go! Let me FUCKING GO YOU BITCH!'

The woman was slipping, an inch at a time, the painted nails that Maddie had seen flash across her face slid lower. Maddie changed her grip, snatching with one hand at the belt that was tight around the woman's middle. She got it on the second go, the weight pulling her down, lifting her onto her tiptoes while the cold steel of the top dug her in the armpits.

'LET ME GO! I KILLED THEM! I KILLED THEM ALL! LET ME GO!'

It was hurting, everywhere. Maddie's shoulder flashed with agony, as if it was coming apart, away from her torso, but the most concerning pain was in her stomach, flashing across like a bolt of lightning. She heard a scream, her eyes clamped shut, it wasn't until it ran out that she realised it had been hers, that her ability to breathe had returned.

'No!' Maddie hissed, opening her eyes to stare at the woman dangling below.

'He's dead too, the ape you brought with you!' The woman hissed back, the words full of glee, her face still obstructed where it was resting against the steel mesh and by dark hair that fell over her mouth and nose to shiver with every spoken word. Maddie grunted with the effort of turning her head, staring back at the door, to where she could see a silhouette that was Vince. It wasn't moving.

'I stabbed him good!' And she licked lips coloured purple, now speckled red. 'So, now's your chance to get the type of justice you really believe in.'

Maddie's vision was blurring with the effort and she clamped her eyes shut. Her fingers screaming out to be opened, to release what they were clamped around. All the pain that she was feeling there and then, all the hurt from the last twenty-four hours, the mess that was the last week . . . it would take just a moment for it to be eased. Her grip loosened, she leaned a little further forward — now at her limit — and the woman slunk another inch downwards.

Among the darkness and the pain, Maddie became aware of another sensation, like being wrapped up, an arm tight around her, the warmth down one side. Her mind conjured an image. It was Harry. He was talking softly and he was right beside her. He shifted to lean down and wrap her hands up in his.

*It's okay, I've got you.*

Maddie let go.

'Woah!' Vince's voice caught Maddie out and she snatched her eyes open to find him next to her, his face a deep grimace where he now had all of the weight of the wriggling woman. The soles of his shoes squeaked where he steadied himself, adjusting for a stronger base. Then he heaved, his hands scrabbling, still leaning over, the woman squawking

352

and screeching. He pulled two legs into view, then scrabbled again to get a fistful of the belt Maddie had just released.

The woman flopped back over to cry out as she lay on the balcony floor. Maddie came back to her senses, dragged back perhaps by the sight of Vince stumbling backwards, his hands now forming around the knife handle sticking out of his thigh. As he fell to a sit, Eileen appeared from the periphery to fuss towards him.

Maddie fixed her eyes on the woman now scrabbling to get up from the floor in front of her and she pounced, using her weight to pin her back down.

'Megan Vrana,' Maddie said. 'I am arresting you on suspicion of murder.'

## CHAPTER 85

DCI Tristan Stepney was not in a good mood. Reputationally and in Maddie's experience, he was never in a good mood, but on that day, he had every reason to be a little upset.

He had stayed silent while the medics did their work. First, they had worked on Vince, keeping the knife *in situ*, trussing it tight, packing gauze tight around the blade to stem the bleeding. Then they had stretchered him to the ambulance that was waiting below, with blue lights that had never stopped and Maddie was able to watch them for miles as they snaked away through the streets.

Then he stayed silent when the sulking Megan Vrana was dragged away. She was checked over too. She had injuries: scuffs and scratches, a suspected broken nose where it had met with a sudden stop against steel mesh — enough for her journey to custody to be via Accident and Emergency. She was chaperoned by four officers, all of them with a look that suggested they were desperate for her to kick off. But Megan Vrana looked like someone who knew that the fighting was over.

Unlike DCI Tristan Stepney.

He lifted his hands to his hips and fixed on Maddie.

'Inspector Ives, care to tell me what the hell you and PC Arnold are doing here? And try to do it in a way that means you still have a chance of a career by the end of the sentence?'

Maddie didn't have an answer. Fortunately, Eileen did and was quick with it.

'We were here to see a friend,' she said and then gestured at a berobed woman who stepped out of the flat directly next to Neil Archer's. The woman nodded a greeting then took a cigarette from a freshly opened packet. The robe she wore had a price tag still attached at the neck that caught in the breeze. 'Julie here.'

"Julie" nodded. 'S'right, guv'nor.' Her words formed out of thick smoke.

'We were here for a cup of tea with Julie and then we heard a commotion from next door,' Eileen explained. 'Seems someone was trying to jump over the railing and cause themselves serious harm. PC Arnold tried to prevent her and received a rather serious injury. Luckily, Ma'am Ives was also on hand to assist, to save her life and then to carry out an arrest when all the pieces fell into place.'

'Saw it with me own eyes, guv'nor.' Julie chimed in. This time the smoke was largely reserved for the smile that followed.

'Is this a joke?' Tristan Stepney was not impressed.

'No joke, sir!' Eileen looked mortally offended. 'But a statement of facts.' At which point, she produced a statement form, filled out in her own impossibly neat handwriting. 'Julie was kind enough to agree to write up her account, though in a little more detail. She was sure to include how we have all been friends for some time and how she invited us along to her home today. That's how we happened to be in the right place at the right time to prevent a terrible incident.'

The DCI stepped over to Eileen, snatching the piece of paper in a movement so sudden and violent that Julie dropped her cigarette from between her lips. She took it well. She merely shrugged, patted her pockets and took out a brand-new carton. There was a moment when everyone present paused to watch her unzip the plastic.

'Just had a big delivery!' She shrugged again, seemingly delighted.

The DCI scanned the front page of the statement. He even flipped it over to pore over the continuations.

'Your *friends* . . .' he spat at the woman now shaking a lighter that had stuttered. 'What are their names?'

'Is there a problem? I'm allowed friends, right? Ain't no law—'

'The big lad with the knife sticking out of his leg. What is his name?'

Julie huffed. She still had the carton of cigarettes in her hand, but she tutted, feeling another pocket, taking out another carton, this one was already opened and she lifted it up and seemed to examine it. 'Ol' Vince, you mean?' She stuffed the carton back where it came from. 'And Mads here . . . Vince and Mads and me ol' friend Eileen? Like I said, ain't no laws against me having friends round for tea.'

'Your cigarette packet. You mind if I see that?' The DCI held out his hand expectantly. Julie glanced at Eileen and was to receive the most subtle of shakes of the head.

'You mean search me? That's what you mean, right? You asking if you can search me? Not a chance!' Her face suddenly burst into a smile that told the story of a woman now enjoying her role. The DCI took a step forward, he looked every bit a man contemplating his next move. At the last moment he spun to talk to Eileen directly, his words through a jaw clamped tightly shut. 'I didn't catch your name.'

Eileen shrugged. 'You'll have all of our names later, sir, as part of the evidential handover.'

He nodded, his eyes narrowing, a flaring of his nostrils the most obvious sign of his internal fight to stay calm. 'Whose team are you on?' he said.

'I'm team Harry Blaker sir, just like everyone else here. Whose team are you on?'

# CHAPTER 86

Acting Detective Sergeant Rhiannon Davies got no reaction from her prisoner when she slapped down the folder of case material on the desk of Interview Room Four. She hadn't expected any. Murder suspects often started out defiant; it was their default position, the one they felt they had to take. But Megan Vrana was a step up from the normal, she was a defence solicitor. She knew this game better than most.

Better than Rhiannon.

It was in keeping with the prisoner who had been described to her by the custody staff tasked with keeping her alive. Vrana had not said a word, not touched her food and not moved from her bed. She was on constant supervision and not long back from a separate area where her forensic swabs, prints and samples had been taken.

Rhiannon didn't start with any niceties or small talk. She had the DC who was with her start the formal questions immediately. Vrana stayed stock-still and Rhiannon couldn't read any emotion from her at all. Then came a slight curling of the lips when she was asked if she wanted the company of a solicitor.

The formal questions ended and Rhiannon waited a beat, enjoying the silence, the fact that it was on their side as the third member of the interview team. Rhiannon had conducted enough interviews to not get nervous anymore, but this was different. This was a whole police force holding their breath, turned to stare down at the dungeons, at that tiny room with the air conditioning switched off. She could feel them all.

Her first question was to ask Megan Vrana straight if she was responsible for murder. This meant that Vrana's first significant input into the interview was explosive laughter. It took everything Rhiannon had not to leap over the table and punch that grinning face until it stopped.

Rhiannon had more questions and she went into them quickfire, keeping up the pressure. She asked specifics around the cars Vrana had been driving, her relationship with Ryan Archer, with Chloe Falconer and then with Neil Archer. She sought clarity on where Vrana had been living too and asked about her history of mental health, quoting the employee from her law practice who stated that Ms Vrana was presenting like she was in one of her 'manic' phases, where she had a history of both manic and depressive.

It was all dismissed. Ms Vrana non-committal, cagey and largely giving *no comment*. But she was getting rattled, more and more and Rhiannon recognised that the moment had come to increase the pressure.

She opened up the folder. It was like a Russian doll; inside was a series of smaller folders and she took her time in taking the top sheet of each of them to lay them out on the table. Each was spun for Vrana to read. She didn't.

'These are seven cases.' Rhiannon took a moment to adjust the papers slightly so they all lined up evenly. 'Seven cases that you took on, seven cases that you actively sought to represent and there is a pattern running right through. Can you tell me what that is?'

Vrana did not respond, did not look down.

'All seven offenders were arrested for assaulting a police officer. For some, it was their primary offence. At least two were targeted attacks on officers, the rest either kicked off when being arrested or as part of an incident that police attended. Why did you want to represent these offenders specifically?'

No response, no breaking away.

'How about if I tell you what we know, what we have been able to piece together and then you can stop me anytime I say something that isn't true?'

No response. Still an unfaltering stare.

'You were a victim when you were young — *very* young. Your own father was arrested and convicted of an abhorrent crime and he was taken away from you. Your father's name was Costin Vrana and it would later be discovered that he had been wrongfully convicted of that crime. That was a discovery that came a little while after he died in prison.'

'He was murdered.' Megan Vrana hissed. A reaction, finally.

'And you were left to suffer the consequences,' Rhiannon said. 'This started an anger in you, a sense of injustice that festered, turned to hate. And you found a focus for that hatred, didn't you? The police.' Rhiannon was still being careful to leave gaps for a reaction. Vrana shifted, her legs slid round on the heavy seats so she was side-saddle, her eyes down to the floor. Rhiannon now faced her shoulder as she still ignored the material on the table.

'You trained as a defence solicitor, the only career you've ever had and I think that was your way of doing your bit to make sure no one else had to go through what you did. But then you realised you were getting good access to criminals, to people who could help. I think Ryan Archer was perfect. These seven cases . . .' Rhiannon waved her hand over the sheets of paper. ' . . . were test beds. You'd been looking for the right subject and then along came Ryan. He told you his MO, how he relieved those people of their posh cars and you saw how that might be transferable. He was smart, strong and angry in a way that you could very easily manipulate. He was also vulnerable, wasn't he?'

No reaction.

'You also knew enough to fit him up. You had access to his records, everything you needed to be sure that we would stop our search when we found him. Ryan went to prison for assaulting someone with an iron bar. You hit Philip Jones with a crowbar. Ryan Archer stabbed someone in the neck when he was in prison, your method of choice in the Day family home was to slit their necks. That's why you chose that method, isn't it?'

Vrana managed a shake of her head.

'Neil Archer's talking to us and he was another piece of the puzzle for you. I mean, he was perfect. When Inspector Ives went out to him to tell him Ryan had died, he talked about his boy, he painted this picture of a lonely man who would do anything for the company of a woman, how it was all that he wanted. But he wasn't describing Ryan, was he? He was describing himself.'

Vrana sniffed. Nothing more.

'Neil told us how you seduced him. He couldn't believe his luck, to be honest and he fell hard — "like a dropped rock" is what he said. You manipulated him. Again, your complete access to Ryan meant that you knew the story of his mother leaving and you saw the gap that created, a family missing a mother, a gap that you could fill. Neil tells us you were exactly that . . . a stepmother, someone Ryan looked up to. Someone who was going to help him build a better life. You had him full of ideas of helping young offenders, a mentor scheme that put them back on the straight and narrow. You were even helping him apply for a grant to start it all up. But what did Ryan have to do in return for all this help and motherly advice?'

A shift in her seat, nothing more.

'He just had to be with you on that first sunny afternoon when you told him you were breaking some windows on a police car. And then you escalated. And the moment you did he was in up to his neck, wasn't he? That's how we can be sure it was you swinging that bar. Neil Archer insists that Ryan went along for some mischief, locking an old man in a hall while he put the windows through, but that was never your intention, was it? You played on the vulnerabilities of what was left of the Archer family, you gave them no option but to do what you said and then you killed Ryan.'

Nothing, not even a flicker.

'And then there was Chloe. You knew her a lot better than you let on to Inspector Ives. You were actually her one phone call when she was in trouble. But it was more than that, wasn't it?' Rhiannon left a gap for an answer and got the silence she expected. 'We have witness statements from her friends who tell us how you reached out to her the day before she went out of the back window of a flat. You scared her, told her she was about to be remanded for something she didn't do, told her she needed to avoid arrest, that she just needed to stay free and you would help her. From her phone records, she called you minutes after she hit Harry Blaker and made off. You were controlling her too. I bet you even told her where to hide.'

'These are just words. You're just throwing shit at the wall in the hope that something sticks!'

'Chloe was perfect.' Rhiannon was straight back on the offensive. 'Just the sort of person we would pursue when stitching up Ryan didn't wash. If this is me just throwing shit, tell me what your relationship was with Chloe Falconer? Why did you talk on the phone each day for five days in a row? Why didn't you tell Inspector Ives the truth?'

Megan Vrana spun back in her seat so they were facing each other, then she looked down, her eyes moving over the printed sheets laid out in front of her. She brought her hands out, steepling her fingers, the backs of her hands carried cuts and bruises, her coloured nails were cracked, one snapped right off. Her lips formed into a smile.

'Circumstantial,' she said, the smile remaining. 'I mean, whimsical, really. You know what I do for a living, right? Is this really the case you're presenting? I mean, I get it . . .' She faded, there were more words she had to say, but didn't. Rhiannon seized on it.

'What do you get, Ms Vrana?'

Vrana shrugged. 'You're desperate. This is about a police force that's humiliated — bruised. Harry Blaker was some sort of cult hero, adored and respected, sent to go head-to-head and you all let him down. I see it all the time. The police take these things really personally and that's why they sent you. I mean, you can call yourself *Acting Sergeant* to start off this process, but we both know what that means. You're a constable, you both are. Two constables leading interviews in a murder investigation?' Vrana snorted laughter this time. 'No one else wants to be tainted by this. Your police force is beaten. Harry Blaker, your finest . . . beaten.'

Rhiannon was still taking her time. She let the silence settle. 'I know what circumstantial means, so let's talk more about facts. You were arrested at Neil Archer's home, is that correct?'

'You know it is.'

'And you were in a relationship.'

'So?'

'And you drive a red coloured Vauxhall Corsa. This one . . .' There was a picture of a Corsa taken from the side Rhiannon laid it out so it was on top of everything else. 'Is this your car?'

'No.'

'But you have been driving it?'

'So what? Oh, I guess I might not be insured? You can do me for that if you want!'

'It's not insured. Because it's not registered to you, or anyone. You do have your own car, of course, one that is entirely road legal. But you have been choosing to use this one. This was one of the cars that Ryan was looking to flip, the only one left. Making it the last one you had access to that didn't have a direct link.'

'So?'

'So, we found it. Ryan uploaded it on social media, for sale, just like he did a black Volvo and an olive-coloured BMW. Do you remember Ryan having those cars?'

'He had a lot of cars.'

'The Vauxhall Corsa . . . we found the keys in Neil Archer's home, upstairs in the bedroom. Neil doesn't drive. He says they are yours. Is that right?'

'Do you have any *actual* evidence or not?'

'I want to talk about Harry Blaker, specifically.'

'I bet you do.'

'The man who was defeated, right?' Vrana gave the briefest of smiles. 'He drove that Vauxhall Corsa too. He was forced to drive it to the location where he was then murdered. Am I correct?'

'You tell me.'

'We found it parked two miles from Neil Archer's flat after you were arrested. It was tucked away in a cul-de-sac. It smells very strongly of bleach, it would seem. The seats have had so much they're discoloured. Why did you bleach the car?'

Vrana shook her head slowly. 'Still waiting for any actual evidence.'

'Bleach isn't enough to wipe all traces, you know that. And that's why you tried to hide it. Forensics will be able to put you in that car, we will find some trace. Harry Blaker, however, that might prove more difficult. He only drove it once, didn't he? That's the sort of contact that might not stick. Which would cause us a problem. Imagine, though, how strong our case would be if we could put you in that car, Harry Blaker too *and* then link it to the scene where Harry was murdered?'

Nothing.

'So, let me tell you about the defeated Harry Blaker and how he managed to do some little things. We're pretty sure he was being watched. Either someone was with him in that car or watching him remotely, from behind a laptop, like a coward. Either way, he would have been restricted in what he could do. That didn't stop him knocking some of the trim out of the car. The plastic trim in the driver's door, specifically. We recovered remnants from where he parked, close to where he was murdered. Do you know what he did then? He spat on his shoe and then he stood on those broken pieces. Not sure how. He would have needed to do it without being noticed. We couldn't work out why we had traces of his spittle on the sole of his shoe at first, but it didn't take long. It's sticky, see. Means the plastic trim he stood in — the tiny bits, fibres really — they stuck to his sole, even if the larger bits didn't make it all the way. Those fibres were still on his sole when you made him take a seat in that garage and when we found him later. Anything you want to dispute yet?'

'I've nothing to say to you.' Megan Vrana's words were more defiant than the tone she used.

'He spun the wheels of that car, too. He might have been hoping to leave a tread, but it was too dry. That was how we knew where he had parked, how we found the trim. We did get a tyre width, so we had an idea of the type of car. He also dragged one of his feet as he walked, judging by the tracks he left. I guess he put on a limp, did he? That's the only way I can think he might have got away with it.'

Megan Vrana made no response.

'So, this defeated man, was able to mark where he parked then dragged out the path so we would know, also finding the time to drape his dog lead over a wooden stile in case we had missed those tracks. Then, when he made it to the garage and took a seat, despite being forced to wear his colleague's handcuffs, he was able to get something into his hand. Something that he then tore up, an action that revealed to us exactly where we needed to be looking. That led us both to this very time and place. He tricked you, didn't he? Do you remember what you let him have in his hands?'

Rhiannon stopped for a breath. It looked like Vrana took the opportunity to breathe, too. She certainly wasn't about to respond.

'You didn't see Harry Blaker coming. At least, you didn't see what problems he might cause you. But you did see Neil Archer and you had a plan for him. Neil's talking to us, like I said and do you know how we got him to start? We told him about the Vauxhall Corsa and what we found inside it. The boot's all packed up like you were planning a holiday and he told us you had something booked — a romantic escape, he called it.

'But that wasn't the kind of escape you had in mind, was it? One of the bags has a forensic suit, a roll of strong tape and forensic gloves and overshoes. What the search team called a "murderer's toolkit". And a jerry can of petrol in a diesel car. You were going to kill Neil Archer and torch the evidence. The car too, no doubt. Neil Archer and that car were the last links between you and the murders. And you know what? When I told Neil what we found he was still trying to make excuses, just like when we told him you killed his son. He refused to believe it, said that the police officer must have killed Ryan, said we were mistaken about that bag and what it meant, said that you loved him and that you had loved Ryan. But even as he was saying that, it was hitting home. The truth was forming in his mind, the mist was falling away, I could see it.'

Vrana's jaw rippled, she blinked too, though it was just too long, as if she had her own mist that was clearing.

'I spoke with Detective Inspector Ives before I came in here to interview you. She insisted it was me, by the way, that's why you get a lowly acting sergeant. I refused at first, I thought — like you — that it should be someone more experienced, but she insisted. She told me that there was no real pressure on this interview, anyway. This is just for us to ask you to make a full admission, to see if you want to save yourself a lot of pain. We already have a remand application ready to go upstairs. We just needed to add that we've held an initial interview. Remand will be granted — you know that better than I do — and you will go to prison. Today. And then the police force that you seem to believe that you outwitted, we will continue to build our case before taking it to court. With what Neil Archer is now telling us, what circumstantial evidence tells us, what forensic evidence will tell us and after what Harry Blaker did, we will have just about the strongest case imaginable.'

Rhiannon left another gap, not for a response, but for the hits she was delivering to land. And she wanted to saviour this next bit.

'Ms Vrana, you are going to prison for the rest of your natural life. You will never see freedom again. You will die there just like your father did and this time it will be utterly deserved.' Rhiannon pushed herself forward a little, her right hand shooting out to make a fist that screwed up some of the material on the tabletop. 'And in those years and years that you will have waiting to die, I want you to know for sure that you never had a police force or any individuals running scared, quite the opposite. I got injured once, doing this job, and I was visited by an incredible detective and what he told me will be remembered long, long after you're committed to the annals as just another statistic. He told me how a police force is just like an ants' nest and now I know he was right. The more you agitate us, the more you dare us, the more you kick us and try and intimidate us, the more of us will come running out to bite you.'

Megan Vrana's scowl broke, its defences breached by a single, thick tear that ran the length of her pointed nose before she was able to brush it away with the back of her hand. She spun in her chair, back to her side-on position so her interviewer wouldn't see her upset.

But Rhiannon *had* seen it and she wasn't finished yet either. She ended the interview, the switch to a formal script saving her a little, dousing emotions that flared again the moment the tapes were stopped.

'You didn't kill Harry.' Rhiannon blurted the words, then followed them by leaning forwards, taking her weight through her knuckles on the tabletop. 'At least, not in the way you wanted to. He died of a massive heart attack, that's what they'll say. We know it already from the blood splatter. His heart had stopped before you even broke the skin, he never felt a thing!' Rhiannon knew she was grinning. She knew she probably looked crazy but it didn't matter. Megan Vrana was

366

still looking down. She rocked a little. It was a subtle reaction, but it was a reaction all the same. It was enough.

Rhiannon stood back straight. She was happy and relieved, sad and desperate all at once and it was overwhelming. She held it together enough to excuse herself to her colleague before bundling out of the room into a corridor that echoed with her footfalls.

The custody desk was at the very end and she was aware of movement, of someone stepping out of the office to greet her, of the inevitable start to the questions. She swept past with her head down, the struggle to hold it all together becoming harder. The internal door out of custody was off to the right and, seeing as she was effectively scampering out of the basement, there were wide steps directly the other side.

And they were full.

Like the bleachers.

Rows and rows of detectives, of uniforms and suits, of canteen staff, of front counter staff, of officers in hoodies who had come in on their day off. To wait. To wait for her, to wait for this. Maddie Ives was front and centre and she stood up, taking her time, as if in slow motion. *Everyone* moved in slow motion. There was a moment of silence that was deafening, a tightly-packed slab of people all holding their breath, unblinking, staring downwards while the door closed behind Rhiannon, the click when it found its place had all the drama of a gun being cocked.

Maddie was waiting to break, the whole of the bleachers were waiting to break. It took nothing more than a nod from Rhiannon, it was all she could do and then a tear of her own sprinted down her cheek to where her lips were shaped into a smile. Maddie Ives had her wrapped up in a tight hug before the next one could meet with it and from that moment, the tears of an entire station, of an entire force, of the entire fucking ants' nest all merged together as one.

# CHAPTER 87

*Three months later.*

'No!' Maddie might never have meant anything more. Her mind was made up, even more so since Vince had seemingly returned home with such a determination to change it. It felt like the sort of argument that could go on forever, be constantly revisited unless one half of the argument made it crystal clear. This was Maddie doing just that. She had her hand flat against a stomach that was starting to show, as part of making her point. 'This is my decision. This is my body and I am telling you we are not keeping it.'

Vince sulked. It was as instant as it was funny. 'I just don't understand what your issue is with blue. It's classic!'

'It's obvious! Cliché.'

'Some things are obvious or *cliché* for a reason, Mads!' Vince whined, 'Because they're a good idea, the only idea that makes any sense! And giving the sprog a middle name of *Harry* was obvious, about as cliché as you can get, but you were still down with that.'

'But I am still not down with your idea of a first name.'

'What's wrong with Dirty?' Vince guffawed now and Maddie couldn't help but join in a little. She took a moment to take in the mess of a room that they already referred to as "The Nursery", though it was currently scraped back walls, holes where curtain poles might go and a cot still disassembled and wrapped in clear plastic. 'I just think a nice, pale green. Then we can match it with browns and vanillas . . . it's . . . earthy!'

'Earthy!' Vince had another guffaw. 'Since when do you like earthy? You been telling me how much you miss the sea, the *blue* sea and now you want topsoil and cow shit!'

'I didn't mention topsoil or anything to do with a cow's arse. I just want a place that is calm . . . sort of steady and dependable and that's what I get from the countryside, the *earth*. And the sea? That doesn't make me think quite like that. Eileen! Back me up on this!'

Eileen stood on the threshold with a steaming mug of tea in an oversized cardigan where the change in the weather was marked and the same blue slippers she had worn from the moment Maddie had told her exactly what they were expecting. She didn't look fazed in the slightest at being thrust into the middle of this latest misunderstanding between the couple.

'I certainly think Harry would approve of *earthy*,' she said, without missing a beat. Maddie grinned. She knew it was the perfect response. Vince knew it too; he slumped on his frame in resignation, took a last look at the patch of blue where he had dared to start and threw the tainted brush into an empty bucket to be washed.

'Harry Blaker,' he huffed. 'Still showing me up.'

## THE END

# THE JOFFE BOOKS STORY

We began in 2014 when Jasper agreed to publish his mum's much-rejected romance novel and it became a bestseller.

Since then we've grown into the largest independent publisher in the UK. We're extremely proud to publish some of the very best writers in the world, including Charlie Gallagher, Joy Ellis, Faith Martin, Caro Ramsay, Helen Forrester, Simon Brett and Robert Goddard. Everyone at Joffe Books loves reading and we never forget that it all begins with the magic of an author telling a story.

We are proud to publish talented first-time authors, as well as established writers whose books we love introducing to a new generation of readers.

We won Trade Publisher of the Year at the Independent Publishing Awards in 2023. We have been shortlisted for Independent Publisher of the Year at the British Book Awards for the last four years, and were shortlisted for the Diversity and Inclusivity Award at the 2022 Independent Publishing Awards. In 2023 we were shortlisted for Publisher of the Year at the RNA Industry Awards.

We built this company with your help, and we love to hear from you, so please email us about absolutely anything bookish at feedback@joffebooks.com

If you want to receive free books every Friday and hear about all our new releases, join our mailing list: www.joffebooks.com/contact

And when you tell your friends about us, just remember: it's pronounced Joffe as in coffee or toffee!

## ALSO BY CHARLIE GALLAGHER

**DI MADDIE IVES SERIES**
Book 1: HE IS WATCHING YOU
Book 2: HE WILL KILL YOU
Book 3: HE WILL FIND YOU
Book 4: HE KNOWS YOUR SECRETS
Book 5: HE WILL GET YOU
Book 6: THE DEADLY HOUSES
Book 7: LAST ONE ALIVE
Book 8: THE GIRL UNDER THE FLOOR
Book 9: THE GIRLS UPSTAIRS

**LANGTHORNE POLICE SERIES**
Book 1: BODILY HARM
Book 2: PANIC BUTTON
Book 3: BLOOD MONEY
Book 4: END GAME
Book 5: MISSING
Book 6: THEN SHE RAN
Book 7: HER LAST BREATH

**STANDALONES**
RUTHLESS

Milton Keynes UK
Ingram Content Group UK Ltd.
UKHW011839120424
441050UK00004B/185